THE
BEAST
OF
BESWICK

THE BEAST OF BESWICK

AMALIE HOWARD

Entangled Publishing, LLC
2614 South Timberline Road
Suite 105, PMB 159
Fort Collins, CO 80525
rights@entangledpublishing.com
Visit our website at www.entangledpublishing.com.

Amara is an imprint of Entangled Publishing, LLC.

Edited by Liz Pelletier and Heather Howland
Cover Artist: Erin Dameron-Hill, EDH Graphics
Photograph by VJ Dunraven/Period images,
Peter Tittmus/123rf.com, and
srongkrod481/depositphotos.com
Interior design by Toni Kerr

MMP ISBN 978-1-64063-741-2
ebook ISBN 978-1-64063-742-9

Manufactured in the United States of America

First Edition December 2019

AMARA

ALSO BY AMALIE HOWARD

For Cameron, the prince of beasties.

CHAPTER ONE

England, 1819

Her pulse drumming at a fierce clip, Lady Astrid Everleigh burst through the front doors of her uncle's country estate in Southend. The flashy coach in the drive was as unmistakable as its owner—the arrogant and deeply persistent Earl of Beaumont. A sickening feeling leached into her as she scanned the foyer. No one would meet her eyes, not the butler, not the footmen, not even her uncle Reginald whose pallid cheekbones had gone an ugly shade of puce.

"You were s-supposed to be at the market," he sputtered in surprise.

"What have you done, Uncle?" she demanded, flinging off her cloak. "Did you arrange this without my knowledge or consent?"

Her uncle's color heightened. "Now, see here," he blustered, "it's demmed high time your sister marry, and you know it—"

Not to *him*. Never to him.

The pit of sickness in Astrid's stomach deepened at the thought of sweet, innocent Isobel in the clutches of such a man. The Earl of Beaumont was scraping the bottom of the barrel as far as Astrid was concerned, even if he was now a peer of the realm.

Throttling the ugly memories his name alone conjured, Astrid turned away from her uncle to her ashen lady's maid, who had appeared upon hearing her voice. "Where are they, Agatha?"

"In the morning salon, my lady. With the viscountess."

Astrid's heart plummeted at the sight of the closed doors. Aunt Mildred's chaperonage would be questionable to say the least. "How long have they been in there?"

"Not five minutes, my lady."

A blink of an eye and yet enough time for her sweet sister to be thoroughly compromised. Isobel was barely sixteen. She'd been an unexpected and much welcomed surprise to their parents, and Astrid had always been protective. To her, Isobel was still a child, no matter their uncle's declaration of her being ready to wed. She hadn't even had a proper Season yet, and already he wanted to marry her off to the highest bidder.

To a liar and a lecher, no less.

Edmund Cain had inherited the earldom from his uncle a handful of years ago. Though a title made him eligible to most, he was still the heartless brute who'd destroyed Astrid's reputation without a qualm during her first—and only—Season, when she'd had the *audacity* to turn down his suit. He'd retaliated with a horrible lie about her lack of virtue, and her entire future had crumbled.

When their parents were taken by illness a year later, she and Isobel had gone into the care of their only living relatives in England. After the year of mourning, Astrid had decided any money left to her would be better saved for Isobel's coming out. She was the daughter of a viscount, and when the time came, Isobel deserved her due.

But that was before her uncle had gotten his hands on their inheritance. Most of it was gone, except for specific, unreleased funds, which would come to them only upon marriage or the age of twenty-six. Astrid was one year away, and Isobel was a decade away, unless a marriage came first, which clearly was the goal here. But now, eight years after her parents' deaths, the girls were nearly destitute, or so her uncle claimed.

Destitute enough to seek a connection with an utterly unsuitable earl? If money was in question, it was a certainty. Uncle Reginald would sell his own soul if he could get a farthing for it.

"Lord Beaumont is a peer now," her uncle said, drawing her attention. "He's not the man you knew."

"A leopard cannot change its spots."

"Now see here, Astrid," he said, blocking her path. "It is done. Lord Beaumont has pledged—"

"You will stay a far step from me, Uncle. And I don't care what that man has promised; he will never—" Astrid broke off, the threat as empty as the power she held…which was none.

Without a husband of her own, the truth was that as their guardian, if her uncle wished to marry Isobel off to a pox-marked pauper, he could, and there would be nothing either of them could do about it. Such was the place of a woman in their world.

Astrid switched tactics, turning toward him, her voice softening. "Uncle Reggie, be reasonable. Isobel hasn't even had a Season yet. Perhaps she can make an even better match, one with greater reward." She let the suggestion hang in the air, knowing the promise of coin would make her uncle salivate.

The viscount thinned his lips. "Better an egg today than a hen tomorrow."

"Spoken by the rooster who has nothing to lose," Astrid said under her breath, though her stomach churned. Had he already made a settlement with Beaumont?

Reasonable discussion was clearly getting her nowhere.

Shooting a look of pure loathing at her uncle, she darted around him to the salon doors and shoved them open, searching for her sister.

Isobel's face was pinched and her spine rigid. With fear or shock, Astrid did not know. Thankfully, her sister sat on the sofa, hands clasped in her lap while Beaumont stood a short distance away. Not far enough away in Astrid's opinion. No one else was in the room. Gracious, where on earth was her aunt?

"I thought I told you I wished to be alone, Everleigh," Beaumont said over his shoulder, annoyance flashing in his eyes for a second before he realized that it wasn't her uncle who had barged in. "Ah, it's the spinster. Have you come to congratulate us?" he drawled, satisfaction creeping over his deceptively handsome features. "I assume you've heard that I intend to court your sister."

She let out a breath, but before she could form a reply, her aunt emerged from the far end of the room, her face pulling tight with vexation. Astrid frowned. Good Lord but Aunt Mildred's designs were transparent. Even though they weren't in London, her aunt well knew the rules of the aristocracy...especially with respect to chaperoning unmarried young ladies.

Astrid swallowed the spurt of anger when she thought of how easily Isobel could have been compromised. Her eyes narrowed with sudden understanding.

Is that what my fortune-hunting relatives intended?

Astrid's frustration pricked as her eyes touched on the smug face of the Earl of Beaumont. She bit her lip, fingers clenching at her sides, her stomach threatening to upend itself. If she hadn't forgotten her market day list, she would never have returned in time…and who knew what else might have happened. Right now, however, Isobel was safe and that was all that mattered. She *was* safe, right? Swallowing a rise of dread, her gaze shifted to her sister.

"Isobel, are you well?" she asked.

Her sister nodded, though her rosy skin was ashen. "Yes, but I do feel a bit of a megrim coming on."

"Perhaps you should rest."

With a grateful look, Isobel nodded and stood, bobbing a hasty curtsy in the earl's direction, and fled the room with Aunt Mildred on her heels.

Beaumont gave a careless wave as she left. "I'll be seeing you soon, dearest."

"You will not," Astrid said.

His stare raked her from head to toe, making her feel as if she were wearing far less than the sturdy gray woolen dress with matching pelisse, buttoned up to her neck. "Tell me, Lady Astrid, what can *you* do to stop me?"

"She's sixteen," she said.

He nodded. "Indeed. Marriageable age."

Astrid swallowed the rise of anger. The same age *she'd* been when he had first set eyes on her in London. His interest, intent, and timing were no mistake. The newly minted earl was back to settle a score.

"Isobel is to have a Season in London," Astrid said.

"Not if your uncle accepts an offer beforehand. She will make a lovely countess, don't you think?"

Astrid scowled, her heart thudding. "Why are you so fixated on her for a wife? She's not part of your set."

"Perhaps because I was denied nine years ago."

And there it was as plain as day—the heart of the matter—the *score*.

A calculated stare met hers as Beaumont approached where she stood, her posture rigid with a sick combination of fear and fury. His victorious smile made Astrid's blood run cold. He'd already wrecked her future. She could not…*would not* let him threaten her sister's.

"No, I won't allow it," she said. "I am her guardian."

"Ah, but Viscount Everleigh is *your* guardian, is he not? And *his* approval has already been granted, or at least it will be once we come to terms. You, my dear, have no say in the matter, and as much as you think you can sway me, you will find that what you desire is of no import. You had your chance, as they say." His grin was slow and mocking. "I told you that you would regret it."

Stifling the retort that she absolutely did *not* regret refusing him, Astrid sucked in a calming breath. "Isobel is barely out of the schoolroom. You are four and thirty, Edmund. Surely you can find a more appropriate wife closer to your own age."

His eyes narrowed at her use of his given name. "It's Lord Beaumont now. Are you proposing yourself as a substitute? Though, for a woman in your situation, marriage would be out of the question now, of course." He canvassed her figure with a lewd glance that made her want to cover herself with a blanket. "However, I could be moved to reconsider with the right incentive."

"I'd rather be mauled by rabid dogs."

"Ah yes, there's that barbed tongue of yours," the earl replied. "You're like a fine-aged whiskey with a bite that has only sharpened with time. Lady Isobel seems much more well-behaved, though it will be my greatest pleasure once we're wedded to discover if she has a stubborn streak like you."

Astrid stiffened. "You will marry my sister when hell freezes over, *Lord Beaumont*. Count on that." With as much effort as she could muster, she tamped down her mounting temper and swept from the room.

Shaking with outrage, Astrid attempted to compose herself in the corridor. Regardless of Beaumont's looks, title, or fortune, she would not wish such a heartless man on her worst enemy, much less her sweet, innocent sister. Given a proper Season, a jewel like Isobel would have her choice of husbands.

Her uncle knew it, and Beaumont knew it, too.

Once the earl had taken his leave, she sought out her uncle, who had retreated to his study, giving her tongue free rein. "How could you? She's only sixteen, for God's sake." She turned to her aunt standing quietly near the desk. "Aunt Mildred, have you nothing to say? What about Isobel's feelings on the matter?"

Her aunt's mouth thinned. "Her future husband will tell her what to think."

"Said no woman with half a spine ever."

"Would you rather her end up like you, then?" her uncle said. "Unmarried, ruined, and a bloody burden to your aunt and me?"

She sucked in a gasp. Her father, the previous viscount, had made sure that his daughters would live comfortably, with the hope that his brother would do his duty by his nieces. Her sister and she had learned early on that that would not be the case. Their father's old family solicitor, Mr. Jenkins, who checked in on them once a year, had advocated for their father's wishes, including a Season for Isobel once she came of age, but Mr. Jenkins had passed away a year ago. His firm oversaw the estate, but there was no one left to keep the greedy Everleighs in line.

"Papa made sure we would not be," Astrid said, striving for patience. "We did not come to you cap in hand."

"That blunt is gone."

Riled beyond belief, she threw caution to the wind. "Where, Uncle? Where did all of it go? Papa bequeathed us a fortune by any standards."

His nostrils flared, eyes bulging as he rose behind

his desk. "How *dare* you, you insolent chit! After your aunt and I took you in, this is how you repay us? With mistrust and suspicion? That demmed money went to gowns, shoes, food, and finishing school." He snorted. "To those books of yours. Your sister's dancing and pianoforte instructors. Do you think it's inexpensive to raise two demanding chits? And what about your horses?"

The horses he spoke of were *his* thoroughbreds bought with his dead brother's money, but Astrid didn't point that out. She glued her lips together, stifling her anger. If Uncle Reginald decided to throw her out on her ear, she would be destitute and homeless. She would not come into her own portion until she was six and twenty, months away, and until then, she had to guard her tongue. Without her, Isobel would be on her own and vulnerable.

"And what about *you*?" he went on, eyeballing her. "You were supposed to make an advantageous marriage. Instead, you've brought ruin upon the Everleigh name." He sneered at her, his eyes cold. "What? You thought your sins would not leach to your poor sister?"

A sound of pain escaped Astrid's lips. Her *sins*. She'd done nothing wrong, and yet she had been the one punished. Excoriated and summarily dropped by the *ton* upon the faithless account of a scorned liar.

"You know what he did," Astrid whispered, hand clutched to her chest and eyes burning with unshed tears. "What he did to *me*, and yet you still welcome his presence. How could you be so cruel?"

Her craven uncle would not meet her eyes. "He is

an earl. And perhaps he wants to make it right."

Her uncle was wrong. Beaumont didn't want to *make it right*. He wanted to make Astrid pay.

"Please, Uncle Reggie," she tried, resorting to begging. "Even if that is so, surely you see how poor of a match it is. Beaumont is twice her age. He isn't fit for someone as tender as Isobel. Can't you see that?"

Uncle Reginald's mouth thinned as he stood and indicated the opened study door. "Nonetheless, he is an earl. A rich earl. And you're forgetting that reformed rakes make the best husbands. He intends to join our estates and revive them. Isobel will be a countess and want for nothing. Now begone and leave me be."

What he really meant was that he and Aunt Mildred would want for nothing. Astrid's heart sank as she obeyed the rough dismissal.

Upstairs, she found her sister in the bedroom they shared. Isobel's eyes were red-rimmed as though she'd been weeping, and Astrid went to her immediately.

"What will we do? I don't wish to marry him." Isobel sniffled. "But Aunt Mildred says I must do my duty to our family."

Astrid took her sister's hands into her own. "You won't have to, I promise."

"But how?" Her pale eyes watered. "He's an earl. And since Uncle approves the match, I have no choice."

"Don't worry, Izzy—fortune favors those best prepared." She hugged her sister tight, her resolve hardening. "I will find a way to see us out of this."

Their options were limited. It was clear what her uncle intended—to sell Isobel's virtue to someone willing to pay for the privilege, in this case, Lord Beaumont. It was unconscionable and it sickened her, but there wasn't a thing she could do about it. Not without help.

Astrid blew out a frustrated breath.

If only her father were still alive or she had a husband of her own...

She blinked, an outrageous idea blossoming.

It would solve everything. It was a dreadful, desperate plan, but it was something. It was a *chance*.

At five and twenty, she was well on the shelf, but she wasn't dead. She might be ruined in the eyes of the *ton*, but she had a sound brain, she'd been raised to run an aristocratic household, and she was the daughter of a viscount. It could work. *It could work.*

She would just have to marry a different kind of beast than the earl to save her sister.

And she knew just the man.

CHAPTER TWO

"You need a wife."

A priceless vase from the Ming dynasty, circa the fourteenth century, crashed into the three wicket stumps drawn along the back wall and splintered into a thousand shards, joining a brightly colored pile of its brethren at the base of a hand-painted mural in the gallery. Lord Thane Harte, the seventh Duke of Beswick, scowled as his valet cast a baleful eye at the ruins, a cricket bat dangling from one hand.

"Your father went through a great deal to collect those, Your Grace."

"My father is dead," the duke rumbled. "It's a *thing*, Fletcher. Now, come on, one more and you're out. Clench those judgmental arse cheeks and let's go for the boundaries with the next ball."

The man grimaced as he lifted the wooden bat with distaste. "Those are not *balls*, Your Grace. They are worth several thousand pounds."

"Expensive and ugly. The devil knows why my father worshiped the absurd things. And for posterity's sake, I need a wife like I need a gash in the head." *Another gash in the head*, he amended silently.

"You need an heir, then."

Thane scowled in annoyance, the battle scars on his skin pulling tight. What child would want or deserve a father with a ruined face like his? And what high-born lady would willingly consent to bed him in the first place? He was lucky his cock remained intact from the war and still functioned.

"I'd rather let this execrable line die out than subject a child to a brute for a father."

"You're not a brute, Your Grace."

Thane clapped a dramatic hand to his chest. "Good God, man, do you even *know* me?"

"Beauty is only skin deep," came the prompt reply.

Thane snorted, his irritation fading. "Did you come up with that clever gem on your own?"

"No, it's from a poem."

"I've told you time and time again, poetry will rot your brain." He peered at his valet. "Unless they're bawdy poems, of course. Those are allowed."

"You have much to offer, Your Grace. If you would only try—"

"Fletcher," Thane warned. "Your loyalty is appreciated, but this conversation grows tiresome." The hint of menace in his tone made his valet pale. "Are you conceding defeat? Or shall I bowl you another?"

He hefted another vase in his hand with forced cheer. This one was painted with tiny blue and white flowers. It was so delicate that if he squeezed hard enough, it would shatter in his palm. Thane felt a sense of disgust as he studied the object. His father had revered the blasted things. He remembered the time he'd wandered into his father's precious gallery as a child, only to cop a caning that had left his bottom raw for days. He'd broken one by accident some years later and had buried the pieces in the garden out of fear for what his father would do.

Thane walked back a half-dozen steps and took a running start before bowling the china arm-over-head toward Fletcher. He felt the pull of scar tissue all along his back and ribs. He was glad the gallery wasn't mirrored, but it was nothing that Fletcher or the rest of his servants hadn't seen. No one looked him in the eye anymore. No one, that is, except for his faithful butler and his longtime valet, who now grudgingly brought his cricket bat to the ready.

The vase flew with calculated precision toward his target. To Thane's surprise, Fletcher swung with an aggrieved expression. The inestimable vase collided with the flat front of the bat and smashed to smithereens. Several of the footmen dodged flying porcelain missiles that sprayed the width of the room.

"Oh, well done, man," Thane said. "Thought you'd lost your ballocks for a second there, caught up in bloody sentiment."

"Your father would turn in his grave, Your Grace."

A bitter sound passed his lips. "My father, God rest his porcelain-loving soul, is *hopefully* having apoplexy in his grave by now. Hence the point, Fletcher."

The servant—though more family than servant, ergo his everlasting gall—slanted him an arch glance. "But as you said, Your Grace, your sire is dead. What purpose does this destruction serve? Consider donating some pieces to a gallery instead."

Thane paused, his eyes narrowing. Trust Fletcher to try to ruin any attempt at joy. "I like cricket."

"Your father's collection was quite extensive and renowned. Or you could auction it. Lord Leopold—"

"Don't."

Fletcher persisted. "Lord Leopold," he said more loudly, "had planned to hold a grand auction in honor of your father."

The flare of pain caught him by surprise. It'd been four years since his brother's death, and he still felt it keenly. Thane hadn't wanted the ducal title. He didn't have the temperament for it. It'd been Leo's from the day he'd been born, and until the terrible fall from his horse that had snapped his spine, it'd been his.

Thane had wanted to live out his remaining days in solitude. Instead he'd returned to a coronet. To duty. To unwanted responsibility.

To acres and acres of fucking porcelain.

"Very well, then, donate the lot."

"*A-All* of it?" Fletcher spluttered. "We would need an inventory at least."

"Hire someone." The suggestion curled his gut, and the thought of having someone new in his domain made him feel slightly ill. Most of his staff were trusted servants who had known him as a boy before the ravaged war hero. He did not take well to strangers. Or staring. The latter almost certainly went with the former.

"In Southend? Finding a credible historian with a knowledge of antique Chinese porcelain would be like finding a needle in a haystack. I'd have to send for someone in London, and that could take weeks."

"Fletcher," he growled. "I do not care. It was your suggestion. Handle it."

The valet bowed. "Of course, Your Grace."

Thane left the gallery and strode toward his study. He'd forgone his daily exercises this morning in favor of some extra sleep. Insomnia kept him awake most nights, along with the recurring nightmares of being cut to ribbons. Sometimes, the dreams were so real that he swore he could feel the blades tearing into his flesh and the hot burn of his separating skin as bayonets punctured and cleaved through it like parchment. He'd saved four of his men in his unit from the ambush, but nearly triple that number had died. All because of one man...one craven turncoat who had abandoned his post.

Thane could still hear their screams.

He stopped to swivel his body, stretching slowly. His entire upper half felt stiff and sore. He was paying the price for not doing his usual exercises, the stitched, cauterized patchwork of skin on his back tight and painful. Perhaps a swim would be in order before dinner. He'd converted one of the unused wings in the manse into a recovery and training facility of sorts, which included an entire room devoted to a heated bathing pool, inspired by the Roman and Turkish baths and some of the extraordinary architecture he'd seen while traveling the Continent.

But for now, he needed a stiff drink.

"Culbert," he said, passing his faithful butler en route to his destination. "Instruct one of the footmen to fire the hearths in the bathing room. I want it good and warm. And I do not wish to be disturbed."

"As you wish, Your Grace."

Finally, he arrived at the study. He loved the solitude of Beswick Park, but the abbey was labyrinthine. After spending so many months in a one-room barrack, he'd needed a map to relearn his way around his childhood home. His study was dominated by a large desk, several comfortable armchairs, and it was dark with heavy velvet drapes covering the mullioned windows. Plush carpeting muted his footfalls as he walked over and sat in the chair behind the desk and poured himself two fingers of fine French brandy. The liquor spread like a warm glow through his muscles.

Thane studied the low fire burning in the grate. He shrugged out of his coat and rolled up the sleeve of his left arm. Shiny, unsightly scar tissue traversed the entire length of it. Most of his body had suffered the same fate, including his back, his legs, and three-quarters of his face. He kept his hair long, but the length did little to hide the stitched filigree of his skin. A beard might have helped, but not when it only grew on the lower, unmarred right side of his face.

Eight years ago, he'd had his choice of women. Now, he'd be lucky to pay someone to even look at him. Not that he was remotely interested in pursuing dalliances with the opposite sex. Or finding a wife. No, Fletcher had rocks in his brain if he thought *that* would ever happen.

Thane pulled the stack of ledgers toward him and glanced over the numbers for the estates. He hadn't visited his tenants in years, though Fletcher said the land was turning a profit despite the handful of farmers who had left. Their departure was probably due to his black reputation, most of it deserved. He'd been a harsh man before the war, and now he was a hundred times worse. Ruthless to a fault. Hard. Intractable. Unforgiving. The list went on.

The rumors of the Beast of Beswick abounded, including the one that he'd committed patricide. And possible fratricide. It was true that his ailing father had died of a heart attack upon his return when he'd laid eyes upon his son's gruesome visage. So, in actuality, he *might* have killed the man. A few unfortunate months later, his brother had died in a fall during a fox hunt. Once more blamed on Thane, though he'd been nowhere in close proximity to him at the time.

Leo had been engaged to a mutual childhood friend whose father had suggested aligning his daughter with the new Duke of Beswick. Lady Sarah Bolton had taken one look at him and walked out of the room. Contracts had been voided. Virgins unsacrificed.

That'd been four years ago.

No wonder Fletcher was in a snit about him being unwed.

Tossing back the remaining brandy, Thane rose and limped to the bathing room. As he'd commanded, the massive fireplaces on either end of the chamber had been stoked and lit. A long rectangular bath lay at the center of the space, beneath which metal plumbing conducted heat from the hearths to the water and to the surrounding slate flooring. He'd designed it himself, and it had cost a bloody fortune. Then again, what was the use of being a rich nob if he couldn't spend his hard-inherited money?

Thane wasted no time in divesting himself of all his clothing and wading in, feeling the warm water soothing his aching muscles. He twisted and stretched until his body felt loose, and then he simply floated, staring out the floor-to-ceiling glass windows that spanned the length of one wall. Stars twinkled in the distance, swatches of the twilight sky blocked by darker bands of cloud cover. Sometimes, when the moon was full and riding high, it was a truly spectacular view. This was another of his favorite rooms at the abbey.

A commotion outside the door made him jolt out of his relaxation.

"No, no," Culbert was practically screeching. "His Grace is not at home to callers, Fletcher. Good gracious, you imbecile, what on earth are you doing? He doesn't want to be disturbed, I tell you. He's… *working*."

Thane wondered who it could be. The Marquess of Roth had developed an annoying habit of turning up in Southend to escape his fractious father. However, Winter hadn't visited in some time, and Culbert wouldn't be in a lather about him.

"You're the imbecile because she followed *you*," he heard Fletcher shoot back. "I told her to wait in the foyer."

Thane blinked. *She?*

"Is the duke in there? I won't be a minute." The voice was decidedly feminine, sultry, and unfamiliar. Thane's lower abdomen clenched at the sound.

"My lady, this is highly irregular." Culbert's voice had notched an octave at the obvious break in decorum. "His Grace is *busy*."

"This cannot wait," she said, impatience lacing her tone. "As I've already stated, it is a matter of some urgency, and I insist on seeing the duke at once. Surely he can put aside his work for a few moments."

He did recall giving the order to Culbert not to be disturbed, and the man was a stickler for instructions. With a huff of vexation, Thane hauled his nude body out of the water and reached for a length of toweling just as a figure barged through the doors.

The room was partially illuminated by the light of the fireplaces behind him, so he could see the woman clearly, front-lit as she was. The fact that she was tall was his first impression, and then he saw her face, only to falter for breath. Her features were exquisite in their cameo-like symmetry—a perfect creamy oval with wide-set eyes, an elegant nose, and lush, unsmiling lips. She was Renaissance art in the flesh.

But even as Thane admired her, it wasn't the kind of beauty that beckoned. Instead, it warned. Or perhaps it was her rigid posture taken with the dour set of that rosebud mouth and the sheets of ice in those eyes. Or the dark hair that was scraped off her forehead into a ruthless coiffure gathered at the nape of her neck. All those sharp angles and cold edges wouldn't hesitate to decimate a man.

A vague sensation of wonder filled him. Who *was* she?

Her eyes found him then, and her mouth framed a small *O* of surprise, a fiery blush heating her cheeks as she averted her gaze with a mortified squeak. Her face turned blotchy with a mix of horror and mortification, and Thane suppressed a flinch. He wrapped the drying cloth around his waist, angling the least offensive view of his wet, unclothed body toward her.

"I b-beg your pardon," she stammered. "I did not realize. I thought this was the study or the library, not your…not your… Oh my *God*."

Thane supposed it was an honest mistake—after all, it was a converted ballroom on the ground floor, not his private apartments. And Culbert *had* said he was working, though probably not exactly in the context she had expected.

"Not God," he murmured. "Just a duke, and an unholy one at that."

As if a spell had been broken, she scrambled to withdraw and collided with a frantic Culbert on her heels. Her arms windmilled madly as she went hurtling in the opposite direction, thrown off-balance. And suddenly Thane found himself sprinting forward to catch her, his hands suddenly full of long-limbed, squirming woman. The only thing holding the thin toweling at his hips in place was the snug clasp of their two bodies.

"Easy," he rasped, his palm easing down the slim curve of her back. "I've got you."

She smelled like warm summer nights, her fragrance swamping him as it rose from her heated skin while she struggled to right herself. He'd gauged that she was tall from a distance, but she still didn't come up to his chin. Then again, at six and a half feet, he knew most women wouldn't.

Their bodies meshed together perfectly, her soft curves yielding to his hard planes. Unlike his brain that was slow to catch on, other parts of his body were taking acute notice of the small but pert breasts that were pressed to his torso and the mile-long, muslin-clad legs that slatted between his very bare thighs.

He'd forgotten what it felt like to hold a woman.

"Unhand me, please," she said, her voice tight with alarm.

Thane realized that he was keeping her wedged up against him, though her face remained averted and eyes closed. With revulsion, probably. God, what had he been thinking? Not with his head, obviously. He released her so quickly that she took two wobbly steps back and rushed from the room without a backward glance.

"I tried to tell you, my lady," Culbert admonished from the hallway. "Would you prefer to wait in His Grace's study?"

"Perhaps I'll come back another time."

Thane paused and then popped his head around the door. Surprisingly, his usual annoyance at facing newcomers was absent. He put it down to curiosity. Hell, a *woman* had sought him out. Voluntarily. And not just any woman…a lady of quality.

What could she possibly want with him?

"Surely if it's so urgent, our *guest* can be persuaded to wait," he called out to Culbert. "I will be there shortly."

A quarter of an hour later, Thane was once more fit for polite company and fully clothed from top to bottom. He took a deep breath at the study door and slipped in. The room was shrouded in its usual shadow but for the light of the hearth and a single candelabra set far away from the desk. Culbert was present, offering the lady a cup of tea. She sat primly in one of the armchairs, her face angled toward the fire. In profile, her nose was a perfect slope, her chin pointed and determined, and a winged brow was pulled into a frown. Every contour of her body was composed into strict, unbending lines. Despite her loveliness, she did not emanate warmth...as if her exterior was made of stone instead of flesh.

Giving her his least damaged view, which wasn't much, he swiftly moved past her to sit in the shadows behind his desk. He had an unfair advantage, he supposed, as the light from the candelabra lit her position, while his location remained in gloom.

"Lady Astrid Everleigh to see you, Your Grace," Culbert announced, bowing, and then took his leave. Thane noticed that he left the door cracked slightly. The fusspot of a butler must have been a governess in a previous life.

He recognized the name, though the faces that came to mind did not include a woman of her age. "Are you related to Reginald Everleigh, the viscount?"

"My uncle, Your Grace. My father was the late viscount, Lord Randolph Everleigh," she said in a crisp voice, that chin of hers thrusting forward like the point of a sword. "Though you and I are acquainted," she went on. "We were introduced many years ago in London during my coming-out before...well, before."

Thane's thoughts snagged. She meant before the war. Before he'd obtained a hideous face and an even more hideous disposition. Well, *more* of a hideous disposition. His good humor evaporated like a breath in the wind. "I don't recall you," he said ungraciously.

"I hardly supposed you would, Your Grace. I was the worst of the wallflowers."

"Fishing for compliments, are we?" His tone was dry. "You won't find them here, my lady. We are fresh out of flattery."

"Of course not. How rude of you to suggest such a thing."

Oh, he was just getting started. Thane lifted a brow. "One could argue, my lady—it *is* my lady, isn't it?— that it's rude to call one's host 'rude,' especially since you were the one to barge in uninvited in the first place. Or has well-bred, ladylike behavior changed so drastically in the years of my self-imposed isolation?"

His emphasis on "ladylike" was not lost as she sucked in an affronted breath, flags of color bursting in her cheeks.

"Then I apologize," she ground out, her eyes fairly sparking with indignation that she struggled to control, though control it she did. "It was a matter of—"

"Some urgency, yes, I'm quite aware. Enlighten me, then, Lady Astringent."

Her eyelashes descended, her cheeks hollowing with obvious frustration. "I do beg your pardon, Your Grace, but my name is Lady As*trid*. Perhaps you misheard."

"Beg away, my lady. I'm quite at my leisure."

Pale eyes flashed. "You, Your Grace, are…are…"

"Abominable? Appalling? Atrocious?" he supplied.

"I was going to say insufferable, but clearly your intelligence is limited to only the first letter of the alphabet."

A bark of laughter burst from him. It was as clear as day that beneath that stony exterior, his guest had quite a temper. It made him want to rile her all the more, to make those brewing passions ignite in her eyes, anything to disrupt her ironclad control.

"So, Lady *Ass*-trid, come to suss out the beast, have you?" he drawled. "Did you not get a good enough look earlier? Duke en déshabillé?"

Her lips pursed as if she'd sucked on a lemon, and he wondered briefly—albeit insanely—what those perfect pink arches would taste like. Whether her nipples were the same shade or darker.

"This conversation is unseemly, sir."

If she only knew the true debauched slant of his thoughts.

"That's an understatement." Thane leaned back in his chair. "Shall we trade insults all night, or will you eventually tell me what you've come here for?"

The lady swallowed what looked like it could have been a blistering response and sealed her lips. She leaned forward to pick up a green-flowered dish from the mantel with deceptive calm. "This is beautiful," she said. "Fifteenth century Chinese?"

He arched a split brow. "Yes. My father collected the silly things."

"Hardly silly, Your Grace."

She examined the dish in her delicate, long-fingered hands. Thane was momentarily fascinated. Those delicate hands were at odds with the rest of her sharp angles and acerbic voice. For an instant, he wanted to be that bowl, being caressed by her palms. He imagined what those long, elegant fingers would feel like circling his hardened length, and his entire body throbbed with a surge of instant need. Lust roared through him.

Holy Christ.

Thane set the heel of his palm on the placket of his trousers hidden beneath his desk, willing the stiffness beneath it to dissipate as his gaze narrowed on the woman still inspecting the antique across the desk's mahogany surface. With the plain clothing and her no-nonsense coiffure, she reminded him of a governess. Thane half expected to see a ruler in her hands, ready to crack down on his knuckles for any hint of misbehavior. She was not the sort of woman who heated his blood…and yet his blood was on fire.

Reverently, she placed the dish gently back in its place, her hands falling to her lap, thankfully out of sight, and found his silhouette with her eyes.

They were light, he guessed, but their exact color eluded him. Pale gray or green, perhaps. He didn't recall meeting her, but before the war, he'd been surrounded by dozens of stunning fresh-faced debutantes and had been just as determined to avoid them all. He wouldn't have forgotten *her*, though. She was lovely…until she opened her mouth. A stunning rose, sheathed in bloodthirsty thorns.

"What is it you want, Lady Astrid?" Distracted by the fire in his veins, his voice was gruffer than he'd intended. "Don't keep us in suspense. Spit it out."

Her delicate brows crashed together, but she cleared her throat, once more fighting for calm.

Thane felt a smile creeping along his lips. "I have a proposition for you, Your Grace."

"Proposition?"

"A *business* proposition," she clarified, gesticulating in midair. Those graceful fingers fluttered, and his entire body hummed in response. "While I was waiting for you to…er…get dressed, I noticed some of the broken porcelain, and Mr. Fletcher mentioned earlier that you might be looking for someone to help you categorize your late father's collection."

He was still caught up in indecent proposals, her flirting fingers, and thinking with his rock-hard lower regions. "And?"

"And I can help. I'm familiar with the period as well as the worth of some of the pieces."

Her matter-of-fact words pierced through his haze of desire. Thane's sex-starved body spun between lust and confusion. He blinked. He wanted to fuck her voluptuous hands, suck her lips from pink to berry, and she wanted to take inventory of his father's blasted antiques?

His dry mouth could form only one word. *"What?"*

"I can catalog the pieces for you," she said patiently. "I'm familiar with the period and the history."

"You're a bluestocking?"

Those distracting pink lips puckered into a little moue of displeasure. "I prefer 'scholar.'"

"Why?"

"Because 'bluestocking' is derogatory," she said with a frown.

He gave a huff of mirth. The second time he'd

laughed in ten minutes. It had to be a record. No doubt the eavesdropping Fletcher would toss it in his face later. Thane shook off the odd feeling. Somehow, instead of unsettling her, he'd only managed to unsettle himself.

A growling sound left his throat. "Why are you here? You barge in uninvited, see some smashed bowls, and decide to seek employment? Don't insult my intelligence. State your business so we can both get on with our lives."

There was no response to his sudden hostility. Rather, her eyes narrowed as she peered into the dimness, her pupils adjusting to the flickering light. It pricked him, the intensity he saw there, as if she were trying to figure out a puzzle. Trying to evaluate *him* like one did with a feral animal, waiting to see if it would bite. He wanted to snarl back at her, to get her to retreat. Run. *Leave.*

"Very well," she said, her jaw firming with blunt resolve. "I need you, Your Grace."

Surely he hadn't heard *that* correctly. "I beg your pardon?"

A sardonic eyebrow lifted at his use of the word "beg," but she clasped her hands together and sat up straight. "Specifically, the protection of your name in exchange for my assistance with your collection, other household matters, and of course, my…er… self, as well, in the production of heirs."

"Heirs," he echoed. He had no idea how they'd gone from porcelain to procreation.

She let out a breath. "Use of my body, Your Grace. As the daughter of a viscount, my bloodlines and background are quite…acceptable, I'm sure."

He didn't miss the minute hesitation or the fact that her captive fingers were clutched so tightly that they were white. Likely, the prospect revolted her. "This will be an arrangement that will benefit us both."

If Thane thought with the head in his pants, his agreement would be instantaneous. But his brain was quite good when he did decide to use it. And now that her outrageously erotic hands didn't distract him, he paused to gather his scattered thoughts.

"Are you proposing marriage, Lady Astrid?" he asked. "Didn't anyone ever teach you that the gentleman is supposed to ask?"

"I prefer to take matters into my own hands when necessary, but let's not be mistaken—this is purely a business proposition, Your Grace," she stated, her composed expression back in place. "One to our mutual advantage."

He couldn't help it. He guffawed, the ugly sound like a choked gaggle of cawing crows. The lady recoiled, her eyes widening further when he rose, uncurling his large frame from the chair. He prowled soundlessly toward her, watching her carefully all the while until he stood directly in front of her. He turned toward the light and heard her indrawn gasp.

Thane didn't release her eyes, reflective like translucent quartz in the firelight, taking in the transition from shock to fright to horror to pity. The darkness curled around him, took his cold, bitter heart into its fist. He felt nothing in the face of her emotions.

"Don't worry, I won't hold your naïveté against you," he murmured. "You are free to leave, my lady, and we can pretend this unfortunate...situation never happened."

To Thane's eternal shock, she rose and moved to stand right in front of him, those pearlescent eyes now giving away nothing. Her breasts were nearly touching his chest, and Thane caught his breath at her nearness, scenting the barest sliver of fear. Her shoulders trembled, and her stern lips, so dangerously close, quivered at the corners. Her distress was a palpable thing, like a hare cornered by a wolf, though the hare tipped its head bravely.

"You need a wife, Your Grace."

Thane had to admire her courage. "As you need a husband?"

"Not just any husband." She swallowed hard, her slender throat working. "I need the Beast of Beswick."

CHAPTER THREE

Oh, sweet merciless Lord.

The duke was frighteningly huge. And his appearance at close range…

Despite all the gossip and the rumors, Astrid had not been prepared. The Lord Harte she'd met in passing years ago had been surrounded by eager admirers, most of them female. A second son and the duke's spare, he'd been born into privilege and wealth and had been handsome and fit, if somewhat standoffish. He would have been sought after if he hadn't secured himself a captain's commission and hied off to war.

A war that had reduced him to this…shadow of himself.

Nothing could have readied her for the bleak vista of his face with its sutured lines and grisly lack of uniformity. A serrated tear ran diagonally from his upper right brow, across the bridge of his nose and cheek, down to his left jawline. It screamed of untold agonies, and the field surgeon's hasty stitching over poor cautery had only made the end result doubly macabre. Like the novel of the modern Prometheus, *Frankenstein*.

Though this duke was wholly human as far as she could tell…his eyes burned with an unholy amber fire, holding her in a glower that seemed better suited to hell. Astrid couldn't control the dread running through her body. His nostrils flared as if he could sense her unease, and suddenly, she felt like prey, well and truly snared by something far bigger and far more dangerous than she.

But fear wasn't the sole cause of her body's instant reaction to the man.

In the pit of her belly, she also felt a shock of pure heat, of raw physical awareness. Seeing a man naked, even in dim lighting, tended to skew one's good sense, clearly. Her brain was split with mixed images—those of him in the altogether, stepping like some beautifully ruined demigod from a shimmering pool, and the foul-tempered, scarred duke standing before her, barely held together by the bonds of civility.

His scars, though terrifying, were the least of what frightened her in that moment.

Courage faltering, her gaze fell away, and then she thought of Isobel. She did not have the luxury to falter in her course. This man—this monstrous duke—was their only hope. She spared him a glance, skating over his marred face. He was waiting for her to do more, she realized. To flee. To scream. To swoon at his beastliness.

And he was, indeed, beastly. Heartbreakingly so. Except for the lower right side of his jaw and his lips. Those were intact. Full, unscarred, masculine. Odd that his mouth felt like the only safe space in the ragged landscape of his face. Even those demonic golden eyes didn't seem so intense at the moment, inscrutable as they were. They'd lost their eerie hunter's glow. Or perhaps she was fooling herself to make her goal more palatable.

Isobel. Beaumont. Safety.

She opened her mouth to speak, but he beat her to it.

"Tell me, my lady, do you still wish for marriage?" The smoky, sardonic snarl of his voice, filled with bitterness, curled around her. "Do you wish to marry into a waking nightmare? Do you hope to see this visage when you wake up each and every morning?" He drew a mocking hand down his person, his lip twisting with distaste. "Provide those heirs you offer without shuddering?"

Astrid did *not* shudder, at least not right then, even though her heart was thrashing like a captive animal in her chest. The very idea of waking in bed with him made her body burn and recoil in the same breath. When she'd been plastered against him in the room with the bathing pool, she'd felt *everything*. Every hard contour, every hollow, every ridge. She blushed, recalling the bulge she'd felt against her belly through the sensible wool of her dress.

Clearly, he was like any other normal, able-bodied man.

Maybe not exactly like *any* other man, she amended. Notwithstanding his ruined face, he was bigger and more intimidating than any gentleman of her acquaintance. On top of that, he exuded an air of unrestrained menace. An apex predator. Would he protect or would he destroy?

Astrid couldn't quite suppress her shiver this time.

She felt his gaze narrow on her. "Don't bother trying to lie, Lady Astrid, or hide your reactions. At least they're honest. I shiver when I look into a mirror most days."

"I'm not," she began, her cheeks on fire. "That's not why—"

"Enough," he said. "Your loathing is as clear as day."

"No, Your Grace, you misunderstand."

He bared his teeth. "Now you seek to impugn my judgment."

God, she was losing him. Beswick was the only one who could help her prevent Beaumont's suit. Isobel was innocent, and *she* deserved better. Her sister was the only reason she was even here. Astrid shoved her chin up and gathered her brittle wits about her. She was no coward and would not back down now. She'd come here for one thing and one thing only.

"Yes, I do, Your Grace. I wish to marry you."

An odd expression passed over his face then. Disbelief? Astonishment? Wonder? After an interminable moment, the duke shifted to resume his position behind the desk. He sat back in the shadows—king of his natural domain. A devil cloaked in perpetual darkness. Again, Astrid felt that lick of self-preservation skate across her senses.

She cleared her throat, focusing on the task at hand and falling to her usual directness. "What happened to you?"

His big body went motionless in his chair, and for a moment, Astrid thought she'd gone too far. Pushed him beyond the limits of genteel courtesy. But then he responded. "I took on a half-dozen bayonets face-first."

The words held no inflection, though Astrid felt the lance of them deep in her soul. God, how he must have suffered. She held back another wince, but the duke was one to miss nothing.

"Don't be ashamed of being revolted. It's not for the faint of heart, is it?"

"No, Your Grace," she said, knowing he would hate any pity. "But I was not revolted. I was thinking that perhaps you might have benefitted from someone with neater stitching skills."

A gasp came from somewhere near the entrance, but Astrid didn't dare turn around. She could sense the duke's astonishment from where he sat.

"Is that one of your skills you hope to bring to the proposed match, then?" Beswick said eventually. "Needlework?"

"I am a lady, Your Grace, and skilled in all manner of gently bred persuasions."

"Is that so?"

She bristled at his tone, though she wasn't sure whether he was mocking what constituted a lady's education or whether he was mocking *her*. "Yes." And then she added, "Among other things."

"Like the study of ancient Chinese relics?"

Astrid sighed. Most men in her experience felt threatened by any females who *knew* anything at all. But she wasn't here to demonstrate her intelligence or use it as a defense against unwanted suitors; she was here to land herself a husband who was a bigger predator than the one she and Isobel currently faced. "I enjoy learning, Your Grace."

"Given your diverse range of feminine…talents, why hasn't some society fop seduced you off your accomplished feet and filled your womb with broods upon broods of future aristocrats?"

A blush crept up her neck. Gracious, but he was coarse. She could hardly tell him that one lying man's word against her own had well and truly barred that door. "Perhaps because I did not wish to be seduced."

"Don't all women wish for seduction?"

His eyes burned into hers, that sultry rasp doing unnatural things to her. A handful of words, and Astrid couldn't tempt a puff of air to enter her shrinking lungs. A rush of prickling heat blazed over her skin. Her entire body felt tight as if the slightest pressure would make her shatter. Gracious, what was the *matter* with her?

"Not all women," she choked out, her face hot, but her addled brain could not stop conjuring images of him naked, limned in fire and candlelight. A sliver of toweling that had barely hid his silhouetted masculine outline or the broad, muscular planes of his chest. She'd even gotten a brief glimpse of his swinging male part, and even *that* had sent a lightning bolt of heat to the base of her spine. The duke might be badly scarred, but he wasn't disfigured *there*.

Focus, you nitwit!

Astrid swallowed and brought her marauding thoughts ruthlessly under control. A fit of nerves hit her hard, one hand rising awkwardly to smooth her hair. No strand had escaped her coiffure, however. She felt his intense gaze track the movement of her palm. He seemed fixated, and her fingers fluttered in midair for an interminable moment before falling back to her lap.

Beswick leaned forward, folding his thick arms

across the desk's surface. Even with the enormous scar that bisected his face, the diamond cut of his aristocratic cheekbones sweeping toward that perfect, luscious mouth commanded attention.

His head tilted in silent ducal command. "If I were to consider your proposal, what would I get out of it?"

"You need my help." Astrid glanced around the room, touching on the priceless antique dish. "Least of all to catalog your antiquities. But as your wife, beyond my marital duties, I shall endeavor to be a proper hostess, should you seek to entertain. I'm also good with mathematics and can assist in your bookkeeping or estate management. Lastly, it's clear that a woman's touch is needed in your household."

She cringed, aware that she'd just criticized his home, but the duke's expression remained inscrutable.

"So when would you propose to do it?" he went on smoothly. "Marry?"

Astrid's heart jumped in surprise. God above, was he *amenable*? She narrowed her eyes. Or was he toying with her? She released a pent-up breath. "As soon as possible."

"Do you have terms?"

She nodded and reached into her reticule for the list she had prepared, then placed it on the desk between them. Despite her optimism, she'd known the odds were slim. "In terms of funds, I do have a dowry. I humbly ask for a certain amount of that be put aside for my sister's Season. In return, I will perform the aforementioned tasks as well as... submit to you as required to procure your heir."

Astrid bit her lip, fighting the sensual quake that rocked through her. "I assume once that is achieved, you will see to your needs elsewhere."

"Elsewhere?"

"I will not begrudge you a mistress, Your Grace."

• • •

Thane was glad to be obscured by the shadows. A *mistress*? Irritation flashed over him. Though many lords kept mistresses in addition to wives, he was not one of them.

At this point, thoroughly pricked pride was all that kept him from showing her the door. Pride and the need to give back as good as she gave. Though his better instincts warned against engaging, he nodded and pushed the inkstand closer to where she could reach it. "You should make a notation of more than one."

"More than one?"

"Mistress," he said. "My physical needs are varied. And quite demanding."

A choked sound met his ears as she reached for the inkpot and the pen, unspooling the piece of foolscap as she did so. The scratch of the pen was loud and heavy as she added an "ES" as a small postscript to the word. "There. Satisfied?"

It hurt to hold his perverse gratification inside. "And we might possibly need to rethink the word 'submit.' It's so outmoded—a wife *submitting* to her husband as though she has no say. I prefer my duchess to be vocal on what she wants."

Those pink lips flattened, splotches of bright

color flooding her cheeks. "What would you like to add, Your Grace? Positions? *Places?*" The little astringent bit of muslin huffed an irritated breath. "If you intend to make this a mockery, then we may as well not continue along this path. We are venturing into the realm of the offensive, sir."

What was offensive was his desire to see her utterly unclothed and open, with nothing but that salty mouth holding him at bay. Thane dug his fingers into his thighs and shook his head to clear it. They both knew that would *never* happen, no matter her asinine terms. She would flee his ill-tempered presence eventually, just like everyone else.

Thane had only humored her to see how far she would go. He did not intend to marry anyone or to sire *any* heirs, as he'd told Fletcher, but in truth, he'd been bowled over by her temerity. The eaves-dropping Culbert and Fletcher were, too, if their collective indrawn breaths through the cracked door were any signal.

His eyes narrowed. "You never answered my question about why you're not yet married."

"I did, but you chose to go off on an unwelcome tangent of ducal innuendo."

God, but she was tart. He grinned, his earlier umbrage dissolving into wicked enjoyment. "True, but I *am* a duke, and ducal innuendo is my forte. Please answer the question as you would to a backward child in your care. Say as if you were a governess."

She frowned at him so hard, he could see the wheels turning in her head.

"I suppose I've been compared to worse," she

said eventually. "Well then, I have not yet married because I have not found the right match."

"No one has asked you?" he asked before he could stop himself.

Wintry eyes met his, her proud chin hiking. "Not that it's any of your business, Your Grace, but yes, I have been asked."

"But if you had said yes and married, you wouldn't be in this position, would you?" he said. "Begging because you were overly choosy."

"I'm not begging," she snapped. "And I wasn't *choosy*."

He arched an eyebrow. "No?"

"I was sixteen during my first and only Season. That gentleman did not know me or have any interest in getting to know me. He desired me for my face, my fortune, and my body."

"Aristocratic marriages are arranged on less."

She loosed an aggravated breath, but her response was noncommittal. "Perhaps."

"And now? You decided to buck tradition and do the asking yourself?"

"As I've said, Your Grace, this is a business arrangement, no more, no less," she replied.

"Such sangfroid from one so young."

"I am five and twenty, so no blushing maiden."

Thane sucked in a sharp breath, his fingers clutching the desk. Her experience did not matter, of course, but now that the chessboard was set and the game was ferociously in play, there was no backing down. "On that point, what may I ask is the status of your virtue?"

Flames obliterated the aloofness in her eyes.

"You are too bold, sir!"

"Come now, in your own words, you are not a blushing maiden, and we are negotiating a marriage contract. A man has to be certain of these things, of whether he will be in possession of a soiled dove or a virtuous swallow."

Her gasp was loud in the silence, as were those of Culbert and Fletcher. If he wasn't careful, both of them would burst in here to defend the poor woman from their master's vulgarity. Not that this woman needed anyone rushing to her defense. Her tongue was her sword, and she wielded it with biting finesse.

Sure enough, a blazing gaze met his. "What, might I ask, is the status of yours?"

"Decidedly *un*virtuous."

That sharp chin of hers elevated a notch. "Then that makes one of us. Clearly I'm nowhere near your sphere of self-proclaimed experience, though I'm hard-pressed to believe any words that come out of your mouth. In my narrow experience, men who boast about their prowess leave much to be desired."

Thane couldn't help it. He threw back his head and roared with laughter until tears were brimming in his eyes. No one had ever stood up to him like this slip of a girl. *Woman*, he amended.

"This was a ridiculous idea," she muttered, standing to leave and then halting mid-motion as if caught in the midst of some raging internal battle.

She bit at her lips and then sighed heavily, clenching her jaw. When she looked up at him, the sparks of fire had gone from her gaze. What remained was desperation, tinged with despair. She leaned across the desk, and Thane knew she could see every one of his scars at such close proximity, but she did not flinch back or drop her eyes from his.

"Please, Duke, I implore you to consider my offer," she said.

Despite her choice of words, it was not a plea. This was not someone who begged for anything, but even he could sense her hopelessness. A flicker of a beat in his barren heart wanted him to agree. But his head knew he could not.

Reason returned with swift efficiency. "Lady Astrid, I—"

"Must get ready for a previous engagement," Fletcher interrupted, bustling in. Both Thane and Lady Astrid turned in surprise. "You can look over the correspondence from the lady later, Your Grace."

"Fletcher, this is highly irregular—" he began in warning, but as usual, the valet took no notice of him. One wouldn't fathom that the man actually worked for him or that his employer was the damn duke.

"Come now, my lady," Culbert said, following in Fletcher's wake and taking the foolscap from her fingers with an elaborate flourish. "Leave this with His Grace."

Lady Astrid looked bewildered at the turn of events and the meddling servants. So was Thane, but he knew exactly what Fletcher and Culbert were about. Clearly, they both thought that she was his only chance at any kind of future. But he knew better—he understood his reality. Hungering for impossible outcomes would only lead to despair. And Thane had had enough of despair to last a lifetime.

He had to end this.

"The answer is no," he growled, halting them in their tracks at the study door. "Not now. Not ever." He turned to Fletcher and Culbert. "Do not ever presume to know my mind, either of you. Leave my sight before you're put out on your deuced heels."

Both men slunk away as he swung back to the silent woman who fixed him with an appalled expression. "Since you found your way into my home uninvited, I trust you know the way out, Lady Astrid. Don't come back."

Hard eyes like polished aquamarine met his, holding them. She did not flinch at his aggression or burst into fits. Instead—admirably—she lifted her chin. "I'm not afraid of you, Beswick. You cannot order me about like those poor men."

"You should be," he snarled. "And they're *my* servants." Mostly.

Astonishingly, she smiled in the face of his wrath. "Be that as it may, you'll find that I'm not a woman who can be intimidated by a temper tantrum better suited to a child than a duke. When you come to your senses, feel free to tender your apologies. I shall be at Everleigh House."

"And pigs will fly with their tails forward."

She spun on her heel, a wintry gaze spearing him over her shoulder. "I would wish you a good day, Your Grace, but I can see for myself that any kind of civilized manners are categorically wasted on you."

And with that, she was gone.

CHAPTER FOUR

Astrid chewed on her nails, her eyes moving from her book to the window overlooking the front courtyard, not that she was expecting visitors. A small—*miniscule*—part of her had hoped he'd send a written apology. Beneath that surly, churlish exterior, Beswick had been born a gentleman, after all. But one day had passed, and then two, and now three. She was dreaming if she thought that man had a lick of good breeding left in him.

Which meant the next move was still on her. *Blast it.* Once more, she cursed her wayward tongue. But no, she had to go and speak her mind and provoke him. And then tell him off. *In his own home.* And now, thanks to her runaway, ungovernable mouth, she and Isobel were out of options. Unless… she went back to Beswick Park again.

Nausea wound through her belly. She could beg, if she had to. Throw herself at his mercy. She'd never bent to anyone, but for Isobel's sake, she could. Even to a hard-hearted, rude, ill-mannered brute of a man.

"Well, what was he like?" Isobel asked for the fortieth time, no longer put off by Astrid's vague answers. "Is he as bad as they say? Cook said that he fired another housekeeper. She says he's so terrifying, he can't seem to keep a full household."

That did not surprise her. She'd seen the shards of porcelain gracing the foyer and several of the dusty corridors. She pursed her lips in thought. Perhaps she could convince Beswick that *she* would make an excellent housekeeper. It wasn't the worst idea, even though it was contingent on him hiring her. She hadn't exactly left the abbey on the best of terms.

Astrid sighed and faced her sister. "Cook should not be gossiping."

"Was he hideous?" Isobel asked.

"His face is badly scarred from battle," Astrid said, the twisted ropes of the duke's many scars coming to mind. "But it's not as dreadful once the initial shock has worn off."

Her sister shuddered. "I've heard people in the village say that his skin looks like a stitched sack, and he's so awful to look upon that children have night terrors. His own father had a heart attack and dropped dead when he saw his face."

"You know better than to listen to rumors, Isobel. He's not as bad as all that."

Inside, Astrid's heart clenched with pity. She'd heard the same stories. No wonder the man was so closed off and prickly. Though in truth, the duke was doing little to dissuade that opinion with his atrocious attitude. People always assumed that if someone looked like a monster, then they had to be monstrous. But as crude and abrasive as he was, Astrid did not feel endangered in his presence. He *did* make her want to pull her hair out, but that was completely unrelated to his appearance.

Astrid stared blindly at her novel, trying to distract herself from her constant thoughts about the confounding duke. For all her intelligence and insight, she'd read the man wrong. She'd thought with him being a recluse, he would be desperate for a wife and heir. She knew how the aristocracy worked. Noble lines mattered. Primogeniture mattered. She couldn't fathom any duke worth his salt wanting his ducal heritage to pass into oblivion.

Then again, the Beast of Beswick was no ordinary duke.

Oddly enough, as crude as he was, she'd relished matching wits with him. He was nothing like she'd expected.

Inquiring about her virtue, for heaven's sake. She'd almost swooned from the sheer gall of it. A secretly delighted part of her had trilled, however, that he hadn't treated her like a piece of precious china whose feminine ears were in danger of fracturing from a bit of bawdy conversation. Deep down, she'd *liked* it.

Besides, from what she'd seen at his residence, he needed her as much as she needed him. And not just for the categorization of his antiques, though her fingers itched at the chance to go through the gorgeous collection. She'd also seen how he'd treated his poor servants. The man needed someone to take him in hand…someone to see past the rages and sulks, who wouldn't let him get away with his bad behavior.

But how could she convince him a match between them was necessary?

There were no other lords in Southend who could come close to standing up to the Earl of Beaumont or her uncle. Otherwise, she would have to put another plan into place. And that entailed pawning jewelry and running away, which wasn't much of a plan at all for two unmarried women. She needed time to persuade Beswick, to plead her case.

Perhaps she could talk to the duke's man, Fletcher, about the inventory of Chinese antiques in the meantime. He'd seemed desperate to hire someone. She could barter her skills in exchange for a safe place to stay for her and Isobel. Once again, it wasn't the worst idea she'd ever had. But it still wouldn't protect Isobel from their uncle's rights of guardianship if Astrid couldn't convince the duke and remained unmarried. And then, there was also no guarantee that Fletcher would hire her without his master's say-so.

God, it's hopeless!

Astrid focused on her book, determined to put her negative thoughts out of her mind, at least for the moment, when a red-faced maid came bustling up the servant stairs. "Lady Astrid, one of the horses has gotten loose, and Patrick sent me to get you at once, if you please."

"Which one?" she asked, leaping to her feet, but she already knew. The head groom would send for her only when Temperance or Brutus was giving trouble. Both thoroughbreds had a long history of racing in their veins. Her mare Temperance was decidedly temperamental, despite her name, and Brutus was a mischievous three-year-old that needed a firm but gentle hand. Unlike the rest of the horses, they belonged to her and had been gifts from her father.

"Will you be all right for a moment?" she asked Isobel.

"Of course. Agatha is here," she said, indicating their shared lady's maid who sat quietly with a basket of mending.

"I'll be back in a bit."

Hitching up her skirts, Astrid raced through the house and down to the stables. Sure enough, it was Brutus who had escaped and was causing trouble. The stallion was surrounded by three grooms, rearing up on his hind legs and snapping with his teeth.

"How did he get out, Patrick?"

"I dunnae ken, my lady," the big Scottish groom said. "His pen was latched, but it came open on its own. It must have no' been closed properly. I'll have a word with the lads."

Astrid approached the skittish stallion with care. Brutus was unpredictable when he was riled, and she needed enough distance to protect herself if he decided to bite or kick. She'd suffered the ill effects of two badly bruised ribs when she'd made that mistake once when he was a colt. He was much bigger now and no less skittish.

Signaling to the men to back away, Astrid approached, her hands wide. "There, boy," she crooned. "It's only me. I won't hurt you."

Brutus reared up again, his hooves thrusting out, but it wasn't wild. After some more male posturing, he allowed her to approach and take hold of his bridle; all the while she kept murmuring soft endearments into his ear. Within minutes, she was leading him back to the stable as quietly as you please.

"Ye're a miracle worker, ye are, my lady," Patrick said, his eyes full of wonder and respect. "I swear he was going to take a chunk out of my hide this time."

Astrid stroked the horse's lathered black coat. "He's just high-strung. Put him in the stall next to Temperance. She seems to calm him some when he gets in these moods."

The Scot eyed her. "Do ye ever think to breed them, my lady?"

"Someday," she replied with a fond pat to the stallion's glossy hindquarters. "But not if my uncle intends to sell the foals to the highest bidder. Once Isobel gets settled safely into a new position, perhaps then."

Astrid made her way back to the house, thankful that it hadn't been worse. The horses were two of her most prized and valuable possessions. She halted mid-step at the thought. If worse came to worst, she could sell them, but that, too, would take time. The thought of parting with either of them left her cold, but if it meant Isobel's happiness and safety, no sacrifice would be too big. Gracious, she'd already offered herself to a duke with a terrible reputation.

As she went past the courtyard, Astrid squinted at a coach in the drive. Her heart rose and fell in the same breath. It wasn't an apologetic duke but an entirely unwelcome Beaumont. What was he doing there? Her aunt and uncle had business in the village and weren't at home. Astrid hefted her skirts and ran, nearly skidding around the corridor where the earl had discovered Isobel in the morning salon.

"Get Patrick," she whispered to Agatha who stood close by, her face white.

"Lord Beaumont," Astrid said, hoping to God her voice sounded stronger than she felt. "To what do we owe the honor of your unexpected visit?"

Beaumont turned, a smile forming. "I was invited."

"By whom?" she replied with a cool hauteur she did not feel. Fear for her sister swamped her. "My aunt and uncle are not at home."

"They expressed an invitation for me to visit today."

Astrid's heart sank. Of course they had. They did not care if a notorious rogue compromised their niece as long as he married her. Notwithstanding that said rogue had already ruined one niece. She kept a tight hold on her unraveling emotions. "I'm sorry, my lord, but you will have to return. Without my aunt as a proper chaperone, I fear this is quite improper."

"Surely you can suffice," he said, "while I call on my future wife?"

Her skin crawled at his tone, but she forced herself to remain calm. For Isobel's sake. For *both* their sakes. "I am also unmarried, my lord. It would not be proper. I must, regretfully, ask you to leave."

"I'm not pleased with your lack of proper respect or welcome, Astrid. I *am* a peer of the realm."

"Then do everyone a favor and act like one," she retorted. "And it's Lady Astrid to you."

With a scowl, Beaumont advanced into the room as if she hadn't protested his presence at all, but no more than two steps in, he stopped, his eyes fastened on the doorway where Patrick stood with two hefty grooms.

"Lord Beaumont was just leaving," Astrid told them.

"Your uncle will hear of this," the earl hissed.

"Mark my words."

But he departed without more of a scene, thankfully. After the carriage left, Astrid slid down into a nearby chair. Her hands shook with delayed fear. She had no doubt that Beaumont would complain to her uncle, and that reprisal would be swift. Would he send Astrid away? Post the banns for Isobel? Oh God, what were they going to do?

"Astrid?" Isobel whispered. "Will he come back?"

Her sister's voice pierced her fog of indecision. Without a doubt, the earl would. There was nothing to be said for it—they had to leave. Astrid composed herself, rose, and met Patrick's eyes where he still stood in the doorway to the salon. "Saddle Brutus and Temperance and call for the carriage." Astrid turned to Isobel and her maid, Agatha, her voice low. "Gather our things. Pack anything you can fit into our trunks."

"Where are we going?" Isobel asked, wide-eyed.

Astrid shook her head. There were too many eyes and ears still about. "Somewhere safe."

• • •

Hell and damnation. Not even the brutal hours-long ride back from London to Beswick Park had chased the bunched energy from Thane's muscles. He had worked himself to the bone for the past three days, pushing himself further than he'd ever done, and nothing seemed to help.

He'd taken a trip to London to meet with his estate solicitor, Sir Thornton. The overnight trip had turned into a week, with him restlessly pacing the halls of his London home. He knew why he was in a froth, of course.

It was because of *her*.

Thane supposed it was guilt for sending her away as callously as he had. But the truth was, he couldn't agree to her proposition. Though he couldn't stop thinking about it—or her. One bloody hour of conversation, and he craved more of her delicious wit like an opium addict. It was madness. By God, the chit invaded his every waking hour. Sleeping ones as well.

Before he'd gone to London, he'd ridden over to the Everleigh estate in the dark of night, trying to figure out which bedroom was hers. And then he'd imagined her in a transparent night rail lying in bed, and his renowned self-control had been shot to hell.

He'd left for Town that very night.

Thane couldn't remember the last time he'd felt so uncertain. He was a man who'd been valued for his discipline, his unerring ability to know what action needed to be done in the moment. His war unit had been effective because of that mind-set. On the battlefield, it was that certainty that had made him take on six armed Frenchmen alone. In hindsight, in view of his personal sacrifice, it might not have been the best decision, but it had spared the rest of his unit from being slaughtered.

Throwing his reins to his waiting groom in the mews at Beswick Park, his eyes fixed in the distance on a massive black horse being exercised in a paddock by a large redheaded man he didn't recognize. When had he acquired another horse? Or a groomsman the size of a small mountain?

Culbert would know. But as he pushed open the door, no butler was there to greet him. In fact, *no one* was there. He hadn't sent notice ahead when he would be arriving, but he was the sodding duke. Certainly some of his ungrateful staff should be present to welcome him home! It was far too early for anyone to be abed. Scowling with displeasure, he went in search of his missing servants.

On his way to the staircase, he heard what sounded like music and laughter.

Female laughter.

His scowl went so tight, it threatened to decapitate his brow from his face. If those two impertinent louts of a butler and valet thought to entertain village wenches in his absence, they were in for a rude awakening. He would follow through on his threats and dismiss them immediately.

Following the voices, what he saw when he turned the corner into what used to be the ballroom and was now a room of no special purpose made him freeze. It was a veritable crowd. And not villagers. Most of his absent servants, in fact.

The notes of a jubilant country song filled his ears, the lilting voice accompanied by a tune on the pianoforte. Thane blinked in disbelief. His traitorous butler and valet were dancing a reel! Along with his surly French chef who hated everyone, most of the footmen and the maids, and two well-dressed ladies…one easily identifiable and the other unbeknownst to him.

Thane ignored the leap of his pulse and the violent need to dismiss everyone from sight.

Everyone except *her*.

"Will someone please instruct me on what the fuck is going on?"

. . .

Astrid had never seen people scatter so quickly, servants scurrying to their positions at the return of the master of the house. In moments, the boisterous group had dwindled to Fletcher, Culbert, herself, and Isobel. Her eyes flicked to the imposing figure at the door. The duke was still wearing dusty riding clothes as well as his hat, pulled low. She was grateful for it, though Isobel was staring at him in slack-jawed morbid curiosity, which likely had more to do with his foul, oath-spewing attitude than his sudden appearance.

Fletcher opened his mouth to respond, but Astrid beat him to it, drawing the fire to her instead. "Language, Your Grace."

He tipped his head back just enough for those blazing amber eyes to capture hers. Astrid almost shrank back from the burn of his glare. He was furious. "It's my house," he said, that smoky voice doing unnatural things to her senses. "I'll say what I damn well please."

"Not in the presence of gently bred ladies you won't." She reached for her sister's hand and squeezed in a reassuring manner. "My lord duke, may I present my younger sister, Lady Isobel Everleigh."

Isobel dipped into a curtsy. "Your Grace."

Astrid could tell he wanted to shout and swear more foully from the look on his face—possibly at her and it was likely deserved—but he gritted his teeth and bowed, keeping his face hidden in the shadow of his hat. "A pleasure."

"Mr. Culbert," Astrid said gently, turning to the butler whose jowls had gone ruddy. "Will you kindly escort my sister to her rooms while I have a word with His Grace?"

"Astrid?" Isobel whispered, looking scared. "Will he cast us out?"

"It will be well, Izzy. I promise."

Fletcher moved to follow Culbert and Isobel but was cut short with one word from the duke. Frankly, Astrid was happy. She did not want to face the man on her own. Not after she'd invaded his domain without so much as a by-your-leave. *Again*.

She drew a breath. "Have you reconsidered my offer, Your Grace?"

"No." He glared at her, tearing his hat off and stalking to the mantelpiece. Strangely, the swift sight of his ruined face did not distress her. "My answer is the same."

Astrid had fled to Beswick Park after Beaumont's visit with the intention of changing the duke's mind, only to learn that he was in London, and then she'd decided to beseech Fletcher for a job or at least somewhere for her and Isobel to stay for a day or two. He had taken pity on them. However, from the look on the duke's face, his master would not be so easy to convince.

She had to try. "How many housekeepers will you scare away before you come to your senses? I've heard you dismissed another one."

"She was incompetent."

Astrid lifted an eyebrow. "And the previous three?"

"I don't need a housekeeper," he snarled, lifting a green and white Ming bowl from its stand and throwing it into the hearth, an act that made *both* her and Fletcher flinch.

"I can see that you have everything under control," Astrid said. "Clearly a quick wedding would be in your best interests."

A furious stare met hers. "I fail to see how I require your approval for my staffing needs, Lady Astrid, as a wife or otherwise." The tension rose to the murals on the ceiling as the three of them stood there in silence. Then the duke turned on his heel with a sound of displeasure. "Fletcher, unless I'm paying you to stand there and flirt, I require a bath."

"I gave the order for a bath to be readied the moment you arrived." The cheeky valet smirked with little care for his own well-being. "And flirtation's always free, Your Grace."

The duke's mouth went flat, and Astrid hurried to intervene. "Your Grace, surely you can see that this—" she began with a frown as he whirled on his heel and strode away, leaving her standing with her mouth open.

Good God, but he was rude! Where was the man going mid-conversation? What would she and Isobel do if he did not give her an answer? Where would they go?

"You may follow if you have something more to say," he told her over his shoulder.

Head high, she walked past the nearby footmen, two of whom had wonderful singing voices, as Astrid had discovered earlier before Beswick's arrival. She'd only meant to cheer Isobel up with some music, and then it seemed that everyone else in the dismal manse had needed some cheering as well. It was all her fault, and she would explain it to him, if only she could keep up.

"Your Grace, please do not take your anger out on the staff," she gasped, running to match his ground-eating strides. "Or Fletcher."

"I am not angry."

But he was. She could feel it emanating from him like rolling thunder. He was seething with it. Astrid exchanged a look with Fletcher, who had hurried ahead and was waiting at the entrance of the duke's private suite, and halted. "I cannot go in there."

"It's a sitting room, Astrid, not a bedchamber," the duke said coldly.

The sound of her given name was a startling flick of pleasure along her senses, and she shoved the odd response away to be pulled apart later. "Regardless, it's not proper."

"If you wish to explain your presence here and not see you and your sister booted out on your un-welcome behinds, you will explain wherever I see fit. And right now, I want a fucking bath."

She grimaced at the oath. "Do you kiss your mother with that mouth, Your Grace?"

"My mother is dead," he said, peering down, amber eyes flaring. "But if it's kissing you desire, then we should be having another conversation."

"I wouldn't kiss you if you paid me."

"And yet you offered much more than that. Which is it, Lady Astrid?"

She faltered, her face heating, but then tossed her chin. "Lying there and thinking of England is hardly the same."

Beswick stopped dead to stare at her, those hot eyes burning into hers, his fists clenching and unclenching at his sides. Good God, had she gone too far? Even Fletcher gaped. But Astrid held her ground, chin high. Someone had to stand up to the duke. His temper was too foul for words, and she was only giving him what he doled out...what he deserved.

A short, hard huff of breath left his lips, and after an interminable moment, he spun on his heel and stomped past his valet. "Follow me or leave. Your choice."

The tension left her body in a wild rush as she stood in the corridor debating what to do. He hadn't ordered her thrown out, at least. She heard the faint rustle of clothing and froze. No, he wouldn't be so vulgar, would he? Somehow, she had to convince him to let them stay, even if entering his private quarters wasn't proper, and even if he made her want to rail and scream like a fishwife.

Isobel. Beaumont. Safety.

"I'm waiting," he called out after long minutes of indecision on her part.

With a bracing inhale, Astrid inched forward on leaden feet, but the duke was not in the adjoining bedchamber. Fletcher met her eyes with an apologetic expression, but he, too, said nothing, as if he were on uncertain ground himself. His position was at risk, Astrid realized with belated horror, because of her. She could not let him take the fall for having a kind heart, when clearly, his master had none.

Briskly, she closed the distance to where Fletcher stood. It led to another room. A brightly lit bathing chamber, to be precise. Astrid bit back a gulp. Not at the opulence of the high-backed tub that dominated the room but at the man lounging inside of it, facing away from her. She couldn't see much over the tub's sides, but mere feet away, her brain processed that the duke was *naked*.

"Speak," he commanded.

Hurriedly averting her eyes and banishing the phrase "naked duke" from her vocabulary, she rushed into her explanation, outlining Fletcher's kindhearted offer and his need for a capable historian. Astrid didn't miss the side glower that pinned the poor valet in place at the last.

"He only wished to help," she said. "If you won't agree to wed, for your…hospitality for a few paltry months, I will do your inventory. Think of it as employment, if you cannot find it in your heart to consider it charity."

When she turned six and twenty, she wouldn't be so powerless. That money was hers, and she would fight tooth and nail to claim it.

"Look at me," the duke said.

Astrid raised her gaze, careful to keep her eyes fastened to his, but peripheral vision was a dratted thing. His sable hair was damp, wet droplets beading his golden-hued skin. She couldn't see much scarring on the right side of him, and Astrid lost her breath at the sight of a glistening sculpted shoulder. As if sensing her thoughts, Beswick angled his face sharply toward her. She swallowed a gasp at the view in full light but refused to look away even when she felt tears prick her eyes.

"I don't want your pity," he said. "I'd prefer your loathing."

"I don't loathe you."

"You might, when I decide what to do with your sister and you," he said. "You cannot stay here in a bachelor's residence." She opened her mouth to protest, but he lifted a finger, stalling her, a notch of irritation appearing between his brows. "Not without a proper chaperone. Your sister's reputation, and yours, will depend on it. I will agree, aside my better judgment, for you to stay here if my aunt, the Duchess of Verne, consents to be in residence for the time you require. You will perform the inventory as agreed, but that is the extent of my generosity."

Relief, followed by elation that they would not be cast out, swamped her so much that she took a handful of steps forward before she thought twice. His indrawn hiss stopped her, but it was too late. Her eyes dropped to the clear surface of the water that hid nothing.

Not the scars and gouges and missing flesh that marred his left arm and peppered his left side. Not the sleek bronze hair covering his massive chest and arrowing down a tapered belly. Not the scarred tapestry of his lower limbs. And certainly not the unmistakable evidence of his arousal.

Astrid did what any self-respecting lady would do. She fled.

CHAPTER FIVE

Christ, he wanted to fuck her into the wall.

Lift her lithe body against the bathing chamber door, wrap her legs around his dripping wet body, sheathe himself in her, and come until he had nothing left. Thane groaned and threw an arm over his eyes. Evidently, those parts of him weren't as dead as he'd thought.

"Fletcher," he said wearily, knowing the man was still standing there.

"Yes, Your Grace?"

"You'll pay for this. You know that, don't you?"

He could feel the grin in the man's voice even without looking at him. "Yes, Your Grace."

"Good, now get out so I can drown myself in self-pity and frustration." He slitted open one eye to see his valet wearing a smug grin. "Write my aunt and see if she's amenable to a long, overdue visit."

"I already took the liberty, Your Grace."

Of course he had. The wretched man knew his own worth, which was probably why he'd taken in the waif and her sister in the first place.

"Lady Verne will be arriving in time for dinner," Fletcher said from the other room.

Thane frowned. "When did you send a messenger?"

"Four days ago, Your Grace, when Lady Astrid arrived on your doorstep. I thought it prudent to be prepared in case you decided to offer employment and safe refuge."

Safe refuge? Thane nearly hooted with laughter. People didn't run to him. They ran *from* him. The Beast of Beswick did not harbor young innocents, nor was he the hero in any story. He was a recluse, a monster of a man, and a beast by all accounts. Having not just one but *two* highborn, unmarried females in his domain was unthinkable. Absurd, really. Their precious reputations would be smudged in the dirt by morning.

"And you did not think to send a missive to me in London?"

Fletcher appeared for one moment in the doorway. "I did, Your Grace. At Harte House. Though you had not been seen since your arrival."

No, because he'd been working with Sir Thornton during the day and drowning his demons at The Silver Scythe at night. A vision of frosted aquamarine eyes set in a heartbreakingly lovely face, dark hair scraped back with fastidious precision, and a tart pink mouth framed in a perfect *O* at the sight of him nude filled his mind.

Christ, he was a depraved, unfeeling bastard for forcing her to plead her case *while he bathed*. He hadn't intended to, of course, but then that sharp tongue of hers had drawn blood: *Lying there and thinking of England is hardly the same.* Salty minx.

After Fletcher departed, Thane washed and lay in the water until his skin became the consistency of a prune and the water had cooled considerably. He was still as hard as steel, however. Thane fisted his length and, with a few short strokes, brought himself to release. It felt mildly hollow, but he didn't care.

He'd resort to his own hand a dozen times a day if it meant not obsessing about her...a beautiful woman with the spiciest mouth this side of England, whom he'd just invited to stay under his roof for months.

Clearly, he was a glutton for punishment.

He dressed in the clothing that Fletcher had left out for him and descended the stairs. He hoped dinner would be prepared and served, and he wouldn't walk into another impromptu amateur musicale. Thane shook his head. His country staff, like his London staff, was silent and efficient. The epitome of a duke's household. The footmen were large, competent, and quiet. The chef was French and proud of it. In the absence of a housekeeper, Culbert kept the maids and everyone else in strict order. But never had Thane seen them partake in such bold, happy revelry, heedless of rank between upper and lower servants, as he had earlier.

He'd only been gone a bloody week.

And he knew exactly who was to blame.

Scowling, Thane grabbed a hat from the foyer as he clomped to the dining room. He didn't want to scare the younger chit. Isabella or Isabel or some such. He'd only glanced at her briefly, taking in her pretty features. She was indeed a perfect English rose with her golden ringlets and sparkling blue eyes. Though he'd been more concerned with the prickly bit of bramble who had been standing beside her, her sharp chin high and eyes bright. Ready to do battle with the lord of the manor on account of a few paltry servants.

Astrid.

Even her name made him feel invigorated, like

an icy burst of sea spray from a winter ocean. Hard-nosed and stubborn, she was the opposite of her sister in every way, not just in looks. She was no meek English rose, no sweet-tempered maiden, no delicate miss. She was a fiery hothouse bloom that made his blood burn and drove him to intolerable distraction.

Culbert was waiting at the entrance of the grand dining room. "Your Grace," he intoned and pushed open the door. "The Duchess of Verne is already in residence and is awaiting you."

Thank God for small mercies. He didn't want the destruction of a debutante's reputation on his conscience. The old duchess was alone, he noted with some relief. He wanted to speak to her briefly before his uninvited guests arrived.

"Aunt Mabel," he said, walking over to the tiny but plump woman who was sipping on a glass of sherry and flirting with the footmen. He bit back a smile. Some things never changed. At five and sixty, she was incorrigible. Last he'd heard, she'd taken a lover who was half her age. Thane faltered briefly. Perhaps she wasn't quite the best choice of a chaperone, given her proclivities. Then again, she was family, and she could be trusted.

And she was accustomed to his face.

"Darling boy, how are you?" she said, embracing him fondly. "I've heard nothing but naughty tales of you for months, living in seclusion and terrorizing your staff. Come now, Beswick, will you not settle down? You're getting on in age, you know." She paused, eyeing him. "Why are you wearing a hat for dinner?"

He bussed her cheek, accepting the glass of cognac from one of the footmen, and ignored everything but for the last question. "One of the young ladies is quite tender in years, and I don't wish to frighten the spit out of her, Aunt."

The duchess didn't miss a thing, those sharp green eyes fastening to his. "And the other? Fletcher said there were two. Will she not be frightened?"

"The other is a harpy who is immune to fear," he muttered, downing his drink. He did not mention that the lady in question had in fact propositioned him with marriage a mere week before. It would likely set darling Aunt Mabel into a fit of histrionic laughter. Or she would force him to the altar herself. "I suspect people tend to cower in that lady's presence."

Mabel's eyes brightened. "She sounds like my kind of girl." Thane scowled, and she patted his arm. "That she's not cowering from you, I mean." She studied him. "Though it's remarkable how much I no longer notice your scars. Perhaps I've grown used to them."

"Or perhaps you're losing your eyesight in your old age."

She swatted him. "Dreadful boy!"

Thane felt his ill humor slip away. Mabel would manage the undesirable invasion, and if push came to shove, he would simply return to London until it was all over. Which he had no idea when that would be. He recalled the older chit saying something about a twenty-sixth birthday and coming into an inheritance. Months, she'd said. He tried not to balk at being in London during the Season. Not that he had anything to worry about in terms of marriage prospects or being pursued, it was just too over-crowded.

Thane valued his solitude. And he sodding hated London even when Parliament wasn't in session.

"Lady Astrid Everleigh and Lady Isobel Ever-leigh," Culbert intoned.

Thane turned, his gaze touching on the younger girl for a moment and then resettling on the older sister. Both were dressed for dinner, Isobel in a pastel-colored dress and Astrid in a simple dove-gray gown that made her beauty seem more remote, more untouchable. His fingers itched to demolish that ascetic collar, her severe hairstyle, and that tight, dour expression. One that softened marginally when she saw his aunt.

"Lady Astrid, Lady Isobel, may I present the Duchess of Verne, my aunt."

"Aunt?" Astrid murmured as if confused that he had relatives.

"I wasn't raised by wolves, if that's what you were thinking," he said dryly. "My late father's sister."

"I wasn't." She shot him a black look that could rival any of his and curtsied to his aunt. "A pleasure, Your Grace."

"Ladies." Mabel greeted them with a warm smile.

Under the duchess's cordiality and guidance, dinner passed without discomfort. The food, as always, was of exceptional fare. André would die if anything not fit for French court left his kitchen. As it was, the cream of turtle soup was as light as air, the duck *à l'orange* melted in one's mouth, and the braised rabbit was succulent. It was a wonder that

Thane wasn't two stone heavier with such rich foods, but he made it a point to stay physically active. After being a soldier for so many years, he refused to live too dissipated a lifestyle.

Conversation was pleasant, with Mabel and a surprisingly chatty Isobel leading most of the talk. It was strange that the two of them took to each other so well, given the age gap, but not surprising. His aunt could make anyone feel at ease. Even when he'd returned from the war, she'd been the one to hold him firmly and ask him if his brain or his heart or his spirit had been destroyed.

"Beauty is fleeting, lad," she'd told him. "You have your life."

His response had been predictably grim. "A half life."

"It's only what you make it, my darling. Half, quarter, full. It's all in your power, and everything you had before, you still do."

"I don't have a *face*, Aunt."

"Then, perhaps you'll have to depend on your other redeeming qualities for once."

Thane almost laughed at the memory. His aunt Mabel was a hoyden with a heart of gold and a core of pure steel. But he'd still disappointed her. Unfortunately, there was nothing left in him that was worth redeeming. His own father hadn't thought so, and neither did most anyone else.

He felt eyes on him and glanced up to meet Astrid's. She hadn't said more than two words since they'd sat down, though she did not seem unhappy. More pensive. Though that wasn't quite the right word, either. She seemed focused as though she were in the middle of a performance. "Is the meal to your liking, Lady Astrid?"

"Oh yes," she said. "It's delicious."

"When do you expect to start the inventory?"

She faltered as if surprised by the question. Thane lifted an expectant eyebrow. It *was* how she'd intended to barter for her stay, of course.

"Tomorrow," she said crisply. "I've already spoken to Fletcher."

"Inventory?" Aunt Mabel asked.

"Father's cherished antiques," Thane answered. "I haven't decided whether to sell or donate the lot of it. They're just here gathering cobwebs. It was Fletcher's idea. Me, I'd rather use them for sport. There's nothing like the sound of shattering porcelain. Quite invigorating, I tell you."

Astrid's lips turned down. "Your Grace, some of those pieces are priceless."

"So you keep saying."

"If only you would listen," she shot back. "But alas, you would have to stop speaking long enough to do so."

Thane sat back in his chair, aware of his aunt's suddenly interested gaze panning between the two of them. "When a voice is all one has, one tends to indulge."

"You know what they say about noise and empty vessels."

He couldn't help it—he gave a dry chuckle. "Touché, my lady."

Although Astrid Everleigh was a fascinating contradiction and a spark of life in his otherwise barren landscape, it irked him how much he actually enjoyed the verbal sparring. How much he seemed to enjoy *her*. And that was a certain recipe for disaster.

Thane sipped his wine with a frown. Aside his body's interest, which hadn't been interested in anyone since the war, she wasn't afraid of him, and she amused him…a feat in itself. Her protectiveness toward her sister intrigued him. Though she was guarded, he was determined to find out what she was hiding. And what he'd gotten into.

After dinner, when his aunt decided to retire to her rooms after her journey and Isobel hastened off to bed, only Astrid remained at the table. Thane stood and offered her a glass of brandy, gesturing for her to follow him to the adjoining terrace. Though it was dark, soft lamplight illuminated the grounds, the lush scent of the gardens wafting around them.

"This is beautiful," she said, joining him at the balustrade. They stood in silence, sipping their drinks and staring into the shadows, before Astrid spoke again. "I want to thank you, Your Grace, for your kindness."

"I am not in the least bit kind, Lady Astrid," he said quietly, his eyes pinning hers in the darkness. "What are you running from? Tell me the truth."

Her gaze fell away, and she took a bracing sip of brandy before answering. "My uncle intends to marry Isobel off, and unfortunately, I do not come into the rest of my inheritance until my twenty-sixth year to take her away. I have no prospects, and my uncle is a greedy man concerned with his own fortunes, no matter the tender years of my sister. Isobel wasn't safe there."

Thane blinked, not entirely sure what he'd been expecting. "Marriage to whom? A peer?"

"The Earl of Beaumont."

He froze. Now *that* was a name he hadn't heard in years, and one he wished to keep buried in the past. Though, in truth, he did not have fault with the earl, only his nephew. Thane's fingers curled in anger around his glass. Last he heard, the pigeon-livered Edmund Cain was hiding on the Continent. After he'd abandoned his post in Thane's regiment, sacrificing half their unit to a French ambush, Cain had defected to parts unknown.

"Why are you so against the match?" he asked. "Beaumont might be old, but he's not objectionable."

"My sister is only sixteen. A man like him will destroy her."

Thane's brows rose. He couldn't say he knew much of Cain's uncle, but he supposed he might. After all, the man had to be getting on in years, and Isobel was so young. Not that it wasn't common practice in the aristocracy for peers to take much younger wives.

"Was that the reason for your proposition?"

Astrid nodded, sliding him a sideways glance. "Beaumont plans to offer for Isobel before anyone else, and I cannot allow that to happen. If I am to marry, my husband will have the final say in Isobel's future, not my uncle." She sighed into her glass. "You were my only avenue of influence to thwart the earl."

"Why me?" Thane wanted to kick himself for asking.

She finished her drink before walking back to the terrace doors and pausing there. Shuttered ice-blue eyes met his, her voice low. "Because sometimes a girl doesn't need a hero to save her. Sometimes she needs the opposite."

• • •

Ensconced beside Temperance, Brutus seemed content in his new stall of the roomy stables at Beswick Park. Her mare was calm as well, but Astrid guessed it had to do with the superiority of the staff. Beswick would not demand less than excellence. The superb quality of his horseflesh—two pairs of matched Andalusians, as well as a handful of spirited Arabians—was to be admired as well, though many of the spacious stalls remained empty.

Patrick had insisted on staying on at Beswick Park and had bunked down in the quarters with the other grooms. Astrid had been glad. She would not have wanted him to suffer at Beaumont's or her uncle's hands, given how he'd come to their rescue. She would have to find a way to pay him, perhaps by garnishing some of what she might earn from the sale of their jewels. Or perhaps the duke would be amenable to giving him a job, though she wouldn't count on it.

She hadn't seen Beswick in a week. After the evening she'd told him the truth about Beaumont— as it pertained to Isobel—the duke had disappeared. Culbert had assured her that His Grace had urgent business in London and sent his abject apologies for his sudden departure. Astrid hadn't been able to stifle her snort at the resigned expression on the butler's face. She suspected that neither "abject" nor "apology" were words in the duke's current lexicon.

A relieved Isobel had been grateful for the reprieve from any additional close encounters.

"I'm glad he's gone," she'd said that first night. "He's terrifying."

"His servants wouldn't be so loyal if he were a bad master, Isobel. Furthermore, it's clear that his aunt cares for him. And you like her well enough, don't you?"

"I do," she'd said. "But his *face*, Astrid. It's frightful."

"The duke is a war hero, Izzy. A few scars don't make him unworthy of our compassion or our gratitude."

"Yes, but he seemed so angry," she'd carried on. "So rude and overbearing."

Astrid hadn't bothered to explain that his caustic nature was probably because of reactions to his appearance in the first place. It wouldn't occur to Isobel that the duke had worn a hat during dinner— eschewing centuries upon centuries of blue-blooded dining etiquette—for *her* sake. But Astrid had noticed, and her heart had been grateful to him for it. It was a kindness she had not expected.

It had made her reply to Isobel sharper than she'd intended.

"We are indebted to His Grace, Isobel," she'd said. "Think upon where you would be if it wasn't for his hospitality. In the clutches of a true monster. He could have turned us away, and as such, your contempt is undeserved. Now, go to bed."

A chagrined, teary-eyed Isobel had nodded, though she'd found it difficult to sleep in a strange place. Astrid had silently empathized. Her own body had been strangely agitated, a coiling energy brimming within her that had made it difficult to sleep as well. But she knew her disquiet had to do with the duke himself, as if she could *feel* him prowling the corridors like some territorial wild animal whose boundaries had been crossed.

Despite that, however, their first week in the duke's home hadn't been a hardship. After the first night, Fletcher had insisted that there was not enough room in the servants' quarters, and as a result, they'd remained in the guest wing. She suspected he was lying but didn't want to press the matter. The opulence of their chambers had awed both Isobel and their lady's maid, Agatha, but Astrid was too worried about the duke's response to even appreciate the exquisite decor. After all, they weren't actually *guests*.

"It's good that ye're taking Brutus out, my lady," Patrick said, interrupting her thoughts. "He's been chomping at the bit to get a good run in, ye ken."

"They're happy here, then?" she asked with a tiny frown.

"Of course. Ye ken they're happy wherever ye are." His frown matched hers. "There's no telling what yer uncle would have done. Ye did the right thing, my lady."

Astrid sensed he wasn't just speaking of taking the horses. She sighed and placed a hand on the man's sleeve. "That remains to be seen. He'll never suspect we came here, so we're safe for the moment, but we cannot be indiscreet. Or anger the duke."

"Speaking of the devil," Patrick murmured, and the hairs on her nape rose.

Astrid whirled to see Beswick marching down the path from the manse, hat pulled low, but she could sense his irritation even as far away as he was. Her pulse escalated instantly at the sight of his large form bearing down on them. "You should go."

"Are ye certain?"

"Yes, he won't harm me. He's a gentleman."

Patrick scowled. "So is Beaumont."

The two men were as different as night and day, and while Astrid was wary of the duke and his volatile humors, she did not think she was in mortal danger from him. At least for the moment. She nodded reassuringly and patted the groomsman's arm. The duke's stride increased until he was nearly running. "Go, please, Patrick."

He did not argue this time and disappeared just as the duke came to a seething halt in front of her while she tightened the cinches on Brutus's saddle. Beswick was so angry, his golden eyes glowed like hot coals beneath the brim of his hat. Astrid was fascinated, though she did not know what she'd done to incur his ire, considering he'd been gone the whole week. She hadn't been able to get an answer out of Fletcher or Culbert on his whereabouts.

"Who the hell was that?" he said in his smoky rasp, his burning eyes following Patrick's departure. The low, possessive pitch of it made her chest squeeze. "And just what do you think you are doing?"

She patted the horse's glossy flank and lifted a

brow. "What does it look like I'm doing, Your Grace? I'm knitting a doily."

He opened his mouth and snapped it shut, those demon-hot eyes fastening on her and narrowing to pinpricks at her dig. A different sensation curled over her. Perhaps she shouldn't provoke the beast more than necessary. "I'm going for a ride. Brutus needs the exercise, and I need fresh air."

A muscle jerked in his jaw, his eyes flicking to the stable. "Who was he? That man?"

"Patrick is my groom."

His eyes glowered. "You treat your grooms so familiarly?"

"He's family," she replied, wondering at the terse note in his voice but casting it off as part of his usual surliness. She did not presume to understand the man. Or his mercurial sulks.

"I do not recall giving you leave to bring your help to my estate."

Astrid sobered instantly. "Patrick protected us. If you send him away, then we must go as well."

"Must you?" he murmured. She felt his gaze on her, sweeping her from head to toe along with a low rumble of disapproval, and she waited for the question that would inevitably come. "What the devil are you wearing?"

"A riding habit, Your Grace."

Astrid saw no need to explain her unusual riding dress. It was what she wore to train and exercise the horses. Though it was far from acceptable for a highborn lady and she would not wear it in London, she'd learned early on that she needed both thighs to manage Brutus. As such, she'd designed the full-skirted trousers with their draped pleats herself to preserve modesty over a pair of breeches.

Dragging his eyes away, Beswick changed the subject. "Fletcher said you've made good progress on the porcelain."

Astrid nodded but wasn't surprised that the ever-efficient valet had reported on her job. She'd been astounded at the vastness of the late duke's collection and the astronomical value of some of the pieces. When Fletcher had jokingly mentioned the duke's love of indoor cricket, she'd been appalled.

"Yes, your father's pieces are rare." She pursed her lips. "Perhaps a smidgen better than using them for cricket balls."

A smirk crept into a corner of his mouth. "In whose estimation?"

"Christie's in London, Your Grace." Astrid allowed herself a small gratified smile. "They have agreed to host the sale after receiving my detailed letter on whose property it was to be auctioned. Apparently, your father was quite the famous collector. His collection will fetch a considerable sum."

"Donate the proceeds to charity."

Astrid felt her eyes pop. "You're speaking of hundreds of thousands of pounds at least, Your Grace. Shouldn't you put such a fortune in trust for your heirs?"

"*Heirs?* Like the ones you offered to procreate?" His eyes fairly sparked heat, though his voice was silky, making the hairs on her nape stand at nervous attention. Other needy parts of her went soft and molten.

Cheeks aflame, Astrid lifted her chin. "You

declined, remember? That offer is no longer up for discussion."

Tension exploded between them as that golden-hot gaze scorched hers, burning past every defense she could possibly erect against him, but Astrid held her ground. If she wasn't careful, she'd be nothing but a charred cinder by the time he was through with her.

"I've been known to change my mind," he said softly.

Her mouth nearly fell open, but Brutus chose to rear and snap his teeth in the direction of the duke then, his eyes rolling slightly as if taking offense to Beswick's suggestion and his mistress's agitation. Astrid brought him smartly under control with a soothing sound, reaching for the reins. Beswick's eyes focused on the enormous, skittish horse as if just seeing him.

"You are *not* riding that beast."

Astrid's eyebrows launched into her hairline, her own tense nerves snapping. "Brutus is mine, Your Grace, and I will ride him if and when I please."

"He is not a mount for a lady."

She glared at him. "Don't order me about. I'm not one of your servants."

"Aren't you?" he said coolly.

"God, you're insufferable!" She turned to lead Brutus away, though not toward the stables as he no doubt expected.

His eyes narrowed as if guessing her intent, once she was out of his reach. "Astrid, I forbid it."

Oh, *no*, he did not! Without hesitation, she hopped nimbly on to the low fence where she'd directed the horse and climbed into the saddle. She heard the growl behind her, felt it in the marrow of her bones, but ignored it.

Wheeling Brutus around and urging him into a gallop out of the yard, Astrid felt unburdened for the first time in days. She did not wait, nor did she care, to see how the duke had responded to her dismissal.

Arrogant, controlling man.

CHAPTER SIX

Thane stood stock-still in amazement—that reckless little harridan had just defied him. Swearing a blue streak, he stalked into the stable, making several grooms leap to instant attention.

"Get me Goliath. Now," he ordered.

He scanned the space for the groom who'd been talking to her, but the redheaded man was nowhere in sight. Lucky for him. When Thane had seen her place her fingers on the man's arm, he'd been unprepared for the surge of violence that had filled him.

Rage? Jealousy? He hadn't cared to examine the feelings, only acknowledging the fact that he'd wanted to snap the man's arm in two.

Seeing *her* had been both bliss and purgatory. It was as if he'd been starved for the sight of her. He'd gone to London to deal with the sale of one of his many properties in the city with Sir Thornton. And the minute he'd arrived there, he'd only wanted to leave. And the second he'd arrived back at Beswick Park, he'd sought her out. Though he knew maintaining distance was wise, given his erratic moods where she was concerned, Thane couldn't help himself.

Goliath was brought forward, and he mounted the thoroughbred with a wince of pain as his fatigued body pulled tight. He usually enjoyed a brisk ride, but not on days when he'd traveled hours in a cramped coach or forgone the daily swimming routines that kept him pain-free and limber.

Thane grimaced, setting his horse after hers. It didn't take the powerful Arabian thoroughbred long to catch up to her mount. *Brutus*. The aptly named brute that had tried to take a bite out of him was as unpredictable and as touchy as his mistress.

Looking over her shoulder, she urged her horse on faster, rising into the stirrups. Thane caught wind of what echoed like her laughter, and the sound energized him. He couldn't help but admire her expert posture and her graceful handling of the massive horse. Or the fact that the split skirts of those indecent trousers flared wide on either side of her, baring glimpses of trim legs wrapped in worn buckskin.

Thane very rarely pushed Goliath to his limits, but he did so now. That stallion of hers had champion bloodlines; any idiot could see that. But then, so did Goliath. He had to admit the ride was exhilarating as he felt the bunching and elongating muscles of the animal beneath him.

Unlike other horses bred of racing stock, Goliath no longer raced. The loyal steed had gone with him to war. Had borne him from danger when he'd collapsed in a ditch and been left for dead. It'd been a miracle that the horse had led him to a tiny hillside village in the Spanish countryside. The doctor there had taken one look at him and summoned the priest. But he'd survived. They'd both survived.

Shaking his head clear of the past, Thane nearly collided with the lady and her horse, perched atop a hillock, acres of Beswick lands spread out below them. Patches of the lush green landscape were dotted with grazing sheep and tenant cottages, the sun climbing into the sky over the hills to the east making the bucolic scene a picturesque one, even to his jaded senses. But it was a windblown and smiling Astrid who took his breath away.

The apples of her cheeks were rosy, and the elegant column of her throat was flushed with healthy color. The bright sunshine turned the tendrils escaping her tenacious coiffure to sun-burnished chestnut, and Thane wanted to sink his fingers in the silken mass of it. He wanted to loosen the rest of it from its pins and bury his face in it.

"Goodness," Astrid said. "It's so beautiful."

"I suppose it's better than the alternative," he said, angry at his constant desire where she was concerned. "Fields soaked with blood."

Wide crystalline eyes met his as Astrid stared at him for a prolonged minute, but she did not respond. Thane appreciated the fact that she did not feel compelled to fill the air with unnecessary platitudes…about him being alive for a reason or some such.

"War is a terrible thing," she said eventually.

He nodded, his scars pulling tight on his scalp and along his rib cage. The tug of lust faded away, only to be replaced by ghosts. Phantom pain fired along his nerve endings, the cuts of a thousand bayonets blooming, his lifeblood seeping away, the burn of a blade and the agonizing tug of thread. He acknowledged the pain, felt each one of his scars, but for the first time since he'd returned to England, he did not feel like burying himself six feet deep.

It was…strange.

They stared at the rolling countryside in a quiet, companionable silence.

"Is this all yours?" she asked after a while.

"Yes," he said. "Beswick Park encompasses thousands of acres and has hundreds of tenants. You are one of many in my employ."

It was an intended barb.

The small smile of wonder dropped from her face as she turned to him with a stony calm once more, that faithful composure battling every other emotion into line.

He wondered what—or who—had made her that way. A stone queen, constantly on guard. He didn't know much about her past, but he'd tasked Fletcher with finding out whatever he could…knowing one's enemy and all that.

Thane only knew from her own lips that she'd spent just the one Season in London. It made him also wonder why she'd remained unmarried even if she'd told him it was by choice. He simply couldn't fathom some gentleman not snatching her up. She'd admitted that she was an innocent. Though she didn't look like one at present. Now, on that horse, dressed in partial men's clothing, she looked like a defiant warrior goddess. One who had blatantly disregarded him.

"Do you disobey every command?" he asked.

She stared down the length of her nose at him. "You are not my uncle or my husband, Your Grace. I do not have to obey you."

"But I *am* your employer," he said.

Her mouth flattened with mutiny. "That does not

include dictating which of my horses I should or should not ride."

As if listening, her stallion reared, his feet pawing empty air in a fit of mischief. Raising herself slightly in the saddle, she hauled him under control with a firm click of her tongue and an expert touch on the reins. The skirts of her dress had parted when the horse had risen upward, baring her breeches-clad legs for a moment before she smoothed them into place. It brought Thane's attention back to her odd if intriguing ensemble.

"That doesn't look like any women's riding habit I've ever seen."

Astrid glowered at him. "Not that it's any of your concern, but I needed the extra mobility to manage my horses, and, well, it's not the acceptable thing for a woman to wear trousers. The combination is of my own design, not unlike the harem pants of women in the east."

Thane's mouth opened and closed—an act that was becoming common in her presence, it seemed. The image of her wearing the clothing of such women invaded his brain. The fabric she wore was not transparent, but it well could have been with the illicit direction of his thoughts. Her fitted breeches gave enough fodder for his imagination to sketch out a pair of trim legs, finely molded buttocks, and shapely hips draped in voluminous yards of gossamer, and Thane went instantly hard.

Christ. He set his jaw, furious at his body's re-sponse. "Regardless, when I give an order, I expect it to be followed."

Her eyes flashed. "While you may control all of

this, Your Grace, you do not control *me*."

"Would you rather I send you and your sister packing back to your uncle?" Thane asked silkily. "Or to Beaumont?"

He regretted it the minute he said it when her entire body reared back as if she'd been struck, but it was a matter of pride. He could not give in. Astrid stared at him, fists going white-knuckled on the reins and eyes teeming with furious emotion. He could feel the heat of them from where he sat, all fire and brimstone. But then suddenly, the anger drained from her face. It was as though the light—along with all her fight—had been leached out of her.

He'd been the one to take it from her by threatening her sister, and suddenly, guilt daggered him. It was the only reason for his next words.

"You will take a groom with you," he said through his teeth. "Whenever you ride him on the estate."

Her eyes met his, and resentment, not gratitude, shone in them for a long moment before her eyelashes lowered with demure, if false, obeisance. As high-spirited as her stallion, she was not accustomed to taking orders from anyone, even though it was her place in life to do so. She would have been raised to be an aristocratic, *biddable* wife, but clearly, Lady Astrid did not fit that mold by a long shot.

Thane bit back a smile. What he wouldn't have given to have seen her in her first Season, putting all those society matrons in their place and offering crisp set-downs to the dandies who ventured too close.

"Why didn't you have more than one Season?" he asked abruptly.

She kept her face trained on the hills in the distance. "My parents died."

"And after mourning?"

She did not immediately respond, but he could see that she was thinking about the question. Thane waited. "It was clear to me during my first Season that another would not…gain the result I hoped for, and it made more sense to save the money for Isobel."

He frowned. "Why?"

"What's the point of this?"

"Humor me."

"I was ousted from society, Your Grace, because of bad judgment." She flushed deeply. "Isobel doesn't deserve to be punished for my mistakes. And I want her to be happy. She deserves to be happy."

"And you don't?"

Her throat bobbed. "This isn't about me."

"Why not?"

It seemed like she was going to answer, but after a moment, she wheeled the stallion around and galloped back toward the manse. Thane stared at her retreating form with a thoughtful look. He'd seen loyalty in his men on the battlefield but had scarcely encountered it in the real world. The men and women of the aristocracy dealt in secrets and intrigues, and many a gentleman would sell his own brother if it meant some kind of gain.

But not Lady Astrid. She would swallow the mountain of her pride whole if it meant protecting her sister. He admired that more than he cared to admit.

• • •

Insufferable, persistent beast!

What could she say? That her own naïveté had destroyed any chance for happiness? That she'd trusted the wrong man? That said man was *back* and out for vengeance? Beswick would probably laugh in her face or tell her to stop caviling over trifles. As if her life were a trifling matter. God, he was unspeakable!

Her chest heaving with exertion, Astrid threw the reins to a waiting groom and slid off the horse once she arrived back at the stables. Normally, she would groom Brutus herself, but she was far too agitated with the duke. How *dare* he? How dare he question her about her sister and her decisions? He was no one to her, no one to them.

He's your employer, her inner voice reminded her.

"That doesn't make him my owner," she muttered, stomping the caked mud off her boots. "He has no right."

He's a duke, one of the most highborn peers in the land, and you're living on his charity. Arguably, he has some *right*.

"Shut up," she half snarled to herself.

"My lady, are ye well?" the young groom asked.

Astrid nodded with a scowl. Of course she wasn't well; she was talking to herself like a bedlamite.

All because of one thoroughly aggravating man. She wasn't by any means a society darling who expected men to fall at her feet, but most of the men she'd met had been gentlemen. They did not ask impolite questions or say whatever came to mind. They did not look at her as if they wanted to incinerate her very bones or demolish the defenses that had served her well for nearly a decade.

She blew out a breath, stalking from the stable toward the house. Gentlemen didn't pry. Not when the answers led to ugly places. Astoundingly, Beswick did not seem to know of her past, but Astrid knew he would find out. Eventually. And if he was anything like the rest of the aristocracy who'd equated the fallen Everleighs to scum on their bootheels, then she and Isobel would be out on their laurels.

Astrid wanted to put that off for as long as possible.

Agitation and worry coursed through her. She was much too frazzled to go into the house and speak with anyone, so she headed for the gardens. A good walk would help to calm her down. The pathways were wild and covered in rosebushes, but something about their ungoverned nature appealed to her. In truth, it reminded her of Beswick himself.

Wild, unruly, savage.

Gracious, why was she still thinking about him? With a hiss of frustration, Astrid wrenched her thoughts away from the vexing man and focused on the problem at hand. Namely, Beaumont. A part of her wished she'd never set eyes on the cad. He'd ruined everything. Her parents had been in raptures when the charismatic and handsome war hero *and* the nephew of an earl had offered for Astrid. Giddy with delight, she had fancied herself in love, until she'd tumbled from grace and realized that love was a lie for starry-eyed fools.

God, she'd been so naive and gullible. She hadn't known she was in trouble until it was too late. Until her drunken, overly amorous fiancé had ushered her to a deserted music room, expecting his husbandly *due*, barely a month after their engagement. The memory was still razor-sharp, her thoughts flicking back to the darkened room where he had escorted her.

Fending off his roving hands, Astrid had backed away behind the pianoforte. "Please stop, Edmund," she'd begged, "you've been drinking."

"You want this," he'd said. "Don't tease. You belong to me."

"I'm not your property."

His smile had been predatory. "But you are, sweet. Mine to do with as I wish, when I wish, *however* I wish. We are to be married, after all."

"We are not married yet." Astrid had shaken her head, stunned at the side of him she'd never seen. The truth was his kisses repulsed her, and she'd endured them, but the thought of him touching her in any intimate way made her feel ill.

"Now, in a few months, what does it matter?"

He'd lunged for her, his wet lips slavering over hers, and Astrid had ripped herself away, wiping her mouth with the back of her glove.

"It does matter, Edmund. Oh God, I don't want any of this. I simply don't feel the same as you do. I thought I could, but I cannot do this."

"Who are you to refuse me?" he'd said to her, eyes blazing. "You're nothing but a silly country girl who's lucky to have an offer from me. I'm the heir to an earldom."

Trembling at his hostility, she'd held her ground. "That may be, but I am a woman of sound mind. I don't wish to marry you, Edmund. More than ever, now I see how ill-suited we are. Surely you know it as well."

He'd glared at her for so long, her legs had cramped, but after what seemed like forever, he'd nodded, his face unreadable. "Fine, if that's what you want."

"It's for the best."

It was only the next day that Astrid had learned what he'd done.

Edmund Cain had taken it upon himself to ruin her good name…saying *he* had broken the engagement on account of her not being a virgin. Astrid had laughed it off, certain that the truth would prevail—she'd never been intimate with a man. But in the end, she had never stood a chance against the poisonous gossip that had raced like wildfire…to her parents, to the entire *ton*.

Despite Astrid's claims, she'd been judged as guilty. After all, how could one prove one's innocence, especially when impugned by a male peer? Such was the power of a man's word versus a woman's. And like that, without any defense whatsoever, she'd fallen from grace, her life over. *Finished.*

Never again, Astrid had sworn.

Never again would any man have that kind of power over her.

And yet, here she was, nine years later and considerably wiser, and beholden to one. Though from the little she knew of him, the Duke of Beswick was a man who answered to no one...yielded to no one.

Astrid plucked a nearby rose from its bush and held the delicate blossom between her fingers. The blushing pink petals felt like velvet. If fate had been different—and she'd met a different gentleman—Isobel would have been safe.

If she, Astrid, hadn't been naive...

If Edmund hadn't been such a bastard...

If anyone had believed her over a scorned, small-minded man...

If...if...if...

Her life could be a constellation of *if*s.

She discarded the flower and kept walking. None of that mattered anymore. It was all in the past. To take care of Isobel, Astrid needed to look forward, not backward. But a part of her couldn't help worrying that when the duke found out the truth—and it was only a matter of time before he would—he might turn out to be just like everyone else in the *ton*.

CHAPTER SEVEN

In dumbfounded silence, Thane sat at the massive mahogany desk, staring at the neatly rendered parchment pages and then up at Fletcher. "What in the hell is the meaning of this? Is this supposed to be a joke?"

"You asked for a report, Your Grace."

Thane read the preposterous text again. And then a fourth and fifth time for good measure. According to Fletcher's notes, Astrid had been affianced—to one Edmund Cain, that lily-livered bastard of a traitor. However, the engagement had been called off because of some scandal, and after that, she and her family had left London.

Thane blinked, his thoughts racing. Had she given herself to Cain? Was that why it'd been so easy for her to barter herself for his protection? Offer herself in marriage to the Beast of Beswick? His chest clenched in a nauseating combination of bitterness and fury. What else had she withheld or lied about?

God, she must have taken him for a desperate fool.

Didn't she?

In the short time he'd known her, he could tell Astrid had many secrets, but she didn't strike him as a liar. A small thread of reason pushed through the haze, reminding him that she'd been ousted from society because of bad judgment. Had she meant in men? Thane frowned. Cain was a snake. A deserter and a blackguard. Had he been the one behind her fall from grace?

He inhaled and crumpled the sheets of paper in one shaking fist before spearing an accusing glower at Fletcher. "Did you know who she was when she came here that first day? That she had been engaged to Cain?"

The valet had the grace to look guilty. "Yes, Duke. Though in my defense, it was not immediately. It was only after she left that I recalled the name Everleigh."

He scowled. "And you did not think to inform me then?"

"It was a short betrothal." Fletcher shook his head. "Barely a month because of the scandal. Your father took it personally. Cain was a part of Lord Leopold's set, as you know."

Thane was aware. His father was the sole reason Edmund Cain had secured a position in Thane's regiment, as a favor to his friend, the Earl of Beaumont. The old man hadn't batted an eye to send his nephew off to war, despite Cain being his heir presumptive, when most peers kept their successors close. Perhaps the earl had hoped for a different outcome.

"Explain," Thane demanded of Fletcher, curious despite himself. Not that he would have cared about his father's *ton* machinations while trying to do Wellington's bidding and not getting himself killed in the process. He hated the intrigues of the aristocracy.

But this was Astrid...

Fletcher hesitated, his expression pained. "Cain cried off, declaring she'd had lovers."

Acid churned in his stomach. He knew more than anyone what a slimy bastard Edmund Cain was. "Was there any proof?"

The valet shrugged. "Even if there wasn't, you know how gossip is, and you know as well as I do that His Grace, God rest his soul, did not love scandal. Given his friendship with the earl at the time, he was the most vocal in denouncing her and her family. Keeping up appearances was his only goal."

Oh, Thane understood that far too well. It was the reason he'd taken the captain's commission and sought his freedom from beneath his father's thumb. Leopold had been the golden son, groomed within an inch of his life to be the perfect heir. But every step Thane had taken had been to provoke his father and to flaunt his disdain for the Harte family name.

But as it turned out, fate had a twisted sense of humor, since he was now duke. The very life he'd deplored had become his responsibility. Thane was now accountable for the dukedom and for passing the title and the entailed lands to his descendants. His *heirs*.

For some reason, Thane thought of Astrid's delicate, beautiful hands. Those pristine fingers sweeping down the length of his lacerated flesh with desire, not disgust. His chest seized, and other parts of him responded more insistently. Even if she had been with others—including *Cain*—he still wanted her. He almost hated himself for it.

Thane sighed and glared at the folio.

"Where is Lady Astrid at present?" he asked.

"In your father's private study, Your Grace," Fletcher replied. "Off the ducal apartments."

Four years of being duke, and Thane didn't recall that the ducal apartments ever housed a study. Then again, he only slept in the bedchamber and bathed in the bathing chamber. The rest of it remained untouched. The staff did an efficient job of cleaning, but Thane had little interest in entering any of those rooms. They served only to remind him of who he was…and how sorely he was unfit for the position of duke.

Fletcher hesitated. "You won't cause a scene, will you? Regardless of her family name or ancient gossip, she's doing a fine job cataloging His Grace's antiques." He paused again, swiping at an imaginary speck of dust on the desk. "And it's been a pleasure having her and Lady Isobel at Beswick Park."

"Surely you know me better than that, Fletcher?" Thane drawled, leaning back in his chair.

"That's just it. I do. You'll chase her away, and then where will you be?"

Thane fought his irritation at the valet's complete lack of respect. He settled for staring Fletcher down with a protracted, honed look. It was one that made hardened generals quail on the battlefield, but the man did not cower or scurry away.

"If you mean to intimidate me, you're wasting your time," Fletcher said.

"I pay you to be intimidated."

His valet arched a brow. "Very well, then. Pretend I'm quaking in my boots if it suits you."

Thane huffed a disbelieving laugh and shook his head. Since when had Fletcher gotten so mouthy?

Devil take it, Astrid's rebelliousness and defiance were catching. Soon it would infect his entire household…if it hadn't already.

He sighed and scanned the rest of the report that Fletcher had prepared. Her thirst for knowledge hadn't been a fabrication. Her father had indulged her with a complete education, rivaling the ones he'd had at Eton and Oxford. She'd had tutors in mathematics, science, history, languages, and anthropological studies. And she was a voracious reader.

She was indeed five and twenty. Her birth date was in four months…the day when she would legally come into her portion. The date when she would no longer need his help. Not that he'd offered it in the first place. Somehow, she'd wormed her way into his household and into his thoughts. Though now, he didn't know what to think.

Especially about her engagement to a man like Edmund Cain.

• • •

In the narrow but elegant study, Astrid blew a stray curl out of her eyes and squinted at the neatly scripted sheets of foolscap. Her fingers were covered in ink spots, and she was sure she'd managed to spill ink on her dress as well. She'd filled pages and pages of painstakingly written notes, but luckily, the former duke had been meticulous in his own transcripts. She'd found several bound journals in the desk containing dated records of sale, which had been invaluable in her efforts of confirming the worth and age of the pieces.

She rubbed at her eyes and yawned. She'd missed lunch, only munching on a piece of cold toast from breakfast, and her stomach growled. At least she had made some real progress. It was tedious work, but the benefits were worth it. She and Isobel were safe. Astrid didn't know how long that would last. She dared not go into the village or inquire about comings and goings at the Everleigh estate. Someone might take notice or, worse, recognize her. At best, she and Isobel were in hiding, which meant they could be found and returned to their owner.

It infuriated Astrid that women were valued like property, to be married off and handled like transactions of sale. Much like the pieces she was in the middle of cataloging. The London marriage mart was little more than a glorified auction room, where the best merchandise was displayed and purchased by wealthy, titled gentlemen. And women went like chattel from their fathers to their new proprietors.

Astrid sighed. She'd avoided matrimony for ten years after the scandal, but there was no doubt that marriage offered some degree of protection. Marriage to a man like Beaumont, however, would have a distinct quality of hell.

And marriage to Thane…

Goodness, she had to stop thinking of him by his given name, which she'd learned from his aunt.

With her luck, she'd blurt it out in front of him and never live it down. At the thought of the duke, Astrid felt a muddled sentiment—one part irritation and one part fascination. One could not call him handsome by any stretch of the imagination, but parts of him were beautiful in isolation, like his eyes when they were lit with amusement or his mouth when his mood was indulgent, which wasn't often. Astrid wondered what those lush contours, so at odds with the pitted rest of him, would feel like against hers.

Warm. Alive. Sinfully sweet.

She shook herself with a short laugh. She was a hopeless cliché, fantasizing about kissing the lord of the manor. She'd do better to start spouting Byron or swooning over Austen. Astrid had been so busy that she hadn't had a chance to visit the library properly, and Beswick Park's was truly exceptional, as she'd discovered.

Thinking of her own books that she'd left at her uncle's house made her feel dejected. She'd been able to pack only one trunk of her favorites — including her worn copies of *Paradise Lost* and Homer's *Odyssey*, several Shakespearean plays gifted to her by her father, poems by Byron and Keats, as well as several instructive essays on science and education by Locke and Rousseau that she could not bear to leave behind.

With a tired sigh, Astrid lounged back in the chair and let her eyes wander the length of the study. It'd been a disappointment that the glass-covered bookcases had housed only antiques and not books. But perhaps that was for the best — she did not need any distractions…or any reason for the duke to assume she was not up to the task.

Astrid had stopped herself from exploring further when Fletcher had first shown her to the tiny study, only to discover that it adjoined the duke's private chambers, where she'd seen the present duke naked.

Damnation. She'd sworn to stop using those two words together. Duke and naked. Naked duke.

Naked duke naked duke naked duke.

Good God, she was so tired that even her brain had mutinied to the point of stupidity.

Astrid rubbed her eyes and chuckled beneath her breath. Shoving back from the chair, she rose, her limbs protesting at the movement. She rubbed her stiff shoulders and winced as her stomach let out what sounded like a roar. A break and a meal might be in order. She would wander down to the kitchens and see if Cook had saved any leftovers from tea.

It didn't take long after meandering aimlessly down several identical, narrow wood-paneled corridors with thick carpets for Astrid to realize that she was lost. *Again.* The place was a dratted maze, and as usual, there wasn't a maid or footman in sight to help. She paused and peered down yet another hallway before retracing her steps to a wide staircase that looked familiar.

Just as she was about to cry aloud for help—surely there was a footman prowling about somewhere—the sound of low voices reached her ears, and she made her way toward them with relief. As she got nearer, however, she recognized the voices. One was Fletcher's and the other was Beswick's, and they were coming from a nearby room.

For no reason at all, Astrid's pulse started to leap madly in her veins. She had no idea why the Duke of Beswick affected her so. He was *just* a man. No, not just a man…a churlish, inflexible, terrifying beast of a man who terrorized his servants and scared the living daylights out of everyone around him.

She should not be *fascinated* by him. It wasn't fascination, she decided in the same breath. He was like a splinter in her thumb. More like an aggravation.

As she neared the study, her footfalls cushioned by the thick pile of the carpets, Astrid made to announce herself, only to freeze as she heard her own name on the duke's lips.

"Come now, Fletcher. Lady Astrid is no damsel in distress."

Hesitating for a few rapid heartbeats, she vacillated between wanting to eavesdrop and doing the proper thing and declaring her presence. But in the end, curiosity—and irritation at his condescending tone—won out over propriety.

She inched closer, the duke's voice filtering out clearly.

"She was affianced to a snake of a man, for God's sake."

His snort was derisive, the sound accompanying his heated words like a dagger to Astrid's ribs. Oh no, he *knew*. She pressed a fist to her lips. For some reason, it sounded like he was more upset about *her* engagement, rather than the gossip or his father's edict about Everleigh unsuitability. Then again, everything she did seemed to vex him.

"A decade ago," she heard Fletcher reply. "Admit it: You're afraid because you're drawn to her, and now you've found a stupid reason to thwart it."

Astrid held her breath, her heart taking on an erratic pitch.

"Attracted to that shrew? Hardly. She's more of a

beast than I am."

"Your response to her would say differently," Fletcher replied snidely.

The duke snorted. "What are you going on about? She's vexing and irritating and too much of an insufferable know-it-all. I respond to her like I do everyone else."

"Yes, but you don't *look* at her like you do everyone else, do you?"

Silence stretched for a moment as Astrid released a shuddering breath. When the duke spoke again, his voice was dripping in ice. "Once more, Fletcher, you've proven that your irritating and unsolicited opinions are completely erroneous."

Fletcher's reply was fast and full of amusement. "His Grace doth protest too much, methinks. You're petrified, plain and simple."

Thane laughed, the sound devoid of any humor, and once more, his words cut through Astrid like hot blades. "If you think I'm afraid of anyone, man or woman, you've gone addlepated. She is the last person in England whom I would ever choose to be the lady of Beswick, even if I was in the market for a wife, which *I am not*. So stop trying to meddle before I make good on my promise to sack you for good this time."

"Very well, Your Grace. But you're wrong about her."

Astrid warmed at the valet's stalwart defense, though the duke's brutally efficient words had done more than enough damage to her pride.

"Do I pay you to disagree with me, Fletcher, or is this another one of your overly generous handouts?"

"The advice is free, though whether you choose to listen is up to you."

"Let me put this simply, then," she heard Beswick go on, his voice grim. "Any advice with regards to the lady is unsolicited and unwelcome. I'm not so desperate to be duped into marriage. I might be scarred, but I am a fucking *duke*." The thud of a large fist striking wood made Astrid flinch. "No. Hell will freeze over before I marry her—or anyone."

The widening knot in Astrid's throat threatened to choke her. His callous words felt like lead ballast, tearing into her without mercy, and she'd let her guard down so thoroughly that she felt the brutal, ugly bite of each one.

God, she couldn't believe she'd been fantasizing about him not ten minutes earlier! The duke wasn't some romantically tragic figure who needed saving in some silly fairy tale. He *was* the cold, cruel villain…the unfeeling monster, inside and out, who chased everyone away.

The sound of movement—a chair scraping along wood floors and heavy footsteps—jolted Astrid's numbed limbs into action. As she turned to flee toward her chamber, tears stung her eyes. She should have been over the pain of the past by now. But no. It never got easier. The shadow of the scandal would always be a black stain on her existence. In the eyes of the *ton*, she was ruined. *Worthless*.

And now apparently worthless in Beswick's as well.

She would *not* cry, not for him.

In the safety of her room, Astrid slumped against her bedchamber door, composing herself roughly.

With slow breaths, she reached for the cool pragmatism that had been her shield through the first few years following the scandal. It had never failed her, and it would not fail her now. She would persist. She had a job to do, and that was to keep her sister safe.

Beswick was a duke, yes, but he was also a man. And now she knew that he wasn't immune to her. His cruel words might hurt, but he *did* look at her differently. She'd been the subject of enough heated glances from the opposite sex to know what that meant.

He wanted her.

And if wedlock to a peer was the only thing that would protect Isobel without fail, Astrid would do whatever it took.

Even if she had to seduce a beast.

CHAPTER EIGHT

At dinner the next night, Thane nearly lost his mind, his morals, and his good sense when an angel with a siren's soul was sent by fate to tempt him to folly.

He'd lost his breath the second Astrid had been announced, his every sexually deprived nerve on fire. Her gown had been simple—a creamy ivory silk with a blond lace overlay—but on Astrid, it had clung to every feminine curve. Curves he'd felt that very first day beneath his hands—a fine bosom, small waist, flared hips—curves that had been buried since under yards of plain, serviceable fabric. The panels of translucent chiffon and lace could have been cannons for all the destruction they'd wrought upon him.

Once he'd gotten past the dress, other hints had been harder to ignore. A glance here, another there. A tart response. A secret smile. Low, throaty laughter. And then there was the way she looked at him. She'd never shied away from his face since that first day, but this was different. He had almost forgotten what it had felt like for a woman to *look* at him. Eagerly, and with what felt too much like yearning.

What *was* her game? Because it had to be a game. Astrid had never been so forward.

The absurdity of it—of even contemplating her desiring him—unsettled him. Threw him out of balance. Made him snap and growl throughout the first courses like the uncivilized beast everyone took him for. Even Aunt Mabel had been appalled. She'd chastised him once early on, but his hard glare had silenced her completely.

Astrid had borne his irascible mood with remarkable grace. On occasion, a small pleat would form between her brows, but for the most part, she'd smiled and conversed, waving those elegant hands at every turn. Taunting him with all that he could not have. And *hell* if he didn't want it all. Those hands, her mouth, the body under that indecent silk. The excruciating, endless ache in his trousers was proof of it.

Yet another reason for his rapidly fraying temper.

Did she truly think he was so despicable and so desperate that he would be *grateful* for her attention? For her bold offer? Her arrogant proposition made with the assumption that he wouldn't be able to find a suitable wife on his own?

Not that he wanted a wife, but still…

Thane clenched his jaw as she sent him a serene smile, tugging her lower lip in between her teeth and demurely lowering her eyelashes. His mind recoiled, but beneath the table, parts of his anatomy leaped with excitement. Christ, even his brain and body were at fucking war.

Conversation had all but dissolved into verbal grunts over the last quarter of an hour. Isobel had left halfway through dinner, claiming a queasy stomach. His aunt had fled after the last course, throwing a sympathetic glance to Astrid and a fulminating one to him, but Thane was well beyond redemption by then.

If a fallen angel had come to lure…she'd succeeded.

He drained his glass as the servants cleared the plates and brought in dessert. At least the wine took the edge off the concoction of lust, misery, and bitterness curling through him at present. The object of his considerable frustration smiled at one of the footmen, waving him away and declining the offer of dessert.

"No, thank you, Conrad. I simply could not eat another bite."

"Of course, my lady."

Who the flying fuck was Conrad? Thane's eyes narrowed when the man gazed adoringly at her. Was that the footman's name? Apart from Fletcher and Culbert, servants at Beswick Park came and went. Thane hired them for their discretion, nothing more, and he certainly did not avail himself of their names. Or watched them fawn over his guests.

"Have you finished flirting with all the servants?" he snapped.

Astrid gave him a cool look. "Is that what I was doing? I thought I was just being courteous and well-mannered."

"You made the man blush."

"Well then, at least I can congratulate myself for being moderately successful," she said in a teasing voice that went straight through his agonized groin. "I am not by any means, you see, an accomplished flirt."

Jealousy tore through him like a hammer, and he let out a sharp exhale. Good God, was it possible he was jealous of a footman? Thane dismissed the remaining servants with an irritated command. He noticed that Astrid watched their departure with what looked like relief, though he could not be sure whether it was for him or for her. Or for poor sodding Conrad. Thane's anger folded in on itself as he filled another glass with wine to the brim.

"Is something amiss, Your Grace?" she asked, her stare colliding with his once they were alone. "You seem…aggrieved."

"I'm fine." His reply emerged like one caustic grunt of a word.

His mood unraveled further as his eyes caught on the delicate lace overlay of her bodice and the creamy, flushed expanse that rose above it. Had *Conrad* noticed her radiant skin? Had she *wanted* him to? Was that why she'd encouraged the man? Thane was spoiling for a fight and he did not know why.

And though every sense warned against opening his mouth, he did it anyway. "That's an unusual choice of dress for you."

"Why? Because I'm a spinster? Because I'm tarnished in the eyes of society?" She lifted a slim brow, taking the wind from his sails. "Or because I'm not a blushing debutante? Tell me, Your Grace, which of the above offends your esteemed sensibilities?" Astrid didn't wait for his answer. "Perhaps I chose white because I like it. It's a woman's prerogative, you understand, to wear what she favors. Her wardrobe is one of the few things in her control."

"And what of a husband? Would he have a say?"

She canted her head. "I imagine so, though I am unmarried, as you well know. I enjoy my freedoms where I can, Your Grace."

Her previous engagement to Edmund Cain shot back to mind, a fresh wave of jealousy surging with it. The man must have slunk back to England, after leaving his men for dead, only to search out a bride. Had he touched her? Kissed that pert, impudent mouth? Discovered the sinful secrets under those yards of demure white silk? His temper flared.

"Red would be a better choice," Thane growled, thinking of what he'd read in Fletcher's report. "For a fallen woman."

A hint of hurt passed over her eyes before it was gone. "Fallen but not dead. I'm still here, Your Grace, with all my purported sins accounted for. Do you think to judge me for them on account of a simple color?"

The guilt was instantaneous. *Pot, meet kettle.*

She was right, of course. People judged him on what they saw, and they judged her on what they thought she'd done. Astrid had clearly been the root of a scandal—she'd admitted as much—but whether or not the accusations were true, who was *he* to punish her for them? No, his reactions stemmed from something else, something he didn't wish to dwell on too deeply because it felt too much like jealousy.

Thane exhaled. "I suppose one should not throw glass stones when having dinner in glass houses."

"Unless, of course, one enjoys breaking things."

It was a dig at his affinity for throwing his father's porcelain, and he smiled before he thought the better of it. "There is that. It's quite liberating. You should try it sometime."

"In your own words, Your Grace, pigs will fly with their tails forward before I lay a harmful finger on any one of those precious antiques." Astrid let out a musical laugh, shaking her head with an exaggerated roll of her eyes, and Thane couldn't help himself. He chuckled, too.

He'd said that very thing when they'd first met, and suddenly, Thane felt shame for his behavior. A better man would have apologized, but he wasn't much of a gentleman, not anymore. Though for some inane reason, she made him want to remember how to be one.

He pushed off his seat and walked to the open terrace doors. "Come," he told her gruffly. "I wish to show you something."

For a second, Astrid looked uncertain, but then she gave a short nod and followed silently in his footsteps to the outdoor balcony.

"Where are we going?" she asked after they'd cut back through the darkened gardens and past several well-lit follies.

But she went quiet when the large glass building, and their destination, came into view. The flickering light from internal lamps made the panes of glass glow with internal fire, and he heard her gasp in awe. Thane pushed open the heavy doors, and a rush of warm air and the scent of orange blossoms surrounded them.

"Oh, goodness, what is this place?" she breathed, wonder threading her voice.

"My greenhouse. I built it."

She gaped at him. "*You* built this?"

"Yes."

Inside the glassed-in structure, lush orange trees stood laden with blooms and fruit at its center, the fragrant scent unique and invigorating. Colorful shrubs and plants occupied the rest of it, with a stone footpath cutting through them. Whimsical water features punctuated its meandering shape. Flowers of every hue lay at the edges, climbing intricate trellises set against the paned glass walls.

It was his solitude. His sanctuary. While he'd been at war and later on the Continent, Thane had almost expected what had been only the bones of the conservatory to have fallen into disrepair or neglect, but neither Fletcher nor Culbert had allowed it. When he'd returned, he'd finished it.

"Oh, Thane, it's *incredible*," Astrid breathed as her gaze turned up and up and up, following the path of flowers that climbed on vines all the way to the top. "It's like we're in another world."

He startled at the sound of his given name on her lips, but from her captivated expression, she hadn't even realized that she'd used it. He instantly wanted to hear it again. Astrid's eyes were wide with wonder, and it made him ache to give her more. To make her look at him with such softness and admiration in her eyes. He wanted to give her everything.

And that thought made him go cold with dread.

Because he *couldn't*.

Fear was a devil with sharp claws and large teeth…and it was relentless.

Had he truly thought showing her this would make her forget what he looked like? *Who I've become?* What had he been thinking? Letting her in wasn't some miracle that would suddenly turn him into a better man. He was and would always be a beast. Someone to be reviled and isolated. Keeping people at arm's length was what he did...who he was.

Thane's entire body compacted into a sick ball of fury, misery, and bitterness. Astrid would never want him in that way. No woman would. Lady Sarah Bolton, whom he had known his whole life, had looked at him with total revulsion at the thought of being touched by him. Stared at him as if he were an animal and fled his presence. No, he could never expose himself to such humiliation again. He whirled to escape the darkness creeping in on him and nearly knocked Astrid over.

With a laugh, she gripped his shoulders to right herself, her elegant fingers landing like humming-birds on the fabric of his coat. His breath caught. His heart hitched. Time and intent came to a pained halt at the sight of her beautiful, *beautiful* hands. Touching him. Holding him.

"Thank you for showing me this," she whispered. "It's beautiful."

You're beautiful, he wanted to say.

He expected her to push him away, but instead her fingers tightened on him. Her face was grave, eyes like pale crystalline chips boring into his. He wanted to drown in the pools of her irises. If he were a poet, he'd describe them as the color of a lake on a winter morning, touched by a pale-blue sky backlit with sunshine. But he wasn't a poet, far from it. He wasn't a dreamer. His dreams were nightmares, and she didn't belong in them.

Thane drew a shattered breath, ready to step aside, when those perfect lips of hers parted, her pink tongue darting out to wet her lower lip. Transfixed, his starved senses reeled as desire swallowed him whole, fracturing practicality and logic, erasing concern and consequence. Demolishing restraint. Obliterating fear.

Leaving only want and need and one inevitable outcome.

He crushed his mouth to hers.

• • •

The feel of the duke's lips stole every coherent thought in Astrid's head. What had started out as a dismal attempt at seduction had dissolved into a pantomime of awkwardness over dinner, but *this*… this was unexpected. He'd brought her here…to a place that meant something to him. The conservatory was magical. As was the rare glimpse into who this man was, perhaps who he'd been a long time ago before tragedy struck.

And now he was kissing her as if she were the air he needed to breathe. As if she were *life* and he only subsisted because of her. She breathed in his scent and relished the sweet violence of his mouth, basking in his heated urgency. Astrid's hands wound up his lapels and twined around his nape into the silky curls above his collar. She met his intensity with a wildness of her own—that fire and fight that he always seemed to bring out in her.

"So sweet," he groaned into her mouth.

Without warning, the kiss gentled, his touch featherlight on her swollen lips. Beswick's mouth was warm and pillow-soft and so reverently tender that she ached at his extraordinary gentleness. It was completely at odds with the needy ferocity of the first, and Astrid couldn't decide which she liked more.

He cradled her jaw in his large hands, grazing her cheeks, her jaw, her brow with his lips. His voice against her ear was an agonized rasp. "My God, you are lovely."

Astrid blushed, but his mouth sought hers again, and she pushed herself up on tiptoe to meet him, greedy for more of the sensations bursting like wildfire inside. When he licked deep, ribbons of pleasure unraveled in her veins, making her gasp against his mouth. She clutched at him, at those broad shoulders, winding urgent fingers into fabric and slanting her mouth on his, desperate to match the delicious, decadent flex of his tongue.

He tasted of brandy and spice and his own special brand of sin.

She wanted *more*.

Never had she felt such an intense reaction to a man's kiss—the weightlessness of her stomach, the trembling of her limbs, the liquid heat between her thighs. The all-encompassing storm of it barreling through her.

"Thane," she whispered.

With a low growl at her plea, he drew her up against him, giving her exactly what she wanted. More of him. Their mouths crashed into each other, ferocious now. *Hungry*. His lips teased hers, his tongue dominating her mouth with deep, delectable licks. Desire shook her. Her senses quaked and crumbled.

She was caught up in his universe, filled with

combusting stars and streaking meteorites, her own need climbing in its pursuit of pleasure. Incoherent moans burst from her as she reached up to cup his jaw, fingers connecting with roped, raised skin. Her eyes flew open as she froze in place, her palm recoiling in shock.

Instantly, he jerked away, breaking the kiss, his golden eyes blazing like twin suns, his lips full and swollen.

"Thane, I—"

"Enough," he rasped. "That's enough."

Beswick stepped back, eyes feral, and Astrid had the sudden urge to calm him as she would a wary, skittish Brutus. She watched as his knuckles skidded across the curve of his lower lip almost in wonder, and the unconscious act made her heart squeeze. His fingers slid to the deep scar that carved into his left cheek only to fall away. Pain, anger, and raw need swirled in those beautiful eyes, regret and shame swift to follow.

He'd flinched because she had touched him. Had she hurt him somehow?

"I'm sorry," Astrid whispered.

"Don't. Pity. Me." The words were doused in agony and no small amount of anger. Then all traces of emotion bled from his face. "I should not have kissed you."

Inexplicably hurt, she responded in kind. "It was just a kiss, Your Grace."

But even as she said it, Astrid knew it for the lie it was. There was no *just a kiss* with a man like him. Even now, her lips felt like they'd been conquered, like they still belonged to him…no longer hers. She fought the urge to run her fingers over them.

Instead, she peered up at him through her lashes…and a lump formed in her throat. Beswick looked bitter, his beautiful mouth twisted into an ugly, distorted shape. She couldn't tell whether it was directed at her or at himself. With him, one could never be sure. Cold and remote one minute, hot and entreating the next, his humors were impossible to read or predict.

Either way, his regret was clear.

Squashing the spreading ache in her chest, Astrid turned and pretended to inspect the downy petals of a striped orchid. "One would think you'd never been kissed before."

"As you have?"

There was a subtle shift of tension in the fragrant air that made the hairs on her nape stand at attention. Those hunter's eyes speared her, something dark flashing in them, and Astrid bristled. She had nothing to be ashamed about. There wasn't much lower to fall when one was already ruined and well acquainted with rock bottom.

"I've had my share," she said softly.

Her *share* she could count on one hand—one or two hasty ones with Beaumont that had made her skin crawl and bile pool in her throat. And once later, long after the scandal, in a moment of reckless defiance with a stranger, when she'd felt nothing but indifference. Not that she had to tell him that. Let him think what he wanted.

Everyone else did.

CHAPTER NINE

Astrid slammed her pillow over her head and screamed. Every nerve ending in her body, particularly the ones centered between her legs, was on fire. For the third night in a row, she was hounded by some of the most erotic dreams she'd ever had in her life, involving a silken-tongued duke and a decided lack of clothing.

Though she knew he'd regretted kissing her — they'd parted soon thereafter in awkward silence, and he'd been avoiding her ever since — Astrid wished she could say the same as a wicked pulse throbbed low in her belly just from the memory of his lips, his scent, his *taste*. Regret, unfortunately, was the least of her opinions.

In her fantasies, Beswick was a demanding lover whose hot, talented mouth trailed wet kisses down her entire body, from her lips to her breasts to where it ached the most. Dream Duke didn't stop there, either.

No, Dream Duke strummed her womanly parts like a violin.

Staring up at the darkened ceiling, Astrid pressed her damp thighs together and half giggled, half groaned into the pillow. God, she was shameless! Though she was an innocent in the ways of passion, she'd attempted to explore once with a nice-enough young man she'd met at a country fair, telling herself that if she was going to be accused of being ruined, she might as well know the crime, but she hadn't been able to go past a single kiss.

Unsurprisingly, she had not cared to try again, at least, not until recently. With a scarred, fractious, broken duke who had the emotional proficiency of a flea.

Astrid screamed into the pillow again and kicked her feet for good measure.

Despite not having seen Beswick for days following their interlude in his conservatory, for which she was thankful, he wasn't ever far from her thoughts. Or dreams, clearly. But something had awakened in her at the duke's touch. Something dark and demanding, as if the thread of sin that had shadowed her fall from grace had been resurrected.

Astrid kicked off the covers in a fit of frustrated pique, her damp skin cooling in the night air, and then realized that she wasn't alone. There was a lump beside her in the bed. She nearly shrieked and then remembered that her sister had climbed into bed late last night with a nightmare of her own. Astrid doubted with a sour scowl that Isobel's night terrors were of the erotic naked-duke variety.

"Are you well?" Isobel murmured, her voice thick with sleep, when Astrid sat up and eased herself to the side of the mattress.

"Yes, Izzy. Go back to sleep. It's early yet, not even dawn."

Through the upper window, the moon was still visible, the first hints of light now starting to speckle the inky skies to the east. Going for a walk or ride would be out of the question. It was still too dark. Perhaps some warmed milk would help. She yawned and stretched, feeling the contracted points of her nipples scrape against the soft lawn of her night rail. Her body tingled from top to bottom, the memory of her dream lover's hands making her blush. A cold bath would be a better choice. An ice-cold dunk in the Arctic preferably.

"Where are you going?" Isobel whispered when Astrid stood with an aggravated groan.

"To fetch some milk from the kitchen," Astrid said, pulling on her wrapper and tightening the sash about her waist.

If I don't get hopelessly lost, that is.

She'd spent most of the last three days inundating herself with work and navigating the mazelike twists and turns of the abbey. It was getting easier but not by much. Counting the hallways under her breath, she made her silent way toward the servants' staircase and narrow corridor, the light of her candle flickering on the walls. She didn't want to think of what she and Isobel would do once the categorization was completed.

Though she enjoyed cataloging the priceless antiques, she knew the work was a temporary fix at best. And not if their uncle discovered them first. Patrick had learned that the Everleighs had hired Runners to find them, no doubt at the insistence of the Earl of Beaumont. Astrid shivered. If that were true, it wouldn't take long for them to be found. Any of the servants at Everleigh House could have seen them packing their trunks or observed which direction the wagon had taken.

If push came to shove, they would have to leave England. Maybe they could go north into Scotland.

They didn't have much money, but perhaps Beswick might be persuaded to lend them the funds until she came into her inheritance. The idea wasn't completely outside the realm of possibility. It was clear that he didn't lack for coin if he was playing cricket with priceless antique Ming dynasty dishware.

If he wasn't amenable, she would find another way. Go to London and find a destitute lord for a husband, if she had to. And if that didn't work, she could get a job in some remote village in Northern England. Perhaps Chetham's Library in Manchester would not be opposed to a female librarian, though Astrid suspected that tiny male brains would explode in simultaneous solidarity should such a progressive thing come to pass.

Astrid came to a halt, peering down an unfamiliar hallway.

Where on earth are the dratted kitchens?

Good God, she was lost again. She glanced over her shoulder, noticing that the wall paneling had turned to beveled stone in the light of her candle. It'd been unnoticeable in the dark. She'd taken a wrong turn somewhere, but she couldn't think whether it'd been an extra staircase or one on the same floor.

"Better to go forward than back," she murmured to herself and winced as the eerie echo of her voice came back to her. It would not do to think of ghosts while she was walking about alone in a deserted abbey in the middle of the night.

Shivering slightly, she hurried down the wide hallway and found herself in a gallery she recognized from the shields and weapons that adorned the walls. Beswick's family had descended from generations of fierce Viking warriors. She could easily imagine the duke dressed head to toe in armor and wielding one of those broadswords or axes hung across those massive crests. His wide shoulders beneath her fingertips had been compact and hard with muscle.

Astrid slowed, studying the portraits of his ancestors in the next hall. Beswick favored them with his dark hair and burning golden eyes. She moved along the gallery until she came to the paintings of the family. A blond toddler in the arms of a beautiful blond woman stood next to a swarthy dark-haired man who bore a resemblance to the current duke. Beswick was nowhere in the portrait.

Several paintings later, she found him. This time, the blond boy was older, and the woman in the portrait was auburn-haired with a swaddled infant in her arms. The duke was the same, though his dark hair held a spate of gray at his temples. The next frame depicted the half brothers. The younger child beside him wore a sullen scowl on his face as if he wanted to be anywhere but there, standing still for a painter to immortalize him.

Astrid bit back a smile. The young Thane would have been about twelve or thirteen, but his square jaw was already pronounced and those uncommon amber eyes of his already burned with inner fire. A lock of burnished brown hair curled onto his forehead.

She lifted a hand to his youthful, unmarred face, her fingers tracing the rounded curve of his cheek. He looked nothing like the man now, of course.

Beswick had been to hell and back—a journey that had taken more than its pound of flesh and left its imprint upon him. He was no less alive for it, though Astrid knew he carried more than his fair share of pain. But she mourned for the boy he'd been and for innocence lost.

Fate could be ruthless.

Astrid supposed she was the same. Her scars, however, were twisted ropes hidden on the inside of her body and encasing the organ currently beating in her chest, while his were on the outside, visible to all.

Would things have been different if Beswick hadn't gone to war? His appearance wouldn't have been altered, but would he have been a softer man? She couldn't countenance it. He had too much strength. Too much innate dominance.

Would *she* have been different if she hadn't met Beaumont? Or would she have been happily married by now with a child or two of her own? Before her ruination, her bloodlines and her dowry would have ensured a suitable match.

In a perfect world, they could have both been happy.

But perfect worlds did not exist. They both had the marks—metaphorical and physical—to show for it.

Leaving the gallery behind, Astrid entered another corridor. This one she instantly recognized. It'd been the one she'd stalked down when she'd first met the Duke of Beswick. A very wet, very naked duke. She felt a shame-faced grin creep onto the corners of her lips—that particular combination of words didn't seem to want to be erased from her lexicon.

Even though she could have easily found her way to the kitchens now that she knew where she was, her feet followed the path toward the bathing chamber. It was unlit, the air chill against her skin, but no less impressive. The water looked black, reflecting the darkness beyond the paned windows. She hadn't had the time to appreciate the architecture before—she'd been too concerned with an eyeful of nude male musculature—but the space was truly magnificent.

Much like his conservatory.

Astrid wondered if he had designed and built this room as well. She had never seen the bathing chamber's like, though in some Turkish and Roman history books, she recalled drawings of similar public baths.

The thought of Beswick floating at the pool's center like some indolent pasha slipped into her mind like silk.

Lord above, but she was obsessed with ducal nudity.

Kicking off her slippers, she wandered to the edge and dipped her toe into the water. To her suddenly over-warm skin, it was delightfully cool. She wouldn't dare go in, but the temptation was too much to resist. Discarding her wrapper near her abandoned footwear, she sat at the edge and hiked up her night rail to her knees. A fit of nerves made her glance over her shoulder, but nothing stirred in the shadowy corners of the room.

She sighed at the sublime feel of the water on her

submerged legs. There was something decadent about the soft splash of the water lapping at her bare skin. The urge to wade in grew, but it wasn't just a matter of bravery; it was a matter of logic. She had no idea where the servants kept the toweling, and she also didn't know if she could find her way back without dripping everywhere. As such, she contented herself with submerging her feet and watching the dawn's fingers creep across the sky.

Astrid had no idea how long she sat there staring through the windows, watching the sunrise, but it was incredible. Like experiencing nature's artistry coming alive with long, elegant brushstrokes. Pale-gold swatches, tinged with pink and orange, appeared first, catching on the edges of the trees and gilding them in light. And as the sun chased away the darkness, the shimmering hues spun and danced, bathing the world afresh in color.

A distant clatter reached her ears—one of a household awakening—and Astrid launched to her feet. Her toes were the texture of prunes.

"Blast it!"

Her faithful candle had near burned down to a stub. Grabbing her slippers and dressing gown, she almost skidded on the wet floor but righted herself with a gasp. The echo of her gasp reached her, but she was too focused on not being discovered by the waking staff that she put it down to the room's acoustics. She made her way to the foyer at the front of the abbey.

From there it was a simple task to find her bed-chamber.

• • •

"There you are, Your Grace, good morning," Culbert said, making Thane's cramped body flinch painfully as the butler walked into the room that Lady Astrid had vacated only moments before. "You should have summoned me to light the hearths. Did you fall asleep in here again?"

"Good morning, Culbert."

Thane blinked, uncurling his long body from the position it'd been in for the better part of an hour. The oversize chaise was situated in the far corner of the room, designed as a sitting area, and he'd been occupying it for most of the night. He'd been about to ring for the butler to light the stone flues when the object of his fantasies had wandered in. Thane had been shocked. Had he summoned her with his lewd thoughts?

But no, Astrid hadn't been a figment of his lust.

Thane had almost alerted her to his presence, as any gentleman would have, but then she'd approached the pool. He'd held his breath while the wheels turned in her head. She'd dipped one dainty toe in and then discarded her wrapper.

Thane couldn't have announced himself even if he had wanted to.

The silhouette of her body limned in moonlight had stunned him to silence. Long and lithe, she'd walked like a nymph to the water's edge and crouched down. She moved like a silken ribbon caught in a breeze, with an elegant and fluid economy of motion. An outstretched leg, an exquisitely arched foot. The curve of a sleek calf as it sank from view. She moved like music. Like poetry. And he'd been spellbound.

She'd sat there and watched the sunrise.

He'd sat there and watched her.

Watched the shadows creep from that regal profile as the dawn's light replaced them. Examined the curls that had sprung free from her bedtime braid, haloing the beautiful oval of her face. Seen the way her lips had parted in astonished delight and the soft rise and fall of her breast. Heard the erotic sounds of water sloshing against skin and wished he could be the one at her feet. Caressing. Lapping. Enveloping.

He'd gone as hard as stone.

And stayed that way.

"Shall I have the footmen light the hearths, Your Grace?" Culbert asked.

"Yes."

"Do you wish to have your breakfast here, then?"

Thane shook his head. "No, just coffee will do. I will break my fast later with my aunt and the young ladies Everleigh."

"Very well, Your Grace."

After Culbert took his leave, Thane discarded the robe and strode to the pool, sinking to where Astrid had sat. It gave him a cool thrill to enter the water at the exact point where she'd dangled those pale sylphlike legs of hers. The glimpses of her well-turned ankles and shapely calves had made him lose his breath. He'd wanted more. Much more. A vision of her with her curls unbound and draped in soaking-wet, transparent lawn invaded his mind, doing nothing to lessen the erection he still sported. A brisk plunge would help with that.

Some hours later, after a lengthy swim, a bracing round of exercise that combined gymnastics and stretching, and Fletcher dressing and grooming him into civility, Thane descended to the breakfast room, all parts of him in compliant, civilized order.

Voices reached him as he pushed open the door and then went silent. They all rose upon his entry.

"Don't get up on my account, please," he said. "Sit. Continue."

But the youngest of the trio of ladies at the dining table stared at him in wide-eyed alarm. He turned around, wondering which fiend had rode in on his heels. Was he missing some vital item of clothing? A cravat? He glanced down. His trousers? No, everything was in place.

Except for...

Hell, he'd forgotten the blasted hat.

Thane blew out a breath, feeling both relieved and irritated. Relieved that the pretense was over and everyone could move on. And irritated because it was his bloody house and he couldn't skulk around it any more than he already had, just to avoid offending the sensibilities of some delicate debutante. He was only scarred, for God's sake, not the devil incarnate.

"Isobel," Astrid hissed to her sister. "Compose yourself this instant and greet the duke properly."

The girl's mouth immediately snapped shut and her head ducked to her plate. "G'morning," she mumbled.

"Good morning, Your Grace," Astrid said in a

stricken voice. "Please excuse my sister's poor manners. She's usually not so ill-behaved."

"No insult taken," he said.

"Beswick," his aunt greeted, a concerned look falling to the young lady who remained ashen, eyes downcast.

Thane filled his plate and took his place at the head of the table, half regretting his decision to join them. Already, he felt on edge. And not because of Isobel's reaction but because of the woman who sat a few feet away. Despite her efforts to avoid him, the draw of her was magnetic. Impossible to ignore, especially after the kiss in the conservatory several evenings ago and *especially* after her early-morning exploration that had left him in such a sorry state.

Clad in a dove-gray morning dress, Astrid's dark hair had been brushed off her brow into that pristine bun. He almost wished he could see it fully unbound, not just the tantalizing curls he'd viewed loose earlier in the bathing room. It would be pure chaos. A dark, wanton mess he could wind his hands in, bury his face in, do thoroughly indecent things in that would make a courtesan blush.

"Did you sleep well, Lady Astrid?" he asked in a voice like gravel.

Clear eyes lifted to his, the hint of a smudge beneath them, but then they dropped away. "Of course, Your Grace."

"She did not," Isobel volunteered, as if desperate to make amends for her faux pas. "She left for hours in the middle of the night."

The duchess looked up from her toast. "Where did you go, dear?"

"I...I couldn't sleep, so I attempted to find the kitchens for some warmed milk...and got lost," Astrid replied, clearly flustered and peeved at her sister for mentioning her nighttime wanderings. "It took some time for me to find my way back to bed."

Thane ignored the way that one word lit an ache in his gut. He shoveled a forkful of eggs into his mouth, chewed, and swallowed. "You should have rung for a servant or sent your maid to get it for you." He paused, trying to recall her stout lady's maid. "Aggie or Agnes?"

"Agatha." Astrid shrugged. "She was asleep. Why wake her when I'm hale enough to fetch it myself? Honestly, the lack of resilience expected in the female nobility these days is trying."

Thane blinked, his fork arrested halfway to his mouth. Her unusual viewpoints constantly surprised him. Most aristocratic ladies wouldn't dream of doing anything themselves. But then again, she was unlike any lady of his acquaintance. He glanced at his chortling aunt and revised his statement. Aunt Mabel had been flaunting society's expectations since the dawn of time.

"A girl after my own heart," Mabel said. "Though I quite agree. This place is quite a maze. Wonderful for childhood hide-and-go-seek games but not for old ladies in their dotage."

"You're not in your dotage, Aunt," Thane said loyally and glanced at Astrid. "Did you find the kitchens?"

"No," she said. "But all was not lost. I did see the sunrise."

"Oh!" Mabel clapped her hands. "You must have

been on the east side of the abbey then." She frowned to herself. "Was it from the gallery? That's the only floor with partial views to the east."

Twin flags of color rose into Lady Astrid's cheeks after a sidelong look in his direction. "No, er, it was a room with a rather large bathing pool."

"A pool?" Isobel perked up and then instantly dropped her head.

"The sunrise was indeed spectacular this morning," Thane murmured. He was careful not to make eye contact with Astrid, but he felt the touch of her stare nonetheless. "And yes, Lady Isobel, there is an indoor bathing pool at Beswick Park. Perhaps when you are no longer so frightened, you may allow me to show it to you and your sister."

"I'm not afraid." An interested gaze rose and dipped comically. "Can we go after breakfast?"

"Certainly, if Lady Astrid does not object."

"She doesn't!" Isobel clapped her hands, bright eyes a shade darker than her sister's meeting his. "Do you, Astrid?"

"I do not think we should impose on the duke's time, Isobel."

"It's no imposition," he said. "I spend most of my time there."

"Why?" Isobel burst out.

He met a second pair of ice-blue eyes, ones far more guarded than the first. "When I can't sleep, swimming helps with insomnia."

Thane almost grinned at the moment Astrid realized that he might have been there as well when a bright splash of color bloomed along those regal cheekbones. She dragged her eyes away on the pretext of taking a sip of her tea, but the hue of her cheeks belied her fraying composure. Thane followed the blush as it stole along her skin, only breaking concentration when his aunt cleared her throat.

The duchess stared at him with a suddenly fascinated look, and he scowled. "My poor nephew has been plagued with insomnia since he was a boy."

Astrid replaced her teacup. "I've read an academic text on alternative remedies where meditation can help with sleeplessness as well. Besides exercise, I mean."

Aunt Mabel nodded with interest. "Where did you find it?"

"Careful, Lady Astrid," Thane said. "The color of your stockings is showing."

Isobel gasped, and Astrid shot him a disparaging look. "The color of one's intimate garments is inappropriate conversation, sir."

"If I recall correctly, you called yourself a blue-*stocking*."

"I called myself a scholar," she returned. "That bigoted term was yours. And you know very well it has nothing to do with women's garments. It came from the *men* who attended literary salons wearing informal blue hose. You attempt only to shock, Your Grace."

He leaned back with a slow grin. "Alas, shocking tender sensibilities is my only source of amusement."

"Then, I should hate to be as bored as you," she fired back. "And pray tell, what is so wrong about a woman who enjoys literary or intellectual pursuits?

Or reading scientific texts?" She rolled her eyes. "The horror of it! No one faults the men for their education."

"I, for one, do not see the point of a man's education for a female," Isobel said primly. "A young lady should be accomplished in the *feminine* arts. Music, singing, dancing, art, and whatnot." She tossed her blond curls. "My erudite sister here, however, does not agree."

"And yet you exhibit your own superior intelligence with simple word choice." Astrid sent the girl a wink. "The mind is a muscle," she said. "If not exercised, it will weaken. And we erudite females shouldn't let the patriarchy rest on their laurels, should we?"

"Hear, hear!" Aunt Mabel crowed. "I always did like a chit with some spirit."

"Says the woman who lived to scandalize the matrons of London in her hoydenish younger years and had quite a number of the patriarchy on their knees," Thane said dryly. "And still does."

"When one is a duchess, one can do as one pleases," she said with a grin at Astrid.

To his surprise, the lady laughed, her eyes shining with intelligence and humor. "You are truly a shining beacon of our underestimated sex, Your Grace," Astrid said, smiling at the duchess. "I, for one, should love to hear more of your adventures in hoydenism."

"That is not a word, Madame Scholar," Thane said with a laugh, drawing the surprised attention of his aunt as well as Culbert, who stared at him as if he'd grown two heads. His laughter cut off abruptly.

"What?" he snapped.

"Nothing," Mabel said with another of those fascinated stares. "I haven't heard you laugh in some time."

"I laugh all the time."

"Perhaps when you're terrorizing young children," Astrid said and covered her mouth with a shocked giggle.

Isobel gasped. *"Astrid!"*

But Aunt Mabel's guffaw simply took precedence. She laughed until tears were leaking from the corners of her eyes, uncaring of propriety or decorum. "Oh, indeed. Priceless. Terrorizing…young…children." And off she went into gales of laughter again.

Thane rolled his eyes. "I'm glad to see I'm such a source of amusement, Aunt."

Astrid looked as though she were torn between laughing and running from the room, while her sister had a bewildered look on her young face. The difference between the two of them was remarkable. Thane couldn't fathom the composed and poised Lady Astrid ever being so young and green as Lady Isobel. But according to Fletcher's notes and by her own admission, she would have had her London Season at the same age, when Cain had proposed marriage.

Had her thoughts been as eccentric as they were now? Most men of his set, including Cain, would have been appalled at the idea of a woman challenging his manly intellect or spouting revolutionary notions of female parity. Her dry, clever wit would have been lost on him or any of them. A lady of

Isobel's temperament and philosophy would have been far better-suited to the *ton*.

Not her...not Lady Astringent.

He bit back a grin. A man like Edmund Cain would have rejected any spark of originality. He would not have been able to handle her, which made Thane question how the engagement had come about in the first place.

The words were out of his mouth before he could stop them. "Why did you accept Cain?"

A guarded gaze met his, Astrid's soft response equally so. "Edmund, though he wasn't yet the Earl of Beaumont then, was a gentleman of means. I suppose to my father it would have been an acceptable match."

The name hung in midair like a billowing red banner. Thane's eyes panned from Astrid to Isobel and then narrowed. "Edmund Cain is the Earl of Beaumont? Since when?"

Astrid stared at him strangely but nodded. "His uncle died some years ago, and he inherited the title. When he was discharged from the war, I believe."

Discharged? More like deserted.

"*He's* the man who's wanting to marry Isobel," Thane said slowly. He hadn't known the old man had passed. Then again, he hadn't kept up with much in the *ton* for obvious reasons.

When Astrid nodded again, Thane felt a chill wind through him. Though many debutantes were married young, a part of him understood Astrid's concern—a girl like Isobel in the hands of someone like Cain was unconscionable.

The official report was that Cain had been shot in

Spain trying to escape the enemy, but Thane didn't believe that for a second. A gunshot wound to his left shoulder at close range, according to the War Office's reports he'd read years ago, reeked of a self-inflicted wound. A screen for his defection. When Thane got his hands on him, he intended to find out the truth.

Nonetheless, any man who had left his so-called brothers to die on a battlefield while claiming to be a war hero would be lacking in common decency. Missing a moral compass.

What would he do to an innocent like Isobel?

Thane loosed a breath. What did he care? Neither of the chits was his problem.

But as soon as he thought it, he knew he was lying to himself. Honor would not allow him to let either of them be at a man like Cain's mercy. His eyes slid to Astrid, drawn to the movement of those slender long fingers, reminding him of the sinuous way her limber form had knelt at the pool. The way her mouth had clung to his…the honeyed taste of her.

A blast of tension gathered in his groin. Who was he fooling?

Honor was the least of his motives.

CHAPTER TEN

"We should not be going near the village, Isobel," Astrid said, pulling the cowl of her cloak low over her brow as they cantered along the grassy paths toward the outer edges of the village of Southend. Agatha and a young groom accompanied them. Isobel must have been desperate if she'd actually climbed on top of a horse—albeit a very placid one—to escape Beswick Park. "It's not safe."

Her sister tossed her head. "This is *Southend*, Astrid, and it's perfectly safe. We've come here for years, and no one bats an eyelash at anything. You may enjoy being cooped up with your books and papers all day long, but I do not. I need some fresh air. And normal people who don't…"

She trailed off, but Astrid knew what she meant to say: *normal people who don't frighten the living daylights out of their guests.*

Despite thawing toward the duke, Isobel continued to be at odds around him. It wasn't difficult to grasp the whys and wherefores. She was a sheltered, sweet girl, and Beswick was an imposing, terrifying presence whose constant fractious attitude didn't help matters. In truth, his scars were the least of it. If the duke worked at being less of a bear with a thorn in its paw, he could actually be quite…nice.

Isobel dismounted and walked over to an oak growing atop a knoll that looked down over the village, her expression longing. Astrid did the same and followed her, letting Brutus graze under the watchful eye of their groom.

"I thought you liked the duke."

Isobel goggled at Astrid. "*Like* him? Just this morning, Cook said he'd been in one of his rages and not to go anywhere near the east tower if I didn't wish to be frightened. By all accounts, the man is a beast with a temper to match."

"A man who is providing us his protection, Isobel, and we will do best to remember that. Uncle Reginald hasn't given up in his search. Money is a powerful motivator for even those we think are on our side." She let out a breath. "Has the duke ever hurt you or given any indication that he would?"

"No." The admission was soft.

Astrid sighed. "I'm doing the best I can, Isobel. For both of us. Until I come into my inheritance, we don't have much choice in the matter, and we must prevail upon His Grace's generosity."

"I know. I'm just lonely, and I miss my friends."

It was true that Astrid had been busy, and as a result, Isobel had been left to her own devices. She had not inherited their father's love for horses, and she preferred dancing and needlepoint to more intellectual pursuits, with the exception of reading *Ackermann's Repository* for needlework patterns. To which the duke did not have a subscription.

In the absence of social pursuits, it meant that Isobel had spent more time than she normally would in the company of an embroidery hoop, thread, and needle. Perhaps Astrid should have recognized the signs of her sister's isolation earlier, but she'd been so wrapped up in her work and keeping Beswick at a distance that she simply hadn't noticed Isobel's growing unhappiness.

"Is it truly that bad?" Astrid asked, softening. "It's only been a few weeks."

Isobel bit her lip. "No, you're right, it's not. After all you're doing and what you've done to keep us safe, it's nothing. I don't know what's come over me."

Astrid blinked, taking in her sister's wan coloring and pinched smile with fresh eyes. She was trying so hard to grin and bear it, but Astrid could see the lines bracketing her mouth and the tightness of her pale face.

"I'm sorry, Izzy. I wish things were different."

Her sister's shoulders slumped. "Don't be. You're doing the best you can. And I feel like I'm doing nothing. That I'm a burden and you wouldn't be in this position because of me." She swallowed hard, a tear tracking down her face. "Sometimes, I feel so lost. Maybe it would be better if I just married Beaumont, and then you wouldn't have to worry."

"Never say that." She grasped her sister's shoulders and pulled her close. "We're in this together, Izzy. Do you hear me?"

"I do," she mumbled into Astrid's neck, hugging tight. "I love you, you know."

"I love you, too."

Astrid pulled away and glanced down to the deserted streets of the village. It was Sunday, and it was quiet. Most people would be at church, and it was unlikely that Beaumont would even venture into town. Surely a few moments couldn't hurt.

She squeezed her sister's hand. "Since we're

already here, how about we have an ice? I suppose it will be fine for a few minutes if we try not to draw attention to ourselves."

"Oh, thank you, Astrid!" Isobel shrieked, flinging her arms about her again. "I promise I will be as insignificant as a beetle!"

They rode in and stopped for a cream ice before dismounting in front of Howell's Emporium, the village shop that carried everything from fabric to bonnets to fans and various other items. After instructing the groom to wait with the horses, she and Agatha followed Isobel into the shop. It would be too much of a miracle to hope that Howell's was empty, but Astrid was counting on one thing...that her uncle had not made a public declaration that his nieces had run away, out of sheer embarrassment on his part. And fueled by greed, of course. No, he would try to find them quietly with some acceptable excuse as to their absence. So far they hadn't encountered more than a handful of villagers. Perhaps they would continue to be lucky.

"Why, Lady Astrid," a nasally voice called out.

Or not, Astrid thought as her heart sank when she turned to greet Mrs. Purley, the worst gossipmonger in Southend.

The woman raised an eyebrow. "I thought your uncle said you and Lady Isobel were visiting your late mother's relatives in Colchester."

And there it was—the "excuse." Astrid shrugged noncommittally.

Mrs. Purley frowned. "Though I do recall your mother being an only child."

"Distant relatives."

The feeling of panic started to spread as she noticed Isobel in conversation with Mrs. Purley's spinster daughter, who had almost as big a mouth as her mother's. She hadn't strictly told Isobel not to say anything, but slips could be made, especially when someone wanted to be nosy. Murmuring her apologies to Mrs. Purley, she hurried over to where Isobel stood.

"I would love to go to Lady Ashley's ball," her sister was saying. "However, I do not think we will be attending."

Lady Ashley was a widowed marchioness and the reigning *ton* matriarch of Southend. They had been invited to previous balls in the past, but Isobel had been much too young to attend. And in Astrid's case, well, there was no real reason for a committed spinster to socialize.

"But everyone is invited," Miss Purley said, lowering her voice to a stage whisper. "You simply must come, Lady Isobel. I've heard the Earl of Beaumont is in residence. Isn't that exciting?"

Astrid frowned, nerves taking flight in her belly at the mere mention of the man and Isobel in the same sentence. She moved to her sister's side. "Come now, Isobel. We're late, remember?"

Isobel nodded with a quick goodbye to Miss Purley, and Astrid breathed a sigh of relief that her sister had caught on. She wanted to get back to Beswick Park before too many people, namely the Purleys, could gossip about their presence. They'd risked too much already.

As she stepped out of Howell's, blinking in the sunlight, she could hear the murmur of voices before her vision narrowed on a small crowd surrounding a particularly flashy carriage. With distinctive red trim. At once, her stomach took a painful nosedive to her feet.

Oh God, is the earl here?

"Quickly, Isobel," Astrid said, turning on her heel to seek out her sister, only to stare into the grim countenance of Lord Beaumont.

"And where, pray tell, have the two of you been?" he asked, a gloved hand catching her elbow. "You've driven your aunt and uncle and *me* nearly mad with worry."

"But, Lord Beaumont, surely you know that we've been visiting relatives in Colchester," Astrid said in as innocent a voice as she could manage, but every muscle in her body was screaming with fear. They were in grave danger. If the earl decided to take them into his coach, as she fully expected him to do, no one would do anything to stop him. He was a peer. Nobody, not even villagers who had known them for years, would oppose the nobility.

His eyes narrowed. "Have you?"

"Isn't that what my aunt and uncle told everyone?"

Astrid's desperate gaze spanned the street, searching for their mounts, but the horses were nowhere in sight. Where was that dashed groom? How had Beaumont *known*? He must have had someone on watch in the village. Of course he would have. She should have known he wouldn't give up so easily.

"Get in the coach." His command was loaded with soft menace.

"We have our own means of travel, my lord," Astrid said. "We shouldn't like to inconvenience you. I'm afraid we really must decline."

His voice lowered to a hiss. "I said get in that coach."

Isobel let out an exhale that sounded like a sob, and Astrid's heart slammed against her rib cage. Could they make a run for it? Not hampered by skirts and improper footwear, they couldn't. And she didn't know where the bloody groom had run off to!

Astrid squared her shoulders. "No."

His mouth tightened with displeasure, and his fingers pinched the tender flesh above her elbow, and she braced herself for public humiliation, but not before the sound of thundering hooves entered the square. People screamed and leaped out of the way as a curricle careened to a stop within inches of Beaumont's coach, driven by none other than the Beast of Beswick himself.

Sans hat, sans cravat. And utterly magnificent. Astrid had never felt so deliriously happy to see anyone in all her life.

"I believe, Cain, the lady said no," he said in that smoky snarl of his as he dismounted.

The earl's lip curled, revulsion flashing in his eyes, his hand falling away. "This is none of your affair, Beswick. And it's Lord Beaumont now."

"You'll always be a dunghill of a deserter to me."

Beaumont sputtered. "I-I was honorably discharged."

"You and I both know the truth, *Cain*, and you can't hide from it forever."

"Are you threatening me?"

Beswick's response was silky. "Do you feel threatened?"

Astrid goggled from one man to the other, but by then, the whispers in the crowd had become roars. Someone screamed, and a child started to wail. The duke was inscrutable, ignoring the chaos around him, his stony expression making his patchwork face seem even more gruesome in the full light of day.

"In any case, this is my affair, you see," Beswick went on. "Two females who clearly do not want to accompany you will always be of concern to a gentleman."

"You're no gentleman," Beaumont snarled. "And I am escorting them home."

The duke's smile was a showing of teeth, no more. "According to Debrett's, I outrank you." Beswick's amber eyes turned to Astrid, and she fought not to throw herself into his arms as though he was some dark avenging angel come to the rescue. "Do you wish to accompany Lord Beaumont?"

To Astrid's surprise, it was Isobel who answered. "No, Your Grace. We do not."

Beaumont scowled. "They are no one to you, Beswick."

"Ah, but you are mistaken," the duke drawled with an exaggerated flourish. "She is my future wife."

• • •

The declaration had left Thane's mouth before he knew he meant to say it. But it was either that or beat that craven peacock to a bloody pulp. The sight of the earl's hand restraining Astrid had made him want to commit murder without a second thought.

"Your future *wife*?" Beaumont scoffed. "Isobel is betrothed to me."

"No, not Lady Isobel. Lady Astrid."

Thane heard Astrid's soft inhalation but didn't take his eyes from the earl. Astrid was smart enough…she would take his meaning. However, he wouldn't put it past the man to snatch Isobel and shove her into the conveyance, exposing her to public ruination.

"You wish to marry that dried-up old spinster?" Beaumont laughed, lifting an eyebrow. "I didn't think used goods were your style, Beswick."

The chatter soared around them, and Astrid went crimson with shame. While the beast inside him growled on her behalf, Thane kept it under control. This wasn't a battlefield. This was the Southend village square—the home of his ancestral seat. Beaumont was baiting him, wanting him to disgrace himself, but Thane hadn't come through hell and survived only to be goaded into stupidity.

He gave no indication of the rage ballooning inside him. "Careful, Beaumont. That's my fiancée you're speaking of, so watch your tongue."

"Then, you're more of a fool than I gave you credit for." Beaumont's eyes shone with malice, lips folding into a sneer. "Enjoy her. Unfortunately, I found her to be quite frigid."

Astrid gasped. "I never touched you, you lying cretin."

That time, it was only by a supreme effort of will that Thane kept his body from surging forward. His gaze panned from Astrid's heated face to Beaumont's smug expression, but he was careful to give no reaction. No doubt, the earl *wanted* him to react physically so that he could have him thrown into gaol.

"You should get back into your coach, Beaumont," he said in a low voice. "Or I will have my seconds call on you forthwith, if that is your wish."

The man had the good sense to blanch. "This isn't over."

"Come near either of them again, and you will face me at dawn."

After a seething Beaumont departed in his coach, for the first time since he arrived, Thane took in the stares of the villagers around him. He sensed the fear and the loathing, heard the dread in their voices, understood their horror. He hadn't shown his face in public in years, after all. He was both man and myth. Both legend and the ugly, glaring truth.

And he'd forgotten his bloody hat.

The furor rose in crescendo, and he felt the world start to crowd him. The voices rose and rose, and the countenances of the villagers whirled, their faces merging. His head felt hot, and the earth started to spin.

"Breathe," a low voice said, slim gloved fingers weaving with his larger ones and squeezing. "I'm here."

"Astrid."

Her palm was like an anchor, tethering him back to reason. Like a cloud fragmenting, his senses cleared, just from her palliative grip.

"Help Isobel and Agatha up." She nodded to the waiting curricle, her voice low. "I've got this."

"You can handle the team?" he rasped.

She shot him a jaunty grin and winked. "I made our coachman teach me."

He shot her a dry look. "Why am I not surprised?"

"Don't trust me, Duke?"

"You'd be surprised to know how much I do trust you."

When they were all settled, he climbed up beside her. She rode for home much more sedately than the life-threatening pace he'd taken getting to the village, after the groom he'd tasked with keeping an eye on the ladies returned with the news that the earl had been spotted.

Naturally, she managed the horses with a deft, expert touch. But despite his admiration, by the time they took the turn at the start of his estate, Thane's earlier annoyance returned in full force. Things could have gone far worse if he had been a minute or two later. He kept his mounting irritation in check until they pulled into the courtyard at Beswick Park, but as soon as they stopped, his control broke.

"What were you thinking?" he thundered, handing her down from the driver's perch and keeping her hand caught in his as he practically dragged her inside.

Her beautiful ice-blue eyes widened. "I—"

"It wasn't Astrid's fault," Isobel cried, hurrying behind them, their maid on their heels. "It was mine, Your Grace. I wanted to go to the village. She tried to warn me, and I wouldn't listen. Please don't be angry with her."

"I'm not angry."

"Then, why are you manhandling me?" Astrid asked. He released her like she was a hot stone, and she stumbled backward, nearly crashing into her sister.

"In my study," Thane ordered, throttling his ire. "Both of you. *Now*."

He didn't look to see if they followed but went straight past his desk to pour himself a liberal glass of brandy. When the door closed behind him, he turned to see Astrid standing there alone. *That is for the best*, he thought. Isobel would probably burst into a puddle of tears for the blistering he had planned.

Thane opened his mouth, but Astrid lifted a palm. "Thank you," she said. "That must have been hard for you."

He blinked. Did she not realize how close they had come to being at Beaumont's utter mercy? "Hard for *me*?"

"Being out in public."

"I didn't think of it until there at the end." He raked a hand through his hopelessly tangled hair. "Astrid, do you have any idea the danger you were in?"

"You prevented that," she said softly.

"This time," he said. "But Edmund Cain is not a man to be deterred, and now that he knows you are here, things could get worse. Much worse."

"I know." Astrid approached where he stood, her scent curling around him, and Thane went stock-still as she lifted the snifter from his hand and took a long draught before handing it back to him. He stared at it and then her in dumbfounded silence.

"Did you mean what you said?" she asked, her voice husky from the bite of the brandy. "Or was matrimony only a ploy to discourage the earl? It seemed like you were already acquainted. How do you know him?"

"He was in my regiment." Thane did not want to talk about Cain and dredge up those memories. "And marriage is the only safe course now," he went on. "If your uncle comes looking for you—and he will—without a husband's name behind you, you have no power."

"And you wish to give me yours?"

"I wish for you to be safe."

She canted her head at him, her eyes unguarded and full of emotion. "Why do you care? When you didn't before?"

Thane gulped the rest of the cognac, focusing on the hot burn in his stomach instead of the insistent burn elsewhere. "You work for me. Without you, the stupid auction will never happen."

"Is the auction the only reason?"

"What other reason would there be?" he shot back, needlessly vexed. "That you and your sister stormed into my perfectly ordered life and left nothing but mayhem in your wake? That I happened to enjoy my existence as it was before you decided to employ a woman-shaped hammer to it?" He stood, breathing heavily, unwilling to meet her eyes because he had no doubt she would see right through his bluster, right through his lies. "I care now because I *can't* in good conscience turn a blind eye. My mother would roll over in her grave."

"How chivalrous of you, Your Grace." Her tone implied the opposite. "One would think that you'd never rescued a damsel in distress."

No one was worth rescuing before.

Thane sucked in a sharp breath. "Not to my knowledge, no. Women tend to be more trouble than they're worth. Case in point. Which is why I've made it my business to stay away from your species."

"We are the same species, Your Grace." Her defenses were up, the vulnerability that had been in her eyes long gone. "I take it you mean my gender."

That haughty pedantic tone of hers had returned, putting them both back on safe ground. Thane mourned it and celebrated it in the same breath. "Quite," he agreed. "In any event, you strike me as a lady who is more than capable of rescuing herself, and I mean that as a compliment."

"Thank you, Your Grace. In most cases, I aim to be. But you have my everlasting gratitude, and Isobel's, for what you did today."

Thane's chest clenched at her words. For once, he was the hero instead of the villain of the story. He'd forgotten what it had felt like to be truly *esteemed*. For a moment, he found himself choked with emotion. "You're welcome."

"You do not have to marry me, Your Grace. I've decided that Isobel and I should leave for Scotland. Beaumont and my uncle won't follow us there."

"You are wrong about Beaumont. And don't underestimate the power of greed."

Astrid lifted an elegant shoulder. "My problem to handle."

"And what of brigands and highwaymen en

route? How do you propose to deal with them? To keep your sister safe?"

"We will have Patrick with us," she said.

The groom who had been familiar with her. Thane felt an indescribable urge to flatten something. Preferably something Scottish. And large. With red hair.

"His family will offer us refuge," Astrid said.

If Thane hadn't been watching her so carefully, he would have missed the slight twinge of doubt that passed over her face. He'd bet his last farthing that she hadn't approached the groom yet with her asinine plan. Fleeing to Scotland? They wouldn't be able to lose the track of seasoned Runners, not in a carriage with two ladies, a maid, and a single groom for an escort. And Beaumont would have Isobel exactly where he wanted her—in a place celebrated for its elopements and anvil weddings. He felt his anger return as if it was attached to a pendulum.

Thane arched an eyebrow. "Have you told him of your plan yet?"

"No, but he'll agree."

Good Lord, but she was stubborn. Thane wanted to force her to listen, but intimidating her would never work. Her tenacity and pride rivaled his, and she would dig her heels in if she had to. He needed to change his tactics.

"I never took you for a coward," he said.

"I beg your pardon," she shot back. "How dare you? I'm no coward!"

Thane grinned. "And we're back to you begging. I already like where this conversation is going."

"Go to the devil." She whirled on her heel, but he

blocked her path easily, barring the door with one hand. "Let me out, Beswick."

"I like it when you call me Thane."

"And I'd like it if you dropped dead."

He pressed his free hand to his heart with a mock sigh. "So bloodthirsty for such a puny female."

Her eyes flashed blue fire. "I know what you're trying to do, Beswick, and it won't work. You see, I actually have a working brain, unlike the other females of your acquaintance."

Thane grinned, his arm lowering to capture her waist. "That big brain of yours is what I'm counting on."

And then he took her lips with his.

CHAPTER ELEVEN

Astrid's very capable brain was supremely *incapable* of thought, blanketed as she was with a huge, determined duke. And truth was, she didn't want to. She'd wanted to wrap herself around him and kiss him the moment he'd thundered into the village, and she wasn't about to deny herself the occasion, no matter how irate she was.

Dreadful know-it-all man.

Though sweet Lord in heaven, he knew how to kiss.

It was as if he were born to it. Born to use that sinful mouth of his in every decadent way. Even now, it nipped at hers, coaxing her lips to part wider, his tongue sliding in and out in silken, teasing strokes. Taking, giving. Demanding, worshipping.

"Take this down," he muttered thickly, his hands going to the pins in her hair. She felt the mass tumble down her back and heard his satisfied groan as he dug his fingers into it, cupping her nape in his large palms as his mouth found hers again.

This was only their second kiss, and though it tasted the same—hot and dark and sweet—it *felt* different. This kiss was evocative of winter nights in front of a fireplace, of spiced wine and delicious secrets.

"Say my name," he whispered between breaths.

She wanted to resist, but her lips wanted his more. "Thane."

The reward was explosive as his mouth slanted hotly over hers. His clever tongue ignited a pulsating ache in her breasts and between her thighs and sent shivers over her skin. She was awash with sensation. With *fire*, and she wanted to burn.

Astrid wound boneless arms around his neck and clung to him, even as he lifted her easily into his own and deposited them both into a nearby armchair. Cradling her body to him, his lips left hers to travel down her throat in sensual nudges and bites until all she could do was sigh in pleasure and give in to his skill. Vaguely, she became aware of his straining arousal beneath her thighs, and she murmured a half protest about servants, which he promptly smothered with his mouth.

She was so lost in the web of passion that she didn't hear the commotion at the door until it was too late. Far too late.

"Good God, Astrid, what are you *doing*?"

Isobel's shocked face swam into view when Astrid tore her lips away from Beswick's. But it wasn't her sister who made her scramble out of the duke's lap, it was the veritable entourage behind her. Including her aunt and uncle, Lady Mabel, a gentleman she did not recognize, an openly gloating Fletcher…and Lady Ashley. Astrid cringed at the last. The stylishly appointed lady was the pinnacle of Southend society. And its arbiter.

Astrid blinked in horror, staring down the tableau of her own ruin.

Again.

Lady Ashley's presence at Beswick Park was no accident.

Once more, she'd been betrayed by a man, only this time, it wasn't a lie. And there were witnesses. Witnesses whose expressions ran the usual gambit upon seeing Beswick in the flesh. Fear, loathing, and horror were written on her aunt's and uncle's faces, though those were quickly eclipsed by hostility. Isobel and Lady Ashley looked properly scandalized, Lady Mabel stricken. The unfamiliar man wore no expression at all.

Astrid glared accusingly at the duke, who had risen to stand beside her, her voice a low hiss. "Did you arrange this?"

She moved to step away, but one muscular arm came down around her, holding her in place. "Not this way."

"Explain."

The duke nodded to Culbert. "Please show our guests to the morning salon. Lady Astrid and I will be along shortly."

"But she is unchaperoned," a pinch-faced Lady Ashley said. "It's not proper to be alone with an unmarried lady, Beswick."

The expression on the duke's face was comical, given the scene they'd interrupted. Astrid would have snorted if she weren't stinging from his betrayal. Nine years ago, she'd only had her word and the truth, and she'd lost everything anyway. Now, being caught in flagrante delicto only compounded what people had once believed of her. That she was a loose woman.

"I intend to rectify that, Lady Ashley," he replied calmly.

"Now, see here," Uncle Reginald said. "This is

demmed outrageous."

The low rumbling growl came from the man at her side. Astrid could feel every muscle in the duke's body bunching as if he were an animal readying to strike. Without thinking, she braced her palm against his, not for any other reason than to prevent bloodshed.

Lady Mabel cleared her throat, her amber eyes falling to their joined hands, and Astrid hastily dropped her hold. "You have five minutes, nephew."

When the room cleared, Astrid lifted her gaze to Beswick's eyes. It was a mistake. He hid nothing from her in their swirling whiskey-colored depths— not his regret, not his intent, not the embers of desire. A lock of silky brown hair curled onto his cheek, making him look almost boyish, like the young man in his family portraits. Unbelievably, *impossibly*, she wanted to kiss him again.

Astrid tore her eyes away and broke free of his clasp. "By my count, you're down to four minutes, Duke."

"Astrid."

She clenched her jaw. "Beswick."

The corner of his lip twitched at her tart reply, one tawny eyebrow tenting as if to signify the obvious fact that she'd been moaning his given name not moments before.

He poured two glasses of cognac and offered her one, which she accepted with an ungracious huff. She wasn't *that* stubborn. She took a bracing sip and then another. And then an indelicate gulp.

"Slowly," he said, watching her over the rim of his own glass.

"Don't tell me what to do. Three minutes, Duke."

He canted his head after a sip of brandy. "I directed Fletcher to summon Viscount Everleigh the minute I rode for the village. I preferred to have the advantage, should he come barreling in here with demands. Lady Ashley was to be my insurance in case your uncle accused me of abducting you or Isobel."

Astrid shook her head. "He wouldn't go so far. Who would believe such a lie?"

"Wouldn't he?" Beswick swilled the rest of the brandy, his face going hard and drawing attention to the ropes of scars beside it. "You don't think they speak of me in London? They think me a beast. A shadow of a man wrecked by war. Outside and inside. The *ton* will believe any piece of salacious gossip that makes them salivate. The fact that I possess a coronet only makes it more sensational."

Astrid sucked in a breath, her fury forgotten. "You're a *duke*."

"You say that as if it's a magic wand."

"Isn't it?" she asked. "You're one of the most powerful peers in the realm."

Beswick smiled, and it was as dark as anything she'd ever seen. She suppressed a shiver. "People don't like monsters, Astrid."

"You're not a monster."

He gestured to himself. "The world sees otherwise."

The explanation made sense, though it didn't take away the sting of his method…that he'd taken her choices from her in a manner that stank of what Beaumont had once done. It wasn't fair to compare the two situations or the two men, but Astrid couldn't help feeling deceived.

"Why marriage?" Taking his empty tumbler, she walked to the mantel and refilled both their glasses from the decanter. She handed one to him, and they sipped in silence. "I seem to recall overhearing something about hell freezing over before you would marry me."

"I was wrong then. And angry at what I'd discovered." His mouth twitched. "I didn't take you for an eavesdropper."

"Trust me, I hadn't planned to."

He held her stare. "Regardless, we seem to have an indisputable…rapport, and while lust isn't always a basis for marriage, I'm willing to concede on that point."

Her cheeks burned at the bald admission, an instant pulse beginning to throb between her legs. "Lust?"

"Yes." Beswick nodded, answering heat sparking in his eyes that made her already erratic throb deepen. "But this isn't only about that. If it makes it more palatable, then think of protecting Isobel. Isn't this what you wanted? I'm offering you both a way out."

Astrid swallowed hard. He was right. This was what she'd wanted from the start. For Isobel's sake. But when she'd proposed marriage to him before, she'd meant it to be bound by the practical, sensible terms of an agreement. Before there was any attraction between them and before her decisions had become clouded by sentiment. She knew all too well where such things could lead…and how easily it could turn to heartbreak.

• • •

Astrid looked so conflicted that Thane wanted to pull her into her arms and kiss her into agreement. However, he knew she had to take the last step on her own. He hadn't lied about the attraction between them being an incentive for marriage, but his deeper intentions had everything to do with protecting her from Cain.

The moment in the study had gotten away from both of them, and while Thane had not planned for them to be discovered so flagrantly in each other's arms, the outcome would be the same—a marriage.

"I have new terms," Astrid said eventually.

"I wouldn't expect you not to."

Astrid huffed a breath. "Unlike my previous offer, apart from the necessary consummation of the vows, this will be a marriage in name only."

"Done."

"One more thing," she said, a slight tremor in her voice. "What happened between us here cannot happen again. Kissing, to be clear."

Before he could reply, Aunt Mabel pushed open the library doors, her face anxious. Though the worry wasn't for them, it seemed. "Hurry, Beswick, before things escalate further. Culbert and Fletcher are not helping matters, and the viscount is voicing all manner of threats." She breathed in deeply. "You should also know that Beaumont has arrived with the local parish officer in tow."

"Beaumont?" Astrid said, striding for the door. "The parish officer? Whatever for? Does he mean to take Isobel?"

Thane opened his mouth to reassure her, but she'd already sped past his aunt, her face drawn with worry. He caught up with her easily, and when they arrived at the entrance to the morning salon, it was complete chaos. Everyone was shouting, the viscount was red in the face, and Beaumont wore his usual sneer. Apparently, the man hadn't taken his earlier warning seriously. Thane would simply have to be more convincing.

He cleared his throat, and the room fell silent. "We have a wedding to plan."

The viscount spluttered anew. "Now see here, you bounder, she is my niece. I have the right to thwart any fortune hunters and the like."

"I beg your pardon, Lord Everleigh." Aunt Mabel looked down the length of her aristocratic nose at him as if he were lower than a slug. "The Hartes have no need of fortune."

He reddened but scowled. "The duke falls into the category of *the like*."

"What do you mean, sir?"

"Look at him," Everleigh scoffed, his disgust plain. "With a face like that, he'd have to coerce any woman to wed him. There's no way a beautiful niece of mine would have accepted willingly."

"She looked rather willing when we arrived, eh, Culbert?" That was from Fletcher, the insubordinate rascal. Thane bit back a smile at Astrid's instant blush.

"Begone," Viscount Everleigh said. "Servants have no place here."

Thane hiked an eyebrow. "You'll forgive me,

Everleigh, if I take offense at you ordering about my staff. Fletcher is more than welcome to share his opinion."

"Well, I never," the viscount fumed. "If you think I'm going to give my blessing to this union, you are wrong, sir."

"Your Grace," Lady Ashley corrected.

The viscount glowered rudely at her. "What?"

"The duke outranks you and so you must address him as Your Grace, Lord Everleigh," Lady Ashley said with a sniff of disdain. "It is only proper."

"I do not approve of your suit, *Your Grace*," Everleigh mocked. "The answer is no."

"We don't need your approval, Uncle."

Thane's gaze pivoted to land on Astrid, who was standing to his right beside her sister, her chin high. She would hold him to task and blister him with her tongue behind closed doors, but she would not dishonor him publicly.

"I've reached my majority, and it says clearly in my father's will that in my own sound judgment, I may pick a husband of my choosing." Her smile was tight. "As long as he is of good birth, titled, and not a fortune hunter as we've already established, my choice shall stand. The Duke of Beswick is a sound match."

"Sound? You're not of sound judgment, more like it," he accused. "*Look* at him," he shouted again. "He's a bloody beast who doesn't even possess the manners to exist in polite society. Is that what you want? To accept that savage *creature* into your bed?"

Isobel gasped, her face flushing at her uncle's crudeness, and the older ladies present tittered with disapproval.

"Uncle!" Astrid cried, her gaze flying to Thane's, but he was used to it and more. He kept his expression shuttered, despite the urge to smash his fist into the viscount's mouth, but he would not give him or Beaumont the satisfaction or an excuse to call his mental capabilities into question. He wouldn't put it past either man to undermine him with accusations of violence. Founded on the battlefield though such claims might be, Thane would never harm a woman.

Lady Ashley huffed. "For shame, Lord Everleigh—you venture into the obscene. And in the presence of gently bred ladies, no less. For *shame*, my lord."

"It is the duke who has no shame. He has ruined my precious niece. *Forced* her."

And there it was—accusation number one.

"Is this true, Your Grace?" the parish officer who had accompanied Beaumont asked, speaking for the first time.

"Why not ask the lady?" Thane replied. "Lady Astrid is more than capable of speaking for herself."

He'd expected her to reply, not to move to his side and take his hand firmly in hers. Thane's throat felt tight. A tremble passed over her shoulders. "The duke did not force me. I accepted his suit of my own free will."

"Good Lord, see how she's shaking with fear," Lady Everleigh cried. "I saw it. The girl is terrified. An imbecile could see it!"

Thane opened his mouth to silence the absurdity once and for all, but Astrid beat him to it. She met her aunt's crazed eyes with cool composure, the hint of a smile on her lips. "I assure you, Aunt Mildred, it's not fear that makes me shiver."

God. This woman.

Thane was so fucking proud of her in that moment, he wanted to crush her to him. Fall to his knees and worship her as she deserved. His own avenging angel. Others saw it, too. He could see the sheen of tears in his aunt's eyes and the surprise in Lady Ashley's. He ignored the disgust in everyone else's, as if it was so inconceivable that a living, breathing woman could feel anything but revulsion for him. Thane felt an odd sensation in his chest… as if the organ that used to be there had suddenly started working.

"You are sick and wicked, child," Lady Everleigh whispered. "That you would bed the devil himself."

"That is enough," Thane said in a dark, deadly voice. "Leave, all of you."

"Isobel, retrieve your things," the viscount commanded.

"No," she said calmly. "I'm staying here with Astrid."

Astrid moved toward her sister, but Beaumont blocked her path. "She is betrothed to me," he said. "Perhaps a double wedding will be in order."

"Over my dead body," Astrid snarled.

"There's nothing you can do about it," he said. "The settlement has already been reached."

Thane's longtime solicitor, Sir Thornton, cleared his throat. "According to the documents of the late Lord Everleigh, which I've secured from Jenkins and Jenkins, the viscount's prior solicitor, it is clear to me that should Lady Astrid take a husband, he will act as guardian in the interests of both his wife and Lady Isobel."

"Isobel is already betrothed," Everleigh insisted. "It is done."

Sir Thornton went on as if the viscount hadn't spoken. "Since your niece's nuptials have yet to take place, approval must be granted by Lady Astrid's husband."

"Then we will do it via special license," Beaumont hissed, reaching for Isobel.

"Do *not* lay a finger on her," Thane said, the soft words as effective as if he'd roared them. "I warned you what would happen, Beaumont, if you came near my fiancée or her sister again. Now pay heed or you will not like the outcome."

"Are you calling me out?" he asked, throwing a look to the parish officer. "Dueling is illegal."

"Do you wish me to spell it out? Very well. I dislike your style. I dislike your small mind. I dislike the knot in your cravat. I dislike *you*. Shall I continue? Or have I insulted you enough?"

A bead of sweat formed on the man's brow. "You go too far, Beswick."

"Do I?"

Beaumont's eyes widened, and Thane almost laughed. Had the coxcomb really thought that he would be cowed by the presence of the parish officer? No one terrorized a duke in his own home, much less one like him.

"By God, Beswick, you've gone mad."

"No, on the contrary, I'm perfectly sane." Thane turned to the jowl-faced man standing behind him.

"Parish Officer Jones, unless you have something to charge me with, I bid you good day."

The man blanched and bowed. "No, I do not, Your Grace. Good day."

"Aunt Mabel, Lady Ashley, if you'll excuse me, it seems I have some business to cover with Sir Thornton. Fletcher, if you'll accompany Lady Isobel to her room." He did not acknowledge Beaumont, the viscount, or his odious wife.

Thane reached for Astrid's hand and lifted it to his lips. "My lady," he murmured.

Unreadable ice-blue eyes met his, though she did not remove her hand from his.

On the way past, Fletcher shot him a gratified look, an aggravating grin gracing the man's mouth. "Do you require a blanket, Your Grace? Perhaps a scarf or muff?"

"No." He stared quizzically at the valet. "Why do you ask?"

Fletcher's grin widened. "Heard it's been snowing rather heavily in hell."

His future duchess made a strangled noise at his side that sounded like she was trying not to laugh and failing miserably. Thane shook his head, the sound of her muffled laughter a balm to his damaged soul, and he chuckled, too. He'd never hear the end of it now.

Winter had come in hell—the Beast of Beswick was to be married.

CHAPTER TWELVE

Over the next fortnight, Thane had reservations about leaving for London to procure an expedient marriage license, if only because Beaumont still lurked in Southend. Though the time had passed without incident, Thane would not put it past him to try something sly with Lady Isobel. Most overindulged aristocrats, when denied anything, only made them more determined to have it. And Beaumont was no exception.

Although Thane was not a pauper by any means, he'd been shocked when he'd learned of the astronomical size of Astrid's and Isobel's dowries. No wonder the viscount had been so desperate to get his hands on part of them. Sir Thornton had reported that the viscount was in debt up to his ears, and he had also discovered from Jenkins & Jenkins that the money had remained untouched because of the ironclad terms surrounding it.

Astrid, too, had been convinced that her uncle would not give up without a fight.

"I'm certain my uncle would have found a way to take both mine and Isobel's," she had told Thane. "As a woman, my rights are restricted without a man breathing down my neck like a dragon hoarding its treasure." He had not missed her bitter tone. "My only goal was to make sure Isobel had a proper Season, but then Beaumont came sniffing around."

"Why did he? As much as I despise the man, he is

not strapped for coin. With his title, fortune, and looks, he'd be a desirable catch."

Her glare had nearly set him on fire.

"Then, *you* marry him. Beaumont is a toad. Perhaps you can kiss him and live happily ever after."

Thane had laughed, but she wasn't wrong that the man was a toad. "Turns out I'm partial to saucy-mouthed harpies, not toads."

He'd been hard pressed not to kiss the tartness off her tongue.

In the past weeks, they'd seemed to come to some sort of unacknowledged truce, and despite her moratorium on physical contact, Thane found himself enjoying spending time with her.

He'd discovered that one of her favorite collections of stories was *The Thousand and One Nights*. He'd contended that Scheherazade had willfully entrapped the king with her storytelling gifts, and she'd countered with the argument that women throughout history had always had to use any tools at their disposal to survive.

Granted, the king in the tale of Scheherazade had killed his queen and all his concubines and subsequently every maiden he married thereafter. Subtlety, Astrid had claimed, was the key to overthrowing the patriarchy. Dukes included, she'd added with a sly look. Thane had laughed at her utter irreverence.

He appreciated the way her mind worked and how she viewed the world. Her ideas on education and female empowerment intrigued him. And while he liked challenging her, he especially loved when she took him to task. Her quick mouth and shrewd brain might deter a lesser man, but not him—he'd come to esteem their verbal duels.

But most of all, he liked figuring out what made her tick. Loyalty. Learning. Passion. And she *was* passionate. About her sister and her interests. About her beliefs. It made Thane want to discover if that passion extended elsewhere.

In bed, particularly. *That* desire he squashed firmly.

Thane's bottled-up physical wants didn't stop him from seeking out her company in the warmth of the conservatory, where they'd taken to walking after dinner, her with a book and him a nip of brandy, before retiring for the evening.

As such, after finishing up with his estate business, Thane found her curled on her usual bench, her shoes discarded and her feet tucked beneath her, a book in her lap. He handed her a glass and filled it with a flask from his pocket.

"Thank you," she told him with a soft smile.

"How is Isobel?" he asked, checking on a few of the flowering plants.

Astrid shrugged. "She has gone to bed after a very full afternoon. Patrick has been teaching her how to ride. And Fletcher has been teaching her how to shoot."

"Has he?" Thane arched an eyebrow at that information. Fletcher had taught him to shoot when he was a boy. The man had annoyingly good aim. "What about you? Did you not wish to learn as well?"

"I have a job to do, Your Grace, if you recall, of

categorizing your father's antiques," she replied. "Which I am very close to finishing, I might add. However, my eyes were so tired that I was afraid I would hit the wrong target."

"Good thing I wasn't out there," he joked.

"If you had been, Your Grace, then I would have insisted on my turn."

Thane grinned at her teasing. "An untrained woman, deep-rooted dislike, and a pistol do not a good combination make."

"I am not untrained," she said as she took a sip of her brandy, licking a drop off her bottom lip, and he fought back a hiss of breath. "My father taught me how to shoot. Isobel was not inclined to learn anything outside the normal realm for girls, but me...I wanted to know everything that boys did."

"He indulged you."

Intractable eyes met his. "I prefer to think that he gave me a fighting chance to stand up on equal footing with other men."

"You are a lady, Astrid, not a man."

Her eyes flashed and her chin rose, both signs that she was ready to do battle. "And that gives me the right to be inferiorly educated? To be treated as the weaker sex? To be discounted at every turn? To excel at waltzing and whimsy?" She said the last three words with so much heated contempt, it was a wonder they did not cinder the nearest shrubs.

"That's the way the world works."

Not that Thane agreed. Women in other communities across the globe had different roles, fought as hard as their men, and were treated on near-equal footing. His own mother had not been a weakling. She wouldn't have survived, not with a father like his. The Duchess of Beswick had understood her role, but she had not let society's rules govern her. Much like his aunt Mabel. Thane smiled inside. Female revolutionaries surrounded him, it seemed.

"Wollstonecraft would disagree," Astrid countered. "She contended that the value of a woman extends beyond the value of her womb and that education is the only thing that separates our sexes."

For a moment, his mind blanked at the sound of the word "sex" on her tongue. Her eyes shone with indignant passion, lips parted, breasts heaving. Suddenly, Thane was overtaken by a slew of lewd images that left him breathless. He blinked and shook himself. He'd gone to half-mast in his trousers. *Hell.* Hurriedly, he turned to check on one of the pipes that fed the irrigation system.

"Is that why you're hell-bent on learning?" he said over his shoulder. "You want to be like a man?"

Astrid threw back her head and laughed, and Thane went full tilt at the uninhibited sound, swelling against the placket of his breeches. Hell, she fired his blood like nothing else. He sat on the bench beside her, hands folded over his lap to disguise the bulge in his pants.

"No, of course not," she said, her tone amused, "but I do want to be *valued*. I want to be a partner, a companion, instead of a broodmare whose only worth is to procreate. Women are *not* property to be traded like chattel, Your Grace."

God, but she had passion in spades.

"I, for one, am glad you're not a man," he said.

Her attention fell back to the book in her hand, but the movement did not hide the rosy tint seeping into her cheeks. Good. Thane counted that as a victory.

"What are you reading tonight?" he asked, examining the volume she held in her elegant fingers. The sight of her hands made his insides clench as they always did. It baffled him that he'd be so tied up in knots over a woman's fingers. Who knew he'd be such a quixotic fool? Peering down, he read the title on the book's embossed cover. "Byron?" He chortled out loud. "You surprise me. Wollstonecraft is quite a shift to the prince of poets."

With a blush, Astrid mumbled that she loathed the poet as a man but enjoyed his poetry from time to time.

"If you dislike him, why read his work?"

"It's interesting to compare the man with his poems. He was terribly indiscreet about his lovers." She paused. "Men can get away with so much, but shame if it's a woman. Then, she's vilified for life. Like Wollstonecraft."

Thane nodded. "One of Byron's mistresses was linked to Wellington."

"My point exactly. Lady Annesley inspired 'When We Two Parted.' Beautifully composed, but honestly, love isn't found in haste, is it? Although," she remarked cynically, "it can be lost just as quickly."

He stared at her. "What do you know of it?"

Throat working, her face contorted with something like pain as she ducked her head, hiding her face from view. Was she speaking from experience?

Had she fancied herself in love with Cain?

"Nothing," she said.

"How many poems and novels have been written as a result of broken hearts?" Thane said, shifting closer on the bench. "Complete drivel, I say. Love is for fools."

"You don't believe in love?" The question was soft, almost inaudible.

"No."

"Neither do I."

Thane was intrigued at her firm assertion and the undercurrent of raw pain in her voice. "What happened with Cain, Astrid? Why did he cry off?"

Crystal-blue eyes fastened to his, buried hurt visible for a stark moment before it was banished. She'd alluded to it in his study after they were discovered, but he had never asked her about it outright, to hear it from her lips. "You know why. Beaumont called off the engagement when rumors of my indiscretions surfaced," she replied in a dispassionate tone, shutters descending over those expressive eyes.

"Did he compromise you?"

It didn't seem like she was going to answer, but then she nodded as if to herself.

"He tried," she said. "He thought because he was my fiancé he was entitled to"—she glanced at him, flushing—"his marital rights. Even though I knew he was to be my husband, I said no." She exhaled and closed her eyes for an interminable moment. "I felt ill when he touched me, and it was then that I realized I had made a mistake in accepting his offer—we simply weren't suited—and I suggested that we end the engagement amicably."

A puff of deprecating laughter left her lips. "*Amicably*. It's such a mild word, isn't it? It makes you think everything is going to be fine. God, I was so naive. Edmund agreed, only to turn around the next day spreading vicious lies about my character and that *he* was forced to cry off the engagement. No one believed me. He destroyed any hope of a future I had without a qualm. Because he felt scorned. Because a woman had the gall to tell him no."

"He ruined any chance you had for another match," Thane discerned.

"Yes. The Everleighs had suddenly become outcasts. Friends abandoned us; invitations were withdrawn. We were shunned and cast aside." Astrid stared down at the book in her hands. "Poor Isobel…to be caught in the sights of the same man who destroyed me. I fear it's history repeating itself, and I'll lose my sister for it."

Thane felt a muscle start to tick in his jaw and saw her eyes flick to it. Her eyes hardened as though she expected him to doubt her account. But he couldn't begin to articulate the feelings crowding his chest—the sympathy for what she'd been through, the fact that all he could see in her eyes was pain and the fear of being hurt yet again.

Thane wanted nothing more than to gather her into his arms and soothe away the hurts she'd suffered. But he sensed Astrid would not welcome the overture. She was anything if not proud. Proud and strong and unbelievably resilient. Most women would have crumbled in the face of her past. She hadn't.

"None of it matters anyway," she said quickly. "People will believe what they want to believe."

"Beaumont is a snake."

"Perhaps, but he wasn't alone in the *ton*'s vilification of me. Everyone loves a good scandal, no matter who gets incinerated in its wake." A hint of a smile ghosted her lips. "Don't worry—he didn't quite get away unscathed. I believe I called him a grasping, oversexed gutter rat in front of the entire assembly."

Thane barked a laugh. "The least of what he deserved."

She lifted a shoulder in a half shrug, though he could still see the old injury in her eyes. "Beaumont is just an overindulged, entitled prick." She blew out a breath. "My story is not so different from other women who have been silenced. That's why I'm so fond of Wollstonecraft's essays. If women were treated equally, I would have been allowed to plead my case. To tell the truth. Instead of having to live with the assumptions and sentencing of others." She smiled ruefully. "But you said it yourself—that's the way the world works."

"It shouldn't be," he said quietly. "Beaumont took something from you. It might not have been your virginity, but the truth is, he stole something valuable just the same. Part of *you*."

A look of vulnerability crossed her face that she quickly hid. She set the volume of poetry aside and reached down for her slippers. "If you will excuse me, Your Grace, I am for bed."

He leaped up and knelt at her feet, taking the

shoes before she could grasp them. "Allow me. And it's Thane."

A blush rose to her cheeks. "What are you doing?"

"If we are to be married, it's the…"

But Thane lost his ability to speak at the sight of her bare toes and the pale, high arch of her instep. She wasn't wearing stockings beneath her skirts, and *fucking hell*, her slender feet were just like her hands—fine-boned and elegant, as though carved by some master sculptor.

"It's the what?" she asked, breathless.

He blinked. "Chivalrous thing to do."

Thane's greedy hands engulfed her narrow foot, a wild current bursting between them. He expected her to jerk away, but she didn't move, as caught up as he was in the fragile, beautiful intimacy of it. Time stood still, a soft gasp escaping her lips when he slid one slipper on, followed by the next.

He couldn't trust himself to speak as he rose and held out a hand, his skin aching and on fire. Mute and trembling, she took it, rising to meet him. Her breasts were almost grazing his chest with every inhale. Thane wanted to touch her so badly, his body vibrated with it.

She wanted him, too. He could see it in her fluttering pulse, feel it in the shallow breaths breaking from her lungs. Her slim body swayed toward his, caught in the same magnetic pull that held him in thrall. He wanted to sweep her into his arms, kiss her until neither of them could breathe. Hold her close and tell her over and over again that she was worthy.

"Astrid," he whispered. "May I kiss you?"

His whisper broke whatever spell had held them together.

Her eyes widened as she pulled away with a harsh sound. "Please don't. I *can't.*"

And with that, she turned and ran from the greenhouse.

• • •

Astrid flew back to the house, past a stupefied Culbert and an even more astonished Lady Mabel, and slammed the door of her bedchamber shut behind her. She caught her breath in fits and starts, clutching at her quivering belly. Heat from her tingling feet speared up her limbs into her abdomen and settled low in the cradle between her legs where a warm, insistent ache throbbed. The look in Beswick's golden eyes had made her feel unhinged, as if she would come apart at the seams if he *didn't* touch her.

Astrid blinked, breathing deeply. During the last two weeks, what had simmered between them had gone well beyond attraction. This was all-consuming, heart-fracturing need, the force of which terrified her. One touch and she'd been ready to ignite, fall at his feet, and plead for those warm, clever fingers to continue their wicked path up her leg.

It would have been so easy to say yes.

What are you so afraid of?

She'd asked herself the question almost every night. Beswick wasn't making her do anything. He wasn't Beaumont, trying to force his unwelcome attentions on her. The duke had simply asked for a kiss, and the truth was, she *liked* kissing him. Maybe that was it—she wasn't afraid of Beswick. She was afraid of herself...afraid of what kissing him would mean for *her*. Hence, the *no kissing* rule she'd insisted upon.

But being afraid did not line up with her basic ideals of living life on her own terms. It made her a coward. Astrid walked over to the mirror in her chamber and stared at herself in the reflection—eyes glowing, hair askew out of her bun, cheeks aflame.

She touched her fingers to her lips, imagining Beswick's there.

You are a strong, enlightened female...a modern woman who can choose to embrace her own desires. You want him, you daft chit, and he wants you. What would one kiss hurt?

One kiss had the power to ruin lives—she knew that well enough. But Beswick was not Beaumont.

Hauling a breath into her lungs, Astrid marched back downstairs.

"Have you seen the duke?" she asked Culbert.

"His Grace has retired for the evening, my lady," he said. "Is there anything I can assist you with?"

"No," she said and turned on her heel, disappointment settling in her chest and then resolve. She stopped at the staircase. "Er, where are the duke's chambers?"

The normally unflappable Culbert stood agape before stammering the answer when she arched an imperious eyebrow. "The east tower, my lady, adjacent from yours and Lady Isobel's. Might I escort you there?"

"No, thank you, Culbert. I'm sure I can manage."

She hoped.

Her newfound nerve kept her spine straight and legs moving forward until she came to a pair of gilded, intricately carved double doors in what appeared to be the family wing. It was even more lavish than the guest wing, done in hues of cream and gold with pale-blue accents.

Biting her lip, she knocked on the first door and quailed as the echo of the sound reached her ears. Oh God, what in heaven's name was she doing? The spike of courage deserted her in a whoosh. She whirled around, ready to race back the way she'd come, when the door was opened. By a woman wearing a plain dressing gown and cap.

"Oh, I'm so sorry," Astrid blurted out. The lance of jealousy took her by surprise.

Who is she? Why is she in the duke's quarters?

"Who is it, Frances?" The muffled voice was preceded by footsteps, whereupon Lady Mabel appeared behind the woman. "Astrid, dear, what are you doing?"

Astrid's mouth opened and closed, her hands rising to her throat. Heat flooded her cheeks. "I'm… lost."

Mabel smiled and dismissed the woman. "Thank you, Frances, that will be all for tonight." Her eyes took in Astrid's expression. "Frances is my new lady's maid." Ushering Astrid inside to a charming sitting area, she lowered her voice to a stage whisper. "The last one left because of the footmen."

"The footmen?"

Mabel grinned. "The ones in my bed, dear. Tea?"

"No, thank you," Astrid said, swallowing her

amusement at the duchess. The woman was incorrigible.

"Gloria was too high in the instep for a maid, if you ask me," she went on. "Luckily, Frances had just left another position locally and came highly recommended. Now, where were we? You said you were lost?"

Astrid nodded, pinning her lips between her teeth at the lie. "I took, er, a wrong turn."

"You weren't looking for my nephew, perchance?"

"No, of course not!" she replied much too quickly.

Mabel shot her a knowing look. "I wouldn't fault you if you were, you know. You are an engaged woman, after all. And beneath all that coarse bluster, Thane is the same red-blooded man he used to be."

"He's not coarse," Astrid said before she could stop herself and then flushed to the tips of her ears. "I wouldn't know about the hot-blooded part."

"I said *red*-blooded, dear," Mabel corrected with a sly look. "Anyone with eyes can see the attraction smoldering between the two of you. Honestly, I'm surprised none of the rest of us have singe marks."

Astrid's face heated. "We agreed on a marriage in name only."

"People have been known to change their minds, dear." Mabel peered at her face, and Astrid was afraid her wanton desires would be written all over it. "I think you've been hurt in the past, and you're letting it interfere now, but you need to let go of your fear. Even if I did not love my nephew, I would tell you this." She patted Astrid's hand. "We radical thinkers need to stick together." Her smile was bright. "Now, if you're looking for the guest wing, it's just down those stairs. If you're looking for the duke's chamber, it's at the end of this corridor."

"I'm not," Astrid said, her ears burning. "I was lost."

"If you say so, dear."

After she'd bid the duchess good night, Astrid stood at the top of the stairs, her insides pulled in different directions. She wished she were as brave as Mabel, but the woman had several decades of bucking society under her belt. And she was a *duchess*. An unrepentant duchess.

Astrid was neither of those things.

At the heart of it, she was just a girl with too much to lose.

CHAPTER THIRTEEN

"Where is His Grace?" Astrid asked Culbert two days later when she'd not seen hide or hair of the duke. Or Fletcher, for that matter. Then again, she'd been finalizing the items for the auction and had been buried in the study from early that morning.

"He's gone to London, my lady," the butler said.

Without telling me?

Astrid felt a snap of discomfort. Had he left without a word because he was displeased? Because she'd told him no? Her past swung back to taunt her. She'd said no to Beaumont, and he'd turned around and punished her. Was Beswick doing the same? He hadn't struck her as that type of man, but she'd been disillusioned by men before.

No, he must have finally gone to arrange for the marriage license, and if he went for other reasons that didn't bear thinking about, why should she care? But Astrid couldn't help being annoyed. With him for leaving without informing her and with herself for feeling anything at all.

"For how long?" she asked the butler.

"He didn't say, my lady." This time, she let her annoyance show, making Culbert back up a sharp step. "I'm certain he will be back soon."

Very well, then. She would do as she pleased, too. Which would include a long ride on Brutus and perhaps a trip to the village. Isobel would like that, and they would be safe enough with the men

Beswick had hired to keep an eye for trespassers on the estate. They were men loyal to him, she knew. He wouldn't trust anyone else with their safety.

Why did he leave without a word to me?

The slight niggled at her. But then she thought of how they last parted—she'd run from him and she'd kept on running. She had avoided him, and he'd left for London without a word. Astrid didn't want to analyze the feeling in her chest. Disappointment? Regret?

May I kiss you?

The whispered plea had crushed her soul. Because she'd wanted his kiss more than anything in the world. The sheer force of the yearning inside her had made her weak with desire. The clasp of his big, warm hands on her foot…the indescribable need to feel those fingers elsewhere. She'd wanted to give him *everything*.

A man like Beswick would swallow her whole.

And she could not afford that.

"Agatha," she said, striding into her bedchamber. "My green riding habit, please. Agatha?" Astrid looked around the spotlessly clean room, but the maid was nowhere to be seen.

Perhaps she was with Isobel. It was no hardship to dress herself. Most of her special riding habits had been tailored with closures in the front, and since she planned for a bracing round astride Brutus, she would not need the regular habits designed for a lady's sidesaddle.

The brisk ride might also take away the fullness between her thighs that had not dissipated in days. In private moments over the years, Astrid had found release on her own, but she couldn't risk being caught. Not here. Though in one of the volumes of private letters she'd discovered in the upper echelons of Beswick's library, a woman touching herself was not shocking at all. In fact, the author, Ninon de Lenclos, who had been a French courtesan, encouraged it.

One part of her restraint was because she was in someone else's residence, but the other part was the duke himself. The thought of Beswick even suspecting the madness to which he drove her was so dreadful that she resisted the impulse, even knowing the relief it would bring.

Did he touch himself and think of her in the same way?

A wicked image of the Duke of Beswick lying in bed, head flung back with his hand caught over the fabric of his bulging breeches, assaulted her. She lost all feeling in her legs as breath and bones went on hiatus, making her sway and nearly stumble.

Good Lord, this was becoming ridiculous.

A ride. A ride on Brutus would solve everything. In her haste to get to the stables, she didn't notice the uproar coming from the foyer until she was upon it. She almost crashed into Culbert arguing with Patrick, who was so white-faced that she didn't recognize him. His naturally ruddy complexion was ashen, his red hair sticking up on end.

"What is it?" she asked, taking in the duke's men who patrolled the estate grounds. Her stomach tilted in premonition. Was it Beswick? Had something happened in London?

"It's Lady Isobel, my lady." Mrs. Cross, Beswick

Park's newest housekeeper, stepped forward from the melee. "She's gone."

"Gone?" Astrid repeated. "Where?"

"She left a message with one of the undermaids saying that she has gone to London with her aunt and uncle. Agatha is with her." Mrs. Cross look troubled. "Lord Everleigh sent his carriage several hours ago."

"London? Why on earth would she—?" Astrid broke off, her hand flying to her mouth. She should have seen it coming, especially when Isobel had mentioned feeling like a burden that day in the village of Southend. Her sister might be frivolous at times, but she had a spine of steel, especially when it came to those she loved. Without a doubt, she'd gone to London to take matters into her own hands—to save Astrid from having to marry for Isobel's sake.

"Why did no one summon me?" she demanded.

"You said you weren't to be disturbed, my lady," Culbert said, looking a bit shamefaced. "And Lady Isobel said she'd already discussed it with you."

Of course she had. Astrid's thoughts spun. What was her sister planning? As much as she pretended not to be clever or value intelligence, Isobel had quite a formidable brain in her head. And if she thought she was *saving* Astrid from an unwanted marriage, nothing would stop her. At least she'd had the presence of mind to take a lady's maid with her. Astrid trusted Agatha to keep her sister safe.

"She left you a note, my lady," the housekeeper said, handing it to her.

Sure enough, the note was in Isobel's neat

handwriting, saying exactly what Mrs. Cross had communicated. Isobel had accompanied their aunt and uncle to London for the start of the Season and promised that she was going to fix things. She'd added that their uncle had promised new gowns and jewels and to give her a chance to choose a suitor who pleased her.

Astrid gritted her teeth. Of course he had. He'd promise anything to get his greedy hands on Isobel's dowry. And Astrid wouldn't discount the fact that Beaumont wasn't still involved somehow. Her brain whirled furiously. What were her conniving relatives up to?

Or better yet, what was her *sister* up to?

Culbert made a pained noise, distress written all over him. "I'm sorry I didn't stop her, my lady. She was so convincing. Is Lady Isobel in trouble?"

"It's not your fault, Culbert. Isobel is headstrong. It tends to run in the family," Astrid said. "Whether she's in trouble remains to be seen. I suspect this is yet another ploy of my uncle's. And it's my doing, too. I should have seen this coming."

"Shall we send word to the duke?"

Astrid shook her head. "No, if Isobel has gone to London, I will go myself."

• • •

Sitting in his study at Harte House in Mayfair, Thane stared hard at the documents in hand—a marriage license granted by the Archbishop of Canterbury. It seemed incongruous that such a small piece of parchment would hold so much power to bind two people together without the customary posting of the banns. And yet it did.

He and Astrid would be married.

Thane hadn't seen her before leaving for London. He'd left that task to Culbert. The truth was that he couldn't face her, not after she'd fled his presence. Not after he'd begged for her favors like a schoolboy begging for sweets. God, he was pitiable. Not even his own future wife could stand to be in the same space as him.

He toyed with the idea of visiting his club. The idea of drowning himself in a bottle of port while fleecing other men of their fortunes at the gaming tables had merit. It was better than sitting here, waxing philosophic over a piece of foolscap.

"Summon Fletcher," he called out to a nearby footman. "Tell him to ready a bath. I'm going out."

"Of course, Your Grace."

The master bathing chamber at Harte House had also been updated to match the ones installed at Beswick Park, with bathtubs large enough to fully accommodate his size and his needs. When the bath had been readied and Thane lay submerged in water as hot as he could manage, he felt some of the tension slowly start to melt away.

"You may go," he told Fletcher. "I'll be a while."

"Your outing, Your Grace?"

"I'll decide when I've finished."

"Very well." Fletcher nodded, his normally pleasant face austere. Thane felt a spurt of annoyance. He knew his longtime valet and friend had something to say, and normally he was more than liberal with his advice.

"What would you do in my place?" he heard himself ask.

Fletcher paused at the door. "Marry the lady. Make a life. Be happy."

"The lady in question doesn't want me. At least, not in that way."

"She doesn't know you, Your Grace."

Thane rubbed his temples. "You know what I've been through. I'm not built for a life like that. With love, and laughter, and sodding rainbows. Look at me." Thane gestured to the puckered flesh of his left side and the ugly terrain of scars on his legs visible beneath the water. "I'm a fucking monster. Who deserves to lie with this?"

"So what?" the valet said, biting off the words as if they came from somewhere dreadful. "You have more than a few scars. We all have scars, Your Grace. My father killed my mother in front of his four children because another man looked at her. She did nothing to deserve his abuse but took it for years."

Stupefied, Thane stared at him as Fletcher broke off, chest heaving and fists clenched. "I didn't know."

"Why would you?" Fletcher shrugged. "I let hate poison me so much that I walked away from any chance at happiness. And you know what, Your Grace? Pride is a lonely bedfellow." He smiled sadly. "Just because I'm not marked on the outside doesn't mean I'm not hurt. That I'm not wounded. But you need to decide whether you let your scars rule you. And if they do, if that is all you think you are, then forgive me for saying that Lady Astrid deserves more."

"She deserves more anyway," he whispered, but

Fletcher had already left, shutting the door behind him.

Thane sighed, submerging his knotted shoulders. Perhaps he could just stay here instead. Interminably. He let his body slide down the porcelain surface of the tub, sinking his head beneath the water, until his heartbeat roared dimly in his ears.

Behind his closed lids, visions of Astrid appeared—ones of her curled on the bench in his conservatory, all peach-colored skin and fierce-witted intelligence, and others of her spread out on his bed in tantalizing glory, all sin and desire and naked torment. Unable to help himself, he focused on the latter. Her full lips were pink, those ice-blue eyes of hers warm pools of want. Handfuls of glossy hair spilled over her shoulders, hiding her ample curves from view and playing peekaboo with rosy nipples.

His already hard cock twitched. Never one to deny himself, he reached down to grasp himself in one fist, stroking upward almost roughly. He repeated the movement several times more as his breath shortened and his ballocks tightened. Head flung back, he gave himself up to the release streaking through him until he was spent. It felt less satisfying than usual. *Loneliness.* He knew why, of course. His body craved *her*.

Hell, he was as fucked as Fletcher.

Reaching for a length of toweling, he stood and dried himself. He would go out. He would fill his mind with other things. Anything but the woman he could not have.

Shrugging into his robe, he stalked into the adjoining chamber. "Fletcher, send for my carriage—"

His words broke off. The lady of his fantasies stood there in the flesh at the entrance to his bedchamber, mere steps away from his bed. She looked beautiful and flushed as her eyes swept his half-dressed form. Though not with mutual desire… with fear and with worry. Thane blinked, sanity returning.

"Astrid, what is it? Why have you come?"

"Thane, it's Isobel," she rasped, her hands going to her face. "She's with my aunt and uncle here in London."

"She's here?" Conscious of his nudity, he fastened his robe before going to her and gathering her into a loose embrace. "Start at the beginning. Tell me what happened."

In a few short sentences, she told him about the note and the fact that Isobel had gone willingly. "She said they were happy to let her decide for herself. They've promised her gowns and trinkets, more than enough to turn a girl's head. My uncle is up to something, I know it."

"Fear of the debtor's prison drives men to many things," he said. "And trust your sister. From what I've seen, she's very much like you."

"Isobel is nothing like me. She's kindhearted and sweet, and people will take advantage of her. Especially my uncle, who has probably convinced her of his good intentions."

He brushed the hair off her brow. "I think you underestimate what she's capable of."

"At least Agatha is with her," she said eventually, closing her eyes and leaning into his touch. "She will look out for her as well as she is able." Thane held her for a few more minutes until she gently extricated herself. "I had to come."

"Yes," he said, turning slightly so that his hips hid his renewed erection. Despite the circumstances, the feel of her long, warm body in his arms had been the sweetest kind of punishment, and while his reaction would most likely not be welcomed, it could not be controlled. The fiery tint of her cheeks, however, led him to believe that she'd already discerned the unruly state of his body.

"We need to marry before Uncle Reginald tries to find some loophole in my father's will."

"Yes, I have the license."

Her eyes flew to his. "You do?"

"What did you think I came to London for?" he asked, frowning.

Astrid swallowed. "I don't know. I assumed it was for business. Culbert didn't say much other than you had gone. I thought maybe you left because you were angry." Her eyes snagged on the evening clothing that Fletcher had set out. "Were you going out?"

"No."

Her fingers dipped to stroke the superfine jacket. "It looks like you were."

"I was, but I'm not anymore."

"Beswick," she began, and he sighed at the address. They were back to formality. She'd called him Thane when she'd first arrived, and the welcome sound of it had made his barren heart fist in his chest. Her beautiful face was devoid of emotion, but he could see those slender fingers of hers winding in her skirts as if they were too undisciplined to be contained by the force of her will. Those expressive hands always gave her away. "Do you have a mistress?"

His mouth fell open. "I beg your pardon?"

"Here in London. Do you?"

"No."

"I thought that was why you came to Town. Because I could not…would not…give you what you wanted." Astrid stared at the ground, her cheeks crimson. "I know when we first spoke about terms and mistresses…"

She gulped and trailed off miserably. Thane wanted to laugh, but he was sure she would not appreciate his humor in the situation. When she'd first propositioned him, he'd only been toying with her to see what she would say. He took her hands in his.

"Astrid, I assure you, I do not have a mistress *or* mistresses. And I was not on the way out to sow my wicked and wild oats, if that was what you were imagining." Her blush deepened, and he cleared his throat. "However, as it so happens, I *do* have something quite important planned. And now, so do you, in fact."

She glanced down at her dusty, wrinkled riding habit, her brown eyebrows raised in surprise. "I am not dressed for society. What is it?"

"Our wedding."

She blanched, her voice lowering, though no one was around to hear her confession. "I am wearing breeches, Your Grace."

Thane's deep chuckle filled the room. "Somehow, I wouldn't have it any other way."

CHAPTER FOURTEEN

It was nearly over before Astrid could even blink.

And she did indeed appear for her own wedding in a riding habit and *breeches*. Though she had brought a few of her sturdy gowns with her, Beswick seemed happy enough with her current state of dress. The minor mortification was eclipsed by the solemnity of the moment. Matrimony. To a man she barely knew but somehow trusted enough to hand over everything most dear to her.

Her sister. Her inheritance. Her future.

Her fragile heart, however, she would guard for as long as possible.

A vicar had been sent for, and the nuptials were to take place in Harte House's empty ballroom. Though she mourned her sister not being present, it was for Isobel's very sake that their vows were taken so hastily. Astrid would not put it past Beaumont to ruin Isobel given the chance, but her uncle and aunt would not welcome the scandal. Perhaps the earl, too, had secured a special license and intended to wed Isobel.

Well, no matter. She would now be the Duchess of Beswick.

A duchess.

Astrid drew in a smothered breath as the vicar's terrified eyes rose to the imposing duke—standing without covering over his face—and fell away to begin the service. Oddly, the vicar's ungoverned reaction made Astrid want to kick him. She understood what he was seeing. Beswick's appearance *was* chilling, though she herself had grown used to it.

She saw the *man* beneath.

Thane repeated his vows in a deep, resonant voice, no hesitation in it. "I, Nathaniel Blakely Sterling Harte, take thee, Astrid Victoria Everleigh, to be my wedded wife."

His Christian name is Nathaniel?

The vicar cleared his throat. "Will you take this man to be your wedded husband, to live together after God's ordinance in the holy estate of matrimony?"

Astrid started as the vicar's eyes fell upon her. He shot her a look as if to ask, *Are you certain this is indeed of your own free will?* She nearly laughed through her muddled nerves. "I will," she said.

She sucked in a breath but was distracted by the exquisite sapphire ring the duke slid from his pocket and placed onto her finger. "With this ring, I thee wed, with my body I thee worship, and with all my worldly goods I thee endow."

"Then, those whom God has joined together, let no man put asunder," the vicar said.

Thane turned to her, his beautiful eyes a shade of amber that was so clear, she could see a myriad of gilded golden flecks in it. Would he kiss her? It wasn't the custom, but he never did anything the way it was supposed to be done. She closed her eyes, just as his lips brushed her cheek. "You and Isobel are safe now."

And then it was done.

Clapping pulled her out of her thoughts as she

turned to see Fletcher and the rest of the staff of the townhouse. They were blurred by her tears. "Congratulations, Your Grace."

"In lieu of a wedding breakfast," Thane said as she discreetly wiped her eyes, "we shall go to my private club for a wedding supper tonight. The staff will be dismissed from service this evening in celebration."

As he escorted her upstairs, Astrid leaned in. "I don't have any clothing appropriate for dinner, Beswick."

"Thane," he corrected.

"Not Nathaniel?" she asked with a smile.

Her husband grimaced. "Not if you value your tongue."

A stunned giggle burst from her at the ferocious but empty threat. "Why do you hate it? It's a lovely name."

"I've never used it," he said. "I couldn't pronounce it when I was a child, and Thane stuck. I've always felt it was more...*me*. My father hated it, but when I refused to answer to any other name for nigh on a year, he eventually gave in as well."

Astrid had to agree. Thane suited him perfectly. Nathaniel, by contrast, seemed too complicated. Too old-fashioned. Thane carried individuality and strength and an innate simplicity—that what one saw was what one got. If one looked beyond the obvious, that was. Astrid's glance slid up to the ragged scar splitting his face and the vines of smaller ones creeping down the left side of his cheek and jaw. He was a tapestry of pain but held himself proudly.

Thane.

She ignored the sudden pressure behind her eyes. "I left in such a rush that I didn't bring a gown for dinner."

The duke gave her a benign smile and ushered her toward the suite of rooms belonging to the Duchess of Beswick. "Since Agatha is with Isobel, I've arranged for the sister of one of the footmen to assist you." He bowed, mischief in his eyes. "I will see you for dinner shortly…my lady."

Curious, Astrid walked into her chambers. It was, like everything else in Harte House, exquisitely appointed, in a subtle pale-gold and green color scheme that was pleasing to the eye. An enormous bed sat at the center of the room, its bedposts draped in filmy gauze. A connecting door at one end led to the duke's own chambers. Her heart stuttered at the thought that the wedding night would have to be consummated, especially to those who might push to have it annulled, but she was grateful that she had her own privacy. For now.

"Good evening, Your Grace," a young girl said, bobbing a curtsy. "I'm Alice."

"Good evening, Alice." Astrid walked toward the bed where the girl stood, her jaw going slack at the sight of the gown on the bed. It was a frothy ice-blue creation of tulle and silk. "Where did that come from?" she whispered.

"From Madame Pinot," Alice piped up. "She's the most famous modiste in London, Your Grace. My brother was sent by His Grace to fetch it during the wedding. You are to see her yourself at the end of the week for a full wardrobe."

Astrid was dumbfounded by the duke's thoughtfulness. It seemed she had underestimated her new husband, as well as his influence and bottomless coffers if he was able to get a dress in less than an hour *and* commission an entire wardrobe from a celebrated modiste during the busy start of the Season. She stared at the lovely gown that Madame Pinot must have had on hand and wondered whether it would fit.

"His Grace ordered a bath prepared for you as well." Alice held out a folded piece of parchment. "Also, a letter came for you, my lady."

"A letter?" Astrid blinked. "From whom?"

"I'm not sure, Your Grace, but it was delivered to the kitchens a few minutes ago, addressed to Lady Astrid."

She took the folded piece of foolscap with shaking hands and opened it. Her knees gave out at the sight of the urgently scrawled handwriting, and she collapsed onto the armchair in the sitting area. It was from Isobel, and it was exactly as she had suspected.

My dearest Astrid,

I hope this note finds you well. I've just heard from Agatha by way of Fletcher that you arrived in Town only today, and she has promised to see this to you.

First of all, I am well, so do not worry yourself. Please understand that I had to do this, for both our sakes. You should not have to marry under duress, not Beswick, not anyone. I only want for your happiness, Astrid. And mine, too, of course, but never at the expense of yours. You've always taken care of me, and it's my turn now.

In other news, Uncle Reginald is very cross with us but says that I can make it right by securing an expedient match. He says that we are here for the Season so that I may be courted properly and have my choice of suitors. The Earl of Beaumont is also in London, and he remains Uncle's top candidate for marriage. I have overheard that he means to seek the Prince Regent's favor to overturn Father's terms of approval.

Please do not worry about me. If you need to reach me, send word to Agatha. I will be at the Featheringstoke ball a week hence. It is a masquerade. Perhaps I will see you there.

I remain yours, faithfully. Your loving sister, Isobel.

Her sister sounded…normal. Astrid hadn't expected that, but then again, recent events had been more surprising than not. And Isobel had come to London of her own free will. Perhaps Beswick was correct. Her sister had come from the same willful stock she had. Despite her youth, she was strong and resilient. And she was loyal to a fault.

Astrid's heart raced as she reread the note. The Featheringstoke ball. It would be a chance to see Isobel for herself, and since it was a masquerade, she would be disguised. She would plan to be in attendance if it killed her. If only to see for herself that her sister was well.

She placed the letter down and followed the maid into the bathing chamber that connected both suites. It seemed somehow far too intimate that she and Beswick would now share such a space. A tub half full of heated water awaited her. It was more than enough for her needs, but she suspected it had been designed with the much larger duke in mind. Astrid couldn't help the rush of heat along her veins at the scandalous thought that they would both be nude, though at different times, in this very bathing tub.

Undressing quickly, she peeled the dusty riding habit from her body with Alice's help and then stepped into the deliciously hot water. With a happy sigh, she lathered with the lemon-scented soap that Alice held toward her in a small jar and washed her hair.

The door at the far end of the chamber cracked open, and Astrid squeaked as the master of the house—and her new husband—leaned against the doorjamb. Alice scurried from the room when he gave a dismissive wave of his hand.

He didn't come any closer, and though the water was opaque with soap suds, his golden stare caressed Astrid from head to toe…even the parts he couldn't possibly see—causing her to erupt in tingles everywhere. Mortified at her instant reaction to him, she crossed her arms over her tightening breasts.

His broad frame dwarfed the space. He was still dressed in his clothing from earlier, though his cravat looked like it was about to give up the ghost, hanging on to within an inch of its life. His golden-brown hair was endearingly rumpled, curling into one eye and giving him a rakish look. Astrid had to look to pinpoint his facial scars, when all she could see were those brilliant jeweled eyes of his and that firm, sculpted mouth.

"This is my favorite room in this house," he said softly. He crossed his ankles, one booted foot over the other, and Astrid couldn't help but notice how snugly his black breeches encased his lean, muscled thighs. Or how the white lawn shirt beneath his open waistcoat hugged the sleek abdominal muscles beneath it.

"It's lovely," she managed, entirely too conscious of her own nudity and his disturbing nearness. Not that she expected him to pounce upon her, but she felt defenseless. Astrid cleared her tight throat. "I'm not late, am I?"

"No."

"Oh," she replied.

He cleared his throat, a deep flush suffusing his skin. "I know you might wish to wait to...consummate the vows, but given the circumstances, sooner might be in our best interest."

Her lungs seized. Good Lord, he was talking about their wedding night. While she was *naked*. In a tub. The sensible part of her knew it had to be done, even for a marriage that would be in name only, but other parts of her quivered and quailed. Astrid reached for detached poise and failed miserably. "Quite so. I agree, Your Grace."

His eyes held hers. "Thane."

"Thane," she repeated, her hand sloshing the water.

He didn't respond, his burning eyes focused on a point below her chin. The sapphire ring on her finger, she presumed, but her assumption was corrected with one glance down. A peach-tipped nipple peeked from the suds floating on the water's surface. Mortified, she shifted her hand to cover herself.

"Don't," her husband said thickly, moving so fast that when he knelt at the edge of the tub, she bit back a hushed gasp. He stared in fascination, his lips flattened, a muscle flexing in that lean jaw. His index finger rose to circle the bud, causing the wet skin to tighten more. "You're beautiful."

Astrid sucked in a ragged breath, but the duke seemed utterly mesmerized. Without a word, he rolled the pebbled peak between two fingers, and she couldn't hold back her moan as lightning shot from her breasts to her thighs. Unconsciously, she arched her back like a cat, pushing her body into his caress. Wanting more. Wanting *all*.

"Thane, I ache," she whispered.

His cheek flexed as he froze, his frame rigid, and then scooped her up into his arms, soaking wet. Astrid didn't even have the decency to blush as he took her to his adjoining chamber, kicking the door shut behind him. He placed her in the middle of his large bed, uncaring of his now drenched sheets, and snuffed out the single candle in the room before she heard the telltale rustle of clothing.

In the moment, she wasn't afraid. She wanted this. She felt restless, her nerves on edge, warmth pooling through her limbs like honey, that ache inside her demanding to be soothed. After a beat, the mattress dipped under his weight, and as his long body hovered over hers, Astrid almost laughed. If there was a time for her brain to put "naked" and "duke" together, this was it.

Although he wasn't completely naked. He still wore his shirtsleeves. Astrid could feel the fabric grazing her overly sensitive breasts, and compassion surged through her as she recalled the scars she'd glimpsed for a half second when he'd been in his tub at Beswick Park. But then a pair of lean, hair-roughened, bare thighs slid against hers, and her brain went deliciously blank. He was obviously naked *down there*. And thick and hard and ready.

Her breath sawed out of her lungs.

She was on the cusp of losing her virginity. Losing the very thing that had plagued her every waking moment ever since Beaumont's accusations. *No!* She didn't want to think about him. Not now, not here. She'd chosen to marry Beswick, and she'd chosen to be here in his bed. Chosen to be his wife. These were *her* choices…on her terms.

"You're wet," he growled.

"I just had a bath," she said without thinking.

His low laughter warmed her as his fingers brushed her curls at the apex of her thighs, and she almost bowed off the bed. "*Here.* You're wet for me."

Astrid sucked in a breath but lost it the minute those big hands started caressing her bare legs… over her calves, behind her knees, her inner thighs. Thane settled his large body between them, his fingertips finding sensitive areas that made her nerve endings scream, and by the time he returned to the heart of her quivering core, she was an overwrought mess of want.

"God, Astrid, you feel like warmed satin."

The mattress shifted with his weight—the only warning she had before warm lips kissed her *there*.

Right where it ached the most. She nearly shot off the bed as his tongue swirled against her hot flesh. Suddenly, Astrid wished she could see in the darkness, as she imagined those wide shoulders ensconced between her legs, but all she could do was feel.

And feel and feel and *feel*.

Thane took his time, mapping each fold like a master cartographer, learning each spot that made her writhe and moan against his unhurried onslaught. Astrid had seen lewd drawings in the pages of erotic books, but nothing prepared her for what such a thing felt like. In the darkness, it felt sinfully decadent. Lush. Raw. Powerful.

"It's too much, Thane. I can't…"

"You can," he said, cool air blowing on the exposed heart of her. And then he proceeded to torture her once more, this time adding fingers to the mix. Astrid's back arched as his lips and tongue worked against her, lapping, sucking, and circling without mercy, while two of his long fingers sank inside her.

Beneath his ruthlessly skillful attentions, pressure built and then broke, bliss cresting over her in sweet, hot waves. But her sneaky husband didn't stop until he'd coaxed another paroxysm from her in quick succession. Astrid's body felt deliciously boneless, her mind gloriously blank. Her head fell back against the pillows as Thane made a sound of pure male satisfaction in his throat and levered himself over her upon his muscular forearms.

"You are splendid, Astrid."

"Now, Thane, please," she whispered before her

courage deserted her. "Make me yours."

Her cheeks burned. She might as well have ordered him to take her like the virgin sacrifice in some lurid Viking penny novel. But the space between her hips pulsated in agreement. She bloody well *wanted* to be taken.

Good gracious, can I be any needier?

But she didn't have time to ponder on it as her very large, very skillful husband chuckled at her demands and positioned himself between her legs. Her knees fell apart to cradle his hips, and she gasped at the wickedly erotic position. It was almost too much…the sensitivity, the weight of him, the texture of his firm male body. A brief twinge of anxiety rolled through her, and her muscles tensed in anticipation.

But she didn't have time to dwell on it when she felt the warm prod of him at her entrance, and slowly, he pushed inside. Astrid gasped and clutched at his shoulders. The pinch of friction took her by surprise, as did the feeling of fullness, even though she'd known to expect the discomfort, but her body gradually relaxed to accommodate him. And then he began to move with slow, deep thrusts that made her toes curl and her palms fall to fist in the bedsheets.

True to their agreement, he didn't kiss her on the mouth, but his marauding fingers plucked at her nipples, making her spine arch and driving her mindless with pleasure. Thane's hand slid down between their joined bodies, pressing that slick, needy spot between her thighs where all sensation seemed to converge. Astrid moaned as his adept fingers worked her, his hips quickening in their movements even as his movements grew more uncontrolled.

Heat sparked and ignited once more, and then she was bursting into a million pieces as her release crested and shattered. With a final thrust and a guttural groan, the duke yanked himself from her body and collapsed against her, panting heavily. She could feel a sticky warmth between them on the skin of her belly. He did not speak, though she could feel him breathing, his heart hammering wildly against hers, communicating in a language all their own.

"Astrid," he rasped after several minutes, his voice deep and sated. "Are you well? Did I hurt you?"

"No, it was wonderful," she whispered. "Did I...? Was I...?"

Her husband gathered her into his arms, his lips feathering her damp brow. "You were perfect. You *are* perfect."

• • •

Thane refastened the buttons of his waistcoat and remained still while Fletcher replaced his earlier rumpled cravat with a fresh one. Honestly, the thing was worse than a damn noose. The valet slid his jacket over his shoulders and brushed at several imaginary pieces of lint on the raven-black fabric. Fletcher turned to grab a comb from the mantel and studied him as if he were a horse to be curried. "Might I suggest some pomade?"

"No." Thane scowled. "I already look enough like a dandy as is. Astrid knows who I am and what to expect of me."

Fletcher grinned, uncowed by his expression. "That she does, but it's your wedding day, Your Grace. You're supposed to make an effort for your duchess."

His duchess.

Thane's heart thudded against his rib cage. He had a wife. One who had made him spend in a handful of minutes like a randy lad, just from the warm, wet clasp of her body. Though she'd been a virgin, her responsiveness had demolished him. And the divine flavor of her. *Fuck!* He could still taste her on his tongue—the savor of rosewater and ocean breezes. It only made him want her more.

He couldn't recall the last time he'd come so hard and so fast. At least he'd had the presence of mind to withdraw. The prevention of pregnancy was something they would have to discuss later. But for now, he hoped to repeat the experience. Though they'd only agreed to consummate the marriage, if Astrid permitted, he intended to make it up to her after dinner tonight, when he would take his time. Sample every inch of her. Make her scream his name and come so many times, she'd lose count. He wanted to worship her the way she deserved.

Hell, he was getting aroused just thinking about it.

Thane tamped down his lust, allowing the valet to unsnarl his hair and smooth the locks back into place. He stared at himself in the mirrored glass, the familiar sight of his patchwork face looking back at him. Thank God he'd taken her under the cover of darkness and kept his shirt on. His face was a fair sight better than the rest of him.

Descending the staircase, he entered the foyer. Even though they were going out for dinner, his staff had gone beyond the call of duty to brighten up the place. Soft candlelight illuminated the room from the chandelier, and vases of fresh hothouse roses added bright spots of color. His bride had not yet arrived. Thane signaled for a finger of brandy as he lingered, but he didn't have to wait long.

His throat went dry as he felt her presence. Astrid looked equal parts ethereal and regal...like a fairy queen visiting from some mystical land. Her dark hair had been twisted into loose coils and pinned to her crown, and she wore no jewelry save for the rings on her finger. He'd been right. The diaphanous silvery blue fabric matched her eyes perfectly. The dress itself was modest, but Astrid in it made it a tool of seduction. It hugged her frame to perfection, the bodice molding her breasts and reminding him of the way her slender but voluptuous body had felt beneath his.

His groin tightened instantly.

Christ.

Thane grazed his lips over her gloved fingers before tying her cloak over her shoulders. "Your Grace," he murmured, leading her to where the carriage was waiting. "You look exquisite."

Bright eyes met his. "As do you."

He took his place across from her and rapped on the roof, and the coach lurched into motion. "Where are we going?" she asked.

"The Silver Scythe. For dinner. It's not far from here. I thought it would be a pleasant outing."

"Oh." She wet her lips. "I would have been happy to stay in."

"It's your wedding day, Astrid. You deserve for it to be memorable."

A blush bloomed over her cheeks as she canted her head, a gleam in those transparent eyes of hers. "It already is."

Thane stifled the rush of pleasure at her words, along with the urgent need to instruct the coachman to turn the carriage around at once and head back to Harte House. He wanted her again. Badly enough to plead for her favors, agreement be damned. Thane had never begged for a single thing in his life, but he'd drop to his knees for her in a heartbeat.

"I do admit that I want to show off my beautiful new bride," he said.

"Hardly beautiful, Your Grace," she said, that gorgeous blush deepening. "Isobel is the beauty in the family, not me."

He arched a brow. "Beauty is in the eye of the beholder, is it not?"

"I think this particular beholder might be biased because of what just happened between us, and his brain is still fuzzy," she said dryly. "If he's thinking with his *actual* brain, that is."

Thane barked a laugh. He might be temporarily influenced by the appendage in his trousers, but Astrid *was* beautiful. Though hers was a beauty sheathed in danger—in those sharp eyes, that fine-edged intelligence, and that barbed tongue. Even now as he craved her body, he also wanted to hear her converse and laugh. A strange feeling bloomed in his chest. Dare he call it optimism? He bit back a grin. Christ, he'd never hear the end of it from Fletcher.

"Are you saying I'm ruled by my passions, Duchess?" he asked just as the carriage rolled to a stop in front of his club and the coachman rapped on the door. He helped her down from the coach, his fingers flexing on her slim, silk-clad waist and instantly recalling how velvety soft her bare skin had been.

Astrid's teasing glance slid to the bulge in his trousers, a playful smile on her lips. "I don't know, Duke, are you?"

He groaned. "Do you blame me? All I can think about is having you in my arms again."

Her reply was so quiet, he almost didn't hear it.

"I wish that, too."

Thane stopped so suddenly that his poor wife nearly went pitching forward through the doors of The Silver Scythe. Hardly daring to hope, he turned, his eyes meeting hers and holding them. "What are you saying, Astrid?"

Her smile was pure seduction. "How quickly can you eat?"

Before he could form a coherent reply, they were being welcomed and ushered by the proprietor to an opulent dining room. Though Thane could hardly focus, his nerves were so jumbled by Astrid's shattering admission. Heads turned as they were led to their table, and already Thane could hear the murmur of whispers.

However, when a particularly unkind sentiment reached him, he frowned. People were staring, but it took him a moment to realize that their stares were full of pity, not admiration. He blinked, fists clenching. He was used to the insults, but his glance slid to his bride, whose face had tightened as the word "beast" filtered through the air. She flinched at the sudden peal of loud, cruel laughter, and he resisted the impulse to growl his displeasure.

Her face paled when more whispers reached their ears. "How do you deal with this?"

"I don't."

And he didn't. For the most part, the rest of the aristocracy tended to shy away from him, not just because of the way he looked but because his temper was notorious. No one cared to be mauled by the Beast of Beswick. But now, with Astrid, he felt exposed. Every flicker of her eyes, every pained twitch of her lips felt like a new blow to him. A lash to freshly vulnerable skin.

Determined to enjoy the evening for her sake, Thane sipped on chilled cucumber soup and chewed tender lamb before sparing his duchess a glance. Her brow had knitted with a curious combination of confusion, discomfort, and annoyance, but she seemed focused on her food. As he ate, he felt her gaze upon him from time to time, but she remained steadfast upon her own meal. He worried that if he looked up, she would see the rage brewing in his eyes and think it directed at her when it wasn't.

Even now as the mention of "bestiality" reached him followed by noxious laughter, Thane found himself holding on to his temper by a thread. Every muscle in his body was locked. It was as though they didn't even see Astrid—the jewel she was—they only saw *him*. He wanted to rail and rage, but at the same time, his tortured soul filled with powerless anger. Powerless to prevent it. Powerless to protect her.

God, how could he be so blind? So stupid?

No matter what, his appearance could never be changed. People would always stare, and they would always whisper, and the *ton*'s cruelty knew no bounds. They thought him a monster, and she was now the monster's bride. He could not protect her by virtue of who he was—the duke. He could only hurt her by *what* he was—the beast.

No woman deserves to be tied to this.

The only answer would be to keep her at a distance. To close himself off.

As if she could sense his turmoil, her low voice pierced his hateful thoughts. "Your Grace, do you wish to leave?"

He clenched his jaw, swallowing hard. "No. Finish your dinner."

Despite her concerned glances, he made no attempt to converse, no attempt at refined politesse, and his behavior, without question, bordered on rude. If she was confused at the peculiar turn of events or his conduct, she did not show it. But Thane knew that if he opened his mouth, only vitriol would follow. He'd cause an unforgivable scene, and as furious as he was, it was still her wedding day. But by the time they finished the last course, the strain on Astrid's face was clear. Whether that was because of their avid audience or him, he could not say.

"Have I done something to displease you?" she asked in a low voice after they were back in the privacy of the carriage.

"No."

"Then, what is bothering you? Why are you shutting me out? Are you…regretting your decision?"

Thane drew a deep breath and voiced the resolution he'd come to at dinner. "Once your sister is safe from Beaumont, I will move back to Beswick Park. You may remain here in London. Harte House is yours. If it is not to your satisfaction, I will buy you any other property that suits you."

Astrid blinked. "I don't understand."

"Since this marriage is a means to an end, it is preferable that we reside separately," he said. Her stare met his, pale-blue chips of ice, when they arrived at his residence. Her expression was riddled with hurt and confusion.

"Why?" she asked. "Because people were staring and whispering? I don't care."

"You will after a while. Trust me that this is for the best, Astrid."

The air grew thick with tension between them. It was his fault, he knew, but he had to protect her from herself. And from him. This was the only way to keep her unscathed. If the *ton* believed it was a marriage of *in*convenience, she might have a chance to join their ranks unscathed. Thane knotted his fingers into fists.

He owed her that much for the price of being the unfortunate Duchess of Beswick.

CHAPTER FIFTEEN

"Fletcher," Astrid called out, entering her husband's suite via the shared connecting door the moment she knew the duke had departed the residence.

She'd deliberately waited after another silent meal—a repeat of their first horrid wedding dinner and each meal since—and overheard the duke talking to the valet about a midday meeting with the Marquess of Roth.

The duke had not made any overtures to her over the past few days, nor had he sought out her company once. He was scrupulously polite when their paths crossed, of course, but no more than necessary. The sudden and unexpected coldness had stung, but Astrid was determined to not let it affect her. Theirs was a marriage of convenience, after all.

He'd made that more than clear.

A part of her still ached for him, for what he'd endured in public at his club, but any further overtures or attempts at conversation had been harshly cut off. He was stony and cold to the point of cruelty. Enough for it to sting, enough for her to stop trying. Though he hadn't yet left for Beswick Park, he might as well have already gone for the little she did see of him.

Astrid took in the minimalist decor of his chamber in the daylight. She'd barely spared it a glimpse on her wedding night, concerned with other things before he'd snuffed out the candle. Unlike hers, it was overtly masculine, with dark mahogany furnishings and navy and cream accents. It was spare, much like the man himself.

Astrid averted her gaze from the bed, however, which was massive and luxurious and the complete opposite of the rest of the room. Her brain might have taken the hint, but her body was slower to listen. The memory of them in that bed, joined together in the darkness, tied her up in knots.

Swallowing her emotions, she turned to the valet, who had stalled with a pair of the duke's trousers over his arm and was staring at her expectantly.

"Has the duke received any recent invitations?"

The valet eyed her with interest. "Some, Your Grace."

"Please, Fletcher, call me Lady Astrid, or Lady Beswick if you must, but I simply cannot abide by the constant Your Grace-ing."

"You're a duchess, Your…er…my lady." She could scowl just as fiercely as Beswick, with much the same effect, as the valet backed away in alarm. "Culbert has the duke's invitations."

"Culbert?" she asked in surprise. "He's here?"

"Yes, His Grace sent for some of the staff from Beswick Park as well as for his aunt. They arrived early this morning, and Lady Verne took straight to her room."

He smirked, catching sight of the butler loitering in the corridor, and raised his voice. "You see, poor Culbert feels quite left out if he isn't included in some menial way. Doesn't think the duke's life can go on without his constant supervision. And now you will endure the joys of being smothered as well."

The butler spluttered, shooting daggers at Fletcher, and then bowed in her direction. "May I offer my congratulations, Lady Beswick."

"Thank you, Culbert, it's wonderful to see you," she said, making the older man beam. "Will you kindly look through the stack of invitations and see if there is one from Lord and Lady Featheringstoke, and if there is, please send back a reply in the affirmative."

"And the rest?" Culbert inquired. "There are quite a few."

Astrid halted. Beswick did not entertain, nor did he attend any of the *ton*'s festivities. She wasn't in London to socialize, either, but she also needed to keep an eye on Isobel, which she would do by any means necessary. Subterfuge, if she had to.

"I'll take a look. Keep me informed if more arrive. I'll speak to the duke once he returns."

Culbert cleared his throat. "His Grace also bade me remind you of your appointment at the modiste, Your Grace. The carriage has been readied at your convenience."

Astrid nodded. She'd completely forgotten. Then again, she was going to need fashionable clothing if she meant to take her place in society. She sighed. She hadn't quite determined whether a covert approach was wiser so as not to cause problems for Isobel or making a grand splash as the new Duchess of Beswick and facing her uncle head-on. The masquerade would give her the perfect opportunity to suss out the situation.

"Thank you, Culbert."

Once the efficient butler bowed and left, she

lowered her voice and leaned toward Fletcher. "Find out from Agatha where Isobel plans to go," she whispered. "And, Fletcher, do be careful. I wouldn't want anything to happen to my favorite valet."

With a jaunty nod, he departed, and Astrid went back to her suite. It would have been lovely to see Aunt Mabel, but the duchess must have been tired from the journey if she had retired to her chambers. Astrid called for Alice and set out for Bond Street. She received several odd looks as she descended the coach, ranging from shock to curiosity, and only belatedly realized that Beswick's bold family crest—a roaring lion with crossed swords—was displayed on the side.

"Come, Alice," she said, tugging on her bonnet and entering the shop, which thankfully was empty. She did not want to run into any society ladies, if she could help it. The reclusive, scarred, and scary Duke of Beswick taking a wife would be gossip fodder for the ages.

"Your Grace," a musical voice said. "What an honor to have you."

"Madame Pinot, I presume," Astrid said, turning to greet a petite brunette.

"You presume correctly, Your Grace," the modiste said, ushering her to a private salon in the back of the shop that was filled with gorgeous bolts of fabric and pages from *La Belle Assemblée* detailing the latest Parisian and English fashions. "May I offer you some tea? Some wine? Something stronger? Sherry, perhaps?"

"Tea would be lovely."

The modiste gave the order to a waiting assistant

and then brought forward some pages with preliminary sketches. Madame Pinot smiled. "The duke was very specific in his requests for colors, but I think you must tell me what you like as well, *oui*?"

"His Grace was here?"

The modiste gave a coy smile. "Earlier. He instructed me to treat you like a queen and spare no expense." Her smile widened. "It is nice to have such a devoted husband, *non*?"

"I suppose," Astrid replied.

Barely a word from her husband in days since his declaration, and yet he'd gone out of his way to visit a lady's modiste to provide carte blanche on his wife's purchases. Truly, the man was incomprehensible.

She tilted her chin. "Well, then we better get to spending His Grace's money."

"I like the way you think."

Hours—and a half-dozen cups of tea along with a few glasses of sherry—later, Astrid finally emerged from Madame Pinot's exclusive salon. She'd been measured, taped, and draped to within an inch of her life, but the modiste's tastes were truly spectacular.

When Astrid had inquired how she had known her sizing for the premade gown she'd worn, Madame Pinot—or Silvie as she'd insisted she be called—had given a sly smile and said that the duke had provided the measurements. Astrid hadn't been able to hide her blush.

The modiste promised to have one of her premade creations altered and sent to Harte House for the Featheringstoke ball. It'd been made for another lady who had had to go into unexpected mourning and would not be needing the gown.

It was fate, she had declared. Astrid had hesitated at the near-transparent silvery white confection, but Silvie had been adamant that Astrid was meant to be Titania, queen of the fairies. It was ludicrous. The gown even came with a pair of gossamer wings and a mask that covered half her face. The good thing was that she would be unrecognizable.

"I count on your discretion, Silvie," she'd murmured before leaving.

The modiste had laughed. "In my profession, Your Grace, discretion is as important as currency. Your secrets are safe with me."

• • •

Thane passed yet another sleepless night while his bride of a week slept like a baby on the other side of the wainscoted wall between their chambers. At least, she never made any noises that he could hear, not even when he pressed his ear to the connecting door like an obsessed fool. And he *was* obsessed. He grilled Fletcher incessantly as to her daily activities, desperate to know every detail.

"Why don't you do us all a favor and talk to your wife?" the valet had sniped the day before, and Thane had nearly put him through the wall.

"Because I'm asking you," he'd snarled.

Fletcher had obliged under threat of losing his position, informing him of her walks in the garden, her time exploring Harte House's library, her meeting with the head of Christie's for the auction, the letter she had received from her sister, her acceptance of the invitation to the Featheringstoke ball, her successful visit to the modiste, her suppers with his aunt, and the time she cleaned her teeth and retired for bed.

Thane had almost lost his temper at Fletcher's sarcasm, but he was more worried about his headstrong, willful wife. He didn't want her going to any *ton* events without protection, but he wasn't very well going to accompany her. He hadn't attended a ball since he'd left for war. Already at the thought of formal togs, he could feel the garrote of a heavy cravat against his throat and the stifling heat of a ballroom crammed with hundreds of sweaty bodies.

No, thank you.

Aunt Mabel would no doubt be ensconced at Astrid's side, protective battle-ax that she was. It wouldn't take society long to put two and two together and guess Astrid's identity. Perhaps Sir Thornton would be amenable to lending a hand. He'd married the daughter of an earl, Lady Claudia, and they were both well received by the *ton* during the season. The solicitor could keep an extra eye on his stubborn duchess.

Following his morning ablutions, Thane strode from his bedchamber only to discover from Culbert that Astrid had already had her breakfast and had gone for her usual morning constitutional in the gardens.

"The duchess," Culbert informed him, "rose at an ungodly hour, and Lady Verne is still abed."

No wonder Thane hadn't heard anything on the other side of the wall. It was a marginal comfort to know that she, too, had been unable to sleep. He deliberated between finding her and going to his study to work. While he did not take his seat in Parliament for obvious reasons, he still liked to know what was going on. Sir Thornton's reports on those matters were painstakingly detailed.

Considering he actually hadn't seen his wife since the morning before—like two ships sailing past in the dark—a part of him was desperate to take his own measure of her after Fletcher's mutinous account. And this was his house, after all. His gardens, too.

It didn't take him long to find her. Astrid sat on a bench, an apple core in one hand and a book in the other. Thane found that he missed their after-dinner brandies in the conservatory at Beswick Park and their rousing discussions of life and literature.

Well then, he'd seen her. He should turn around and leave.

"What are you reading?" he asked instead.

Ice-blue eyes peeled from the page, the brief uncertainty in them replaced by aloofness. Without responding, she hefted the book for him to read the title. Ironically, it was *Frankenstein; or, The Modern Prometheus*. He'd bought the thing when it'd first been published anonymously a year ago. Percy Bysshe Shelley, a poet and distant acquaintance, had penned the foreword, but Thane had heard rumors that the man's wife, Mary, was the true mind behind the gruesome story.

He lifted a shoulder in a cynical shrug. "Felt like comparing notes?"

"Do you need something, Your Grace?" she returned coolly.

"He dies," Thane said. "At the end, the monster dies after he kills everyone."

"Thank you, I've read it." She shot him a stony look. "Though if I hadn't, you would have spoiled the ending for me."

"The author was right; he didn't deserve to live."

He didn't know why he was provoking her, only that he needed to. He wanted to drag some reaction from her, something other than that rigid composure that turned her into an ice sculpture.

"Why? Because he was different?"

"He was an abomination."

"Who wanted love. He wanted a mate." Her voice trembled on the last word, and she ducked her head back to her pages. "Isn't that what we are all searching for? A partner in life? Companionship?"

"Not everyone." He clasped his hands behind his back. "Mary Shelley, Percy's wife, was Wollstone-craft's daughter, did you know? I've heard she wrote the novel, not her husband. From women's rights and the feminine mystique to unnatural monsters and unhappy endings. Quite a leap for a female author, don't you think?"

Her expression peaked with curiosity, her mouth parting as though she might respond, but then she chose to ignore him, focusing studiously on her book. After a while, she looked up. "Do you mean to stand there and hover?"

"I like watching you."

"That's not disturbing at *all*." Sighing loudly, Astrid snapped the book shut and stood, looking everywhere but at him. "Very well, I shall leave you to it, Your Grace. I, however, do not enjoy being incinerated by a pair of eyes belonging to a man who has hardly made the effort to say two words to me in the short time we have been married. Clearly, you have much better things to do than manage a wife. Or even pretend you have one."

God, I miss her tart tongue.

She swept past him in a flurry of skirts, and the faint waft of her scent hit him like a log to the head. Without thinking, Thane reached out to grasp her elbow. She gasped but held herself like a statue, clutching her book to her chest.

"Astrid, look at me."

Rebelliously, she did. At a distance, the power of her gaze had been supportable. At close range, the fire in them was lethal. Her mouth twisted into a grimace, and Thane had to fight with every ounce of sanity in him. He wanted to bend his head and kiss the salty defiance from those lips. Set her on that stone bench, toss her skirts over her head, and lash her with his tongue until the only thing left in her eyes was passion.

"About the Featheringstoke ball—" he growled. He'd meant to tell her about Sir Thornton accompanying her in his stead, but she didn't let him finish.

She reared back, her eyes flashing bloody murder. "You cannot think to forbid me to go."

Thane forgot everything he'd been about to say, reacting only to her tone. "If that is my prerogative, certainly I can. I am your husband."

"In name only."

He arched an eyebrow. "Name is the only thing that matters."

"Go to hell, Beswick."

Thane drew her closer to him, tightening his hold on her elbow even as she tried to wrestle out of his grip. He laughed at her. "What a filthy tongue you have, dear. You sound like a peevish child. Are you a child? Do you know what's usually done to punish such childish displays of temper? Naughty children are put over the knee."

Her eyes went wide as she took his meaning, though his fierce little virago didn't cower one bit. "You wouldn't."

"No, but don't tempt me."

Thane dragged her so close that her upper body was crushed against his, the book sealed between them. Beneath her loosely fastened cloak, her breasts heaved. He wondered if she were having the same arousing thoughts about a thoroughly erotic spanking and being splayed over his knees, her pert bottom bared to the sky. His other hand moved to the small of her back, his last finger grazing the start of that tempting curvature, and held her against him.

Now that he had her in his arms, Thane could think of little else. Not his decisions, not keeping her at a distance, not engaging with her at all. All his good sense fell by the wayside.

They stood there for an interminable moment, panting against each other. Her, standing frozen in his arms. Him, fighting desperately not to take her to the ground and give them both the release they craved. Her tongue snaked out to wet her lips, making his body jerk in response.

"Thane," she breathed.

Her eyes were wide with defiance and desire, her mouth parted. Long fingers fisted in the folds of his morning coat, not pushing him away but not encouraging him, either. He would not ask the question he'd asked that day in the library. No, if she wanted him, she would have to be the one to bend this time.

"If you want me to kiss you, Astrid," he told her, "you simply have to ask. You made the rules, after all."

"You're a beast."

He shrugged. "I've never claimed to be anything else. If you want me, say please."

She grasped at his lapels as she pushed to her tiptoes, her gaze lit with equal parts anger and passion. Thane's heart thudded in his chest. Would she do it? Would she give in? Her lips parted, and he leaned forward a fraction, his body stiff and aching. Desire hummed between them, so thick he could taste it on his tongue.

Put us both out of our misery, he willed her.

Her lips grazed his, a puff of air feathering against his mouth. Glacial eyes lifted to his. "I wouldn't beg you to kiss me if you were the last man in England."

Then she wrenched out of his grasp and whirled away, stalking toward the house.

A pained chuckle burst from him. *Stubborn little minx.*

• • •

Good God, but the man turned her into a raving lunatic.

"Of all the bloody nerve," she seethed, storming onto the terrace and into the residence. Culbert and the rest of the maids gave her a wide berth, no doubt crossing themselves as she muttered witlessly to herself. "As if I would ever beg to kiss that loathsome, arrogant jackanapes."

Although she was angrier with herself for *wanting* to kiss the man. And she *had* wanted to, quite desperately. She'd heard the thread of pain in his voice when he'd compared himself to Frankenstein's monster. Astrid hadn't meant to hurt him by selecting the book. She'd been curious to see if *she* felt differently after getting to know Beswick, who lived such a self-imposed solitary existence because deep down he felt that he was a monster.

Admittedly, she'd flown off the handle about the ball, but he didn't own her.

He does, a smart, know-it-all inner voice reminded her.

As his wife, she was as good as his property. She clenched her jaw—she'd sworn to herself that she would be at no man's mercy, and here she was, exactly that. Her face heated at the words she'd flung at him. It was a wonder he *hadn't* put her over his knee to deliver the punishment he'd described.

Astrid felt a throbbing pulse deep in her core. The thought of his bare hand on her equally bare behind turned her brain to mash, twisting dark knots of sensation between her legs.

Sweet Jesus.

She needed to do something or she would go mad.

"Culbert," she said. "I wish to go for a ride."

"Of course, Your Grace, I will send one of the footmen to the mews at once."

"Tell the man the faster the horse, the better," she told him, since Brutus and Temperance were both still at Beswick Park. "And no sidesaddles. A regular saddle will do."

Culbert frowned at the unusual demand but nodded. "As you wish, Your Grace."

She was taking a risk riding astride down Rotten Row, but it was still absurdly early for anyone of import to be about. By the time Astrid had changed into her riding habit and breeches, a horse had been saddled and waiting. The mare that was brought around was a racer. Astrid could tell from the sheer size of the chestnut beast, along with its refined head, muscular hindquarters, and long graceful neck. She was a beauty. She pawed at the ground, steam bursting from her nostrils into the slightly chill air.

"She's perfect."

"This here is Luna," the attending groom said and leaned in conspiratorially. "As in luna*tic*," he amended. "But don't tell the duke I said that. She used to be one of his favorites before Goliath. She's a right brute."

Astrid grinned. *This* was the mount she needed— one that demanded a strong hand and an enormous amount of concentration. They would work each other to the bone. She didn't want to think about anything. Not her marriage. Not the duke. Not the loss of any freedom she'd ever known. The young groom helped to boost her into the saddle, and Astrid took off with him in tow on another horse.

She waved to Beswick, who stood on the side terrace, his eyes widening upon seeing her mount. He opened his mouth, but she couldn't hear a word beyond the rush of wind in her ears.

"Keep up," she called back to the groom with a laugh and braced her knees into the mare's sides.

Astrid rode like the wind through Hyde Park until she came to the south end and Rotten Row. And then Luna staunchly refused to obey her commands. Astrid was an expert rider—this mare wanted to run. She'd been stabled far too long and relished the exercise. Under normal circumstances, Astrid would have hauled the horse under control, but she wasn't thinking straight. No one deserved to be trapped. To be caged at someone else's whim. To wither away and die. She and Luna deserved some modicum of freedom.

She gave Luna her head.

CHAPTER SIXTEEN

Thane's heart lodged in his throat as his eyes tracked Astrid's breakneck pace into the south end of Hyde Park. She was truly insane.

He'd wanted to take a piece out of the groom's side when he'd seen that she'd been given Luna. The horse was unpredictable at best and hadn't been ridden in some months. Normally, he was the only one to handle her, but he'd been busy. Busy marrying a termagant who was going to snap her fool neck.

"Her seat is incredible," Fletcher had said, trying to calm him down. "Better than yours, in fact." He'd cowered at Thane's glare. "Culbert said she asked for a spirited horse."

"Spirited, not demonic," Thane had muttered.

But now, though, as he thundered on Goliath in her wake, he did catch sight of her expert seat. For a moment, he felt real relief that she rode astride, because Astrid rode the horse as if they were one, fluid and effortless. He'd seen her on Brutus, but this was a whole other level of proficiency. Thane couldn't remember the last time he'd seen a woman—or man for that matter—seat a horse so capably. Despite his anger, he felt admiration.

Until his eyes fell on the broken tree branch in the path.

Luna had jumped higher obstacles, but Astrid didn't know that.

"Jump it," he yelled. But she was too far away to

hear him.

Astrid yanked on the reins, which only served to confuse the horse. Luna stumbled and slammed to a halt, and her rider went flying.

"Oh God, Astrid," Thane shouted, reining in Goliath at her side where she lay staring up at the sky, her body shaking as he leaped down to crouch beside her. Was she convulsing? Had she hit her head? Sustained some internal injury? He blinked, his jaw falling open as she clutched her sides, great gales of laughter coming from her chest. "Are you bloody mad? You could have been killed!"

"I know how to take a fall, Thane," she said, her eyes sparkling.

"You should not have been on that horse."

"She was magnificent. *Is* magnificent." She pushed up to her elbows and grimaced slightly, watching as the groom trailing behind her finally caught up and went to secure Luna, who was grazing nearby. "Why do you keep her here and not at Beswick Park?"

"She's for sale," Thane said. "There's something wrong with her."

Astrid shook her head and tugged at his coat for him to help her up. "She needs a loving hand, Thane, and room to run. There's nothing wrong with her. When I got Brutus, he'd been abused mercilessly with the crop. He wouldn't let a soul near him, and now look at him."

He stood there, rapt, watching her in mute fascination. The woman confounded him. She was stubborn to a fault, that sharp tongue of hers could flay like a blade, and yet she worried about the future and care of a deranged horse. Something indefinable squeezed his chest as he reached an arm down to her. She accepted his help, stood, and dusted the leaves off her riding jacket.

"You are extraordinary," he said, shaking his head. "How is it that you see promise in the things that most people want to discard?"

"Just because something is fractured doesn't mean it has lost its value."

They were talking about something else entirely, but spectators on the public path had begun to gather. Nowhere near a crowd or anyone from high society, but enough for the horrified whispers to start getting loud. And once more, he'd forgotten a damn hat in his haste to leave Harte House. Thane squared his shoulders and glared at the stunned onlookers before mounting his horse. Before Astrid could call for the groom who had Luna in hand, he'd reached down to scoop her up and place her across his lap.

"I can ride perfectly well," she protested.

He did not pause but urged Goliath into a gentle canter. "You winced just before. You're injured somewhere. Where did you get hurt?"

Thane looked down, registering the flags of color in her cheeks.

"It's...impolite to say."

He blinked, confused, and then understanding dawned. She'd injured that spectacular seat of hers. Dozens of lewd propositions sprang to mind—a massage, a closer look, a warm bath—but Thane bit his tongue. "You should not have been on that horse," he repeated.

She stiffened. "Will you forbid me to ride as you have forbidden me to attend the Featheringstoke ball?"

"I didn't forbid you."

"*What?*" She twisted to glare at him, the grinding motion of her soft thighs against his half-masted cock making him see stars for an endless moment. "You were about to…"

"You made an assumption, little hellion. An incorrect, *hasty* one. I was simply going to inform you that Sir Thornton will be there, along with my aunt."

Words appeared to fail her. "Oh."

"I must say it's quite gratifying to see that the cat has gotten your tongue." Thane pulled Goliath to a stop and peered up at the sky, a mock expression of fright on his face.

"What are you doing?" she muttered grumpily.

"Making sure that lightning won't strike us where we sit."

"Not funny." She elbowed him in the ribs and then gasped, cradling her arm. "Gracious, Beswick, you're as hard as rock."

He wasn't, but he was certainly getting there. Thane wasn't sure she would appreciate his bawdy observation, so he kept his mouth shut.

"Why won't you go?" she asked. "With me. To the ball."

"With this face? You saw the reaction of the working classes in Hyde Park. Don't think it won't be worse among the nobility. Their cuts are sharper. They don't hesitate to go for blood."

"It's a masquerade."

"It's a ball."

"Isobel will be there," she said.

"I know," he said. "Which is why I'm asking Sir Thornton to attend. His wife, Lady Claudia, is the daughter of an earl. She's as boisterous as you are. You should rub along famously." He frowned but couldn't quite suppress his amusement. "On second thought, perhaps that's not the best idea."

"What if I begged you to come?" she asked quietly.

His fingers clenched on the reins. "I won't, Astrid. I vowed never to subject myself to their scorn. The *ton* turned its collective back on me while I was out fighting for their freedoms, for their way of life. And all they see is the Beast of Beswick." He was getting so agitated that even Goliath nickered softly. "A nightmare of a thing."

"You're not a nightmare, and you haven't let any of them get to know you. You've closed yourself off. You've turned your back on them before they can do it to you."

Thane didn't argue her logic because it was true. He sucked in a breath as they pulled to a stop in front of Harte House. Several passersby paused to point and stare, proving his point that he would be nothing more than a lurid curiosity. "Regardless, Astrid, I cannot. I will not."

"Not even for me?"

Thane set his jaw. "Not even for the Prince Regent himself."

• • •

Alice put the finishing touches on Astrid's cheeks—a smudge of silver dust along the crests of her cheekbones—and the barest hint of rouge on her lips. Silver dust was sprinkled liberally on her eyelashes and in her hair, which hung in thick curls down her back, a diadem of diamonds clipped to her crown. As agreed with Isobel, she tucked a bright-red rosebud behind one ear.

Astrid could scarcely recognize herself in the looking glass. The dress that had been delivered as promised by Silvie was truly outlandish. And gorgeous. It seemed even more diaphanous than before and exposed a scandalous amount of décolletage. Astrid was certain that the fairy queen would have gotten herself into a dangerous amount of trouble if this had truly been her ensemble of choice. Then again, many of the artists who tried to immortalize *A Midsummer Night's Dream* had painted Titania as naked.

Small mercies.

Astrid tied the mask in place. Well, at least she would be incognito even if her dress was at most a strategic placement of chiffon, satin, and lace. As she made one last twirl in front of the mirror, she felt a twinge of disappointment that Beswick would not be attending. Perhaps she should find him before she left. There was a good chance he would not want her going anywhere alone in this dress. Then again, he had been adamant that even the Prince Regent could not sway him, much less *her*.

She'd felt hurt, but she'd tucked it away where it couldn't do her harm.

He would never change, not even for her.

When Astrid went downstairs, Aunt Mabel, with a glass of sherry in hand, was dressed in a Cleopatra costume, complete with eyes ringed in kohl, arm bracelets, and a costume that hugged every one of her considerable curves. Astrid would bet money on the fact that Aunt Mabel intended to break a few hearts tonight.

"Lord Oberon is not going to like that," the duchess predicted with a laugh.

Astrid's lips twisted down. "Beswick would not care if I were Lady Godiva riding naked through the streets of Coventry."

Aunt Mabel shot her an incredulous look but then laughed in delight. "Now, why didn't I think to do that? Next year for sure!"

Though the journey to Grosvenor Square was quick, Astrid was sweating when she arrived. She was going to see Isobel. Unlike most balls, there were no announcements of formal names—only masquerade titles made up at the whim of the host. In this case, an already foxed Marquess of Featheringstoke who was dressed as Poseidon, if his trident was any indication. The fumes on his breath could start an inferno.

"Who might you be, beautiful lady?" he slurred. "Persephone? No, Venus!"

"Queen Titania," Mabel said, poking the marquess in the side. "And Cleopatra."

His eyes widened with recognition. "Mabel, is that you?" He blinked and swayed. "I must say, I heard a devil of a rumor about some rushed nuptials. So if it is you, this young vixen must be the new—"

"Don't say it," Mabel warned. "Or other secrets

will come to light that you will not like, *Feathers*."

Astrid almost giggled at how sober he became upon hearing the nickname, with an askance glance to his wife, who was dressed in what looked like a siren's costume. Either that or someone had spewed copious amounts of seaweed all over her ample breasts.

"Of course," Poseidon murmured with a smart bow that was ruined by a loud belch. "Away then and be merry."

They descended the staircase together, and Astrid searched the crowded ballroom for Isobel, but she saw no one else with white roses tucked into her coiffure. Had she decided not to come after all? Had Aunt Mildred or Uncle Reginald forbidden her to attend? Astrid's heart sank, though it was still early yet. She followed Mabel toward the far end of the room where a few of her acquaintances stood.

As luck would have it, Astrid was free to look for Isobel once introductions were made with Mabel's set. She was more than aware of a few probing glances from the duchess's friends, as if they sought to place her. No one would remember a scandal from a decade ago, would they? But of course, she was not so lucky.

"You were engaged to Beaumont," a rotund lady dressed like a bee—Lady Bevins, a notorious busy-body—pronounced in a stage whisper. "Everleigh or some such."

Astrid nodded stiffly.

"Your younger sister was presented her voucher to Almack's earlier this week," the woman went on. "She's a beauty."

"Is she here?" Astrid blurted out at the mention of Isobel, but the lady had already been guided away by the clever Mabel. Astrid was grateful.

Her eyes traveled the crowd and came to rest on a familiar face. Exceedingly familiar because he'd forgone a mask. Of course he would. Beaumont was so arrogant that even at a masquerade, he didn't feel the need to participate. He was dressed all in gold, carried a gold cane, and wore a golden wreath.

"Beaumont is here," Mabel murmured, returning to place a glass of punch into Astrid's hand. "Though I'm not sure what he's meant to be."

"A guinea, perhaps?"

"A golden phallus, and one lacking in girth at that."

"Aunt *Mabel*!" Astrid coughed into her drink. "You shouldn't say such things."

Intelligent amber eyes, so like her nephew's, held hers. "Why? Should it be only the men who objectify the women? We have eyes as well."

"We are *ladies*."

"A dreadful code of conduct beaten into us from the day of our births." The duchess grinned and gave her an outlandish swat on the rear. "But no one needs to know that we are rebels on the inside."

Astrid had to laugh. Several pairs of eyes turned in her direction, one in particular. Someone she had not noticed before. Those eyes burned and scorched, making her feel like a hare that had just been scented by a wolf. A large wolf that looked more like a hound of hell. Or the master of hell himself. The guest was dressed all in black with a hideous horned mask. Astrid's heart hammered uncontrollably in her chest, every inch of her fighting heightened survival instincts.

Who is he? And how dare he stare at me so boldly?

She arched an imperious eyebrow and, with an annoyed jerk of her chin, tore her gaze away. To her chagrin, the stranger started to head straight for her. Luckily, Lucifer's path was intercepted by the appearance of Sir Thornton with a lady in tow who was dressed as an angel.

"Your Grace," the solicitor murmured softly so as not to be overheard and bowed. "Might I present my wife, Lady Claudia Thornton."

Astrid's eyes fell on a pretty blonde whose blue gaze shone with intelligence and humor. "Please call me Claudia."

"Then you must call me Astrid." She glanced at the lady's angel wings with a smile. "We winged creatures need to stick together."

Claudia laughed, her voice low. "I must admit I have been dying to meet you. The one who tamed the beast."

Astrid bristled, but there was no malice in Claudia's tone or expression. She reminded herself that Sir Thornton was the closest thing to a friend that her husband had. "I wouldn't say I *tamed* him. If I had, he'd be here."

"Henry says he's besotted."

Astrid's eyes widened. "Besotted" would be the last word she'd use to describe Beswick. "Hardly."

She was saved from the chaotic turn of her thoughts at the sight of a gorgeous young woman descending the staircase, dressed as the goddess of spring. White roses graced her crown in a wreath, ribbons descending down her back. Even cloaked in a sack, she would recognize her sister. Astrid felt tears leap to her eyes. Two people wearing Venetian masks flanked Isobel. Her aunt and uncle, Astrid presumed. She couldn't help but notice how much attention her beautiful sister was garnering. Indeed, Isobel was a diamond of the first water, and she deserved everything that designation brought—her choice of suitors.

Surely Uncle Reginald would see her popularity as well and would allow her to choose someone other than Beaumont. Then again, most marriages were accompanied by a wife's dowry, not the reverse, and her uncle fully expected to get his share from the *sale* of his niece. Helplessly, she watched as Beaumont sauntered toward them, clear ownership stamped in his gaze. Time was running out for Isobel, and Astrid was low on options. *Out* of options, ever since Isobel had decided to take matters into her own hands. A decision that would be for nothing if the cunning Beaumont managed to compromise her.

"Excuse me," she mumbled to Claudia and Aunt Mabel. "I need some air."

To stop herself from rushing over to Isobel and causing a scene, she angled for the nearest pair of French doors, slipping out to the balcony and hauling huge gulps of cool evening air into her lungs. Astrid gripped the balustrade with numb fingers. Her corset felt laced too tight, pressing in against her ribs and making her light-headed.

Oh God, she was going to swoon. She *never* swooned.

"Drink this."

A tumbler of brandy was thrust into her palms, and Astrid sipped the spirits gratefully. She turned to thank her benefactor and froze. Eyes that glinted an unholy black in the moonlight burned like embers in the depths of his mask.

Hades in the flesh.

CHAPTER SEVENTEEN

Thane's eyes tracked the delicate swallow of Astrid's throat and every muscle in his body locked to the point of torture. Christ, she made even the act of drinking seem like a seduction, innocent though it was. There was nothing innocent, however, about the way her tongue darted out to lick a bead of brandy from her upper lip. His groin tightened to excruciating hardness when her translucent eyes, gleaming in the dim moonlight, met his and those wet lips parted in shock.

He wanted to kiss her senseless.

And to think he almost hadn't come.

Earlier that evening, the thought of Astrid at the Featheringstoke ball had nearly been more than he could handle. She'd looked so beautiful. A goddess just out of his reach.

"If I may, Your Grace?" Fletcher had murmured as Thane had watched her getting dressed and limned in candlelight in her bedroom window from the darkness of the terrace.

"You've never skimped on words, Fletcher, so why stop now?"

"You are a fool, sir."

He'd huffed a laugh. That he was. There was no greater fool than he. "I never should have married her."

"The marriage is done. You need to move forward."

Thane had swallowed, the imprint of his wife's

luscious figure branded onto his brain. "You're right, Fletcher. I do. I need to put her out of my mind."

She deserved more than him.

She deserved a man who was normal.

She deserved a partner and husband she could be proud of.

His body had ached, but it'd been a different kind of ache from the ones that usually plagued him. This one had radiated from inside—an emptiness that had felt like a bucket of rocks pressing into his chest. Thane had hoped that some time at the gaming tables in The Silver Scythe would help as a distraction, and then he would stop obsessing about his delectable wife dressed in nothing but a few strips of gossamer.

And so there he'd gone at first.

But the familiar scents of incense and smoke had done nothing to soothe his agitated spirits. A drink, he'd decided, was in order. A *few* drinks. He'd passed the next two hours at the gaming tables, wagering a small fortune and consuming enough liquor to fell an elephant, all in the interest of distracting himself.

It hadn't worked. None of it had worked.

"Settle my accounts," he told the owner.

"Leaving us so soon?" the man asked.

"I forgot I have a prior engagement," he said and pointed to a particularly daunting mask hanging on a hook. "Might I borrow that?"

"Of course."

Climbing into his waiting coach, he'd given the coachman the address for the Featheringstoke ball. For the first time in hours, the pressure in his chest had eased, and when he'd stood on the threshold to the ballroom and seen his wife, the space there was filled with something other than rocks.

He'd felt it the moment she saw him—that raw pulse of connection across the room. And he'd held her stare hungrily. A faint blush bloomed across her cheekbones, but his fairy queen didn't drop her eyes at his bold appraisal. In fact, her eyebrow tented in aristocratic disdain before she dismissed him completely with a regal sweep of her chin.

Astrid had not recognized him.

She *still* hadn't, even standing a mere foot away, not behind the formidable mask he'd borrowed. Her eyes narrowed in scrutiny, her teeth sinking into her bottom lip in concentration. Lust tore through him, and the desire to kiss her increased tenfold. As if she could sense his wicked intentions, she took a step in reverse, her gaze fairly sparking with warning.

God above, she was splendid.

And she was *his*.

• • •

Hades was enormous, Astrid thought. And he smelled of woodsmoke and whiskey. She could feel his eyes upon her from behind his mask like hot coals.

"While I thank you for your assistance, we have not been introduced, sir," she said primly, resisting the urge to flee. She peered at him, curiosity winning out over propriety. "Who are you?"

His answer was to lean toward her, and she shifted out of the way, her heart in her throat. She'd fought off many overzealous men in her life. He wouldn't be the first, though he was certainly the largest, and she did not want to be trapped against the stone railing.

Astrid whirled to leave. "You are too forward, sir. I am a married woman."

"I am glad to hear it."

The familiar smoky rasp curled around her, and she pivoted on her heel, disbelief making her clumsy as her brain took in his familiar height and the distinct shape of his shoulders. She'd been so fixated on the chilling mask that she hadn't spared a thought to the man underneath. *"Thane?"*

"At your service."

"What are you doing here?"

"My wife demanded my presence." Astrid felt his smile, though she could not see it. "You are exquisite tonight, my dear."

Pleasure at his words flooded her, but she was still in shock. "Isobel is here. And Beaumont. And my aunt and uncle."

"I saw. She's the belle of the ball, except for Queen Titania, of course." He canted his head. "No dancing for the queen of the fairies?"

She smiled. "Not without risking the wrath of Oberon." Her gaze swept him from head to toe. "Though my fairy king appears to have transformed into Hades."

"Perhaps he has devilish intentions."

God help her, every supporting bone in her body dissolved at the husky notes of his voice. "Are you going to lead me astray, Your Grace?"

"Only if that is your wish."

She could merely nod her assent as his gaze

burned into hers from the depths of his mask. "Take that thing off," she said. "I want to see your eyes."

"Not here," he said. "Shall we take a turn in the garden, Your Majesty?"

Astrid glanced back at the ballroom, but it was such a crush that her sister wasn't visible. "What about Isobel?"

"She only just arrived. She will have to make the rounds before she can find you without drawing notice to herself." He reached out a hand. "Come."

In a daze, Astrid slipped her hand in his and followed him off the terrace. Other couples had the same idea, as she guessed from the sounds of muted laughter filling the air. Her body felt on edge, simmering with sensation. A quick look over her shoulder showed that they were already some distance from the house, and the sound of voices had faded to silence. Her husband led her into an arbor where a narrow stone bench built inside a miniature marble folly surrounded a fountain that featured a handful of frolicking fairies.

Thane chuckled, the sound doing odd things to her confused senses. "Appropriate, no?"

She released his hand and went to examine the fountain. It was skillfully carved, the expressions of the fairies mischievous and bright, as if they'd only just been ensnared in stone. "It's beautiful."

"Yes." But he was looking at her when he said it.

Astrid turned toward him, her stomach a coil of nerves, and blurted out the question on the tip of her tongue. "Why did you come, Thane? What do you want?"

"I don't know."

His reply was uncertain and it was honest. Much like how she felt. She didn't know who she was when she was around him. He confused her, muddled her senses. Made her feel like flying and weeping in the same breath. Being with Thane was like being caught at the center of a hurricane while in a tiny skiff. She lost her bearings with one look. And those feelings didn't make her feel weak. How did surrendering to someone make one feel *powerful*?

Thane hadn't moved from where he stood, watching her through the eye slits in his mask. Astrid moved toward him, standing until they were chest to chest, and reached her arms up to loosen the ties that held it in place. He inhaled audibly as the plaster mold came away in her hand, revealing his face. Those angular cheekbones, his finely molded lips, and that smoldering golden gaze that burned away every ounce of her resistance.

"There you are," she whispered.

"I'm not certain that what's underneath isn't more monstrous than the mask."

"Don't do that," she said, her fingers dropping the mask and returning to cup his jaw. "You'll... you."

Maybe it was the moon or the stars twinkling above or the fairies cavorting in whimsical abandon behind her, but Astrid felt bold. The duke made no move to hold her, and she remembered what he'd said. She blushed, also recalling what *she* had said... that she wouldn't ask him to kiss her if he was the last man in England.

He was the *only* man she wanted to kiss her.

She didn't care about terms. She didn't care about

tomorrow. The only thing that mattered was this moment. And the two of them *in* this moment.

Astrid traced her fingers over his firm lips and licked hers. The gold in his eyes darkened to the color of whiskey. "Thane?"

"Yes, my queen?"

"Kiss me."

• • •

Thane didn't know what he would have done if she hadn't asked. Dropped to his knees and begged, perhaps. "Are you certain?"

Because once we do this, there's no going back.

His wife nodded, her slender throat working. "Yes."

Thane stared down at the silver dust coating her eyelashes, making her eyes look like pools of starlight. She was ethereal and lovely, and she was his. He removed his gloves and tucked them into his pocket—when he touched her, he only wanted bare skin between them. And then he gathered her close, softly, softly. Allowing her time to pull away if she chose to. But she didn't. Thane lifted a knuckle and traced the skin of her cheekbone.

"So smooth," he murmured. "I've never felt skin like yours."

She leaned into his caress as his hand drifted down her cheek to the straight slope of her jaw and her stubborn chin. He traced the lush bottom curve of her lip and the arched bow of the top. Her lips parted on a hushed sigh, but he continued his exploration up her slim nose to her smooth brow.

Silvery light glistened on her hair, the thick mass of curls cascading over porcelain shoulders. He drank her in, her beauty transcendent in the moonlight. She was something else—truly a fairy queen come to steal the hearts of mere mortals.

"You dazzle me," he said.

"Is that such a bad thing?"

"Yes. I should stay away from you."

She swallowed. "Why?"

"Because you deserve more."

Cradling her jaw in two hands, he ended the conversation when he leaned down and drew his mouth over hers, back and forth, savoring the shape and texture of her. She tasted of brandy and magic, of beauty and secrets, and he wanted to know them all. Unable to help himself, Thane's tongue flicked along the crease, coaxing her lips to part, and then he licked deep.

With a soft cry, Astrid wrapped her arms around his neck, plastering her entire body to his. And the kiss ignited. Her mouth was hot and wet and open on his, her tongue circling, teasing, and retreating. Thane groaned and sank his fingers into her hair. She was passion embodied, meeting him thrust for thrust and lick for lick. Astrid threw herself wholly into the kiss, holding back nothing. And neither did he.

It was the single most erotic kiss of his life.

As evidenced by the ax handle in his trousers. He canted his hips backward, not wanting to scare her, but she would have none of it, her hips following his until she was arched like a bow in his arms, her body glued to his. He tore his mouth from hers to kiss the long length of her throat, nuzzling into the hollow of her collarbone. She smelled like fresh grass with a hint of rosewater. Essence of a summer thunderstorm in a wildflower garden.

"Christ, you are delicious," he murmured, his tongue darting out to sample her hot skin.

With another breathy sigh, her knees buckled slightly, her fingers clutching at his coat. Thane lifted her easily, sweeping one hand beneath her knees, without breaking the kiss and walked them to the stone bench of the folly. He settled her in his lap. Her plump lips were deliciously swollen, her ice-blue irises nearly swallowed up by the black of her pupils.

"Shall we stop?" he asked huskily, a finger tracing the edge of her bodice.

"God, no."

Thane laughed at her enthusiastic denial. "Good, because I've wanted to do this for days. That first time has been imprinted on my brain."

He pulled her bodice low, exposing her breasts to the moonlight and his ravenous gaze. He full-body shuddered, rocked by a bolt of lust so sharp that it dazed him. That teasing glimpse in the bath hadn't done her justice. The pale, creamy globes spilled into his hand, their peach-tipped dusky peaks tightening into mouth-watering knots. She sucked in a ragged breath as his thumb brushed over her nipple, her back arching into his supporting arm. God, she was magnificent. His pulse thrummed with want.

Mine. Mine. Mine.

Like a cat finding a bowl of cream, Thane lowered his head.

"Wait, what are you doing?" she mumbled, eyes wide and dilated with desire.

"Kissing you," he said. "I'm only fulfilling my wife's demands."

A smile drifted over her lips, and her eyelashes lowered. "Then, by all means, proceed."

And he did, touching his tongue to the sweet peak of her breast, lavishing his attention and adoring the husky moans falling from her lips. He licked into her cleavage and moved to the other breast, feasting on her like a man starved. It astounded him how passionate she was in her response, as if *she* wanted *him* with the same fervor as he wanted her. She writhed her bottom into his straining erection, making him gasp.

"Thane," she begged. "I want…I need…"

"I know, sweetheart. I feel it, too."

That consuming, inexorable need that wouldn't relent until it was satisfied. He took her lips in an untamed kiss, his tongue tangling with hers in blatant simulation of the act they were both beginning to crave. She gave as much as he, licking, sucking, nipping, until they clung to each other, panting. Thane reached beneath her flimsy skirts, sliding up a warm stockinged ankle and then a rounded calf. He skimmed the indent at the back of her knee, climbed past her garter to one silken thigh, the softness pared down from years of riding astride.

He blinked, his knuckles brushing soft maidenhair and bare skin. "You're not wearing any drawers."

"Undergarments wouldn't work with the design of the gown," his vixen of a wife responded, blushing furiously before tucking her head into his neck. "You don't like it."

With a growl, he ground his hips upward. "Does it feel like I don't like it?"

He cupped her sex boldly, one finger sliding between her slick folds. God, she was already damp. She was wet for *him*. Everything male in him crowed like a rooster in a henhouse, satisfaction curling through his lust-hazed mind. He stroked again, and her thighs clamped around his hand, holding him there and rocking gently. The erotic feel of it and the thought of her gripping his cock with those lean muscles made him wild.

As if reading his thoughts, Astrid levered herself into a sitting position and shifted her skirts to the side as she twisted, flinging one knee over his legs, to straddle him. His erection strained against the placket of his breeches, pressed against her hot, bare center as he was. She fumbled at the fall of his pants. He stalled her hand with his.

"Astrid. Not here. Not like this."

He wouldn't take her in a garden, like some shameful, furtive coupling.

She faltered, her lovely eyes meeting his. "Why?"

"Because you're my wife, not some tart."

She grinned at him, though her expression was marred by a touch of shame. "And what if I wish to play the tart, Your Grace? I've been accused of that and more, you know."

Thane blinked, but his surprise gave way to resolve. He wanted to wipe that spark of shame away. Whatever had happened in her past did not define her, did not mar how beautiful she was inside and out. She was a warrior. His goddess.

"If you're a tart," he whispered, "then what does that make me?"

Her lip curled at the corner. "It's different for a man. You're expected to sow your wild oats, while women are expected to stay at home and cook them."

Thane nibbled at her neck. "That does seem unfair, doesn't it?"

"Why do men have to hold all the power? Is it so hard to want equal footing? To be judged on the same merits and by the same standards?"

He traced her lower lip with his tongue, delving in sweetly, just once. "Tell you what—I won't judge you if you don't judge me. We'll go into this…er…" His mind blanked. *Tupping? Lovemaking?*

"Sexual congress," she supplied helpfully.

Thank God for smart women with fertile vocabularies.

"Yes, that," he agreed. "As equal partners. And if you require more, I will happily hand over all my power to you, Queen Titania, as the matriarch, if you will."

"As provocative an offer as that is, I prefer equals."

Her smile was radiant, and Thane wanted her so badly, it was agony. Worse than any pain he'd ever endured. He meant it, though—in this moment, he existed only for her. He thrust his hips hard, making her eyes widen as an indecent shock of pleasure shot through them both. Astrid bolted into action, nimble fingers releasing him from his breeches and shoving her skirts out of the way to position her body. Her eyes met his, and she worked her tight passage down to the hilt.

Fucking hell.

Thane nearly spent himself then and there.

Hubris and the patriarchy were grossly overrated.

CHAPTER EIGHTEEN

If she wasn't seated in the most exquisite position of her life, Astrid would have laughed at her own absurdity. Here she was, half naked in the arms of a *very* virile man, who happened to be her husband, copulating in a deserted garden in the most magical setting possible, and all she could talk about was women's rights.

Thane didn't seem to mind.

Not now, when his eyes were closed and his head was thrown back, the thickness of him lodged inside her, foreign and pulsing and utterly wonderful. Lord above, he felt good. It had been a tight fit—given it was only her second time—but her body had been ready to ease the way. More than ready. Astrid squirmed slightly, adjusting her position, and he let out a ragged groan. The corded muscles of his neck stood out in stark relief.

"Are you well?" she whispered.

Eyelids parted to reveal stormy golden discs. His jaw was rigid, the muscles in his forearms braced against the stone bench even more so. "Yes, but I'll come if you move."

"Isn't that the point?"

He huffed a laugh. "Equals, remember? This has to be good for you, too. Wouldn't be sporting of me to renege on my promise so quickly, would it?"

This man.

Astrid's chest squeezed. In that moment, she

wanted to give him everything. Her body, her soul, her brain. Her heart. And she wanted all of him in return. But then all conscious thought fled her mind as her husband began to move, his hands grasping handfuls of her hips and lifting her up, withdrawing himself almost to the edge of her body. And then he released her, startling matching moans out of them both, as she hurtled back down for him to fill her again. It was better than the first thrust, now that her body had adjusted to his size.

"Again," she commanded.

He arched an eyebrow at her high-handedness but complied. "Bossy."

"I know what I want, and you're not a mind reader," she said and gasped with pleasure as his body sank home a third and fourth time. "I call it leadership."

"I love the way your brain works." He thrust again. "And I love a woman in control."

She opened her mouth to retort, but his lips closed over hers right then. Astrid sighed into the embrace. He tasted of strength, brandy, and spice. She loved kissing him. He was a formidable man who held nothing back, and his driving passion fed the fire inside her. Part and parcel of him being a captain on the battlefield. It made *her* feel powerful to have a man like him acquiescing to her every want.

His tongue challenged hers, luring it into his mouth and then catching it gently with his teeth. He nibbled at her lips and then sipped from them as if they were something infinitely precious. The sweetness above belied the ferocity below—of him completely and unequivocally possessing her with shorter, more uncontrolled thrusts. The two extremes drove her wild.

"You feel like heaven," he murmured.

He groaned, closing his eyes, his control seeming to slip as his pace increased. Thane's hand slid between them, burrowing under the layers of her skirts to where their bodies were joined. He stroked his thumb gently against the slick bundle of nerves, and Astrid almost fell off the seat as white-hot sensation streaked through her body. He did it again, but this time a delicious roll of his hips accompanied it. And suddenly everything inside her coalesced— every thought, every feeling, every sensation—into one giant ball of tension that made her feel like she was being pulled apart in a thousand different directions.

"Please, Thane, I can't take it…"

"Almost there, love. It's yours."

And then it was. The pressure built blindingly and then shattered, spilling through her in waves and waves of undiluted pleasure. Astrid muffled her scream with his mouth, holding on to his shoulders for all she was worth, her body feeling like a limp noodle, aftershocks quivering through her. Thane drove home once, twice, and then his entire body jerked and went still as he clutched her to him.

"Holy hell," he whispered against her hair.

Astrid bit at her lip, wondering if his paroxysm had been half as ferocious as hers. The thrill of discovery had heightened every illicit second. From the dazed look on his face, she suspected it might have been. "Was that good?"

"Very fucking good." His eyes snapped open at his hasty words. "I'm sorry, I—"

"No, I like it."

His eyebrows launched into his hairline, his lips curling at the corners. "Do you just? What would your dear Ms. Austen say?"

"Ms. Austen, were she still alive, probably would have had some choice words to teach *you*, having to write about such conceited, dull, moody men and their fragile male selves. I'd wager she might have whispered one or two filthy oaths in her time."

He laughed. "I think you may be right."

Astrid kissed the bridge of his marred nose, her finger gently tracing the thick, roped scar that cut across it from his right brow to his left jaw. He was so many extremes, this man. Savage on the outside, a passionate but thoughtful lover on the inside. And he did not make her feel foolish with her unconventional thoughts and ideals.

"We should probably be getting back," he said, ducking free of her light caress.

"Yes."

Neither of them moved, unwilling to go back to the ballroom…and to being newly wedded strangers. In a sense, the masquerade had allowed them to drop their defenses and come together as if the battle between them were on hiatus. But such a truce wasn't meant to last. Lines had been drawn, sides formed. She would go back to being the smart-mouthed bluestocking cataloging his antiques, who had married him for security. He would go back to being the recalcitrant irascible duke. And all would be well with the world.

Thane exhaled, seemingly caught up in his own thoughts, and gathered her close before lifting her gently to set on the bench beside him. Astrid tugged her bodice into place as the duke set himself quickly to rights and removed her a small linen square from his jacket pocket.

"What's that for?" she blurted out and then blushed as he knelt. "Oh, you don't have to do that." But he was already dabbing her sticky thighs.

Thane was frowning when he removed the handkerchief. "I should not have been so careless."

She blinked as she belatedly recalled that he'd withdrawn their first time. "It's fine."

"No, it was foolish." He stood and tucked the linen into his pocket. Astrid's blush heated at the thought of something so intimate and marked with her essence being on his person. "We cannot make this mistake again."

"Mistake?"

He stared at her as if she were dull-witted. "I do not want children, Astrid."

The chill of the evening settled on her shoulders. Or maybe it was a chill blooming from inside her… from a place she'd thought well and truly buried. She hadn't thought of babies with Thane before, but suddenly someone telling her that she wouldn't have a choice in the matter made it seem so final. So absolute. She did not deal well with ultimatums.

Astrid's chin lifted. "And what if *I* want them?"

His lips flattened, and his eyes dimmed to frosty amber. The change in him was swift and remarkable. Ah, there he was—her husband, the detached, black-hearted Duke of Beswick.

"If it's company you seek, a pet will do just as well. Might I suggest a foxhound."

"A foxhound?" she echoed in disbelief.

As if he hadn't just destroyed her with his cruel, awful words, he offered her his arm. "Yes, they're loyal and agreeable animals. Shall we?"

Astrid gathered her pride, wrapped herself in it, and rose. "You're a bastard, Beswick."

• • •

Thane downed yet another glass of whiskey. His fourth. Or fifth, he couldn't recall. He hadn't moved since he'd come back into the Featheringstoke ballroom, holding up an unobtrusive pillar near an alcove and watching his wife.

Queen Titania…holding dominion over her court.

Astrid had been shyly reserved when he'd first arrived, conducting herself as a married duchess would, but now, it was as if the very devil had gotten into her. Every time her laughter rang out, he flinched. Every time he saw her smile, it was a bladed fist to the gut.

She remained within the bounds of propriety for decorum's sake, never dancing with the same partner twice, but she accepted a handful of dances from others, including close friends of his like Thornton and Roth, that made him sick with jealousy, when he had little reason to be jealous. He was the one who'd asked them to be solicitous of her in his stead.

God, it wouldn't be long before she grasped how

trapped she was in this marriage with him, and then she would hate him for it, more than she already did. It was only a matter of time before she realized he didn't deserve her. That she deserved *more*. One of *those* gentlemen. Unscarred. Unbroken. With their soul intact. He never should have let her in, wedded her, *touched* her, and now it was too late.

You're a bastard, Beswick.

She was already pushing him away, wasn't she?

Thane gulped his whiskey and signaled for another.

"You're going to keel over if you keep that up," a soft voice said to his left. "Nephew."

"Aunt," he greeted, turning to kiss the duchess's powdered cheeks, unsurprised that she had recognized him. She'd known him since he was in short pants. "Or should I say, Cleopatra. You look lovely tonight. How did you know it was me?"

"I saw you disappear with your wife." Mischief glimmered in her eyes briefly. "For quite some time. I was about to send out a search party."

Her scolding made Thane feel like a disobedient schoolboy. He'd lost control along with all sense of time, it seemed. They were lucky they hadn't been discovered. The scandal would have been dreadful, worse yet if their identities had been discovered—the Beast of Beswick forcing his beautiful new bride to service him in public view. Because of course, no one would believe she'd been willing. He was much too hideous for anyone to want him.

But Astrid *had* wanted him. Until he'd ruined it with his callous response about children, but that was one topic on which he could not be swayed. No child deserved to have a father like him. Just like no wife deserved him for a husband. And he'd gone and married her anyway.

Mabel frowned at him and followed his gaze. "Astrid is having the time of her life, at least on the surface, if one didn't know her."

"What do you mean?" he asked, catching a glimpse of voluminous white silvery skirts as she twirled past.

"She's your duchess, Thane. The only one she should be enjoying is you, which seemed to be the case until she returned to the ballroom looking quite beautiful, furious, and thoroughly ravished—to the trained eye, that is." She tilted her head. "What did you say to her?"

He scowled softly under his mask and drew his aunt into the quiet alcove behind them. "Why would you think I've said anything to her?"

"Because you're you," she said. "And you're absolutely incapable of not ruining things for yourself."

"She wants children."

"So give her some."

"I cannot." Thane huffed a breath. "And you know why."

If there was anyone who knew more about the self-loathing that filled him, it was Aunt Mabel. She had been there in the years no one else was, not even his father. There when he'd smashed every mirror in the house. When he'd locked himself away for weeks. When he'd screamed and growled at everyone like an animal. She'd stroked his stitched face, soothed his volatile tempers, and loved him anyway.

"A child will love his father no matter what, Thane."

"And what of everyone else?" He wanted to pinch the bridge of his nose between his fingers, to ward off the beginnings of a throbbing headache, but the stupid mask was in the way. His scars had pulled tight with the tension crawling all over his body. "I won't allow any child of mine to be ridiculed. Isn't it bad enough I *married* her and forced her into this?" He gestured to himself. "I'm angry and broken, Aunt. I can't love or let anyone close without hurting them. I don't know how to."

"You let *me* in."

He sighed and scrubbed at his face. "You're different."

"Have you considered that you might be pushing her away before she has a chance to leave you?"

Thane stared at her, fingers curling into fists, the familiar bitterness rising like a volcano inside him. He wasn't the paste that kept things together. He was the club that broke them apart. His darkness owned him, inside and out. People ran from him because he made them. All of his friends—save Roth—Lady Sarah Bolton, and most of his servants. They'd all left.

And Astrid would, too…one day.

Allowing her in would only be setting himself up for heartache. But what was the alternative? Letting her go? *That* he could not fathom.

"I must go," he said tightly. "Forgive me, Aunt. You'll see Astrid home?"

"Of course, dear boy."

• • •

Astrid knew the instant Thane went. It was like a great energy had departed the room—as if he were the sun, and she, some lonely oscillating planet, remained helpless in his gravity. Her false smiles and laughter felt heavy, the weight of them unbearable, but she'd forced herself to dance and converse, even knowing that he stood there, watching. Brooding.

How could he be so heated one moment and so frigid the next?

How could he whisper such tender words and then cut her so deeply?

For a few shared heartbeats out in the garden, he'd been unguarded. He'd let her in. She'd let him in, too. But perhaps it'd been too much too soon for both of them. His scars went way past his skin, breaking him irreparably on the inside.

She couldn't save him. Couldn't fix him.

After the last quadrille, Astrid should have sought out Mabel, but instead, she headed to the re-tiring room, where she patted a length of toweling to her cheeks and stared at her reflection. Her hair was hopelessly mussed, though Queen Titania wouldn't care. Behind her white silk demi-mask, her eyes were overly bright, like two frozen aquamarines in her face, and her lips were still swollen from her husband's kisses. She touched the tip of her index finger to her lower lip, reimagining his caress, the stroke of his tongue, and tore her hand away.

Enough, you dolt.

She turned to leave when a cloud of satin nearly

bowled her over. "Oh God, Astrid, it's so wonderful to see you," Isobel squealed. "We only have a moment. I managed to lose Aunt Mildred in the refreshment room. The woman is like a leech!"

Astrid clutched her sister close, her heart swelling with love and relief, her already chaotic emotions untangling within her.

"How have you been?" she blurted out, pushing Isobel back so she could assess her sister's well-being for herself. Her sister looked…well and happy. She seemed composed. Older, even.

"Good," Isobel said with a bright smile. "Uncle Reggie has commissioned me a whole new wardrobe in the hope I find an acceptable suitor this Season."

"Isobel, you can't trust him," Astrid said with narrowed eyes. "You know how he is. He only wants to control you, and giving you all these things is his way of doing that. I'm sure Beaumont is still sniffing around."

The happy smile faltered. "I'm aware, Astrid. I know it's a bribe."

Astrid huffed a breath. Did she *truly*? She was so guileless, and their uncle only had his own best interests in mind. Not Isobel's or anyone else's. And Beaumont was not to be underestimated, either. She frowned. "Beswick will approve the match when the time comes."

"We don't need the duke. I have everything in hand."

"Please don't be naive, Isobel."

Her sister looked stung. "I'm not a fool."

"No, that's not what I meant," Astrid said,

reaching for her, but Isobel shifted out of the way, her face crumpling. "I think you have a soft heart and you want to believe in the best of everyone, including Uncle." Her voice softened. "Isobel, you're my whole world. I've always looked out for you, and I've always been truthful with you about Beaumont and everything else. I only want you safe, you know that. I want you to come and live with the duke and me at Harte House. The duke is your legal guardian now."

Her sister's blue eyes went dull with something like disappointment. "You've married, then?"

"Yes. You knew that was the plan all along."

Her sister's lips trembled. "But I didn't want you to have to marry him! That was the whole purpose of this." She waved an arm. "Of my coming to London to find a suitor, so you wouldn't have to."

"It doesn't matter now, Izzy. You're safe, and that's all that matters."

"But you're not! You're married to a man you don't even want because of me." Isobel's face filled with despair. "Heavens, I waited too long. I should have come to London weeks ago, and then you wouldn't be caught in this predicament. This is all my fault."

"No, it's not. This is what we had to do."

Astrid pulled her into a hug, but Isobel shook free. "I never wanted this at the expense of your own happiness. Didn't you read my letter? I wanted to do this. For *us*."

She stared at her sister, seeing the frustration and misery sparking in her blue eyes, and her heart tightened with emotion. "I know you did, and I love you for that more than you know. But it's done now. Please come home with me. You'll be safe under Beswick's protection. You can have a real Season, and you won't have to worry about Beaumont."

The offer hung between them, but then Isobel shook her head, a determined gaze meeting hers. "No, I wish to stay with Uncle Reggie and Aunt Mildred."

"Izzy—"

"Please, Astrid," she said, a stubborn note in her voice. "If you and the duke are newly married, my place isn't with you, at least not right now. I will be all right for the rest of the Season. You needn't worry about me."

"It's not safe," Astrid said. "I must insist."

"No, sister, I'm where I should be." Isobel smiled softly and kissed her on the cheek. "I have to go. Aunt Mildred will be looking for me." She squeezed Astrid's hands and stood, a grown-up, confident angel. "I love you, Astrid, no matter what happens, but you have to let me go. I need to spread my own wings. Find my own future. And you need to take care of *you* for once. Find the happiness you deserve, and if that's with Beswick, then so be it." She walked toward the door and paused, her expression wry. "Even with his rotten temper. I tried to prevent you from marrying him for my sake, but deep down, I think he might truly care about you."

Astrid didn't bother to correct her sister that Beswick's idea of caring was tantamount to getting a dog. She swallowed the rush of bitterness. But the minute the door closed behind Isobel, Astrid sank into a nearby chair. Everything was spiraling out of control…Beswick, Isobel, her marriage, and there seemed to be not a damn thing she could do about any of it.

And to top it off, she was on the brink of losing the only family she had left.

CHAPTER NINETEEN

Thane stopped at his wife's bedroom door, his hand raised. He hadn't seen her in days. Not for meals, not in passing. God, he'd made a mess of things. The guilt struck him like the lash from a whip. Following his explosion of temper, the shame of his actions had kept him closeted in his study, focused on work. The good thing was that his estates were in pristine order. His marriage, however, was another matter entirely.

Thane scrubbed a hand through his hair and knocked.

"Enter."

He pushed open the door, and his wife's guarded eyes met his.

"May we speak?"

Astrid was freshly scrubbed from her bath, her damp hair curling around her face. She wore a clean nightgown and a loosely tied robe over it. Her lips parted on a guarded sigh. "If you insist." She tightened her arms about herself in a protective gesture that made him ache. "Though I'm still recovering from our last conversation."

Wincing, Thane stepped into her chamber and shut the door behind him, the fresh scent of her filling his nostrils. They stared at each other in silence, so many things between them needing to be said. He knew that he'd hurt her unconscionably. He cleared his throat, forging ahead before he could change his mind.

"Astrid, I want to apologize for what I said the other night…about children. That wasn't fair." He hesitated, seeing the instant tightening of her lips. "I… You took me by surprise."

"What do you mean?" she asked.

He searched for the right words to make her understand. "What happened with you and me and then talk of children. It was too much, too fast." He fumbled with his words, his heart clenching and unclenching in painful lurches. "You're passionate and courageous and beautiful and everything any man could want. The thing is, I'm not worthy of you, and one day, you'll come to your senses, and you'll want more. And I won't be able to give it to you."

"So you're pushing me away, is that it?"

He shook his head, hands reaching for her and then falling away. "I'm protecting you, Astrid."

"From what?"

"From *me*, damn it. Look at me! Who in their right mind would want to be saddled with this? I'm a beast on the inside, too. I lash out at people. Hurt them."

Gutted, he blew out his breath, his heart pounding like a hurricane against his rib cage. His throat ached, his brain ached, his fucking useless heart *ached*. Never had Thane wanted to hide so badly. He wanted to run back to Beswick Park and shut the world out. Shut *her* out. Forget how it felt to feel, how much it hurt to let anyone in. Because now he was paying the piper for not leaving well enough alone.

For not staying in the darkness where he belonged.

"I am looking," she said gently. "I'm not blind, Thane. I see you very well. And you'd never hurt me."

"Not intentionally," he murmured. Those eyes of hers were slaying him…stripping him bare until he couldn't hide. He wanted to lash out. "Don't pity me, Astrid."

"You think what I feel is *pity*?" Her voice rose, her eyes flashing blue fire as they narrowed on him. The look on her face could only be described as incredulous, and for the barest of seconds, Thane felt like he'd entered a minefield wearing a blindfold. "Do you think what happened in the garden was a joke? That it meant nothing to me? Do you think I gave myself to you on our wedding night because I was afraid of you or felt *sorry* for you?"

He flinched, the sentiments hitting too close to home. He sealed his lips together from admitting those very truths, from baring his soul. "Then, why did you?"

She held his gaze. "It was because I wanted *you*, you daft, oblivious man."

"What about the future?"

"What of it?" She shrugged.

"What if—?"

His wife placed a finger on his lips, silencing him. "If there's one thing I've learned it's that what-ifs are dangerous, nasty little beasts."

"But—"

"But nothing." She pushed to her toes and kissed him softly, her voice dropping to a velvety whisper. "I'm here now. You're here now. Thank you for your apology. I'm *yours* for the taking, my lord duke. So what are you going to do about it?"

• • •

Everything froze, her husband's arrested gaze meeting hers.

Astrid's face was on fire. Never in her life had she been so bold, so *shameless* in her demands. He wasn't unaffected from her nearness, she saw. His hands shook, fisted at his sides as they were, as if it took everything in his power to keep from touching her. She didn't have to look down to see the prominent ridge in his trousers.

"I want you," she said simply. His eyes lit with desire, and she reached for boldness, knowing he liked it. She did, too. "If you wish me to be more explicit, Your Grace, I want coitus. Sexual congress."

"Astrid," he warned, those gorgeous golden eyes dilating with lust. A muscle flexed in his scarred jaw.

"Coupling. Tupping. Sex. *Fucking*," she went on, face aflame and licking her lower lip with what she hoped was a sultry look.

He scooped her up so fast that her breath caught. "You have a dirty mouth, Lady Beswick."

"Then give it something to do."

She bit at the tendon on his shoulder, making him growl. The carnal, lust-filled sound made her body hum with arousal. Astrid yanked up her night rail and hitched her legs around his waist, her wrapper falling open, the heart of her abrading deliciously against his clothing and rock-hard abdominal muscles. Desire pulsed through her as he squeezed her rear and hoisted her higher. She gasped at the scrape of his waistcoat.

Groaning, he bit her lobe. "Your bed or mine?"

"Yours. I want to be surrounded by you."

In his bedchamber, Fletcher had left one candle burning, which Thane extinguished on his way to the massive bed. It made her heart twinge, but Astrid didn't mind the darkness. There was safety in it. She understood why Thane needed it with his scarring. And the truth was, she was too afraid of what would be written all over her, what he would be able to see in her eyes.

He wanted to hide his body. She needed to hide her heart.

Scooting to the middle of the enormous bed, Astrid heard the rustle as he shucked out of his clothing. Buckets of desire sluiced down her spine, her anticipation heightening with every sound. Without sight, her other senses were amplified a hundredfold. The mattress dipped as Thane joined her. Warm hands caressed her soles, sending shivery bolts of heat up her entire body.

He licked at her breasts, drawing one nipple into his mouth and sucking. Her entire body shuddered with arousal as he paid patient, decadent homage to the other. "As are you, Your Grace." She smiled in the darkness. "I'm constantly confounded by the fact that your mouth is so…gifted."

She felt his answering grin. "This is only the beginning, darling."

"Confident, too."

"I am a duke," he rumbled. "We are an impressive bunch; ask any one of us."

Astrid wanted to laugh but gasped instead as he pressed that *very* impressive male part against her sensitive sex in response and circled his lean hips in a slow, teasing motion. Her hands, which hadn't been able to explore before, grasped his shoulders, dragging him down to her for a hot, open-mouthed kiss. She gloried in the feel of his body as he draped himself over her. His chest hair abraded her breasts with delightful friction, and she arched her spine, rubbing her hard nipples against him.

"You feel so good," he groaned.

"As do you."

Curious, her fingers wandered over his ruined back and side, and though she felt every rise and bump of his tortured skin, Astrid was careful not to pause. Sorrow and pity surged through her. She wished she could kiss every scar and heal him from the inside out, but she settled for palming every bare inch of him. She marveled at the expanse of his shoulders, savored the long channel of his spine, and delighted in the two wicked indents above his taut buttocks.

Grinning to herself, she grasped his rear at the same time that she brought her knees up to grip his hips. They both gasped at the intimate position.

"Fill me," she ordered in a hoarse voice.

And he did.

• • •

His darling wife was going to kill him.

The smart, beautiful, hot-mouthed little harpy who had upended his world and boldly challenged him on every level. Astrid's natural passion astounded him. Humbled him. And she held nothing back, giving herself wholly and unconditionally, a gift in itself.

The velvet cling of her was exquisite torture, the scent and taste of her combining to make him nonsensical. He'd been in a constant state of arousal from the moment he'd seen her fresh and rosy from her bath. Thankfully, she had wanted him as much as he wanted her.

And now, the feel of her warm, luscious, willing form conspired against years of discipline and experience. Lodged deep, his cock throbbed. Slowly, he inched backward, feeling the soft hug of her passage as she unwillingly relinquished him. Thane swallowed hard, every muscle coiled with tension as he eased back in with a groan.

"I love how you feel inside me," she whispered. "You're my missing piece."

He almost came then. Her words had the power to do that to him, he was discovering. "And you're mine."

His frenzied heart echoed his thoughts: *Mine. Mine. Mine.*

Thane withdrew and plunged forward again, his rhythm gathering speed. He could feel her knees gripping his hips, her hands digging into his shoulders as she met him thrust for thrust. She sought his lips, and he gave them to her, delighting in the hot plunge of her tongue and the assertive way it twined about his. Her movements grew jerkier as she neared her peak.

"Yes, sweetheart, come for me."

"Thane," she cried out, her head falling back as she was gripped in orgasm.

Driving deep, he was quick to follow as her inner muscles clamped down and pulsed around his cock. His ballocks tightened, and pleasure spiked through him as he yanked backward, pulling himself from her sheath at the last minute before his brain went blank. His seed spurted against her belly, and with a guttural shout, he collapsed against her, breathing hard.

Not wanting to crush her, Thane shifted them both to the side, holding her damp body close. His replete senses slowly came back to reality. Thane gave his wife a gentle kiss on the lips, his mouth unerringly finding hers in the darkness. Astrid didn't say anything, but he could feel her mind turning at his withdrawal. He didn't want to spoil what they'd just shared.

After a moment, he rose naked and walked to the bathing chamber to retrieve a pitcher of luke-warm water and a cloth. Thane didn't need a candle to light his way—he was accustomed to moving around in the darkness. His eyes had adjusted enough to make out Astrid's lean shape on the bed. Gently, he washed the stickiness from her belly and her thighs.

"Do you wish to stay here or return to your chamber?" he asked when he was finished seeing to himself.

"Here," she said after several heartbeats.

Inside, Thane was strangely glad. Strange, because in the past after sex, he never wanted to linger. Either he or the women left, depending on location. It was a physical release at best. But with Astrid, everything was different. He climbed back into bed and pulled the sheets over them. Thane gathered her close, pulling the back of her body into the front of his. She fit him perfectly, her rounded bottom nestling sweetly into the cradle of his hips.

After a beat, Astrid turned in his arms to face him. Though they could only see silhouettes in the shadows, Thane still tensed. As if she could sense his discomfort, she soothed him with a few caresses of her palm along the roughened skin of his right shoulder blade, and Thane was astounded at her discernment and care. After what she'd been through, *she* was comforting *him*. His chest tightened painfully.

This rare, clever, passionate, brave woman.

She was everything.

Thane stilled, his heart stuttering and then resuming its steady cadence with startling clarity. The realization was a lightning shock to his system, as if he'd been dead and was suddenly, *brilliantly* brought back to life. He curved himself around her, enfolding her with all his strength, telling her with his body what he could not say with his mouth.

What he could never say.

CHAPTER TWENTY

"Astrid. Gracious, Astrid, are you well?"

At the sharp poke in her ribs, she blinked and startled, Aunt Mabel's concerned face coming into focus. "Yes, yes, of course. I was lost in thought."

Mabel shot her a shrewd look. "Daydreaming about a certain duke, perhaps?"

She felt her cheeks heat. "Thinking about Isobel, actually."

It wasn't exactly an untruth. She *had* been thinking about her sister, at least until thoughts of Beswick had crowded her brain. The wicked man had made her more than fashionably late after he'd removed every stitch of clothing that poor Alice had painstakingly laced and fastened for her outing to the theater. Buttons had been ripped and fabric torn in their haste to devour each other's bodies, but Astrid hadn't regretted a minute of it. Nor had he, clearly.

It was the reason she had missed most the first act of the play.

And it was probably the reason behind Mabel's thoroughly gleeful smile.

Astrid shook her head. The only reason she'd come to the theater was because Isobel was in attendance. She was still struggling with her sister's newfound independence and the fact that Isobel seemed to be thriving. Despite being in the earl's private box with their aunt and uncle, Isobel had continued to seem cheerful and at ease, giving no indication that anything foul was underfoot.

She had met her uncle's glance once, but he had inclined his head politely with no hint of rancor on his face, which made her even more convinced that he was up to no good. Her uncle had always viewed her as an obstacle when it came to Isobel, and offering his sheltered niece some independence had been a brilliant move. If the unthinkable happened, where Isobel somehow chose Beaumont of her own free will and *wanted* to marry the man, there would be little Astrid could do. Short of losing her sister forever.

"Shall we take a turn about the foyer, dear?" Mabel suggested as intermission began. "Lord, but I haven't been to the theater in an age. It makes one work up quite a thirst!"

Astrid would wager that the duchess's thirst was a result of the scandalously dressed actors carousing onstage. She'd been surprised that her uncle had allowed Isobel to attend this particular play, given its bawdy reputation, but with the man, everything was calculated. Perhaps a play like this would make Isobel feel more worldly. In other circumstances, Astrid would have appreciated the over-the-top humor, but she was too preoccupied by her uncle's motives.

"Beswick should be here," Mabel commented.

Astrid sent the duchess a dry look. "You know he would choose torture over appearing at any of these affairs."

"He attended that masquerade," the duchess said with a sly smile. "And don't think I don't know what's going on between the two of you, even for your supposed marriage in name only. He should be here at your side."

Astrid's cheeks were on fire. Dear God. Did *everyone* in the house know?

"That will never happen," she said. "The truth is, I am grateful for your company, Aunt Mabel, especially in the duke's absence. It's good to feel not so alone, so…exposed."

What she meant was facing the wolves as the new Duchess of Beswick. After the masquerade, the *ton* had been afire with the gossip that the reclusive duke had married. And Astrid came with her own fair share of scandal as well. Suffice it to say that the gossip was not exactly kind, not that it ever was.

Some of Astrid's despair must have bled through, because the duchess cocked her head, a sliver of worry skating across her face. "How is he?"

It was a simply worded, if loaded, question. The truth was, Astrid didn't know. Her husband had laughed at the drawings in the gossip rags, depicting him as a monstrous creature devouring his grasping, greedy opportunist of a bride with a fistful of money in her hand. The overt malice had horrified Astrid. The accompanying editorials weren't any more flattering. Apparently, a beast of a duke and a shrew of a spinster were too good to pass up.

"How do you deal with this?" she'd asked Thane when yet another awful parody had hit newsstands.

"Ignore it," he'd said. "They'll move on to something else soon."

But Astrid hadn't missed the flicker of contempt that had couched his words.

Notwithstanding the gossip, the physical side of things was pleasant—more than pleasant—but Astrid couldn't help feeling that Thane still kept a large part of himself locked away. He kept people at arm's length on purpose, never letting anyone in. Her glance slid to the duchess. Well, except Mabel, it seemed. Thane had built himself a dungeon that didn't have room for anyone else.

Astrid decided to confide in Mabel. "He thinks I'll leave him."

The duchess nodded. "Not surprising. That boy has been through hell. So many have left, others he's pushed away."

"But not you?"

Mabel smiled. "Oh, he tried. He can be excessively cruel, but it comes from a place of hurt. He wears the scars we see, but it's the invisible ones that cause the most damage." She drew a breath, her expression somber. "Deep down, he doesn't feel he deserves happiness. So he pushes everyone away. He's twisted himself so much that he can't recognize when something good is right in front of him."

Astrid remained silent, though she'd suspected the same…that the duke would never allow himself to get close to anyone. Not even her.

"I've had many loves and lovers in my lifetime," Mabel went on. "And I see you two together. You fight, you flirt, you—" She broke off with a soft puff of laughter. "Well, we both know what else you're doing. You're in love with him, aren't you?"

Astrid's breath left her in an erratic burst, a thousand denials rising to her lips. What she felt was complicated, and she didn't think it was love. "I…I care for him, I do. But I can't afford to lose my heart, not when there's a chance he won't risk his."

"He will, given the opportunity." Her voice went whisper soft. "I think Thane is in deep, otherwise he wouldn't be fighting you so hard. He's lost, and he needs you more than he knows. Don't give up on him, Astrid. Please."

Her throat was clogged. "You can't force someone to care, no matter how much you wish them to."

"Try for my sake." The duchess smiled brightly, as if she hadn't just begged Astrid to do the impossible, as if she hadn't just laid her own soul bare. "Why don't we find ourselves some refreshment?"

Mabel rose, tucking Astrid's hand in her arm, and went to exit the box. Once the curtains parted, however, they were instantly bombarded by curious acquaintances who, no doubt, wanted to see Beswick's new duchess for themselves. Astrid balked. Oh God, she couldn't do this, not now…but there was no escape.

"Courage, dear," Mabel whispered, giving her hand a squeeze. "Show no fear or they'll sense it like the sharks they are."

Astrid fortified herself, taking her cue from Mabel and smiling like her life depended on it. For better or for worse, she was the Duchess of Beswick.

"Your Grace, you sneaky minx, why don't you introduce us to your beautiful companion?" one tall gentleman drawled.

"Goodness, Lady Verne, where have you been hiding?" another voice asked, a woman whom Astrid did not recognize.

A handsome older man reached for Astrid's

knuckles, bowing over them. "Who, pray tell, Duchess, is this charming creature?"

The rest of them stared unabashedly at her.

"Someone fetch me a glass of Madeira before I expire," Mabel said with a quick slash of her fan. "And then I will humor you lot with introductions."

Once the Madeira was procured—one for Astrid as well—Mabel tugged her forward to their small but rapt audience. Astrid felt a queasiness low in her stomach. No one would know who she was unless they remembered the scandal from a decade ago, and now she was married to a notorious recluse.

"Allow me to present, informally of course, the new Duchess of Beswick, Lady Astrid Harte."

The gasps were intermingled with congratulatory wishes amid remarks about her beauty and rumors over the duke's savaged appearance, and then the questions began in earnest. Astrid shrank back, but not before she saw one woman whisper to another and then another. The word "beast" filtered through, making Astrid bristle. In a few minutes, everyone at the theater would know that the wife of the Beast of Beswick was in attendance. Thanks to the newssheets, the unfortunate moniker had reached London as well.

The noise rose, a man's voice announcing the start of the third act of the play, but Astrid stood rooted to the spot, feeling the weight of dozens of eyes upon her. She held her chin high, staring down anyone who dared meet her eyes. She was a duchess, wife to a peer of the realm. Let them stare.

"Tell us, my lady," a man's voice drawled, "was it a marriage of convenience?"

The voice was nauseatingly familiar. Beaumont appeared with Isobel on his arm. Astrid held her calm, though she wanted to claw him away from her sister with her bare hands.

"The proper address for someone of my rank, Lord Beaumont, is *Your Grace*," she corrected coolly. "And aren't most marriages of the *ton* ones of convenience or, more importantly, alliance?"

The emphasis on "alliance" was not lost. Not on the earl or on her aunt and uncle who rode his coattails. Beaumont's face darkened, but his lips curled with disdain. "It would take a lot more than that for most women to marry the Beast of Beswick."

Astrid laughed, knowing she was under the scrutiny of many, though she took comfort from Mabel standing at her side. "You are correct, Lord Beaumont. Those things are called honor and respect, two principles you will never possess. Good day, sir." She sent a soft smile to her sister. "Isobel, don't you look lovely. Enjoy the rest of the performance."

Astrid forced herself to walk away, despite Isobel. Her battle was with Beaumont, not with her sister. And she needed to prove to Isobel that she wasn't the overbearing, jealous older sister her aunt and uncle were painting her as. It was, by far, the hardest thing she'd ever done—abandoning her sister to the wolves.

"Bravissimo," Mabel murmured, eyes flashing with pride when they returned to the privacy of their box.

"She's so young."

"Darling, if she's anything like you, I'd say you have nothing to worry about."

Astrid searched the duchess's eyes, finding nothing there but admiration. "Surely you must have heard of my connection with that odious man. If Isobel is anything like I was then, meaning starry-eyed and stupid, then I do have cause to worry. I've left her with the wolves."

She attempted to compose herself, not unmindful of the attention flocking toward their box from the rest of the theater. Gossip traveled fast. Titillating gossip, even faster. After the altercation with Beaumont, people would be putting the connections together.

Astrid Everleigh—ruined heiress.

Astrid Harte—Duchess of Beswick.

Both impostors.

"You're forgetting one thing, dear," Mabel said.

"What is that?"

The duchess smiled gleefully. "Lady Isobel grew up with *you* as a role model…as a self-reliant female for the past ten years. You don't think any of that has rubbed off? She may be consorting with the wolves, that is true, but have a little faith."

"I wish it were that easy."

She patted Astrid's arm. "Then, focus on something else. Like the auction you have planned. Last I heard, *everyone's* coming."

Like *that* was better?

Astrid's stomach fluttered at the thought of the auction that was scheduled for the next day, but her nerves crackled with excitement. She had no idea how it would go or whether it would be the rousing success she hoped for, but Astrid knew her antiquities, and she was confident in her proficiency. She might be worried about Isobel and her own new status as a duchess, but there were two things that never failed her…knowledge and preparation.

And in this, she had both.

• • •

The teeming auction at Christie's had gone off without a hitch, thanks to Thane's very clever, very competent duchess. Thane had never felt prouder, standing in the shadows and watching from the private balcony, when the Duchess of Beswick was publicly and profusely thanked by the owner of the auction house. The total monies the collection had fetched was astronomical…and every extra cent of it was going toward a gift for his wife. He grinned, not that she knew about it yet.

"I'll miss cricket," he told Fletcher, who stood beside him.

The valet shot him a dry stare. "I'll buy you a ball like the normal children."

"Where's the fun in that? Doesn't quite give the same satisfaction to not hear that crashing sound or imagine my father's reaction," Thane grumbled, but he clapped an arm over the man's shoulder. "You did a good thing, Fletch. With the collection and with her."

"Do I get an increase in my wages?"

"I already pay you a king's ransom, you ingrate." Thane rolled his eyes. "That reminds me, I haven't dismissed you yet this week, so tread lightly. I'll be waiting in the coach, if you could be so kind as to retrieve my duchess." He took the private staircase to the waiting conveyance at the side of the building.

In the confines of the carriage, Thane removed the heavy metal key from his pocket and felt a shiver of apprehension at the sight of it in his fingers. He was nervous. He couldn't remember the last time he'd given anyone a gift, and here he was, about to embarrass himself with the largest gift ever given. She wouldn't accept, and he'd look a fool.

The coach door opened, and the footman assisted his wife inside. Astrid was glowing as she took the seat opposite him. "Did you see?" she asked breathlessly.

"Yes."

"Thank you for coming," she said, her lovely face earnest. "I know these public events can be taxing."

Thane grinned at her and rapped on the roof for them to be away. "I wouldn't have missed it for the world."

"Well, thank you." A satisfied smile on her face, she stared out the window at the evening crowds, most of them leaving the auction house. "All of those pieces have found good homes. Your father would be happy."

"My father can rot in hell," he said and then bit his lip. He didn't want to ruin her good humor with unpleasant feelings about the former duke. His father deserved to have every single one of those antiques smashed and destroyed without a qualm, just as he'd destroyed Astrid's hopes for her future. Thane cleared his throat. "Speaking of good homes," he began. "I have a present for you."

"A present? For me?" Her sparkling eyes went wide with childlike delight. "What is it?"

His chest feeling oddly tight, Thane handed her the key. "This is part of it."

"A key." She laughed, her eyes brightening. "To your heart?"

Said organ squeezed painfully in his chest, but from the smile on her lips, she was teasing.

"Good God, if I'm ever that sentimental, put me out of my misery." He drew a breath, feeling self-conscious. "I've bought some property with the proceeds from the auction, three connected buildings in Northern London. I was thinking you could use it for a school to educate young girls or a place for young women who have limited prospects to find new ones. A safe space."

Astrid went still, her eyes boring into his, mouth falling open in surprise. "You bought me a building."

"Several buildings, but yes."

"With the proceeds," she said faintly.

"The rest of the money is placed in an account for you to use at your discretion, but yes, all of it is yours to allocate as you see fit."

Her eyes filled with tears. "Oh, Thane."

His smile swayed at the expression in them. "Print some pamphlets. Start an unorthodox revolution. Hire female assassins to hunt Beaumont to the ends of the earth. I don't care as long as you're happy."

His wife launched herself across the carriage into his arms, and then her mouth was on his, hot and sweet and divine. "You dreadful, underhanded man," she said between kisses that she peppered on his face. "Why do you do these things?"

"To make you happy?"

Astrid pulled back, her hands cupping his cheeks, scars and all. He wanted to nuzzle into them like a cat begging to be stroked. Her hands on him felt like a balm, like a benediction. "This is the most wonderful thing anyone has ever done for me. Oh, Thane, it's perfect." She burst into tears. "It's not fair."

"Why?" he asked, bewildered.

"You're making me like you, and I hate it."

"You don't want to like me?" He brushed at her tears.

She sniffed and buried her face in his neck. "No. I want you to go back to being the intractable Beast of Beswick."

"I'm still a beast; look at me."

"I am looking." She lifted glimmering ice-blue eyes to his, the melting desire in them making his body come to instant attention. "Thane," she whispered, "take me home."

He set his mouth to hers, filling his palms with her body…the long muscles of her slender back beneath her cloak, the soft tendrils of hair escaping her coiffure at her nape, the rounded curve of her hip. He squeezed her rump, and she moaned into his mouth.

"God, how I want you," he said thickly.

And he did. Thane wanted to bury himself into her sweet welcoming depths, make her cry out in the heat of passion, lick the sweat from her skin in the aftermath. Kiss her softly. Watch her fall asleep. Hold her. Never let go.

Astrid reached one hand down between them, stroking his hard length boldly and making him so hard, it hurt. "Don't, darling. I can't seem to control myself around you."

"I like when you lose yourself," the minx whispered to him, biting at his lobe and swirling her hot tongue over the shell of his ear. Her mouth found his again, and for a moment he lost himself completely in the feel of her...her taste, her texture, her provocative little noises.

By the time the carriage rolled to a stop at Harte House, they were both panting intensely. They stared at each other and burst out laughing at the same time. Astrid smoothed his disheveled hair, while he ran his palms along hers. They exchanged another kiss when he arranged the folds of her cloak and she adjusted his cravat, only breaking apart when the footman opened the door.

Astrid bit her lip, looking chagrined, but Thane just laughed and escorted his duchess down the steps. "Trust me, love, if you could look desirable when you're shockingly in your cups, a disarranged coiffure won't detract from your beauty."

"The things you say, Lord Beswick." Blushing, she squeezed his arm and rose up on tiptoe as they ascended the steps to the house. "Won't you take me to bed, Your Grace?"

His bold wife shrieked as Thane scooped her up into his arms. "With pleasure."

"Don't drop me!"

"Never."

He'd castrate himself before she came to any hurt at his hands.

CHAPTER TWENTY-ONE

Thane had hoped his epiphany of folly would disappear—that what he started feeling for Astrid had been some emotional consequence of lust—but it only became more fully realized the more time he spent with her. Watching the blushing smile on her lips at the breakfast table the next morning made him feel like a conquering king. Though he usually slept in the nude when he was alone, he'd risen early to don a never-used silk nightshirt and tailored loose trousers before climbing back into bed. He hadn't wanted to be caught unawares in the bright light of day.

Feeling his scars at night and seeing them in daylight were two different things.

Given how he felt about them, it terrified him to think of what her reaction would be. His back and legs were much worse than his face. The bayonets had done the most damage to his back, and several of the deeper gouges had gone septic. It'd been a miracle that he'd even survived the weeks of unrelenting fever and madness, followed by excruciating cautery, and what was left of his body was proof of the horror he'd endured. The only answer would be to never let his wife see him.

Which meant that he could not continue to tempt fate.

Not without severe risk.

"Today looks like it will be raining again...a pity,

as I'd hoped to go shopping for a new spencer," his aunt declared, daintily lathering a piece of buttered toast with jam, her eyes cutting between them. "What are your plans?"

Thane cleared his throat. "I am meeting with Sir Thornton as well as the steward from my northern estates."

"Oh yes," she said, frowning. "I also heard from Culbert that you received some unwelcome news."

Astrid looked up, the instant inquiry in her eyes. Thane hadn't had a chance to speak to her about the missive that had been delivered that morning with his usual correspondence. "Beaumont has formally declared his intention to court Isobel."

"What does that mean?" Astrid asked.

"That an offer is forthcoming, one that I will be tasked to consider."

"He is a scapegrace," Aunt Mabel said. "He's a poor candidate indeed, not for someone as lovely as that child. I hope you plan to reject the bounder."

"Yes," he and Astrid replied at the same time.

He sent her a small smile, one he knew was not missed by his eagle-eyed aunt. "I fear that it won't discourage him, however. The Everleighs have some underhanded agreement with the man, and the earl has somehow curried the favor of the Prince Regent to attempt to overturn the terms of Astrid's father's will."

"With Prinny?" Mabel asked. "And what kind of agreement?"

"They keep Isobel's portion," Astrid said. "The earl isn't lacking in fortune. He only wants her. It's nothing more than a sale, a transaction."

Thane nodded. "And Beaumont's uncle, the previous earl, was favored at court. I can only assume he hopes to use his late uncle's reputation to shore up his own."

The duchess shook her head. "Appalling. Though such tactics seem extreme even for Beaumont."

"I suspect it's related to his feelings about Astrid," Thane said, feeling the rage burn inside him. "She humiliated him, and he's nurtured that feeling for years. Of course, it's no small consolation that Isobel is as beautiful as her sister."

His wife blushed, though a fierce expression remained on her face. "He's a snake."

"That we can agree on, dear," Mabel said. "Though Beaumont is not to be underestimated. We need a strategy to find Isobel another acceptable suitor. Are there any she might deem an appropriate match? We do want her to be happy, after all."

Astrid drummed her fingers on the table. "Agatha writes that she will be at the opera four days hence. Perhaps we can ask her then."

"Then I suggest we marshal our forces." The duchess turned to him. "Beswick, I assume your box is still available?"

Thane nodded. He never used any of his various boxes but retained them nonetheless. It wouldn't do for the Duke of Beswick not to have one, even if he abhorred the society that had shunned him. "I will be there as well."

Two gazes converged on him with shock.

"Are you feeling well, Beswick?" his aunt asked.

"Quite," he responded dryly. "You needn't look so aghast at the prospect. I have been to an opera or two, and my box is quite secluded."

"I was certainly not aghast," she said with an equally dry look in his direction. "Perhaps I will situate my efforts elsewhere. I shall ask Lady Featheringstoke to accompany her, since her box is situated besides the Earl of Beaumont's where I suspect our little diamond and your unfortunate relatives will be." Her mouth curled into a delighted smirk as she addressed Astrid. "There, I shall make an absolute cake of myself and give you the chance to speak with your sister."

"You have thought this through, Aunt," Thane said.

"When one is my age, dear, it pays to be prepared."

• • •

The night of the opera came swiftly. For the evening, Astrid selected a lavender silk gown, with a square bodice embroidered with pale-green lace, with sleeves that came to her elbows. It was one of the bolts of fabric her husband had selected when Madame Pinot had fitted her. The fabric molded to her figure, and the color brought out the violet hints in her eyes.

Astrid had to admit that Thane had exceptional taste.

When she thought of his kindness after the auction and the extravagant gift he'd given her, she'd been overwhelmed. No one—certainly no man—had ever understood her so well. The gift had meant more to her than the crown jewels. And then that same night, he'd made love to her so tenderly that she'd nearly wept. Her own vulnerability where he was concerned made her terrified, and a part of her warned constantly for her to protect her heart.

She had a feeling it was already much too late.

As Alice put the last few touches on Astrid's coiffure, she descended the staircase to where the duke was waiting. Mabel had left earlier to meet with the Featheringstokes, as arranged. Astrid found him in his study, poring over an open ledger book. She was glad for the chance to study him unobserved. Dressed head to toe in midnight blue, with a similar toned waistcoat and snowy white cravat, he made her breath catch. The candlelight flickered on his sable hair, glinting gold in the lock that curled into his brow and limning his profile in gold. He seemed almost fantastical, a man half made of shadow, half made of flesh.

Lord above, but he made her heart flutter.

Astrid exhaled, and he looked up, their eyes colliding for an inexorable moment before he moved, his lion's gaze scanning her from bodice to hem, lingering on the creamy expanse of décolletage revealed by the gown, her cinched-in waist, and the elbow-length white kidskin gloves that covered her hands. After an eternity, his gaze lifted to hers once more. His cheeks had grown ruddy, his eyes glazed, and when he spoke, his voice was gravelly. "There's no word in the history of language to describe how beautiful you are."

Astrid blushed, her cheeks going dangerously hot. "Thank you, Your Grace, you look incredibly handsome."

"That's one I haven't heard in a while." Thane's lip curled in ironic humor, and Astrid felt a stab in the vicinity of her chest. Did he think she would be so callous as to be glib? That she'd meant it in jest? Surely he did not think her so heartless?

"I was sincere."

"Perhaps we should leave it at well-heeled, Duchess." His laugh was hollow. "Money, you see, can purchase clothing so exorbitantly expensive that it's designed to distract from a beastly face. Or that's what the tailor says anyway."

After his heartfelt compliment, the biting sarcasm took her by surprise. She did not know what had suddenly set him off, and she didn't wish to encourage him or become the target of his capricious moods. "Good thing you have lots of it, then," she said mildly. "We are already late. Shall we go?"

"Of course, though later is better for an arrival."

When most of the other guests would already be seated, Astrid realized.

In the foyer, where Culbert retrieved their cloaks, she eyed the duke over her shoulder. His eyes had been fastened on the breadth of bare skin at her back, the neckline of the dress dipping scandalously low on her spine into a V shape. Astrid's skin felt singed just from the burn of his stare. Female satisfaction licked through her as his greedy gaze chased the knots of her spine until they disappeared.

"Do you like my dress?" she asked, hiding her smile. "Madame Pinot informed me that you selected the fabric and color."

He inhaled a shuddering breath and dragged his hot gaze away. "Fabric that was meant to cover you," he said with a scowl.

"It is of her own design. Clever, no?"

"That woman is a heretic and should not be allowed near a pair of scissors."

"Come now, Beswick, surely you're not turning into a prudish fusspot in your dotage?"

"Did you just call me a…a…*fusspot*?"

Astrid laughed as he helped her into the coach. "If the shoe fits."

She'd hoped to make him laugh, tease him a bit, but her hope had been in vain. As he entered the coach, his mouth flattened into a hard white line, and his jaw went rigid. It looked like he'd gone somewhere else in his head. Somewhere dark. A muscle in his cheek took up residence, flexing frantically, a sheen of sweat coating his brow. His gloved fists were clenched on his knees, his posture as stiff as a ship's mast as the carriage rolled into motion.

"Thane, what's the matter? Are you well?"

"Yes," he bit out without looking at her.

"*Thane.*"

"Not now, Astrid. Pray let us get through this evening without incident."

She fell silent, seeing his struggle for what it was. He was beyond panicked. Not to compare him to a horse, but it was much the same as when Brutus reacted to a crop. The duke was stiff with terror. Sure, it was in a private box with a private entrance that he paid handsomely for, but it was out in public nonetheless. A gargantuan feat, clearly, for him.

"You don't have to do this."

Stone-jawed, he flared his nostrils. "Leave it. I'm here."

The rest of the short journey to Covent Garden passed in silence, and when they arrived, they were indeed whisked through a private narrow hallway to the Duke of Beswick's box. It was unlit but for the light that came from elsewhere. The production had already begun, so they sat quietly and quickly to avoid drawing undue attention. Astrid noticed that all the boxes on either side of theirs were empty.

Thane saw her stare. "I bought them all."

She didn't even want to think of what that would have cost. The duke did not put a price on privacy.

"Beaumont's box is over there," he said in a tight voice.

Astrid reached for her lorgnettes and held them up to her eyes. Her sister, Isobel, was indeed in Beaumont's box a few levels down. However, their aunt and uncle were not. Upon further scrutiny, she saw that the earl and her sister weren't quite alone. Agatha, God bless her, sat toward the back. She was only a maid, but Astrid breathed a sigh of relief.

Astrid scanned the other boxes, and true to her word, Aunt Mabel sat in the section adjacent to them. Opening her fan, the duchess's glance flicked upward unobtrusively over its lace edge, and Astrid nodded back.

Time for the games to begin.

CHAPTER TWENTY-TWO

Shortly before the start of the performance, Astrid left the duke's box. Keeping to shadowy passageways, Mabel's footman, Frederick, escorted Astrid to Madame Diamante's suite while the famous opera singer was getting ready to perform onstage. She was as sweet as her voice and made herself scarce soon after the quick introductions. Astrid was grateful for both the lady's and the footman's discretion. People would froth at the mouths if they knew Beswick himself was here. It would not do for her to be discovered.

She waited in the empty sitting room, counting the seconds. They turned into a full minute, then another, then five. And then ten. Isobel wasn't coming. Frederick had indicated he would return shortly with her sister, but as the minutes went by, she grew less confident. Had Beaumont restricted her? Refused to let her leave his side? He *would* be that controlling. Astrid drew a fretful breath and then released it.

Perhaps Frederick was being careful.

Or perhaps Isobel wasn't coming.

In a mild state of panic, Astrid shook her head. She could not risk being discovered, and every moment that went by, she risked someone running into her before the performance started. Just as she rose to leave, the door cracked open, and her sister's beautiful face emerged. They embraced quickly.

"Astrid, I received your message. Are you well?"

"You have five minutes before the performance starts, Your Grace," Frederick whispered.

"Thank you," she said and then turned back to her sister, who looked lovelier than the last time Astrid had seen her. She wore a powder-blue satin gown that flattered her porcelain complexion to perfection. Astrid took her hand and sat, patting the seat beside her. "The question is, how are you, Isobel?"

"Quite well, though I'm certain you know that the Earl of Beaumont has asked Uncle Reggie permission to formally court me. Is that why you wanted to meet?"

Astrid winced at the familiar reference to their uncle. Clearly he still held Isobel in thrall if she was using that nickname. "Partly. How do you feel about his suit?"

"He's persistent for sure, and he's been the perfect gentleman." What looked like a fond smile curved her lips. "Uncle claims no one is good enough for me. And, well, we do have to weed out the fortune hunters."

Fury sparked across Astrid's spine at the man's cheek. He had no qualms about manipulating his own niece, when the truth was that he was the worst fortune hunter of them all. She kept her annoyance hidden. "Have any other young men caught your fancy?"

Isobel blushed. "One or two."

"Which ones?"

"Viscount Morley is more of an acquaintance, but I do enjoy his company. However, I've developed a particular tendre for the Marquess of Roth."

Astrid hadn't heard of the viscount, but she was familiar with the marquess. Roth had danced with her at the Featheringstoke ball. Though she did not know him well, he was in line for a dukedom, and he was a dashed sight better than Beaumont. And he was an acquaintance of her husband's.

"Have either of them declared an interest?" she asked.

Isobel hesitated, a calculating look slipping over her features. "Lord Roth might, though he has yet to approach Uncle." She paused with a tight, proud smile. "I know you think me naive, Astrid, but I do have a working brain in my head. While the Earl of Beaumont has been the very soul of civility, I'm well aware of what both he and Uncle Reggie want. As such, I do not wish to have either of them scaring off any other potential suitors."

Astrid's jaw fell open. Sweet, enchanting, sedate Isobel—moving men like chess pieces.

"So you're here with Beaumont by choice?"

"To be seen, dearest. I'd rather feign interest and be allowed to have a Season than be locked like Rapunzel in a gilded tower. We do what we can with the lot we've been given. You taught me that."

Astrid couldn't remember the last time she'd been shocked speechless. Perhaps Aunt Mabel hadn't been that far off the mark when she'd suggested that Isobel wasn't as helpless as everyone—including Astrid—assumed she was. But all Astrid could think of was the sneaky, underhanded way the earl had manipulated *her*. And how easily he had destroyed her life.

"Beaumont is cunning," she said. "If he realizes

what you've been doing, he will stop at nothing to get what he wants."

"I can handle Beaumont," her sister said.

Astrid frowned. "Can you?"

Isobel reached for her hands, gripping them tightly in hers. "I love you, Astrid, but I'm not you. I won't make the same mistakes you did, and do you know why?" When Astrid flinched and shook her head, she went on. "Because *you* showed me how not to. You taught me how to be smart. How to have courage." Her smile was bittersweet. "I love my music and my dancing and my ribbons, and I know sometimes you think I'm just a silly, naive girl, but you have to trust me. Will you trust me?"

Astrid stared in shock at her sister and felt so much pride that her heart nearly burst. Who was this girl? Mabel's words about having a little faith in the sister she'd raised came back to her. "What can I do?"

"Show up at Lady Hammerton's spring ball in a fortnight. I'll be there all week for her house party with Beaumont, Morley, and Roth." Her sister's eyes sparkled. "It's in North Stifford. Come with Beswick if you can manage it."

Astrid blinked.

All three potential suitors in one place. That can't be good.

"Izzy, what do you intend to do?"

Isobel's smile was decidedly wolfish. "I intend to cause a scandal to end all scandals."

• • •

For the life of him, Thane could not focus on the performance, nor the lush contralto of Madame Diamante during the aria. He'd been the victim of an inconvenient erection the minute his wife had sauntered into his study looking like sex on legs. Thane had wanted to lay carnal waste to her. Suck on the ridges of that long, elegant spine, heft her skirts and devour the feast he knew lay hidden beneath.

Hell.

He was so fucking hard, he wouldn't be surprised if his buttons popped loose.

The moment they'd sat and she'd leaned over the balustrade, opera glasses in hand, he'd been fixated on the sensual bare curve of her back, on display in that salacious dress. And he hadn't been able to focus on anything since. He'd been right about the color. It turned her hair to mahogany and her skin to fresh cream. Thane's eyes resettled on her vertebrae, his cock throbbing.

A woman's spine should not be that erotic. But hers was.

To his left, his wife was so wrapped up in the performance that she hadn't spared him a single glance since her return from her meeting with her sister or guessed at his acute discomfort, and for that he was grateful. The singer's voice hit a note that made Astrid's fingers curl and reach out blindly…to land on his knee. The innocent contact was like flint to tinder. His hand held hers in place as her gaze met his. She read the lust there easily, her own irises flaring with matching passion.

Neither of them spoke, eyes locked. And then

slowly, *slowly*, Astrid edged her fingers out from his, returning her attention to the stage. Thane wanted to curse at the loss, but he was mesmerized as she studiously peeled the glove from her right hand, exposing those elegant, slender fingers. And when she replaced that bared hand on his thigh, he nearly expired from shock. Desire and heat collided savagely within him as her fingers crept upward, each frantic heartbeat bringing them closer to where it burned the most. Where he craved it the most. Almost delicately, with one finger, she traced the outline of his length.

Thane swore viciously beneath his breath.

"Astrid," he rasped.

His vixen of a wife ignored him, deftly unbuttoning several of his buttons, enough so she could reach inside the fall and grasp his straining erection. Her fingers encircled him, her thumb rubbing over his weeping eye at the top of his cock, and then moved back down to stroke him from tip to base. He groaned softly as she repeated the act of sliding upward and then downward, using his own moisture to aid in her carnal exploration.

Her pace quickened, her clever fingers exerting exquisite pressure. Astrid's breathing was ragged, too, and when he removed his left glove with his teeth to run his fingers over that delectable spine, she arched into his palm, moaning slightly. His orgasm roared upon him the second he touched her velvety skin, and he reached into his jacket pocket for his handkerchief. Thane covered her hand with his as he spent himself, his body jerking with the force of his release, pulse after hot pulse emptying into the square of linen.

Thunderous clapping replaced the rushing sound of blood in his ears as the singer completed her act. He wanted to clap, too, but for entirely different reasons. In a sated daze, he watched as Astrid daintily cleaned her hand on an unsoiled edge of the handkerchief and replaced her glove without a sound. The fact that she hadn't said a single word was almost as stimulating as sex in the darkness.

It was intermission, Thane realized dully when people started moving on the floor of the opera house and in the boxes opposite them. Tucking himself away, he refastened his falls just in time for his aunt to announce herself and poke her head around the velvet drapes.

The old biddy smirked, one eyebrow arching. "Enjoying the opera, dears?"

"Very much," Astrid replied in a casual tone, though her cheeks were crimson.

"Did you speak with Isobel?" Mabel asked.

Astrid nodded. "Seems you were right that my sister has things well in hand. I confess that I've never seen her so determined."

"That's just another word for stubborn, dear," Mabel said with a grin. She nodded to Frederick, who stood outside the box with a tray of refreshments. "Shall we have a drink, then?"

Astrid's bright eyes skated over his, and she bit her lip as her cheeks burned anew. "Of course, but first I must visit the retiring room."

That scorching look made Thane want to snatch her up, take her home, and see for himself how aroused she was. How aroused touching *him* had made her. He didn't miss his aunt's sudden interest, either, and for that reason, he simply nodded.

"I shall stay here and keep my dear nephew from accidentally terrorizing anyone in your absence," Mabel said.

Thane wanted to say something to Astrid before she left, but he couldn't find the words. In any case, his nosy aunt was there, and she missed nothing. Instead, he dipped his head briefly before Astrid disappeared. He almost wished Aunt Mabel had left him in peace as well, but she did not. She sat and poured two whiskies.

"Go on, say it," he said.

She smirked. "Say what?"

"That you think I'm infatuated."

"Are you?"

"No."

"You never could lie to me, Nathaniel Harte," she said.

He winced at the sound of his given name. She was right—his feelings for his wife were fast becoming obsession. Thane sighed. Not *becoming*—already past. He hungered for her more than anything he'd ever wanted...her smile, her glances, her kisses. What he felt was beyond dangerous. It wasn't superficial. It was bone-deep. And it was, above all, dangerous.

"If not infatuation, then what?" Mabel asked.

Admiration...passion...affection...love. He couldn't admit any of those things. Even acknowledging those sentiments made it real. Gave it life beyond what he could control. His helpless gaze met his aunt's. "I *can't* do this."

"We don't choose when we fall in love, Thane. Or with whom. We can only decide whether what we feel is worth fighting for. Fate hasn't been kind to you, that's true, but you still have breath in your lungs and blood in your veins, so do yourself a favor and live. Otherwise you're just a walking corpse." She reached over to pat his shoulder, softening her words. "If you push Astrid away because of some misconstrued notion that you don't deserve her, then you're a bigger fool than you know."

A muscle beating in his cheek, Thane glanced at his aunt, who seemed to have said her piece, two grooved lines appearing between her brows. "Finished?"

She glowered at him. "No, actually, I'm not. You're my nephew, and I love you, but you need to remove that stubborn head of yours from your arse before you do yourself permanent damage."

Thane blinked. He couldn't remember Aunt Mabel being this furious, not since the first days when he'd come back from the Continent and attempted to drown himself in whiskey and self-pity. Much as he had then, Thane resented the intrusion. Resented being scolded like an ill-behaving child.

"Not to be rude, Aunt," he drawled, covering his churning emotions with chilly reserve, "but what do *you* know of love? You certainly did not marry for it."

"Aristocrats marry for other reasons," she said, unperturbed by the ice in his tone. "Love matches are rare. Even my marriage to the Duke of Verne was arranged by our parents. Affection and fondness came later, but why do you think after Verne's death,

I took such pleasure in my liaisons?" Thane opened his mouth, and she lifted a palm to stop him. "I know you disapprove of that part of my lifestyle, but I am determined to be open to love before I cock up my toes."

"With indiscriminate affairs?" he asked dryly.

She canted her head, watching him. "Look at you, so stone-cold. There's too much of your father in you, I suppose. Lord knows he was the embodiment of blue-blooded indifference."

The comparison to his father pricked deep, though Thane could not fault her for making it. The man had been a cold, frightening duke. He understood the similarity all too well—because he'd fashioned himself to suit. A stone heart was impervious. An unfeeling man could not be harmed.

Mabel sighed, reaching to pat his cheek. "But there's some of me in you, too, and hope springs eternal that you might allow yourself the chance to be happy. You have to choose, Thane."

"Choose what?" he said.

"Oh, my darling, choose to act with your heart instead of that rigid, fractious brain of yours."

He could hear the hope in her words. *Hope*. It sliced at him, mangling his defenses. Entreated and beseeched like the liar it was. He'd been duped by hope so many times before. His father. Leo. His friends. Lovers. They'd all left him, running in horror from the beast he'd become. And Astrid would, too, once she no longer needed him. He thought of her willing hands upon him…how great his need had been; how great it still was. Already, he needed her like the air in his lungs. It was too much. *Too much!*

Thane thought the war had broken him, but that pain would not even come close to what Astrid could do. He knew without a shadow of a doubt that there would be nothing left of him when she left. The bitterness grew inside him until it became all he could feel. It comforted him like an old, worn blanket. A longtime companion. He drew its familiar, soothing darkness around him.

His eyes met his aunt's, the shadows clinging to him as they'd always done. "That's where you're wrong. You see, my heart withered with the rest of me."

"I fear I've done more ill than good," she said sadly.

"No, you've set me straight, Aunt. I know what I have to do."

CHAPTER TWENTY-THREE

The notorious ill-tempered, stone-hearted, intractable Beast of Beswick was back in residence. The man's erratic mood swings were enough to give a person bloody whiplash! Astrid scowled as Alice fastened her stays at the thought of her husband. He'd gone from tender to tyrant in the space of one evening at the opera, and now everyone in the house was tiptoeing on tenterhooks for fear of incurring the beast's wrath. Even she had not been exempt from his mercurial temper.

The night of the opera, on the way home, she'd ventured to ask if he would attend Lady Hammerton's ball in the interests of supporting Isobel. He'd been uncharacteristically withdrawn during the second half, but she'd put it down to the entire outing being trying for him.

How wrong she'd been.

He'd stared at her in the carriage, his mouth twisting into an ugly shape. "No."

"You said you would help," she'd said quietly. "Protect Isobel. She needs us."

"I am not going to a bloody ball, Astrid."

"What are you so afraid of?"

"Afraid?" He'd laughed, the sound dark and devoid of humor. "Have you forgotten what the monster you married looks like, my lady? Let me remind you." He'd ripped off his hat, leaned forward, and growled in her face, his fury palpable and the

landscape of his scars outlined in stark, gruesome detail.

"If you gave people a chance, they might—"

"Might what?" He'd scoffed. "Allow me into their homes? To sit at their hearths, share stories, and offer me tea? You are naive, my foolish wife."

"And you're being childish."

His eyes had flashed with rage. "Have a care, Astrid."

She hadn't paid heed, thinking only of her sister's request. "It's just that I want Isobel to be safe. And to have a chance to be happy and free."

"None of us is free. Your sister simply hopes to trade one cage for another. Isn't that what marriage is?"

"That's not what we have."

He'd sneered at her. "No, darling, we have convenience. Even better, no? You wanted a name, and all I ever hoped for was a warm, willing body, which I eventually got. Don't make our association any more than it is. What a trade. Duchess by day, doxy by night."

"You're a brute."

"I never pretended to be anything else."

No, he hadn't, and that had been Astrid's own fault. She'd believed in something that hadn't been there. She'd believed in the man he could be, not the one he was. And she had only herself to blame. She never should have trusted him.

After the hurt, the anger had come.

How dare he make promises and then break them? How dare he call her names? He wanted her to be a doxy? Then, by God, that was what she would be. Astrid stared in the mirror at her reflection. Alice had covered the dark circles beneath her eyes with powder. She would have preferred to stay in bed, but the thought of being in the same house with her ogre of a husband rankled.

"Thank you, Alice," she said, once the maid had finished with the final touches of her attire. "That will be all."

Grabbing her reticule, she descended the staircase and, for the first time since the altercation in the coach, came face-to-face with her husband.

"You were not at dinner this evening," the duke growled, amber eyes narrowing on her clover-green evening gown. He looked tired, too. Tired and drawn. "Culbert said you were not feeling well."

She shot him a smile, ignoring the dull ache in her heart at the magnetic tug of him. Despite his cruelty and coldness, she wanted nothing more than to soothe those lines of tension over his brow, draw him close, and find the man who'd wooed her in the conservatory, the man who had bought her buildings for a school, the man who had made love to her with such tenderness that it made her chest ache.

But that version of him had been false…a version she'd obviously romanticized because she'd been lonely, and she'd wanted to believe the best of him.

"I was," she said with forced cheer, "but I am much recovered."

"Are you going out?"

She nodded. "To the Ralston soiree with Isobel." Once more, she pushed a smile to her lips. "You don't mind, do you, Your Grace? I know how much you loathe such things."

He did not respond to her barb. "Enjoy your evening."

"And you, Your Grace."

Their excessively polite interaction had infuriated her to no end, and the following night, it was much the same. Even Mabel had seemed disheartened, her usual optimism absent. She offered no explanation for her nephew's disposition, and every time Astrid tried to get answers of her own and chip past the wall of ice growing between them, he walked away.

If she hadn't caught the naked longing in his eyes one or two times when he thought she wasn't looking, Astrid would have believed he felt nothing. It made her think of what Mabel had told her about her nephew when she'd urged her not to give up on him. *Deep down, he doesn't feel he deserves happiness. So he pushes everyone away.*

Was that what he was doing?

It was definitely possible. Over the past weeks, they'd connected in more ways than one…intellectually, emotionally, physically. And before the opera, she might have even said that Thane had come to care about her. Their intimacy had deepened, blossomed. Astrid blushed. So much so that she had fondled him in public. No one had seen them, obscured in the box as they were, but that was as flagrant a sentiment as any.

The more she thought about it, the more it made sense. They'd come together in darkness—first in the arbor and then in his bedchamber and every other time since. The opera had been a turning point. For both of them. A different type of affirmation.

Was *that* what had sent him running?

The next day, when the duke summoned her to his study to inform her of his intention to send her back to Beswick Park, Astrid had had enough. She would not be discarded like this. A part of her wanted to argue it was for Isobel's sake that she needed to stay, but it was more than that. In her heart of hearts, the truth was that she did not care to be parted from him. What, then, did that say about her?

"That you are a fool who has fallen in love with someone who can never love you back," she whispered to herself.

"Which gown pleases you tonight, Your Grace?" Alice asked, walking in from the adjoining bath.

Astrid frowned. Which gown indeed. She was at a crossroads. She could tuck her tail between her legs and allow him to chase her away, or she could refuse. Make a stand. She was only ever a coward when it came to this man, but she was terrified of what confronting him would bring.

Then again, fear had never helped anyone onward.

Her husband was at his heart a man of war. He understood the push and pull of battle. She needed to rethink her strategy. To reach him, she needed to dig deep into the arsenal she had at her disposal.

"The red silk," she said decisively.

Alice's eyes went round, and Astrid felt a shiver of apprehension chase down her spine. The red silk dress was one of Madame Pinot's most daring creations, with a neckline that covered much less than it revealed. After her bath, Astrid donned the provocative gown. Alice frowned, her eyes fixated on the embroidered edge as if her stare was the only thing holding her breasts in place. Good gracious, if Astrid so much as sneezed, her bosom would tumble out of the bodice. As it was, she was sure she could see the pink edges of her nipples.

"Perhaps it was meant to be worn with a chemisette," Alice suggested.

"Madame Pinot did not say so."

A blush singed her cheeks as Astrid stared at her reflection. The dress was beyond daring. And its indecency didn't stop at the bodice that also left her shoulders shockingly bare. It clung to her corseted form like a second skin, cinching her waist and hips before falling in decadent crimson folds to the floor. A rich blond lace overlay at the bodice, waist, and hem gave the gown an almost Spanish flair.

Astrid paired it with elegant elbow-length champagne-colored gloves and soft matching embroidered heeled slippers. Alice had styled her hair in a simple updo, and she wore no jewelry save for a necklace with a ruby pendant that nestled in the hollow between her breasts.

"His Grace will not approve of you going anywhere in that gown," Alice muttered.

Astrid smiled through her sudden panic. "I should hope not."

When she walked into the dining room, her husband's back was to her. He was deep in conversation with his solicitor, Sir Thornton, and his wife, Lady Claudia. Astrid hadn't realized they were having guests for dinner, and she almost spun around in retreat. But Mabel, whose eyes had sparked with mischievous delight upon seeing her, came to kiss her cheek.

"Bold move," she whispered.

Her smile felt wobbly. "A wise friend told me not to give up."

With a proud look, Mabel squeezed Astrid's fingers as if to say, *Good luck*, and then said loudly, "Astrid, dear, don't you look lovely."

The duke turned in painful slow motion, but when his gaze slid over her, he froze, his mouth going slack and then tight with displeasure. His expression shuttered but not before Astrid saw the flare of lust in those leonine eyes. *Good*.

"Thank you, Aunt," she said in an unusually breathless voice. Her heart felt like it was going to beat out of her chest and gallop from the room. She greeted Lady Claudia and Sir Thornton. The poor solicitor's cheeks went ruddy, but Claudia's admiring glance bolstered Astrid's flagging courage.

She beamed at her scowling husband, whose face now almost matched her dress as he shepherded her a few steps away, out of earshot of the others. The warm, spicy scent of him curled over her, and she had to fight to not close the distance between them and lick the pulse throbbing madly in his neck. Gracious, she was a fool for this man.

"Did I pay for that?"

"Why, of course," she replied, reaching for coolness, despite the fact that his hand was burning a hole at her elbow, sending flames shooting to other parts of her body nowhere near her arm. "I have it on account from Madame Pinot that you specified this color."

"The color," he ground out. "Not"—he gestured at her body with his hand—"*that.*"

Astrid let out a laugh, causing his eyes to drop to her quivering bosom. It was a wonder she didn't go up in cinders at his glower. "This style is all the rage in Paris. Don't be such a prude, Your Grace." He ripped his burning stare away, that muscle in his jaw on the loose again. She lifted her brows. "Won't you pour me a sherry, darling? Or perhaps Sir Thornton will not mind."

With an unreadable look, he stalked away before she could finish and returned with the proffered glass, nearly shoving it into her hand. Astrid sipped the drink and allowed him to escort her to her seat. During all nine courses of dinner, she tasted nothing, not the cream of turtle soup, nor the braised pheasant, nor the beef in béchamel sauce. Though she conversed mostly with Claudia and Mabel about trivial things, she could feel her husband's brooding stare. Poor Sir Thornton had to be getting uncomfortable with the duke's testy one-word answers.

Mabel, who sat beside her to her left, leaned in. "I hope that dress of yours has a plan," she whispered.

"Me too," Astrid whispered back. "I can barely eat in this thing."

"You shall have to give me the name of your modiste," Claudia said on her right, the not-so-innocent comment drawing both the duke's and Sir Thornton's attention. "That gown is rather sensational. Isn't it, Henry?"

Sir Thornton coughed discreetly but not before

sending his wife a thoroughly devilish look that made Astrid bite back a giggle. She hadn't expected it of the stern, composed solicitor. But it was clear that he was very much smitten with his wife.

"Thank you," Astrid said. "Madame Pinot is exceptional, but I fear that the praise for this particular gown has to go to my husband." Thane choked on his wine and opened his mouth as if to deny it, but Astrid did not let him get a word in. "His Grace has impeccable taste."

"Indeed," Claudia toasted, lifting her glass with an impish grin.

Beswick looked like he'd sucked on something awful, and the scars on his face had gone stark white, as if he were holding on to his control by a thread. Thankfully, the rest of the dinner passed with less provoking conversation, and after the last course was served, Astrid put down her napkin as they all rose.

Normally after a formal dinner, the men would adjourn to the library for port and cigars, while the women took tea and brandy in the salon, but the Thorntons had another engagement. They said their goodbyes.

"I'm off as well," Astrid announced. She had no plans for the evening, but *he* didn't know that. Sure enough, her husband froze.

"Off where, Your Grace?" he asked in a silky tone.

"To the Levinson musicale, of course," she said, ignoring the firing of her pulse and the decadent throb between her thighs at his look. "I accepted days ago."

He gripped her elbow, not tightly but firmly enough that her knees went weak. "Please excuse us," he said with a clipped bow. "My wife and I have something to say to each other."

Astrid glanced helplessly over her shoulder as Mabel mouthed *bravo* and Claudia's eyes twinkled with mirth. The duke led her into his study and kicked the door shut behind him.

She opened her mouth to protest his manhandling of her person, and he swore a filthy oath, slamming his lips to hers. She was swamped by more than six and a half feet of large, predatory, sexually aroused male, and Lord help her if her body didn't respond just as savagely to his hot, possessive kiss. Astrid's hands clawed at his jacket, clutching him close as she welcomed the punishing invasion of his tongue and met him stroke for ferocious stroke. He bit at her lips, and she bit back. He licked and sucked and thrust, and she responded in kind.

"This dress is diabolical," he growled, dragging his mouth from hers, his fingers tracing the lace edge of the flimsy silk bodice. It didn't take much coaxing for her nipples to harden. Thane bent his head and suckled, the delicate fabric darkening. Astrid nearly fainted from the friction of soft wet silk against her sensitive skin. He blew against her, making her nipples tauten even more, and bowed to pay homage to the other.

"Thane," she begged, her body dissolving into a mess of need and heat.

Shoving her up against the study door, he wedged a hard thigh in between hers and growled low in his throat. He circled his rock-hard groin against her, making her lightheaded. "I've had you and this gown to thank for the most agonizing arousal I've had in years."

"And I've you to thank for the same," she replied.

His eyes shone, burning with desire as his hands fought her skirts to seek bare skin. Barer still at the tops of her thighs.

"No drawers," he whispered.

Astrid could barely string two words together at the feel of his thumbs, parting the aching place where she was embarrassingly wet for him. But Thane only growled his satisfaction, his free hand moving to unbutton his falls as he gathered handfuls of red silk to her waist, exposing everything to his view. She writhed against him, feeling cool air on her overheated skin.

"Hold these," he ordered, handing her a wadded mound of her skirts.

And then he sank to his knees, setting his hungry mouth to her throbbing sex.

Astrid throttled her scream, the muffled sound turning into moans as he continued his onslaught with his lips and tongue. God, he knew just how and where to touch her…exactly how to circle and lash the gathering knot of tension until she was sobbing his name. Her knees buckled as pleasure streaked along her nerve endings and gathered in the space between her legs, building and building, until suddenly, the climax was upon her, her body splintering apart into aching ripples of sensation.

Without warning, Thane stood and drove his staff into her wet heat, filling her utterly even as she convulsed around him, her orgasm intensifying anew at the magnificent length and breadth of him stretching her to capacity.

"God, Astrid, you feel so damn good."

Wrapping her legs around his hips, he hoisted her up, cradling her back against the door with one free arm, as his body withdrew and slammed back into hers. He was not gentle, mindless with hunger and lust, and she relished every second of it. She loved how undone he was…how the muscles in his shoulders bunched with primal strength, how his lips parted in abandon, how his eyes shone with passion, burning her fears away.

In this moment, he was *hers*. As utterly and irrevocably as she was his.

With a shout, his body worked into hers and went still. For a brief moment, indecision warred in those lovely eyes of his, and then he yanked himself from her, spilling his seed on the waxed and polished floor between them.

Panting, he collapsed against her.

• • •

For a long moment, Thane stood breathing hard, his forehead against his wife's, one unsteady hand braced on the back of the study door. He had completely lost his reason and his mind. All because of a scrap of scarlet silk. Though he didn't blame it *all* on the dress. In hindsight, the tension between the two of them had been building for the better part of a week.

The dress, or lack of it, had been the clincher.

The minute he'd seen her in it, his brain had

fizzled. Everything that had seemed so important before, so crucial to his survival, had fallen away. Nothing mattered. Not his decision to keep his distance, his forced indifference, or his desperate need for self-preservation. Every single thought in his head distilled down to one vital, fundamental thing—she was *his*.

Hanging on to his unraveling self-control by a thread, dinner had been agony, and when she'd announced her intention to go out, *in that fucking dress*, Thane had seen red. Literally. Short of throwing her over his shoulder like a troglodyte, he was lucky they'd managed to make it to the privacy of his study, though everyone within range had likely gotten an earful of what had happened behind the solid oak door. Including—*Christ*—Mabel.

He felt Astrid's eyes on him, their crystalline depths sated. "Beswick, are you *blushing*?"

"What? No, of course not."

Her smile was a siren's. "Your cheeks are flushed."

"I have a demanding lover."

Now it was her turn to blush. Thane smiled and kissed her swollen lips gently, noticing the reddened scrapes on her chin and neck where he'd abraded her with the bristle of his own jaw. He caressed the area with the pad of one finger and frowned.

"Did I hurt you?"

"No." She shook her head and blushed again. "At least no more than I hurt you." She stroked at parallel red lines on his neck. "You've scratches just here."

"Scratches?" he asked with a smirk.

Astrid arched a brow. "You took me against a

door, Beswick. Surely you did not think I could control my passions while yours were on such territorial display."

"Keep speaking like that, little minx, and I shall be forced to put said door to use once more."

He stepped backward, and Astrid nearly fell forward without the weight of his body anchoring hers in place. The silk of her dress was hopelessly crushed, but Thane didn't see her wearing that particular gown anywhere else. Not if he had anything to say about it.

Astrid frowned adorably, releasing the handfuls of her skirts back into place while he buttoned his trousers. "Honestly, why is it acceptable for a man to be passionate, and when a woman shows any sign of lustful urges, suddenly she is Eve incarnate, subverting the whole garden, ergo, the entire world."

He waved an arm to the nearby chaise. "You can subvert me any time. It's not as if the servants haven't already guessed that their mistress shamelessly seduced their master."

Her blush reignited. "Oh, you are incorrigible. They guessed no such thing."

"I will bet you a hundred quid that Fletcher and Culbert are on the other side of this door, pretending to polish a candlestick or some such," he said with a straight face.

"They're *your* servants, so of course they have the most dreadful habits. I would be foolish to take such a bet."

Thane grinned and walked over to the mantel, where he poured two glasses of cognac. He offered one to her, which she took and sat on the sofa, crimson silk pooling over her long, shapely legs. Astonishingly, he felt himself stir again. The effect she had on him was incredible, and though he was hopelessly attracted to her, Thane knew it wasn't just physical. It went so much deeper. No wonder he'd been so afraid after the interlude at the opera. Some part of him knew that he hadn't a chance in hell of resisting her.

"Thane, we need to talk," she said quietly.

He took a sip of his drink and swallowed with a nod. Fear settled in his gut, a dark reminder of what he stood to lose. "Did you know how I would react when you came to dinner?" he asked. "When you wore that gown?"

"I hoped to get your attention," she said.

"Why?"

She stared into her glass, a faint blush on her cheeks. "I felt the distance between us widening, and it frightened me. You were pulling away, and there was nothing I could do about it. I don't presume to know what you were doing or why you were behaving the way you were, but it wounded me terribly. I didn't want you to shut me out."

"I—"

"Let me finish, please," she said. "I also can't presume to understand what you've been through and what you have to deal with on a daily basis, and I want to apologize for asking you to go to Lady Hammerton's. It was truly awful and thoughtless of me."

"It is forgotten."

As if a weight had been removed from her shoulders, Astrid inhaled and nodded. "We are married,

Thane," she said softly. "Regardless of how our marriage came to be, we are not strangers, and…I don't wish us to be. I miss our time in the conservatory and in the library. I miss *you*. I know there can be fondness and mutual respect between us, and I'm not looking for anything more, if that is what you're afraid of."

What if I want more?

The thought came out of nowhere, making Thane suck wind as if he'd been struck in the gut. He'd been the one who'd been adamant that *more* couldn't happen. That *more* was a basket of poisonous snakes that could not be re-closed once opened. That *more* would destroy him. And yet, here he was entertaining the bloody idea.

He scraped a hand over his stubbled chin, his thoughts chaotic. It had taken courage to do what she did…to face him when he'd been nothing but unpleasant and to fight for what *she* wanted. A lesser woman would have given up, thrown in the sponge, and cut her losses. But Astrid was not like other females. She was different. *Unique.* He'd known that from the start when she'd burst into his home and demanded he marry her or give her a job.

"I'm sorry," she said, mistaking the tense expression on his face.

He drew a breath. "It is I who should apologize for the things I said, Astrid, for what I called you. I didn't mean them. You're not a…doxy. Forgive me."

"Forgiven." She bit her lip, a beautiful flush suffusing her skin. "Though I admit, after my recent success, it's shockingly liberating."

Her elegant hands trembled slightly in her lap,

and for once, Thane knew the shiver to be passion. Her responses were too innate to be false. If he still had any doubt, however, the look she shot him from beneath her lashes was pure hunger, and he felt his lower body jerk like a puppet in response.

"Is that so?" he murmured.

Astrid's face flamed as she waved a hand toward the study door where he'd plastered and pleasured her body to distraction. "Apparently," she replied. "But you can't shut me out and withdraw the moment you feel afraid or threatened. This is all new to me, too."

"What is?"

"Trust."

"Then, this is a first for both of us." Thane finished his brandy and stood, holding out his hand. He smiled when his wife took it, drawing her up against his hard body so swiftly that she gasped. At the feel of her, unsurprisingly, he felt his cock stir to life.

"Already?" she asked, glancing down to the rise in his trousers.

"A constant state where you are concerned, Lady Beswick."

Her arms looped around his neck. "That must be uncomfortable. Let's go upstairs and do something about it, shall we?"

In his bedchamber, Thane wrapped his body around hers and made love to her slowly, taking the time to savor every inch of her. He busied his hands with her luscious breasts. He skimmed his palm down her flat stomach and up again. He loved the feel of her…the silken smoothness of her skin, the taut buds of her nipples, the soft tuft of maidenhair at her groin.

Most of all, he savored being inside her, deep within the sleek clasp of her body. He marveled at the delicious friction between them—the tight, hot embrace of her body, as if she were made exactly for him. Retreating and filling her slowly, he kneaded her breast and sucked gently at the tendon between her neck and shoulder. She let out a needy sigh and arched her back, wriggling into him.

"You're so warm and wet." Thane increased his pace, drilling in and out, clamping a hand on the outer flare of her hip. Her spine bowed, allowing him deeper access, and they both groaned as his cock sank home into her.

"Thane," she whispered. "I'm close."

He slid his hand down to where they were joined, his fingers grazing the swollen knot at the top of her sex. His wife moaned her approval. Circling it and rubbing it, he quickened his thrusts at the same time, the erotic combination hurtling them both over the edge. This time when she came, she muffled her screams in the pillow. As he had earlier, he withdrew with a grunt just before his seed spilled in the bedsheets between them. Thane kissed her nape, inhaling the wildflower scent of her.

For the first time in a long time, he felt almost *happy*.

CHAPTER TWENTY-FOUR

"Dratted needle!"

Astrid sucked on the finger that she had pricked for the fourth time, while Mabel shot her a laughing look. It was a *Mabel* look, full of innuendo and mischief. Astrid laid her embroidery hoop aside. With the amount of times that she'd drawn blood, she would have been better off threading the needle through a piece of scarlet cloth.

"Though I'm usually competent with a needle, I loathe embroidery," she said, pouring herself a fresh cup of tea.

"It's good for the spirit."

Astrid rolled her eyes. "Yes, if one wants one's spirit to depart one's body prematurely from sheer boredom."

"It's a feminine accomplishment."

Astrid darted a look at the older woman, focused studiously on her hoop. She wouldn't have taken the duchess as someone with a penchant for needlework. It was too…uninteresting for someone of her passions. But perhaps she was wrong. Isobel hated reading, and they were sisters.

"Learning is an accomplishment. Education. Not threading a needle endlessly over a hoop in ridiculous patterns."

Mabel arched her brows. "So get a book and read, if that pleases you."

Astrid had tried to read. She really had, but her

body had felt too on edge, her mind too busy to concentrate. She had read the same essay a dozen times before giving up. A few days ago, Thane had been called back to Beswick Park…something to do with one of his tenants, he'd said. He wasn't sure how long he'd be gone, which meant she and Mabel were on their own for Lady Hammerton's spring ball that evening. And Isobel's planned scandal. Perhaps that was why Astrid was so on edge. She worried for her sister.

"Do you know Lady Hammerton well, Aunt Mabel?" she asked. Though Astrid knew that she must, considering it was because of Mabel that Astrid had managed to receive an invitation to the exclusive ball.

"Quite well, dearest. We went to finishing school together."

"I haven't seen her or been introduced to her in Town," Astrid said.

"She's been in Bath," Mabel said, her needle flying with small, precise strokes. "Taking the waters there."

"Her house parties, are they usually sedate?"

Mabel smirked. "You do know me, do you not? Suffice it to say that Eloise is twice the rakehell I am."

"Rakehells are male," Astrid pointed out.

"Who says? There are female rakes."

"They're called something else," she said dryly.

"Yes, *rakehellions*." Mabel huffed. "Eloise's parties are nothing more than a buffet selection for her to choose her latest lover. And it is a testament of my fondness for *you* that I am not in attendance, since I, too, am currently between paramours. Why do you ask?"

"Isobel is planning something."

Mabel perked up. "I knew that dear girl had a spine! What is she doing?"

"Apparently three of her suitors will be there, including Beaumont, and she intends to cause a scandal to end all scandals, she says."

The duchess upended her embroidery hoop, sending it flying across the room, and burst into laughter. "Your sister has some big shoes to fill. The scandal to end all scandals went to me nearly thirty years ago when Eloise and I were caught frolicking in the Serpentine at midnight." She paused with a dramatic flourish. "In our undergarments."

"You didn't!" Thirty years ago, Mabel would have been thirty-five, a few years after being widowed.

"We egged each other on terribly. No society rule could bind us."

"Didn't the *ton* shun you?"

"They tried, but I am a duchess. And Eloise a marchioness. After our husbands died, we were untouchable. They deemed us eccentrics and moved on to the next casualty of English superiority."

Smiling, Astrid grabbed the hoop from where it had rolled and stared at it, horrified. And then Mabel's earlier concentration suddenly made sense. The lovingly stitched image was not a leaf motif as hers had been. Instead, it was a…phallus. A very large, very detailed specimen, complete with a pair of embroidered testicles.

"Aunt Mabel!" she whispered. "What is this?"

She grinned without apology. "You're a married

woman; surely you know what that is."

Astrid coughed. "I do, but why would you sew such a thing?"

"I said we had to do needlework," she answered, taking the hoop, her expression all wide-eyed innocence. "I didn't say we weren't allowed to have *fun*."

Astrid couldn't help laughing, her eyes watering. "How many more of these have you done?"

"Oh, scores of them. I've made quite a study of it. They're all different, you know. Long, short, thick, thin, light, dark."

Astrid choked. "I *don't* know."

Mabel stood and put her stitching away into a closed basket, which she handed to one of the young footmen with a wink. Astrid's eyes widened with a sneaking suspicion, and then she felt her cheeks burn as she shook her head. Mabel did have good taste, though—he was very handsome. And if her embroidery was anything to go by, well endowed, too.

She smothered a giggle.

"It's a good thing it's hard to shock me," Astrid said as they walked into the hallway. "Otherwise, I would be properly scandalized."

"That's one of the reasons why I like you, dear." Mabel gave her a fond shove. "Now, hurry along; we must make haste if we want to arrive in time for the scandal of the season. Or this month, at least."

It was early, but Lady Hammerton's country estate was a couple of hours away by coach. For the evening, Astrid dressed in a deep-midnight-blue gown with silver lace accents and embroidered stars that almost made it look like the night sky. She usually favored lighter colors, but the rich color had been chosen by her husband during the fitting with Madame Pinot. A rope of diamonds had been wound into her hair, and light-gray gloves finished the ensemble.

"You look like a duchess," Alice breathed.

"Thank you, Alice. You've outdone yourself, truly."

"I only wish the duke could see how beautiful you look."

Astrid did as well. Perhaps he would be here back from his business at Beswick when she returned. She smiled fondly. Even though he'd been gone only a short while, she missed him. She'd rather be in bed with him than attending a ball, but she had to be there for Isobel. It hurt that he would not be in attendance, but she understood how uncomfortable being in public made him.

A few short hours later, they were off in the Duke of Beswick's crested coach. The interior of the carriage was plush and sumptuous, but Astrid wasn't looking forward to the length of the journey. She focused her attention on the duchess opposite, who had chosen to wear a wine-colored velvet gown that made her look twenty years younger. Her amber eyes sparkled with vivacity.

"Planning to break some hearts tonight, Aunt Mabel?" Astrid teased.

"At least one or two." She reached for a basket at her feet that Astrid had not noticed and pulled out a flask. After taking a sip, she handed it to Astrid. "It's just a spot of whiskey."

Taking the flask, Astrid swallowed some of the liquor.

With Mabel's animated company, the ride passed more quickly than she'd expected. More pleasantly, too, thanks to the whiskey. Astrid blinked as they came to a stop. Perhaps she'd had one too many sips. When they arrived in the gargantuan courtyard, Astrid goggled. Flickering lights were strung everywhere as they walked up the path to the doors, making it all look quite magical.

"It's beautiful," she breathed.

Mabel grinned. "This isn't the half of it. There'll be entertainments and fireworks—just you wait. Apparently, the Regent himself might put in an appearance."

Inside, the decor in the massive ballroom rivaled the outside, adorned in billowing panels of white and gold. And it was packed to bursting with every conceivable color. Mabel ushered her down another set of stairs, away from where the majordomo was making announcements of arriving guests, and they entered the ballroom from another entrance.

"We do not need to be announced," she told Astrid and shepherded her over to where a turbaned woman was surrounded by men vying for her attention. Lady Hammerton, Astrid presumed.

"Eloise, darling," Mabel said, kissing her old friend, who proceeded to shoo away her admirers and shriek with delight.

"You naughty old bat, missing my house party," the marchioness scolded. "You're lucky I even sent you an invitation to the ball."

Mabel laughed. "I'm here now. Allow me to introduce my nephew's wife, the Duchess of Beswick."

Astrid found herself the subject of meticulous attention. "Beswick is a lucky man," she pronounced and then narrowed her piercing green eyes. "You have a sister."

"Yes, Lady Isobel."

"Ah, lovely chit." Her eyes sparked with recognition as she turned back to Mabel. "She's the one you wrote me about?"

Astrid frowned. Mabel wrote Lady Hammerton about Isobel?

"Don't worry—I've kept an eye on her as you requested. She has developed a partiality for Lord Roth. Beaumont, however, proved to be another, more complicated matter. Persistent and arrogant, he refused to take no for an answer. I've had the servants bar him from entry tonight. A pity, since rumor has it his stamina is—"

"Eloise!" Mabel said.

Astrid blinked and pinned her lip between her teeth. The two of them in their younger years would have terrorized England, she was sure of it. She searched the throng of dancers to see if she could find Isobel, but there were too many people.

"So, the Beast of Beswick," Lady Hammerton said, causing Astrid's attention to swivel back, while the duchess was in conversation with a gentleman. "Mabel has been extraordinarily tight-lipped about your marriage. Why did you marry him? We know it wasn't for his good looks. Was it for his money?"

Astrid sputtered at the woman's gall. "I have a fortune of my own, I assure you."

"Beautiful *and* fiery. So why did you marry a man

like Beswick when you could have had your pick of any gentleman with a face like yours?"

"Perhaps like you suggested with Beaumont, his value is *elsewhere*."

The sexual inference hung in the air like a gauntlet, and then the marchioness guffawed and gestured to Mabel. "Oh, gracious, I do like her."

"Have you seen my sister, Lady Hammerton?"

The woman sent her an indulgent smile. "Oh, of course. She went out on the balcony a while ago after her waltz with Roth. Lady Beswick, there's something else I think you should know that concerns—"

But her host's voice faded into the background as Astrid's eyes traced the edge of the ballroom to where the balcony doors stood open. She couldn't see anything beyond the shadowy evening darkness. What she did see on the other side of the room was the Earl of Beaumont cutting through the crowd despite being barred, his mouth tight, and all the blood left her cheeks in a rush.

Astrid didn't care about being rude; she set off almost at a run, not waiting to hear what Lady Hammerton said. She debated threading through the middle, but there were too many bodies. Instead she headed for the perimeter. She'd be lucky to make it before Beaumont did something unforgivable and history repeated itself.

By the time she arrived on the northeast corner of the ballroom, huffing for breath, a crowd had already gathered, spearheaded by none other than Lady Bevins and her entire prattling entourage. Beaumont was nowhere in sight, thank goodness. He must have been waylaid, or perhaps he hadn't known Isobel was outside, *unchaperoned*, in the marquess's company.

Astrid strove to see over the heads of the people in her path and almost started barging through when she caught a glimpse of Isobel, her cheeks red and eyes bright, standing in the arms of Lord Roth, who looked similarly disheveled.

"Scandalous!" Lady Bevins shrieked and fanned herself. "I saw the chit in a lascivious embrace with the marquess. Scurrilous, I tell you. Like her sister."

Astrid froze. But her defense came from an unexpected source.

"Have a care, Lady Bevins," a deep, familiar voice said that sent shivers through Astrid's core.

The Duke of Beswick stood just inside the balcony doors, his ruined face shadowed by the brim of a hat. What on earth was he doing here? He hated balls and crowds. And besides, hadn't he been called back to Beswick Park? Astrid glanced around the room as more people noticed his presence and the whispers mounted.

Astrid was gratified to see Lady Bevins go from red to white as she, too, recognized who had spoken. But then, through the shifting bodies, her eye caught something flash on Isobel's left hand, caught in between the marquess's fingers, something that looked suspiciously like a ring, and she forgot the odious woman altogether. By the time her comically sluggish brain matched the wide gold band on Roth's left hand, her husband was already speaking.

"And since Lady Isobel is now Lady Roth, she

may indulge in any displays she feels necessary with her *husband*. I've given my support for the wedding."

The roar of the crowd felt like thunder in Astrid's ears until it faded to nothing, and all she could hear was silence as time came to a standstill.

She had to have misheard.

But the swell of guests offering congratulations with lifted glasses filled her vision, offering their toasts and felicitations to the bride and groom. Isobel. *Married*. Astrid was filled with equal amounts of relief that it wasn't the Earl of Beaumont and shock that she'd missed her own sister's wedding. Was this the scandal that Isobel had intended? If so, she had to hand it to her sister…as far as making a statement went, it was remarkable.

"Let me be the first to wish the happy couple all of life's many blessings," Lady Hammerton announced from the center of the ballroom, drawing the attention away from the duke, though many prying eyes still remained glued in his direction. "We will celebrate with their first waltz." With an imperious gesture to the orchestra, the strains of the interrupted waltz resumed.

Astrid took a deep breath and pushed to the place where Beswick remained, half hidden in the shadow of a potted fern, tears in her eyes at her sister's obvious happiness as she danced with her husband.

"How did you do this?" she whispered, clutching his arm, her brain still spinning with the announcement and the fact that her recalcitrant duke was *here*. "You went against the Prince Regent? Didn't

Beaumont ask him to overturn the terms of my father's will?"

"He'll understand. I'm heading to Carlton House myself to make sure of it," her husband said, his voice gruff, stepping away so that her hand fell uselessly to her side.

He did not meet her eyes even as he distanced himself. Something was wrong; she could feel the storm brewing in his body, and the fact that he wouldn't look at her was a stab to the heart, knowing how far they'd come and what they'd each sacrificed to get there.

"How did you do this?" she asked, her heart in her throat.

"It was simply a matter of procuring the license. I spoke with the Archbishop of Canterbury myself. Now you no longer need to worry about Beaumont or your uncle."

"I…thank you."

"No thanks needed."

"Thane," she said, a familiar sense of dread filling her veins at his remoteness. "Talk to me. What's the matter?"

"Your sister deserves to be happy," he said so softly that she had to strain to hear. "As do you."

"I *am* happy."

He looked at her then, and the raw agony visible in his eyes for a single heartbeat before it was shuttered nearly drove her to her knees. "No, Astrid. The truth is you're settling. You only married me to protect her, not because I was what you wanted. You deserve more. You deserve someone you truly want. Someone you *choose* without an anvil hanging over your head. I thought I could do this, that I could *have* you, but I can't."

His neutral words were like daggers.

"I don't understand. I thought we were beyond this. We agreed in your study to give us a chance."

"We made a mistake," he rasped. "I made a mistake. Look at Roth and your sister—that's what marriage should look like. The beauty gets the prince. That's how this tale should end."

"This isn't a fairy tale, Thane. This is real life."

"Exactly."

Astrid gasped at the sudden, acute pain in her chest. Didn't the daft man understand? *He* was the only one for her. She didn't want a prince; she never had. No, she wanted the man who made her laugh, who challenged her intelligence, who matched her on every fundamental level.

She was aware of their avid audience, though she couldn't begin to focus on any of them. The only one who had her attention was the man who was intent on smashing her heart into pieces. "Why are you doing this, Thane?"

"Because what we have isn't real, Astrid. You've become infatuated with a man who was little more than your jailor, and no matter how much we pretend, we cannot argue how this all began. I release you from our bargain."

She stared at him. At his overt *lies*. Did he truly believe them? "You're *wrong* and you know it. You were never my jailor. You never kept me prisoner. I stormed into your life, when you categorically pushed me away. I chose this because it's what *I* want."

"You chose it to save Isobel."

She faltered. "Well, at first, yes. But, Thane, you know this is so much more than that."

"I was never meant for marriage. You're more than I could ever deserve. I mean to petition Parliament for a divorce decree, on account that you were coerced into marriage under false pretenses. You did marry a beast, after all, and no one can fault you for wanting to escape that."

He growled at the people no longer trying to hide their stares and strode from the room before she could form a reply.

A *divorce*?

Astrid wanted to rail and scream, but beyond the hurt, deep down a part of her understood his skewed reasoning. The Duke of Beswick had never felt like he deserved her love. He'd saved her sister, and now he thought he was saving her…by letting her go. A divorce was unheard of in the peerage, though one would be granted for a duke, and Thane fully intended for the shame of it to be his. This proud, broken man who shied away from polite society was pushing her away by humbling and humiliating himself.

Her heart clenched.

Oh, Thane.

Astrid pushed through the twittering crowd, ignoring the pitying glances, and caught Mabel's eye where she stood with Lady Hammerton, her hands pressed to her mouth, eyes brimming with tears. She must have heard, along with half the guests in the ballroom. Astrid fought back her own tears, but she couldn't afford to become derailed by emotion.

She had to get to the daft man before he rode off to London.

She had to stop him and set him straight.

With a quick wave of farewell to the duchess, Astrid made her way to the front of the enormous ballroom, only to be waylaid by a looming figure. At first, she thought it was her husband, but when he stepped into the light, she groaned.

"What do you want, Beaumont?"

"You did this," he hissed.

Astrid pinched her lips thin. She'd had enough with men telling her things were her fault, making decisions *for* her, and trampling all over her. For once, she took a page from the duke's book and straightened her spine, uncaring of who heard her in the ballroom. This man had silenced her before. Hell if she'd let it happen again.

"No, Beaumont, *you* did this."

His brows shot to his hairline, his face going dark. "How dare you?"

She raised her voice, head high. "I dare because of what you did. You coveted a woman who did not want you, and when she did not instantly fall at your feet, you smeared her reputation with lies and tried to destroy her in the eyes of society. But you know what, you lousy excuse for a man? I didn't let you destroy me. Instead, I found someone who is proud and honorable, who values me for me, who doesn't treat me like a *thing*."

"That disgusting beast?" Beaumont scoffed.

"He's more of a man than you could ever hope to be," she said. "I'm proud to be his wife, and I'd rather be married to a beast like him than a swine like you." The earl's eyes narrowed with anger, but Astrid wasn't finished. "Sooner or later, Beaumont, you'll try to ruin the wrong woman, and you'll lose everything. But it won't be me, and it won't be my sister. So if you have nothing more to say for your sorry self, I'd advise you to get the *fuck* out of my way!"

"How dare you address me that way, you…you insolent…" he sputtered.

"Duchess," she said. "The word you're looking for is *duchess*."

Astrid suddenly became aware of the thunderous silence. The music had petered out, and almost every eye was trained on them. She could have heard a pin drop in the ballroom, and then suddenly the sound of slow, measured clapping broke through. Lady Hammerton looked positively beside herself with glee.

"Well said, Lady Beswick. I'll deal with this ball-crashing miscreant. Now, go save that fool husband of yours."

Despite a few disapproving glances, there were quite a few gratified ones, including her sister and Aunt Mabel, as well as a number of other ladies who were enjoying Beaumont's humiliation with undisguised relish. They might live in a man's world, but she had a voice, and she wasn't going to be afraid to use it. Not anymore. Astrid grinned, savoring the moment, but only for a second.

After all, she had a duke to rescue.

CHAPTER TWENTY-FIVE

Galloping through the roads of North Stifford, Thane breathed in the fresh country air. Soon, at the very least within two hours, he would be in London. It wasn't too late, and with any luck, he would catch Prinny before he was drowning at the bottom of his cups. It would be hit or miss whether the Regent would already be drunk, given his proclivities, but at least Thane had it on good authority that he was currently in residence at Carlton House.

He'd chosen to ride instead of taking a carriage because it would be quicker. And he needed the grueling pace. Everything hurt. His head, his body, his heart. He wanted to howl like a wounded animal. He wanted to tear at his cursed face, flay his ruined skin, and, most of all, weep for what he'd done. He'd broken Astrid's heart. His beautiful, courageous, clever girl. Oh Christ, the look on her face...it had nearly demolished him. But he had to let her go.

He had to set her free.

Creatures of her beauty didn't deserve to live hidden away. And that was what she would have been, married to him—a caged bride. She deserved so much more than he could give her. Even with a hat, the whispers and glances had been almost impossible to endure, and he'd been hard-pressed not to snarl and growl like the creature he was. But he'd done it, because it was what she had wanted. She'd needed for him to be there, to help keep

Isobel safe. People had stared, and he had let them. They'd simpered and whispered, and he'd held his tongue, kept his composure. Been a gentleman.

But once he'd seen Isobel in Roth's arms, seen the look of adoration on her face, he'd understood just how much he would be cheating Astrid of. She should be dancing in ballrooms with pride, not hiding away from the world in a dark abbey because of him, not enduring the whispers of the *ton*. She'd had enough of hurtful gossip to last her a lifetime. Because no matter how much he pretended, he wasn't a gentleman. He'd never be one.

Cutting her loose had been the only way.

It was the best for everyone.

His head was still pounding when he arrived in St. James on the south side of Pall Mall and into the courtyard of the prince's residence. From the lights and the revelry spilling down the steps, the Regent was entertaining. *Wonderful.* Thane sucked in a breath. He was not in the mood to socialize. He wanted only to get this over with so he could ride back to Beswick Park and sequester himself in solitude.

With a grunt, Thane dismounted and threw the reins of his mount to the waiting groom under the porte cochere. "I'm the Duke of Beswick. I won't be long. Cool him down."

"Yes, Your Grace."

Thane strode through the crowded first hall, knowing he'd likely find Prinny in one of the many drawing rooms or in the great hall or in the gardens. The man wasn't particular about his entertainments. As he strode through the palace, the Greco-Roman architecture with its marbled floor, carved columns, and lush draperies was stunning, but he could hardly appreciate any of it. A few people gathered in small groups, revelers who were strolling past him to head outside to enjoy the warm evening air. Following them, he ignored the stares and the whispers without comment, too focused on finding the Regent.

He was so intent on getting to his destination that he did not immediately notice the group of people he'd nearly crashed into or its royal leader until a heavy hand clapped his back.

"Good Lord, Beswick, didn't think I would see you here."

"Your Highness," he said, recognizing the rounded bulk of the Prince Regent surrounded by his usual fawning entourage. Thane bowed. "I had urgent business that saw me here."

"Must have been important, then, for you to leave the comforts of Beswick Park. I haven't seen you in an age. Too good for Carlton House these days, are you?"

The censure in his tone was just enough to rub Thane the wrong way. He didn't want to be rude, but he was already at the end of his rope. While he could handle the Regent most days, he was not in the mood to deal with his self-indulgent, emotional hysterics of why he hadn't attended one of his extravagant, hedonistic parties. He glanced around at the flamboyant crowd with a measure of distaste—*this* was exactly the reason.

"Apologies, Prinny. I won't take up much of your time."

"You're staying, aren't you?" he demanded. "I've

only just made my appearance. You must stay. My shindigs are marvelous."

"Unfortunately, I must be getting back to Beswick Park," he said. "Though, since I've found you, I did have a small matter to discuss, if it pleases you."

The Regent frowned at the thought of being deterred from his revelry. "What's that? Though you must be quick. I'm famished and thirsty." He laughed and belched loudly, patting his round belly.

Thane focused on the matter at hand, knowing he didn't have long before something or someone else caught the Regent's regard. The man had the attention span of a gnat. "The Earl of Beaumont recently petitioned you regarding his suit to marry Lady Isobel Everleigh, Viscount Everleigh's niece."

"I don't recall, but I've been in my cups of late," he said with a pasty grin. Thane suppressed his sigh. The Prince Regent was well-known for his excesses. Though if he didn't remember his agreement with Beaumont, then that was a good thing. "Beaumont, Beaumont. Yes, I seem to recall something about a chit."

"She has married the Marquess of Roth," Thane said. "With my backing. However, I did not mean to go above any agreement you might have made."

The Regent scratched his chin and chortled. "Roth, that bounder, is married?"

"He needed to inherit."

"Ah yes, our esteemed rules of aristocratic primogeniture." He rolled his eyes as his entourage twittered. "Good, because he owes me a thousand quid."

Prinny's love of gambling was no secret, even coupled with the fact that he was head over heels in debt. It wouldn't surprise Thane if *he* owed Roth money, instead of the other way around.

"And Beaumont?" he said.

"Don't worry—we'll find him someone else."

Thane cleared his throat. "There's one more thing, Your Highness. Beaumont served in my regiment and left his watch post during an ambush. Many men died, and as you know, I barely survived. Several men reported that his gunshot wound was self-inflicted. When I returned to England, it was only to learn that he had been discharged with honor and inherited his uncle's title."

The Regent's eyes narrowed, his irritation clear. "What is it you wish me to do?"

"Open an investigation," Thane said. "That's all I ask. Provide justice for those men who died."

"Very well, I'll get someone on it. But no more, Beswick. You're trying my patience as is." He waved an arm. "Get a drink. Indulge."

He bowed. "Of course, Your Highness."

Thane let out the breath he'd been holding. Given Prinny's capricious nature, he could have gone either way. He could have taken great insult at Thane's accusations. Thankfully, Thane's military service to the Crown spoke for itself, and his reputation preceded him, even with the Regent, whose only goals in life involved gambling, womanizing, and drinking. However, most things with Prinny didn't come without a price, and so Thane waited.

"I look forward to some sport at Beswick Park before the Little Season," Prinny said over his shoulder as he moved toward the entrance to his residence and then gestured for his entourage to follow.

Thane pinched his lips but nodded. The abbey had not been open to guests since his father died, and the last thing Thane wanted was to host a bunch of drunken womanizers in the form of the Carlton set anytime soon. Their type of sport didn't tend to favor grouse or foxes. They had a reputation for debauchery and dissipation, two things he no longer had a taste for.

After doing as requested and forcing down a glass of fine whiskey—he didn't want to insult the Regent in his own home—Thane made his way back to the front as unobtrusively as possible and signaled a footman to retrieve his horse while he waited in the entrance hall. His skin felt tight, and his scars pulled. He needed to get back home. Needed a swim.

"I think you might have forgotten something behind, Your Grace," a lilting voice said.

Thane froze at the sound, his breath stilling in his lungs, and turned to see an angel in midnight-blue satin standing at the top of the steps just inside the doors. He blinked. Surely he was dreaming. But no, when he opened his eyes, Astrid was still there.

He closed his eyes and gripped his thigh with numb fingers, fighting the pull of her voice with everything in him. Footsteps clicked against the polished checkered marble as she drew closer, and soon, her scent curled around him, weakening his resolve even further.

"What's that?" he said without thinking.

"Your wife."

• • •

Astrid stared at him, her heart pounding in her throat.

She'd left Lady Hammerton's not long after he had, but it had taken her a bit longer, as she'd opted to use Mabel's carriage and she knew he'd ridden on Goliath. Even with a team of horses pulling the coach, that was no match for Goliath's stamina or speed. But she was here now, and that was all that mattered.

"Did you follow me?" he asked.

"I had to."

"How could you be so foolish, Astrid?" he chided, steering her into a nearby alcove away from the throngs of people flocking through the hall. "Do you know how dangerous the roads are at this time of night? You could have been hurt, stopped by highwaymen, robbed, or killed!"

"I'm unhurt, as you can see."

"You were lucky. If anything had happened to you, I'd never forgive myself."

Even in his anger, his face looked tortured, but Astrid wasn't going to stop until he was honest with her. "Then, for once, talk to me, Thane. Stop hiding behind this temper of yours and tell me what you're really feeling. You're not alone anymore. *Trust* in me."

"Here?" he asked.

She nodded. "It's as good a place as any."

He scrubbed his hair and stalked to the floor-to-ceiling windows. The leashed danger emanating from his body made the few occupants scurry out of the room. Astrid huffed a breath. He didn't even realize he was doing it—using this ruthless, harsh facade as a front to terrorize people. The menace surrounding him was innate…like a suit of armor.

After a beat, Thane turned to face her and began to speak. "When I fought on the Continent, I fought for duty to king and country, and I've seen and done things that have taken a toll." He swallowed hard, his gaze going inward for a moment. "My scars are the least of it. I'm fractured on the inside, Astrid, and you don't need that. My own father ran from me. My brother, too. And then you came along and confounded every expectation I had. You made me feel again, and for that I'll always be grateful that I met you."

Astrid didn't want his gratitude. She wanted his *love*.

She knew more than anyone that the wounds on the inside were as bad as the ones on his face and body. Her scars didn't hold a candle to his, to what he'd suffered, and she'd barely recovered from those. Thane was stronger and more resilient than he knew, and he was deserving of everything. She couldn't save him, but he could save *himself*. He had to love himself before anyone else could…before he could accept that others *did*.

"Why did you go to Lady Hammerton's, Thane? Was it only for Isobel and Lord Roth?"

He exhaled. "I went to be with you. I *wanted* to be with you, but when I saw Isobel with him, I realized I was being selfish. I wanted you to be free to choose who you want to love."

"I *have* chosen. I chose you. I'm here, aren't I?" She closed the distance between them and reached up to cup his face. "Even if you divorced me, you daft man, I would still choose you. I'd follow you to the ends of the earth. Or to the infamous Carlton House, as it were."

"Why?"

Astrid rose on tiptoe to drag her lips across his ear. "Because I love you. I don't want a sodding prince, you idiot. They're too pretty, too full of themselves, too much maintenance." She rocked back with a grin and waved a hand. "Who needs all this opulence? Give me a dark abbey and a grumpy beast any day."

He froze, the vulnerability on his face nearly bringing her to her knees.

"The thing is, I'm not Isobel. I'm *me*. And I'm imperfect and combative and my mouth tends to run away with me, and I say things before I think about them. I'm bold and outspoken and probably don't belong in polite society."

"I don't, either."

"What a pair we make." She smiled. "But we're made for each other, Thane. Don't you even—"

Breath deserted her as he crushed her to him, his mouth taking hers in a kiss that tore the words from her lips and left her mind spinning. She could hardly draw air into her lungs when he pulled back and positioned her a few inches away.

"What…what are you doing?" she gasped as he wrapped one large arm about her waist and threaded the other into her gloved fingers.

"What I should have done the minute I saw you

at Lady Hammerton's ball. I wish to dance with my wife." He drew her against his lean, hard body and then went still, a ripple of worry chasing across his face. "Unless you don't want to."

Wild horses couldn't drag her out of the haven of her husband's arms in the middle of that room. "No, I do," she said quickly, grasping hold of his sleeves. "But we're not exactly in a ballroom, and we seem to have gathered an audience."

They did indeed have an audience, including several nobles dressed to the nines, blatantly observing their interlude. Astrid blushed hard at the thought that Thane had kissed her so thoroughly in such a public venue. It wasn't *done*. Then again, this was Carlton House, and even she had heard of some of the dissipation that flooded its halls. She blinked, recognizing a few of the faces as some infamous aristocrats from Prinny's notoriously fast set.

"Is that the Duke of Rutland?" she whispered. "And Viscount Petersham?"

"Ignore them," Thane whispered, holding her close as he began to move them in a slow waltz, the faint strains of music from the gardens enough to guide their steps.

"They're staring at us."

Thane gathered her close, placing his large hand on her waist. "Why wouldn't they? They're looking at the most beautiful woman here."

"Or perhaps because we're dancing in the foyer of the Regent's residence, and they think us daft." But she was smiling as she said it, her heart over-flowing.

"Who cares what anyone else thinks?"

She swayed unsteadily, her breath catching. "You usually do. Do you wish to leave? I know you hate this…being out in public."

"I do," he agreed. "But I love you more."

Time stopped, voices and people fell away, and the only things she could see were her husband's beautiful, shining eyes. "What did you say?" she whispered.

He drew her into a flawlessly executed turn, despite the lack of music and despite the rapt attention. "I love you, Astrid Harte, with everything remaining inside me. All of it—the good, the bad, the broken. I'm nothing without you. And if I can't face a few empty-headed aristocrats to make you happy, then I'm not worthy of you."

Her feet, for some reason, had refused to work, along with her brain. Thank God for his excellent timing and impeccable skills because she would be flat on her bottom. But there was nowhere else she would rather be. Suddenly, everything fell into place. Him. Her. Them, together. Dancing like no one else mattered.

Because no one else did.

"Good God, Beswick," a loud voice said. "I said get a drink, not snatch up one of my female guests and force her to dance in the entrance hall."

Astrid sucked in a gasp as the Prince Regent strolled toward them, and she broke away mid-waltz to dip into a deep curtsy. "Your Highness."

The Regent's glassy eyes narrowed as she rose. "You're a beauty. How do I not know you?"

"Hands off, Prinny," her husband's deep voice said, a possessive arm snaking around her waist.

"She's mine. May I present Lady Astrid Beswick, my wife."

To Astrid's surprise, the Regent laughed so hard, his jowls rippled. "I'm shocked anyone would have you with that ghastly disposition of yours." The prince leered at her. "Honestly, how do you put up with him?"

She smiled. "He's not so bad, Your Highness."

The Regent scrunched up his nose, and Astrid had the sneaking suspicion that the man was foxed or stewed on something. His dissipated reputation was infamous. He peered up at the duke. "I suppose I owe you a wedding gift. What do you want besides your earlier demands? More courtesy titles? Estates?"

"God, no," the duke said. "I've more than enough of those."

"A fund for war heroes, then?"

Astrid couldn't help her wayward tongue, knowing what Thane had endured at the hands of the French on the battlefield. "How about simply avoiding war in the future?"

Her cheeks burned at the sudden, awful silence, but then the prince chuckled, and the tension broke. Relief trickled through her limbs as he addressed Thane before marching from the room. "You certainly have your hands full with that one."

"That I do." Her husband smiled down at her after the Regent left and gathered her close. "I wouldn't have it any other way."

"Your Grace?"

"Yes, my love?"

She brushed her fingertips along his hard chest

and let her desire for him fill her eyes. "I know you're all about the grand gestures at the moment, but please take me home."

Thane laughed and swept her up into his arms, crossing the entrance hall as swiftly as those long legs could carry them. Everyone else stared, but she didn't care. Neither did her husband. They only had eyes for each other. Astrid buried her head in the crook of his neck and shoulder as he parted the throng of guests with not one single growl.

She stifled a smile. He was learning, her beast.

CHAPTER TWENTY-SIX

She'd fallen asleep in his arms.

In the coach at Beswick Park, Thane didn't want to wake her. He stared down at his peaceful wife and fought the impulse to hold her tighter and closer.

His brave, fierce lioness.

God, she was so beautiful. He wanted to kiss her lips, bury his face in her hair, claim her forever. He adored her with every fiber of his being, every red-blooded cell in his body, down to his marrow. And miracles of miracles, she loved him back.

Lifting her into his arms once more, he climbed out of the coach and up the stairs. She was so exhausted that she didn't stir one bit. Fletcher opened the door in Culbert's absence, his eyes flaring wide at the sight of his master *and* mistress.

Thane started to carry her up to their chambers and then paused. "Are the hearths in the bathing chamber still lit and heated?"

"Yes, Your Grace."

"Good. Have the cook prepare some food. And thank you, Fletcher. For everything," he added.

It had been his longtime valet and friend who had made him realize what a stubborn fool he was being. Not so succinctly, but his clever mention of Lady Hammerton, her reputation for wild balls, Astrid, and randy males in the same sentence had made Thane see reason, among other things.

His cheeks went ruddy. "My pleasure, Your Grace."

In the well-lit bathing room, he lay Astrid on the sofa and then proceeded to undress her, starting with her gloves.

"Thane?" Astrid asked sleepily. "Oh, we're home," she said, her eyes adjusting and recognizing the room. "What were you doing?"

"Undressing you," he said. "I thought perhaps a swim might be soothing. The water is heated and salted. Unfortunately, Alice is in London. I can get one of the upper maids to assist with your garments, if you prefer." Aware that he was babbling, he sealed his lips.

She slid her palm over his and squeezed. "I confess I've been intrigued ever since the first time I saw you in here."

"And the time when you didn't," he said. "I saw you, though. I was consumed by lust watching you dip these perfect feet in."

She glanced around at the cozy sitting area that comprised two large, overstuffed sofas; an armchair; and a low table. "I didn't even realize this section was here."

A discreet knock on the outer doors had Thane on his feet, but it was only Fletcher with a tray of food. Thane thanked him and returned, sustenance in hand. Astrid's stomach growled loudly, and she giggled.

"I'm ravenous," she said, reaching for a piece of crusty bread and some cheese as he lowered the tray to the table. They didn't talk as she filled a small plate with the offerings on the tray—some cold chicken, along with fresh fruit and a warm meat pie. Thane wasn't hungry, but he watched her eat her fill.

"I was famished," she said, licking her fingers clean with a sigh. He forced himself to behave at the sight of those elegant fingers disappearing into her mouth, but his body had other ideas. Time had not dulled his infatuation with her hands. "I only had a bit of Aunt Mabel's whiskey on the way to North Stifford after luncheon at Harte House."

"She's a terrible influence."

"She's wonderful," Astrid declared loyally, but then she giggled again. "Do you know she embroiders male organs?"

Thane coughed as his mouthful went down the wrong way.

"The phallus," she added casually, as if he didn't know what a bloody male organ was. His own eavesdropping organ perked up in his trousers. "Penis, if we're being pedagogic," she went on thoughtfully.

He choked, unsure if his arousal was because of the first word or the last. He must be the only man on the planet who found his wife's brain darkly erotic. "Astrid, you cannot say such things."

"Why? You are my husband."

"Because, my little tease, you are driving me— and my variously named male parts—to purgatory."

She rose to her feet with a grin. "Good, now come and finish undressing me. I cannot breathe in these stays. And I don't want to be forced to use the filthy words I've read that describe male parts to get you to obey."

Thane swallowed hard. He wanted to hear all the foul words falling from her sweet lips, but he wanted her disrobed more. She toed off her slippers while his fingers fumbled at the tiny cloth-covered buttons down the curve of her spine. Before too long, the gorgeous midnight-blue gown pooled into a puddle at her feet. He unlaced her stays and stared at the soft transparent linen, the outline of her body a fascinating shape beneath it, before kneeling to untie her garters and roll down her stockings.

"Will you undress as well?" she whispered.

Everything inside of him shut down.

Going to the ball and baring his heart in a public courtyard had been child's play compared to this moment. Thane felt the familiar sickness rise in his chest at the thought of what she was asking and the horror that lay under his clothing. It was too bright, much too bright. He couldn't extinguish the hearths—they threw too much light. His body poised to flee, and then Astrid placed a hand on his cheek.

"You don't have to, darling."

Thane felt like a leaf caught in a storm. He was terrified, but he didn't want any more walls between them. And to do that, he would have to drop his. *All* of them.

Slowly, without a word, he unbuttoned his coat and then his waistcoat. He shucked off his boots and stockings and pulled off his cravat. All the while, she watched him, her eyes never leaving his, sending him silent assurances that she was there. His hands shook as he pulled his shirt over his head. He heard her soft gasp, and he shut his eyes, only to feel her warm arms sliding about him and holding him tight. It wouldn't be an easy sight to bear, not even for a seasoned veteran of war, but she did not flinch. Not when she would have seen the tattered mass of his back and side, the gouges and missing chunks, and the grisly tapestry that bound it all. He was not fit for a lady's eyes.

"I love you," she whispered, her lips kissing the ugly scar that ran down the entire left side of his rib cage. "I love you so much."

And Thane wanted to weep. His hands crept around her—this slip of a woman who healed him in so many ways—and he felt whole. He felt *loved*.

After a while, she released him, and the saucy minx lifted her eyebrow. "You're not going to stop there, are you?"

"Astrid."

"Don't Astrid me," she shot back. "I want to see it all. Now, your duchess commands you to strip."

Obligingly, Thane shed his trousers, and he had the distinct pleasure of seeing her shocked speechless, her eyes goggling. "It's rude to stare, Lady Beswick."

"*Th-That's* been inside me?" she sputtered. "You have got to be joking. There's no way that thing—"

"Cock," he supplied helpfully.

Her throat worked, and she licked her lips. "Whatever it is, a bloody rooster for all I care. There's no way that's fitting anywhere."

"I've already been inside you, darling. Several times."

"You must have been smaller those other times." Her face burned hot. "Maybe we should turn off the lights. I didn't realize you were protecting me from bloody Goliath all along."

"I've named my horse Goliath, not that."

He laughed and bent to take her lips in a long, sweet kiss. His wife was panting by the time he was done, her eyes glazed.

"Well, I'm going for a swim," he said huskily. "When you're done being a cowardly little chicken, feel free to join me."

. . .

"Chicken?" she retorted. "I'm not the one walking around with a fowl in his trousers."

"Cock, my love."

Astrid forgot about his impressive front as she watched those scored but taut buttocks walk away and felt her own body grow exceedingly damp. Lord above, he was spectacular. Even with all his terrible scarring, he was so virile, so devastatingly masculine, that she was having a hard time breathing. Or thinking. Or doing much of anything at all.

And that wasn't just because of the jutting appendage that had made her lose her breath. Though that in itself was remarkable. Her husband was nicely formed. Her breasts tingled, and the space between her legs went molten. She watched those muscular thighs of his bend and flex as he climbed into the pool, and she sighed. His legs, she noticed, were as badly scarred as his back, his stomach and chest the only places that had escaped serious injury. He probably would have died if his stomach had been punctured. A red lattice of vines traversed his hips, thighs, and buttocks. It was truly a wonder that he had survived.

She strolled over to the edge and sat, her legs

dangling into the water, and watched him. He moved like a fish, cleaving through the water with ease, until he went under and resurfaced at her calves. He wedged his big body between her knees, bracing his arms on either side of them. Astrid leaned down to kiss him as he pushed up out of the water, and she tasted salt.

"Why is it salted?"

"It's irrigated from the ocean," he said, slipping back down into the water but staying between her swinging limbs. "We are close enough to use water from the river mouth at the southerly end of the property. It's ingenious, the design," he explained, pointing at the large currently closed spigots on either side. "I got it from a Turkish friend of mine whose family built baths for centuries. That one releases the water back to the sea so the pool can be cleaned, and that one refills it." He grinned, gesturing at the glowing fireplaces. "The hearths keep it warm with in-ground copper piping."

"It's incredible," she said.

"Thank you. It's the only thing that helps with the pain when it gets too much to bear."

Astrid trailed her fingers through his wet hair, skimming the patch on his scalp that the slick strands no longer concealed. And then whisper-soft, down his brow to the scars on his cheek. "Do they hurt?"

"Yes, but not as much since I met you."

She frowned. "How is that possible?"

"My physician is of the astonishing opinion that a positive outlook can affect one's health for the better. I thought he was headed for Bedlam, but I suppose he may be on to something after all. I've never felt like this…until you."

She nodded, biting into her lower lip in thought. "I've read that healers in the east have long believed that positive thinking is an essential key to healing. It's been proven to be a potent pain reliever."

"I might need some more persuasion, Madame Scholar." He grasped her wandering hand and brought it to his lips, kissing each finger and stopping at her index finger whose pad had five red spots. "What happened here?"

"The dratted needlework."

Her husband grinned, a wicked light appearing in those golden eyes, as he sucked it into his mouth and made her gasp. "Perhaps you might require a more scintillating change of subject. Phallic inspiration, perchance? I'm happy to oblige my duchess with anything she needs."

Releasing her hand, his palms dipped to slide up her smooth bare calves, pushing the fabric of her chemise up her thighs and making her shiver. Then he turned and placed a kiss to the inside of one knee, making her forget her own name.

"Astrid."

That's it.

She blinked, focusing uncooperative eyes on him. His hands skidded to her ankles and gripped gently. And then he smiled. Right before pulling her in. With a squeal, she surfaced, her mouth full of warmed saltwater, and squeezed water out of her eyes. "You scoundrel!"

"Can you swim?" he asked with a worried look as his hands settled around her waist.

She shot him a smirk. "Does a fish have gills? There was a pond on the Everleigh estate when I was a girl."

He laughed. "Let me guess—you wanted to do whatever the boys did."

"Correct." She pushed off his body in a glide. "I was the best swimmer of all the boys and could hold my breath the longest."

His powerful arms windmilled as he swam to her in three easy strokes. "Shall we put that to the test?"

And then she was the recipient of the sweetest, hottest, wettest kiss as he sank them both beneath the surface of the water. Her legs weaved between his, the water making the coarse male hair on his thighs feel impossibly sleek. He was hairless in patches where his scars stretched but no less manly for it.

Astrid felt his hands at her thighs and the hem of her sodden chemise scraping up along her body as he divested her of the last of her clothing, breaking the kiss only to pull it over her head. Then it was pure heaven as his big, warm body met hers skin to skin, chest to chest, and still, they kissed, an endless tangle of lips and tongues.

She felt him hard against her body and moaned into his mouth softly as he pushed them back to the surface in a shower of droplets. His hands wandered along the length of her back, gliding over smooth, wet skin, down to the curve of her buttocks to hitch one leg over his hip. She gasped at the sudden feel of the broad crown of his erection nuzzling into her sex.

"I want you," he whispered, kissing her nose.

"Then take me." She wriggled her hips, making him hiss as the head of him notched in slightly.

Bringing her to the side of the bathing pool, Thane's palm brushed against her belly and over her breasts, then down to the other thigh, which he hefted to wrap around his waist. Bending his head, he caught a taut nipple into his mouth and sucked hard as he drove up with his hips, spearing himself into her body.

The combination of his powerful body, the feel of him thrusting into her, his marauding mouth, and the sleekness of the water made the experience the most erotic thing Astrid had ever felt. She felt him *everywhere*. The water against her skin amplified every sensation, swilling between their sliding bodies and creating a slippery friction that made every inch of her feel ferociously alive.

"See?" he murmured. "We are a perfect fit."

"I don't know why I doubted you."

He smirked. "Men are always right, likely due to the smaller, weaker female brain."

She squeezed her inner muscles together, wringing a groan from him. "What was that?"

"Men are superior in every way."

She tightened again and made his eyes dilate so much that the black of his pupils nearly swallowed the gold. He retaliated by thrusting hard into her, making her gasp as he filled her to the brim.

God, she loved him to absurdity. Dueling with him. Making love with him.

"Thane," she said, cupping his jaw. "This feels incredible, but I want to see you."

Thane waded to the steps at the near end and,

without breaking their seam, walked them slowly over to the chaise. Every rocking step made Astrid shudder as he shifted inside her, and by the time he sat on the sofa with her on his lap, she was a quivering, whimpering mess.

"I'm going to...*oh*..."

Her release came upon her in a rush so intense that she went blind for a full second. It was like being at the center of the sun. Pleasure streaked through her body in hot golden waves, centering at her groin and shooting into her breasts, until she sobbed his name and collapsed against him.

"I love when you come," he said, and she felt him throb within. "It feels incredible when I'm inside you, but I love to see your face."

"I love *your* face," she whispered, kissing him. Kissing his scars and his eyes and his brow. Leaning back, her hands wandered down his damp injured left side and stroked over the ridges that wound around to his ravaged back. Her fingers trailed over him, mourning his pain, worshipping his strength, and loving him.

Her husband was watching her, breath ragged and eyes shadowed. His pitted flesh flinched at every caress, but he made no move to stop her exploration. Finally, she raised her hand to his heart, feeling the steady thud against her palm.

"Mine."

"Always," he whispered back.

Looking into his eyes, she moved, lifting her hips and sliding back down upon him. Astrid made love to her husband slowly, her eyes never leaving his—ice-blue claiming brilliant gold with every stroke, with every escalating heartbeat. And when his eyes closed and his hips rolled upward with frantic stabs as he neared completion, she moved to lift off him.

"No," he whispered hoarsely, his hands seizing her hips and locking her into place.

"But, Thane, you don't want—"

He took her lips and poured himself into her. "I want it all."

CHAPTER TWENTY-SEVEN

Afterward, when they lay snuggled together and wrapped in plush toweling while snacking on grapes from their leftover meal, Thane felt his wife look up at him. He smiled. "Spit it out," he said. "I can see those wheels in your brain turning like frantic little cogs."

"You said you didn't want children."

"I thought I didn't."

Forehead creased, she pinned her lip between her teeth. "So what changed?"

Thane felt all his old fears rise up into his throat, and he drew a deep breath. Astrid loved him. His courageous wife wouldn't turn tail and run. Either way, he already decided he wanted no secrets between them, and she had already trusted him with all of hers.

"I did, I suppose. I was so afraid of the future — any future — that I couldn't appreciate the present and what I had in front of me. I was letting fear defeat me."

She lifted up slightly to kiss him. "Love can be scary, too. Opening yourself up and being vulnerable to another person is frightening in itself. I'd locked my heart away for a long time, and until you, I didn't know that I could trust anyone with it. It still terrifies me, knowing that it's in the keeping of someone else." She pursed her lips. "Are you still afraid?"

He shrugged. "Sometimes."

Astrid wrapped her legs and arms around him. "Then, I shall have no choice but to surround you with as much love and passion and happiness as possible. I'm not going anywhere."

"You're so fierce," he said, kissing her. "Have I told you how much I love that about you? Duchess of the indomitable spirit."

"I aim to please my duke." She nibbled his lower lip and drew his tongue into her mouth, feeling his length surge against her thigh. "That feels promising."

"You are insatiable."

She licked a hot path on his shoulder and bit gently. "For you."

Thane turned them on the chaise and draped his body over hers. "You really think we have a chance?"

His wild, beautiful, sassy duchess winked. "Does a fish have gills?"

• • •

Many hours later, satiated and replete, long after Thane had carried them both to his bedchamber, Astrid propped herself up onto her elbows, watching her husband sleep as the morning sun washed over the sky. His sensuous mouth was parted, his thick, dark eyelashes with their gilded tips resting against the top of his cheeks. Silky sable hair curled into his face, one muscled arm tucked under his head. He looked too delicious for words.

He had loved her until her body felt weightless, until words had ceased to matter, and until conscious thought lost any meaning.

"Sleep, sweet prince," she whispered.

Climbing out of bed as carefully as possible, she padded to her chamber and dressed in a front-fastening morning dress. She washed herself and cleaned her teeth with the water in the basin. Her hair was a mess, and without Alice, there was little she could do besides pin it into a loose knot before heading downstairs. The breakfast room was already set, and she met Fletcher in the hallway.

"Top of the morning to you, Your Grace," he said in an entirely too jovial voice with a smart bow.

Astrid blushed. It seemed that there were no secrets at Beswick Park. If the duke and his duchess spent all night frolicking in the bathing pool, it would be common knowledge by morning.

"Good morning, Fletcher."

"And might I inquire if His Grace is still abed?"

Her blush intensified. "You know he is, you dreadful man. Now, will you fetch me some coffee before I expire?"

"Certainly, Your Grace," he said with an irrepressible grin. "Oh, and her ladyship is already at breakfast."

Astrid's brows rose. Mabel had returned to Beswick Park as well? Sure enough, she was ensconced at the table being served by not one but *three* footmen. One of whom Astrid distinctly remembered being at the Hammerton ball, particularly because he wore different livery.

"Good morning, Aunt."

"Ah, my beautiful, brave girl. You look wonderfully rested. And by rested I mean ravished."

"Did you return last night?" Astrid grinned, accepting a steaming cup of coffee from Fletcher.

Mabel winked. "I only just returned." Her amber eyes flicked to Lady Hammerton's footman, and her voice lowered to a whisper. "Honestly, it's a wonder I can walk."

"Aunt *Mabel*!"

"You should be one to talk," she said. "Fletcher filled me in. Hopefully it won't be long before this place is filled with lots of little grandbabies for an old lady to dote upon."

"Old lady, my behind," Astrid said with a laugh, struggling to hide the blushes that would not relent. She selected a bit of toast and then turned to the duchess.

Her eyes warmed. "You love him, then?"

"Desperately."

"Then, we can only hope." She reached for Astrid's hand and held it tightly, and Astrid fought the sudden burn of tears behind her eyes. She squeezed back.

"There are my two favorite ladies."

The warm, husky voice sank into her very bones, and Astrid turned to see her husband, fine and still delicious, standing in the doorway. He was dressed in a shirt and breeches with no shoes and no cravat, and he looked utterly mussed and delectable.

"Honestly, Beswick," Mabel teased. "You'd think I've raised a barbarian."

"There are worse things," he said, bending to peck her cheek and then kissing Astrid with a more lingering kiss before sitting beside her.

"Did you sleep well, nephew?"

"As well as you, I imagine. I see we've acquired new help." He grinned, flexing an arm across the back of Astrid's chair and making every hair on her body stand on end as his fingers caressed her nape.

"He rode me home," she said and then widened her eyes in all innocence. "*Drove* me home."

"This is unseemly, Aunt, even for you." Thane rolled his eyes and looked at Astrid. "I told you: terrible influence." He nuzzled her ear. "Did you sleep well?"

"Thane," she gasped, feeling the wet swipe of his tongue. "The servants."

"They all know that the duke is mad over his wife, so whether I kiss you here or behind closed doors is of little significance." He bit her lobe and relented, leaning back into his chair.

Good Lord but the man was sex incarnate. They'd made love for hours, and already, she was ready to race back upstairs and have her wanton way with him. Instead, she demurely sipped her coffee and avoided Mabel's knowing looks.

Fletcher entered the door, once more doing double duty in Culbert's absence, and announced they had callers.

The duke frowned. "This early? Tell them to come back at a reasonable hour."

"Who is it?" Astrid asked at the same time.

"The Marquess and Marchioness of Roth."

None of them was dressed for callers, including a shoeless, cravat-less duke, but they were family, after all.

"Isobel!" Astrid exclaimed as her sister entered the dining room on her new husband's arm. "How are you?"

"I'm well," her sister said. "Astrid, may I present my husband, Lord Roth."

He bowed over her hand. "Your Grace."

Thane stood up, clapping the younger man on the shoulder. "Good to see you, Roth."

"And you, Beswick," the marquess said. "Although good is rather an exaggeration."

The duke barked a short laugh, but Astrid blinked at the man's slightly dry tone. Her gaze panned back to Isobel, who shot her a bright smile. Though her sister was in high spirits, her marquess seemed a bit more…taciturn. Then again, Astrid had only *just* met him. Thane knew him, however, and he'd assured her that Roth was a decent man at the heart of it. Astrid smiled to herself. She was one to talk—she had married a beast, after all.

They exchanged greetings with Mabel, and then Thane invited the newlyweds to join them for breakfast. More hot dishes were brought in and additional place settings arranged. Her sister's obvious regard for her husband was evident, and Astrid felt sad that she'd missed the wedding, but it was a small price to pay for Isobel's safety.

"So, about this marriage," Astrid said. "I, apparently, was the only one in the dark."

"Sorry about that," Isobel said. "I was waiting to see whether Lord Roth would make his intentions known at Lady Hammerton's house party, and he did. However, my plan was a little less thought out. I was hoping to convince him to elope."

Astrid lifted a brow. "That would have indeed been a scandal."

"But Scotland is days away by coach, and Lady Hammerton had a better idea. After the Earl of Beaumont showed up, the duke was able to procure a special license for us," Isobel finished excitedly. "My only regret is that you were not able to be there, Astrid, but it was very small and tasteful in Lady Hammerton's family chapel."

"I am simply glad that you're happy, Izzy."

"I am," Isobel said.

Astrid could not be upset with her sister for so bravely taking hold of her own future. It was more than she had done at that age—when she had naively found herself at the mercy of an unscrupulous man. Isobel, however, had not allowed herself to become entrapped by a society whose rules bestowed all the power to men while women bore the consequences. Astrid could not be prouder of her.

A wolf in sheep's clothing, indeed.

The newly married couple visited for a while before taking their leave. Roth was taking his bride to his family seat in Chelmsford. After they departed, Astrid turned to her husband with a mock pout. "I cannot believe you kept such a monumental secret from me."

He took her hand and kissed her knuckles, the light graze and the desirous look in his eyes making her skin burn. "If your uncle came to Harte House demanding an explanation, I wanted you to have full deniability. As it was, we did have words."

Astrid's eyes narrowed at the thought of her uncle. "What did he say?"

"He was reasonable."

"Reasonable" wasn't a word to describe her uncle,

and she knew her skeptical expression said so.

"I offered him what Beaumont had agreed to give him," her husband said.

"Why would you even give that bounder any money after everything he's done?" Astrid asked. "He'll only lose it all. He bought a fortune in horse-flesh with my father's money."

"I also took possession of those horses at a fraction of the cost and had them sent here to Beswick Park," he said with a grin. "Your groom, Patrick, was kind enough to lead the transaction. That was the business I had to conclude."

Astrid didn't care that they were in the middle of the foyer in view of a dozen servants and Aunt Mabel in the next room—she flung her arms around her husband's neck. "Oh, Thane, I love you."

"Not as much as I love you, Duchess." He smiled down at her. "And speaking of Beaumont, I suspect that after the investigation of what happened in Spain is completed, the earl will most likely be stripped of his title and estate."

"I'm glad," Astrid said feelingly. "He will get his just deserts."

Thane nodded. It would not bring back the lives of his men, but it was a start. If the earl was found guilty, he intended to ask the Regent for a portion of the earl's confiscated fortune to be used for the deceased men's families. It was less than they deserved but more than he'd hoped for.

"Now that we've had breakfast, what would you like to do today?" She bit her bottom lip and blushed.

His laugh was husky. "I suppose we could do that."

He scooped her into his wonderfully muscular arms.

"I am capable of walking," she told him.

"Yes, but my legs are much longer."

She laughed as he flew up the stairs. "I knew I married you for a reason."

EPILOGUE

Nathaniel Blakely Sterling Harte, the seventh Duke of Beswick, paced the corridor, a fine sheen of cold sweat coating his forehead. God, he'd never been so nervous in all his life. He glanced at his pocket watch and then went back to pacing. His valet watched him, not hiding his amusement, as he trampled the same stretch of carpet for the fortieth time.

"Perhaps you should have some brandy," Fletcher suggested. "You're going to wear a hole in the rug."

"It's taking too long," he said. "And since when do you care about carpet? You're turning into as much a fusspot as Culbert."

"Bite your tongue, Your Grace," Fletcher said, looking horrified. "And in any case, her ladyship is a duchess."

Thane scowled. "What does that have to do with anything?"

"Everything," he said dryly. "Ah, here she comes."

Thane perked up at the sight of his beautiful and pregnant wife, accompanied by his precocious six-year-old daughter, Lady Philippa Harte, and her younger brother, Lord Maxton Harte, the four-year-old Marquess of Locke, who were both supposed to be sleeping. He knew that because he'd fed them dinner and put them to bed ages ago, as he did almost every night.

Astrid smiled. "I had to kiss the children good

night, and they wanted a story. Since we aren't going to be back until tomorrow after the race, I said yes."

He frowned fondly at his naughty daughter, whose eyes were twinkling with mischief. He had a good idea who wanted another story. "I'd already read them *several* stories and put them to bed. Why are the two of you little crumpets still awake?"

"We wanted to say good night to Mama," Pippa said, while Max nodded his sleepy head fiercely. "And she's always writing in her study."

"I'm sorry, darlings," Astrid said. "It won't be for much longer, I promise."

It was true; his brilliant wife had been busy of late. After the publication of a few polemic literary essays on the significance of women's voices, including those of writers like Wollstonecraft and Mary Shelley, who had indeed come out as the author of *Frankenstein* a few years before, his duchess had made quite a stir in the beau monde. Some did not agree with her controversial stance that a woman was only as bad as the man behind her, but many did. She was now working on her first novel, a story about a man trapped in a woman's body and the intersection of male and female ideology. It was a bold effort, but if anyone could do it, his intrepid duchess could.

"The coachman is ready, Your Graces," Culbert announced, walking into the room. "Good gracious, I haven't been this nervous about anything since the young master was born."

"It's just a race, Culbert," Astrid said.

Fletcher shook his head, his expression as delirious as the butler's. "It's not just a race, Your

Grace! It's your champion, and he is going to win."

Several years ago, she had bred Brutus and Temperance, and the resulting foal had exceeded all expectations. The colt had been magnificent—a perfect combination of strength, stamina, and speed. She'd named him Dante, and now, the racehorse was unbeatable on any terrain of any length. Tomorrow would mark a monumental day of racing at Ascot. They planned to stay at Harte House overnight.

"Will you tuck us into bed before you leave, Mama and Papa?" Pippa asked, her sweet voice hopeful.

"Come on, quickly then, my little crumpets," Thane said, lifting Max up and tossing him into the air, making him squeal. He knelt and pulled Pippa in for a hug. She was the image of her mother. With a head full of glossy dark curls and in possession of the golden Beswick eyes, Thane had no doubt she was going to be a beauty.

"Why can't we go, too, Papa?" Max complained, tugging at Thane's coat. "I want to see Dante race."

Thane set Max on his hip and ruffled his dark-blond hair. "Because the racecourse is no place for young striplings, but I promise to take you both when you're a bit older."

"Me too, Papa, even though I'm a girl?" Pippa said with wide eyes.

He winked at her with a grin. "Being a girl never stopped your mama, and I'm willing to wager it won't stop you, either, Pippa bean."

"Yes, dearest, you can do anything you put your mind to," Astrid chimed in.

They took their children's hands and shepherded

them back toward their rooms. Thane lifted Pippa into bed, kissed her, and then did the same with his son. A pair of somber ice-blue eyes stared back at him, and it was clear Max was holding back his disappointment and doing his best to be brave about it.

"Tell you what," Thane said to him, fishing into his pocket for a sixpence. "We'll bet this on Dante from you and Pippa, and if you win, you can share all the winnings. How's that? That way, it's like you could almost be there."

"Truly, Papa?" Max said.

"Yes, truly."

He met Astrid's amused eyes as she kissed their children good night and wished them sweet dreams. "We'll be back soon, my darlings. Sleep well. Tomorrow night, we can read one of our old favorites, *La Belle et la Bête*."

The old French tale of the beauty and the beast was a Harte family favorite for obvious reasons. Thane smiled and met his wife's tender gaze from where she stood beside the bed. He couldn't fathom that she loved him so much and that after seven years of wedded bliss, she still made his heart beat faster.

His own feelings for her had grown and matured, though she could still flay him with a word and make his body leap with the flutter of an eyelash. As was evident by the small mound of her stomach, it was nigh impossible to resist her charms. She was his brilliant, beautiful duchess—his wife, his love, the mother of his children, and his light in the darkness.

"Papa?"

Thane paused at the door. "Yes, Pippa bean?"

"My favorite part of the story is when Beauty is brave enough to tell Beast she loves him," his daughter said shyly.

"That's my favorite part, too," he told her, his chest tightening with emotion as he gathered Astrid close. "As your very clever mama once wrote: Love is one part courage, one part choice, and one part luck. And like anything worth fighting for, it's worth it in the end."

Don't miss the next book from Amalie Howard

The Rakehell of Roth

Lord Winter Vance, a notorious scoundrel and the Marquess of Roth, must marry to save his inheritance, but a wife is the last thing he needs. Determined to carry on his rakish ways provoking his straitlaced duke of a father and scandalizing the ton, the minute Winter ties the knot, he dumps his starry-eyed debutante of a bride at his country estate and hies back to London.

But three years later, forgotten in slumbering Chelmsford while her husband gallivants in Town, Lady Isobel Vance decides that enough is enough and she's ready to take matters into her own hands. When a case of mistaken identity leads to a devilish dance of seduction and an indelicate wager is made, this marchioness will show her marauding marquess just who he married.

ACKNOWLEDGMENTS

I loved writing this story so much, but it wouldn't have been the book it is today without my two incredibly savvy, talented, and brilliant editors, Liz Pelletier and Heather Howland. You ladies ROCKED IT. Thank you so much for all your love for this book—it means so, so much. Team LAH for the win!

To the fantastic production, design, quality assurance, and publicity teams at Amara, with special thanks to Stacy Abrams, Curtis Svehlak, Holly Bryant-Simpson, Riki Cleveland, Heather Riccio, Katie Clapsadl, Jessica Turner, Bree Archer, and Erin Dameron-Hill, thank you for all your hard work. To Ginger Clark, who sold this title, thank you for helping to make this book such a gorgeous reality. To my current agent, Thao Le, thank you for your advice, support, and enthusiasm. I'm looking forward to all the things!

I'd like to shout out to my friends and fellow writers—Sophie Jordan, Mary Lindsey, Brigid Kemmerer, Angie Frazier, Wendy Higgins, Rachel Harris, Katie McGarry, Suzanne Young, and Cindi Madsen—you ladies keep me laughing and sane on this roller coaster of a journey. Thanks for always being willing to read, brainstorm, or commiserate. I adore you all to pieces.

To the readers, bloggers, booksellers, and librarians who spread the word about my books and humble me with their unwavering support, I have so much gratitude for you. Thank you for all you do. To my extended family and friends, online and off, thank you so much for your continued love and friendship. It means more than you know. Last of all, but certainly not least, to the loves of my life—Cameron, Connor, Noah, and Olivia—I'd be lost without you.

Keep reading for a
sneak peek at Stacy Reid's

MY
DARLING
DUKE

Miss Katherine Danvers has always been a wallflower. But now with her family on the brink of financial ruin, she finds herself a *desperate* wallflower. To save her family, she'll do anything. Luckily, she has the perfect plan...

She'll impress the *ton* by simply announcing she is engaged to the reclusive and mysterious Duke of Thornton, Alexander Masters, and secure strong matches for her sisters. No one has heard from the duke in years. Surely he'll never find out before her sisters' weddings and she can go back to her own quiet life.

Soon, though, everything is out of control. At first, it's just a few new ball gowns on the duke's accounts. Then it's interviews with reporters eager for gossip. Before she knows it, Katherine has transformed herself into Kitty Danvers, charming and clever belle of the *ton*—with everyone eager to meet her thankfully absent fiancé.

But when the enigmatic Alexander Masters suddenly arrives in the city, dashing and oh so angry, he demands retribution. Except not in the way Katherine expected...

CHAPTER FIVE

The duke's low tone was darkness and sin and something wickedly delightful. And she heard the threat of challenge and warning in his soft, contemplative question.

Before she could formulate a proper response, the sound of the hostess ordering the orchestra to play pierced the air. Too slowly for comfort, the strains of the waltz leaped to life, and those who found the scandalous dance more rousing than Kitty and, presumably, the duke swept themselves away onto the floor.

Suddenly, Lady Sanderson herself was by their side.

"Your Grace, you honor me," the marchioness breathed, dipping into a curtsy, her eyes glowing her pleasure. What a coup it was for her to be the first to declare the Duke of Thornton had been under her roof. "I've summoned my lord from the card rooms, and he shall be here momentarily."

Her gaze lingered too long on the porcelain mask before flickering to the bath chair. The marchioness wrung her hands, her fluster spiking the nervous tension inside Kitty.

It was imperative she find a way to escape the ball, rush home, pack her belongings, and disappear.

As if the duke sensed her silly, panicked thoughts, he spoke. "I will meet with Sanderson before I depart. As it stands, I must confer with my...*beloved* immediately."

Dear God.

He had read the scandal sheets.

The marchioness dipped into a curtsy and hurried away.

"If I recall correctly," the duke continued, turning back to her, "Sanderson has a small drawing room this way, which would offer us privacy, Miss Danvers."

Away from the ball, and safety, and her friends, and possibly flight? Most certainly not.

Yet her tongue would not loosen. A mocking smile ghosted across the half lips not covered by the mask, and Kitty narrowed her eyes, not liking that he perceived her dreadful anxiety.

"Certainly, Your Grace. If you'll lead the way," she said staunchly.

They turned away from the ballroom, and the weighted speculation of the *ton* felt like a boulder pressed on top of her shoulders. As her fiancé, he could converse with her in relative privacy without undue conjecture, and Kitty would still ensure she left the door ajar.

The manservant spoke to him in Greek as he pushed him in the wheeled contraption down the empty hallway.

Why was she merely following like a lamb to the slaughter?

"I believe this to be the drawing room," the duke said smoothly.

His manservant opened the door, and she cheered up slightly to see it was a small study. That, however, did not deter him. There was a fire burning low in the grate, and the room was cast in more shadow than light.

"This is adequate," he said, then addressed the servant once more in the same language.

His servant bowed, and then a silver-handled walking cane seemed to materialize in the hands of the manservant. The duke gripped it and stood.

Oh. He could walk.

The duke was taller than she imagined, and though he had a cane, his posture was impeccable. Her forehead barely cleared his chin, bringing the masculine breadth of his chest into stark review. He was dressed in formal trousers and jacket, complemented by a blue waistcoat and an expertly tied silken cravat.

His body was lean, lithe, powerful, with no trace of softness anywhere. That she did not expect from a man in a bath chair.

How had he ended up this way? While the gossip had hinted of an accident, no details had been revealed. The question hovered on her lips, and she forcibly swallowed it back.

He waved for her to precede him inside, and she sauntered into the room with affected calm. She jolted when he closed the door behind him with a decisive *snick*. "I believe, Your Grace, the door should be ajar. For propriety's sake," she hurriedly added.

It was important to her he did not think her afraid or witless.

"Do you?"

Kitty felt an odd sense of shock at that bland remark. "Yes, of course."

His unswerving gaze made her uneasy. "I cannot

credit you would want anyone from society over-hearing the conversation we are about to have."

Oh dear. This was a disaster.

He considered her in the silence that followed. The duke stood perfectly still, rigidly erect with the aid of his walking cane, and aristocratic. Kitty found his quality of stillness so unnerving.

Then he asked, his tone soft and lethal, "How do you dare?"

Ice lodged in her stomach and her entire body trembled for precious seconds. She gathered herself. Straightened her spine and took a hard, deep breath. "I was desperate and foolish," she said with fearful honesty.

He angled his sleek, dark head to one side and studied her with unflinching intensity. A flare of rest-lessness blossomed through Kitty, and for a moment she could hear only the pounding of her own heart. She barely managed to maintain her calm compo-sure.

"Why are you pretending to be my fiancée, Miss Danvers?"

Lie, her instincts screamed, but she could not. Her sins were already too great against this man. Kitty began to feel the weight of his stare, and it took an inordinate amount of will not to flinch. "Your Grace, when I consider how dreadfully I have imposed upon you, I am stricken with mortification."

A barely there smile touched his lips, then vanished so quickly she wondered if it was her overwrought nerves encouraging her imagination.

"I truly doubt a woman of your ingenuity might be mortified in any situation."

Kitty took a deep breath and tried to be quick in her explanation as to why her pretensions had been needed. "It was ill-judged of me to concoct a plan that shamelessly importuned upon your good name and reputation. My intention was to save my sisters and mother from a life of poverty and unhappiness. I promise I will repay every penny spent on letting the townhouse and the monies and the carriages. I have planned to secure employment as a governess after my sisters are settled comfortably, and by my calculation, I shall be able to repay your unmatched generosity in about…ten years or so."

He smiled. And it was her turn to simply stare. Why was he smiling? The man must be addled.

"You…you are not angry?"

He seemed to consider this. "No."

Something brilliant and cunning glowed in the depths of his eyes. Then the fireplace flickered, the light shifted, and only the most arresting cerulean blue pinned her beneath its piercing stare. His entire body, his very demeanor spoke of strength. A duke secured in his elevated position, the embodiment of privilege.

Who is this man?

"May I ask why, Your Grace?"

"You wish me to be angry with you, Miss Danvers?" he murmured.

"Of course not. I have imagined every scenario in which you confronted me, Your Grace, and none resembles this. I…I fear I am failing to understand what is happening."

There was a disconcerting hint of sensuality in his slight smile. *Oh, what do I know?* She was fighting to keep her wits about her; nothing was making sense. For all she knew, he could be withholding flatulence. Gentlemen tended to do that in a lady's presence.

Heat bloomed through her at her unladylike thoughts, and his piercing gaze sharpened. "Would you like to share more of your thoughts, Miss Danvers?"

"No." Her blush got hotter, and she turned away, lifting her face to the fresh night air coming through the slightly open windows. She walked away to the fire, and after a struggle to regain her composure, she said, "I fear you've lost all good opinions of me before we've had a chance even to converse. Not that I flatter myself to think we would have ever met or that you would find me favorable."

She flushed at her panicked ramblings, took a deep breath to steady her nerves. Kitty lifted her chin, looking beyond his shoulder, finding his mask disconcerting. *Do not be a silly miss*, she chided herself, then leveled her gaze to his face cast in shadows.

She wondered how he had placed himself so well in the ominous shadow cast from the fire. Habit perhaps? Did he feel more comfortable in the arms of darkness? She was being morbid when she desperately wanted the circumstances to be anything but. "May I ask…what is to be done about our situation, Your Grace?"

"I believe these unorthodox circumstances call for informality, Katherine. Please call me Alexander."

Why did he sound so reasonable and unruffled? Certainly the entire affair was beyond remarkable. *Alexander.* Though he had invited the familiarity, she could not be so intimate with a man who made her feel so desperately unsure of her position. Worse, why did his request sound like an invitation to sin and debauchery? Surely it was her overwrought nerves.

"You are awfully silent, Your Grace."

"I am content with observation."

"Of?"

They fell into a striking silence, which was distinctly uncomfortable. A few moments later, it struck her that perhaps he was not a man at ease with conversation. The rumors did say he was a recluse and had been without the proper company of society for many years. Why, she had never imagined anyone could be so unflappable in such a potentially ruinous situation.

"Observation of what, Your Grace?" she asked again, not certain what to do or say anymore. It was simply all too surreal.

"You invite study, Miss Danvers. I've been following your conquests of the *ton* most carefully."

Her heart jolted. "My conquests?"

"The newspaper articles and scandal sheets of your many outings and escapades. Reporters seem fit to compare your laugh with that of a nightingale, your smile to that of sunshine. Quite riveting, I'm sure you would agree. The *ton* declared themselves scandalized by our courtship, but we know they are secretly fascinated and hunger for more. I am not quite certain what to make of you."

The reporters had been merciless in their pursuits for quotes from her about the reclusive duke. It shattered her to think he might have read all the ridiculous flattery she'd claimed he showered upon her. He might have thought her a woman desperate for artful compliments and love.

A flush worked its way over Kitty's body as humiliation crawled through every crevice of her heart.

"I spent most of my journey here wondering what kind of woman you are," the duke said. "I imagined Kitty Danvers in numerous scenarios. A hardened fraudster? A con artist fleecing the merchants on my good name? A jewel thief using my connections to enter the best houses? A bored lady simply stirring mischief and mayhem? I wondered how to best dispose of you."

Her heart lurched, and a shiver went through her entire body. "Your Grace, I—I fear 'dispose' may not be the right word to use in this situation. I daresay it rings too ominously."

Nothing warm lit in his eyes at her miserable attempt at humor. Dratted man.

Still, a reassuring remark would not be misplaced, yet he offered none. The duke merely stared, as if she were an unusual creature that invited the most intense speculation. She could hear the faint din of laughter and clinking of glasses from the ballroom, and she concentrated on those muted signs of frivolity, slowing her heart to normalcy. Her entire family depended on her to be unflappable and courageous in the face of such ruinous uncertainty.

She dipped into a quick, elegant curtsy before lifting her chin and squaring her shoulders. "I never meant you any harm, Your Grace. I truly only wanted to borrow your connections for a few months. If I had dreamed for even a second it would reach your ears, I would *never* have done it. Pray believe that I am sincere."

He took a step forward, and she shifted back. Their slight dance had the visible side of his face cloaked entirely.

"And does that excuse validate your outrageous deception, Miss Danvers?"

The mask staring at her was at once cold and removed, then glowed with sinister intent. A strange roaring thundered in her ears, and she felt a moment's unwilling fascination.

"Of course not, but I pray it may temperate your disgust and anger and allow me the chance to make amends."

A slow, fascinating smile curved his mouth. She began to think that he was a very strange man, and one with whom it was going to be more difficult to deal than she had foreseen.

Kitty glanced away, hurrying over to the far-left corner, and lit a candle atop the oak desk. *There*. Fewer shadows and, indeed, less anxiety on her part. She faced him, frowning her displeasure to see that the candlelight had only served to throw more shadows into the small study, and the wretched man seemed to be…amused? Discerning with that dreadful porcelain mask was hard.

"I have the greatest apprehension my family will never recover from the scandal exposure will bring. I must know, Your Grace. I believe you are too honorable to wilfully subject me to the anxiety I currently feel. Will you please inform me how we are to proceed?"

She prayed he wouldn't send notices to the papers

of her deception. Poor Anna would be wretched for certainly. She would lose whatever admiration the baron possessed. The implication of everything else was simply too frightful to consider. This man could have Kitty jailed or committed.

"Without knowledge of my character, you presume me to be honorable? How naive you reveal yourself to be. Or are you being artful in your flattery for an advantage? You are a beguiling complexity, Miss Danvers."

The dark indulgence in his tone rattled her equanimity as nothing else had done that night. A message throbbed in his voice, one she was unable to decipher, but a ripple of awareness scythed through her. The duke was a man who stood in the gray area of morality. Perhaps that was the reason he'd not exuded disgust at her charade, the reason he hadn't penned a letter to the newspapers denouncing her…and maybe the reason he had traveled to see her.

The very implication of *that* being the reason he stood before her left her breathless with a bewildering clash of fear and anticipation.

"May I ask what you will do, Your Grace?" How odd she sounded, so calm when she wanted to scream her fear at his slow response.

A tense silence blanketed the room for gut-wrenching moments. *Say something*, she wanted to snap. But she worked to be temperate and bury the panic.

"Ah," he said with that odd, fleeting smile. "I believe I shall do nothing."

Kitty laughed and then sobered instantly. In fact, she tugged the white half glove from her right hand

and placed the back of her palm against her forehead. Her skin was surprisingly cool. She understood nothing, and she was uncertain that she wanted clarity anymore.

"Are you well, Miss Danvers?"

The cool mockery in his tone suggested the wretched man knew he toyed with her composure.

"Yesterday I was caught in the rain. I had a mild fever when I went to bed. I am not altogether certain I did wake this morning. There is a very strong possibility I might still be in bed dreaming."

He tilted his head. "You are also peculiar. I like that."

Kitty was even more confident she was stuck in some delirious nightmare. There was a trace of amusement in the odd warmth of his voice. Nothing was clear, and she glared at the mask obscuring the nuances of his features. She wanted to flee from the madness of this encounter, and perplexingly she wanted to stay…to converse with him, to find out why he had truly come for her, what path she needed to traverse to avoid scandal and ruin.

"Why do you wear a mask?" she asked. "The speculation of your peculiarity will be on the lips of everyone within society."

He faltered into such complete stillness, she wondered if he breathed.

"My face is scarred," the duke finally replied.

She had not heard that rumor or even a mention in the newspapers she'd dug up on him. And Kitty was glad there hadn't been rabid speculation that fed his pain to the *ton* for fodder of gossips.

"Show me," she whispered, mildly shocked that

she would dare be so familiar and improper. What madness had overtaken her? She could not credit it. Though her reaction was unpardonable, Kitty lifted her chin, an evidently defiant gesture, and waited.

"Ah…not only are you peculiar but also daringly impudent. My interest soars, Miss Danvers, infinitely so. I wonder, is this your diabolical design?"

She sucked in a breath at that bit of provoking cynicism.

He took one step closer, and the room shrank. How did he do it?

"I only thought to look upon the features of Your Grace. It is decidedly odd to converse with you so masked, as I am ignorant of your full appearance. There was nothing else behind my request."

The hand not gripping the cane pressed against his heart, and two fingers tapped twice. "How disappointing, truly."

He was the peculiar one, and Kitty felt like a leaf floating on the vast waters of the ocean, being churned about in its frothy waves. The duke was a man of consequence, and she sensed the force of the crafty and intelligent personality surrounding her.

While it pained her to admit it…she was intimidated.

Every instinct warned her that it would not do to appear frightened or witless, that he would not mind that she was in possession of an unruly tongue, as her mother often lamented. Yet why should it matter that he would like her oddity? The only thing of import was that her family escaped unscathed, even if she were sacrificed upon the altar of her desperate recklessness.

"Your Grace seems to want me to have another reason for my request; I would not dare disappoint you." She canted her head left, assessing him. "Perhaps you are not the Duke of Thornton...and a charlatan out to deceive me."

He smiled, and her heart beat faster.

"Is that the best you can do?" He *tsk*ed, as if disappointed. "Do you really think I'm not Thornton?"

"I believe you are the duke," she admitted. It was too preposterous to consider another scenario. Only the real duke would know she pretended.

"Why do you think I came for you?"

"Am *I* the only reason you are here?"

"Yes."

Dear God. It was so odd, Kitty could not dismiss him from any part of her awareness, and she so desperately wanted to. "I...am not sure, Your Grace. You are not angry or outraged. Your intentions are elusive to me, and I dearly wish they were not."

The hand gripping the silver-handled walking cane tightened. "Did you think it was mere rumors, wicked gossips, which I'm long used to, that pushed me with the force of a battering storm from my estate in Scotland to mingle with these vipers of society? Did you think I traveled for days and night unceasingly to be faced with pretence from your lips, Miss Danvers?"

She stared at him helplessly, her mouth dry and alarm flipping through her belly with the speed of a racehorse at Aston. It touched his lips again—that unfathomable half smile that hinted at a secret or forces at play only he understood.

"You are different, Miss Danvers. In the cold

silence of my chamber, my thoughts were consumed with meeting you. I fancifully wondered if you had bewitched me; then I wondered if I had become so desperate in my emptiness that a prick of light in the form of deception could rouse me so. Different is always good, welcome, something bright, wonderful, and exquisite from the ordinary drudgery, don't you agree?" he asked with surprising frankness.

What was he saying? Her skin felt sensitized, and her heartbeat was impossible to control. "Your Grace…"

The hollowness in his tone as he referred to his desperate emptiness struck her forcibly. And the notion that her mad scheme had inspired him somehow was too remarkable. She was something bright…and *exquisite*? Her mouth went even drier.

The duke had come for something from her, and she wanted to cry her frustration, for she still could not perceive it. "What do you require of me?"

"Honesty, Miss Danvers." His voice was like a slow stroke of flames across her sensitive skin. "Going forward…let it be honesty that binds us."

She took a quick breath of utter astonishment. "Your words imply a state of future entanglement for us, Your Grace. I question such a possibility. I will, however, at this moment endeavor to be honest…always," she whispered.

He deserved it from her, considering how she had used his reputation without shame or regret.

The cold brilliant blue of the eyes behind the mask glittered with something fierce before his lashes fluttered down. When they lifted, only curious indifference stared at her.

"Tell me, why do you wish to see the face behind the mask?"

"I…" She laced her fingers before her stomach and considered the man who stared at her with such penetrating regard. As if he wanted to strip her of all facade and see the heart of the woman in front of him. *Honesty*… "Perhaps I want to see the face of the man who inspires such vexatious impetus inside me."

A quick flash of intrigue and expectation before he canted his head left and said, "Oh?"

As their eyes met, she felt a shock of some undefinable sensation dart through her. Awareness flowered inside Kitty. He enjoyed the notion she was not cowering before him.

"My heart beats, my palms are sweaty, a thousand questions swirl in my mind, yet I feel more alive than I've been in longer than I can remember. I feel fear but also anticipate something I do not understand."

Pleasure lit in the cold blue beauty of his eyes. "Ahh."

Such satisfaction in his soft exhalation.

Stupidly, shockingly, she stepped closer to the man. "Your Grace. Let me see your face."

Kitty knew she would never be able to look back and know in what moment of this intimate encounter she had decided to abandon all sense of propriety and expectations of her position in society and all the gentle admonishments of her dear mamma over the years. The excuse of honesty felt like the reason she used to reveal the wanton and improper lady who had always existed within.

Silence lingered. Yet she sensed he was inordinately pleased with her. Was it her turn to be fanciful?

Embers sparked from a log in the fireplace. Unexpectedly, he reached up and removed the mask. The revelation was abrupt, the ensnarement of her complete regard immediate.

The twisted skin of his face was so macabre, yet the man so beautiful.

The release of her breath trembled on her lips and settled in the room.

The skin across his left cheek and down to his chin and neck was indeed roped with brutal scars. Kitty wondered how a man who seemed so self-assured and powerful could be wounded in such a manner. It was unsettling to see such imperfection in an otherwise stunningly masculine face.

Without the mask obscuring his features, the bold, arrogant slash of his cheekbones hinted at restrained power. Lips that had seemed full and sensual before now had a ruthless curve. And his eyes without the sunken shadow cast by the white mask…were exquisite in their dark-blue brilliance and piercing intelligence. The unscarred side of his face was smooth, wrinkle free, clear of laugh lines or frown lines. As if he meandered through life, expressionless, his heart reserved with no outward emotion to show.

This time when he moved closer, she stood her ground. They stared at each other. He had a quality of stillness that hinted at unfathomable depth. And helpless curiosity roiled through her, feeling as if invisible strings reached from him to her…

And pulled them closer.

Kitty tried to recall how many glasses of champagne she'd consumed.

He measured her with a cool, appraising glance. "The last ball I attended and showed my face at, at least nine ladies fainted. I believe I can still hear their shrieks of horror."

How had she not uncovered that bit of gossip in her research on the duke? She lifted a shoulder in an inelegant shrug. "That must have been some time ago."

"Seven years if I recall correctly."

"I must say I know no one with such delicate nerves."

The duke gave her an arresting stare. "So you are not frightened, Miss Danvers?"

"I would be the worst sort of lady to be frightened by someone hurt by misfortune, wouldn't you agree?"

He remained silent, studying her with uncomfortable intensity, and she returned his regard with unabashed curiosity. It was then she observed grooves of discomfort bracketing his mouth. *He's in pain*. His posture had also altered, and though now he leaned heavily on his cane, he did not seem less. The duke was the most virile and arresting person she had ever met, and her face heated for having such improper thoughts.

Kitty swallowed her alarm when his hand tightened on his walking stick, and he slowly ambled closer. He stumbled, and with a gasp, she lunged toward him.

He slapped her outstretched hand, but she did not recoil, gripping his upper arm to steady him.

"Your Grace!"

His impossibly beautiful eyes iced over. Slowly she released him but didn't step back. Kitty suspected she had offended him with her instinctive reaction, as fierce pride and a guarded watchfulness burned in the gaze that settled upon her.

This was not a man who relied on others for help, and even now with the grooves of pain deepening the frown on his lips, he did not unbend. There was a stillness in his gaze that spoke of suffering, an unfathomable strength, and something elusive that she might never touch or comprehend. Suddenly her heart ached, and her throat burned sensing the depth of pain he must have endured to be this indomitable.

Finally, he reached for her hand and she allowed it, though she could not say why.

"Forgive me, Miss Danvers. I confess I am not used to being touched by anyone other than Penny."

His lover? Why did the notion make her heart squeeze?

His thumb made a slow stroke down her wrist. "My sister."

Oh. She took a long, ragged breath. "I didn't wonder at it."

"Liar," he whispered with soft amusement. "Your eyes are very expressive. It is a wonder you were able to fool anyone."

He lowered his head, and Kitty stared up at him uncomprehendingly. Then nothing else mattered, for his lips pressed against hers and her senses caught fire. She gasped at the soft featherlike pressure as his mouth gently molded over hers. With a quiet sound of surprise, she parted her lips and stiffened as shock poured through her veins when he touched his tongue to her bottom lip.

"You are truly an innocent. I wouldn't have thought it," he murmured against her lips.

Kitty stumbled back, staring at him helplessly. "Whyever did you kiss me?"

Inexplicably, Kitty's heart pounded, and something long dormant inside her stretched and hummed to life. The ripple of interest to know this man burned through her, igniting a need that was at once terrifying and exhilarating. She was not the fanciful sort. Papa had always praised her for being sensible. This surge of interest felt irresponsible and silly. Yet it was there, roiling through her in confusing waves.

Finally, he said, "You are my betrothed."

Dear Lord. His tone was mocking, and worldly, and thrummed with a tension she hardly understood. The fierce intensity of his gaze sent her pulse into a gallop. "You *are* angry, and you have every right to be so, but I pray you will oblige me to make amends."

"I am not out of sorts in the least. I've already mentioned you invite in-depth study. I am fascinated and curious about our engagement."

Our engagement? Hope stirred in her breast. "Do you mean you will permit me the charade of being your fiancée?"

His dark, arrogant head lifted. Many indefinable emotions tumbled through Kitty. It seemed improbable that he would go along with this. What would be the benefit of an arrangement to a man such as himself? It was astonishingly generous of him to allow her the farce.

"Why?" she demanded, then stiffened as a notion occurred to her. "I'll not be your mistress." That disgusting proposition had been placed to her once, and it had infuriated her that gentlemen truly had no tender, respectful regards for a woman without fortune or connections. "If that is why you took liberties and kissed me, I assure you—"

"You'll not have to worry about ravishment. I am not interested in you in a carnal manner and will never be. Disabuse yourself of the notion."

The force of his reply struck her speechless with mortification. "You kissed me, and I—"

"I am impotent, Miss Danvers. I assure you, ravishment will never be your fear."

The low words settled between them, both icy and heated. The chilling finality in his tone warred with the fiery rage that burned briefly in the dark depths of his eyes before his expression shuttered.

"I...I am dreadfully sorry," she muttered, trying to understand the full implication of this impotence and what it had to do with ravishment. Cleary there was some connection, not that she would reveal her ignorance and naivete. This man was so coldly self-assured, so effortlessly commanding despite his infirmity and scars that she must not falter in their negotiations. Or what she hoped would be the start of a negotiation. "Then, please be explicit with whatever you want from me, Your Grace."

He smiled, and it rendered him charming. "Perhaps we shall be friends."

"Friends?"

"Yes," he smoothly affirmed.

"Surely you did not leave your home to meet me to suggest we be *friends*?" Suddenly Kitty felt frightened. That assessment felt too simplistic to be rooted in reality. The duke must be in possession of a motive he was not ready to share.

The shrewdest of gazes leveled on her. "Perhaps kissing friends," he murmured, his eyes alight with amusement and interest.

Kitty felt a rush of heat, a fiery ache. She was increasingly, unwillingly captivated. She and a duke… friends. *How laughable*.

He wanted something else from her—what, she couldn't perceive, but she was sure of it. "There will be no more kissing," she whispered, because clearly his lips were not impotent. "Unless you are proposing to make our engagement a reality. I am a respectable lady, Your Grace."

She had no notion of why she said that, but icy civility replaced the provoking amusement in his eyes.

"Never that, Miss Danvers," he murmured. "I will never marry."

*A humorous, sexy Victorian romance by
Golden Heart finalist and Maggie Award
winner Kimberly Bell*

A Scandal
by Any Other Name

Julia Bishop has led a very sheltered life. Protected by her family from those who might ridicule her for her secrets, she stays hidden away in the country. But she longs for more, if only for an evening. To kiss a rake in full view of the stable boy. Unchaperoned picnics. Romance. But she knows she'll never experience any of those things.

That is, until a handsome duke with a mysterious past of his own arrives...

Duke Jasper DeVere left London to grieve his grandfather's death privately, away from the prying eyes and gossips of the ton. Seeking solitude at a friend's country manor, he's surprised he finds himself drawn to the company of the shy beauty determined to present the epitome of proper behavior.

That is, until the mysterious woman makes an indecent proposal...

Julia can't believe what she's suggested to the duke. Nor that he agrees a distraction is what they both need. But what will happen when Jasper must return to his duties and leave Julia behind? Will the memories of their time together be enough for a lifetime of solitude for either of them?

Because Julia can never leave her country haven and a duke can never stay...

The Beast of
Aros Castle

by Heather McCollum

Ava Sutton is on the run from a dangerous man and makes her way safely to Scotland. Masquerading as a titled, English lady, she must convince the darkly handsome chief of the Macleans of Aros to wed her before she is tracked down.

Tor Maclean, the new chief of Aros Castle, has sworn off marriage. Despite his efforts to scare away the English-woman his father arranged for him to wed, Tor is nonetheless drawn to her passion and beauty. But he doesn't know if he can forgive the untruths that have come to light for a chance at a once in a lifetime love…

AMARA
an imprint of Entangled Publishing LLC